The
REX
STOUT
Reader

The
REX
STOUT
Reader

HER FORBIDDEN KNIGHT
and
A PRIZE FOR PRINCES

Rex Stout

CARROLL & GRAF PUBLISHERS
NEW YORK

THE REX STOUT READER
Her Forbidden Knight *and* A Prize for Princes

Carroll & Graf Publishers
An Imprint of Avalon Publishing Group, Inc.
245 West 17th Street, 11th Floor
New York, NY 10011

AVALON

Copyright © 2007 by Carroll & Graf Publishers
First Carroll & Graf trade paperback edition 2007

Library of Congress Cataloging-in-Publication Data is available.

ISBN-10: 0-7867-1862-5
ISBN-13: 978-0-78671-862-7

2 4 6 8 9 7 5 3 1

Design by Meryl Sussman Levavi
Printed in the United States of America
Distributed by Publishers Group West

CONTENTS

———⚬———

The
REX
STOUT
Reader

INTRODUCTION

—␣—

BY OTTO PENZLER

*I*T IS OBVIOUS by their titles that the two novels collected here are not mystery stories featuring one of the greatest of all detectives in literature, Nero Wolfe.

Enormous both physically and cerebrally, Wolfe was the pure armchair detective, comfortably ensconced in his New York City brownstone house on West Thirty-fifth Street while his employee, the prototypically tough private eye Archie Goodwin, did the legwork and brought back all the required information for his employer to deduce the solution to even the most complex crimes.

Rex Stout, the creator of Wolfe (who may have been the illegitimate son of Sherlock Holmes and Irene Adler), actually began writing more than twenty years before the publication of the first Nero Wolfe adventure, *Fer-de-Lance*, in 1934.

His first novel, *Her Forbidden Knight*, was serialized in *All-Story Magazine*, one of the first pulp magazines, in five parts from August to December 1913, and had never been published in book form until 1997.

It is a crime story and a romance, fulfilling the desire of the majority of the reading public of the time. It is not revealing too

much of the plot to divulge that, in keeping with virtually all popular magazine fiction of that innocent era before World War I, it has
a happy ending.

To enjoy *Her Forbidden Knight*, it is important to recall that, nearly
a century ago, it was unthinkable for strangers to address each other
by first name, that women's daytime clothing entirely covered their
arms and legs (referred to as "limbs") and that a gentleman would
rarely speak to a lady without being properly introduced, and her
own reputation would suffer if she initiated conversation with a
strange man.

As the novel begins, a beautiful and innocent young telegraph
operator finds herself protected from unwanted advances by a group
of gallant ruffians and gadabouts known as the Erring Knights in
New York's rough tenderloin district. Inevitably, she finds herself
attracted to a handsome ne'er-do-well and they fall in love. There
are crimes (bank robbery, counterfeiting) and police, though it
would not be accurate to call *Her Forbidden Knight* a detective novel.
It does suggest Stout's early interest in mystery fiction, and may be
read with interest and pleasure both for its own sake and as an indi-
cator of things to come.

Stout's second novel was *Under the Andes*, a fantasy/science fiction novel which was first published in its entirety in the February
1914 issue of *All-Story Magazine* and then in book form in 1985.
Here, two American brothers engage in a series of adventures with
a beautiful French *femme fatale* in a lost kingdom beneath the Andes,
battling pre-historic beasts and troll-like descendants of the Incas.

His third book brought Stout back to the crime novel. *A Prize
for Princes* first saw the light of day as a five-part serial in *All-Story
Weekly Magazine* from May 2 to May 30, 1914. Again, as with his first
novel, there is as much an element of romance as there is of murder
and mystery, though it does not have quite so happy an ending.

A young American adventurer, Richard Stretton, comes upon a

scene of terrible violence as a horde of Turkish soldiers storms through a village, raping and pillaging without control. When he sees a convent in the path of the marauding thugs, Stretton breaks in and manages to lead two women to safety. He falls for the one of breathtaking beauty, Aline Solini, heedless of the fact that she is somewhat aloof and cold, although immediately quite willing to marry him. It soon becomes evident that this Russian adventuress, who has no scruples about achieving her goals, is a murderess, though the naive American cannot bring himself to believe it. He tells a friend and ally that he knows it cannot be true because he has asked her.

Incredulous that the American could be so gullible, his friend confronts him. "Stretton, you positively need someone to look after you. It's amazing! It's incredible! I suppose you went up to Mlle. Solini with a polite bow and said: 'Mademoiselle, kindly tell me if you are a murderess.' And when she answered no, you believed her. Stretton, you're worse than a baby. You're an imbecile!"

Significantly, *A Prize for Princes* is set in the Balkans, a background which plays such an important role in the Nero Wolfe novels. The detective himself is Montenegrin, as he often remarks with pride, especially in the novels which refer to his exploits during the years of World War II.

Rex Stout wrote one more pulp novel, *The Great Legend*, serialized in *All-Story Weekly* in January 1916, then published nothing for 13 years before producing the "straight" novels *How Like a God* (1929), *Seed on the Wind* (1930), *Golden Remedy* (1931), and *Forest Fire* (1933). The following year, he wrote his first pure mystery novel, publishing anonymously *The President Vanishes* and, later in 1934, producing the first Nero Wolfe adventure, *Fer-de-Lance*. For the next four decades, he bestowed a gift on mystery readers throughout the world, telling stories about the greatest detective team in the history of American literature.

Her
Forbidden
Knight

~ww~

The Champion and the Lady

"YOUNG MAN," said Tom Dougherty, "that'll do. Remove yourself."

"What do you mean?" said the person addressed, pugnaciously.

Dougherty regarded him with stern disfavor.

"You know what I mean. Go over and talk to Venus at the cigar stand. But as for that"—he nodded toward the telegraph desk, where sat Lila Williams, the operator, her face reddened by the impertinent gaze of the young man—"nothing doing. Stay away, and far away."

"Private, eh?" the young man grinned.

Dougherty's face became sterner still.

"You say one more word," he said calmly, "and I'll punch your face. Now clear out."

At this threat the young man raised his brows in a sort of pained surprise.

"I say," he protested, "that isn't necessary. When you talk about punching my face you offend my sensibilities. I regard it as impolite. Nevertheless, I'm a good fellow, and I'll be glad to seek fresh pastures on your assurance that the little brunette yonder, who is somewhat of a peach, belongs to you. If she does, I wish to congratulate you on having—"

But the voluble young man's oration met with a sudden and effectual interruption. Staggered, but not floored, by the scientific blow that Dougherty planted on his jaw, he fell a step or two backward, involuntarily raising his hands to a posture of defense. Then, as his face colored with anger, he recovered himself and glared at Dougherty with an almost joyous hostility.

"In that case," he said calmly, "where shall we go?"

"To the billiard room," said Dougherty in a pleased tone. There was something to this young fellow, after all, he thought.

The affair was not without its audience. A half-dozen loungers who had observed the clash in the lobby followed on their heels, and the attendant and one or two players looked up curiously as they entered the billiard room.

In the lobby the Venus at the cigar stand, otherwise known as Miss Hughes, stretched her neck to an unbelievable length in an effort to look round two corners at once, and Lila Williams, the innocent cause of the battle, trembled in her chair and covered her face with her hands.

Dougherty soon discovered that there was, indeed, "something to this young fellow." No sooner had he squared off and assumed his favorite guard—for Dougherty had at one time been a prizefighter—than he suddenly felt himself in the midst of a mad, breathless whirlwind.

A thousand arms and fists seemed to be revolving crazily about his head and shoulders. This was bewildering.

And what was worse, sometimes they landed. Nothing more unscientific could possibly be imagined; Dougherty felt aggrieved. This was no man, but a windmill.

Dougherty struck out blindly with both arms, then suddenly felt himself propelled backward by some jolting force, while he clutched frantically at a table to save himself from falling.

He opened his eyes. Before him stood the young man, smiling pleasantly; on either side a knot of lobby loungers, on their faces an expression of amused surprise.

"This is where Tom gets his," observed Billy Sherman.

At this remark Dougherty's strength returned. He leaped at his opponent fiercely and by the mere force of impact bore him to the floor; then, as they both rose, he landed a free swing on the young man's ear.

But the windmill proved too much for him. A succession of jolts on the nose and mouth rattled and unnerved him; his hands waved wildly in the air; and when, after a feeling of delicious repose and a succeeding blackness, he found himself lying flat on his back on the floor, he decided to remain there.

"How about it, old man?" came a voice.

Dougherty opened his eyes and smiled weakly.

"Hello, Dumain! Oh, all right. Only he don't know how to fight. Does he think he's a semaphore? What was it he hit me with?"

Dumain stooped down, placed his hands under Dougherty's shoulders and helped him to his feet. One or two of the others approached and offered assistance, but Dougherty shook them off with a gesture.

"Here, brace up," said Dumain. "What was zee quarrel?"

"Woman, lovely woman," chirped Harry Jennings.

"Shut up," growled Dougherty. "It was Miss Williams," he added, turning to Dumain. "The puppy insulted her."

"My dear fellow," came a voice, "how can you call me that after what has just happened? Do you require additional demonstration?"

Dougherty turned and glared at his late opponent.

"No, thanks," he said dryly. "You've already proved you're one.

Just because I've lost my wind is no sign you're a man. And anybody who insults Miss Lila Williams is a puppy, and remains so till he apologizes."

"You are, I take it, the young lady's champion," the young man observed.

"Call it anything you like. But I'm her friend," said Dougherty.

"And I," said Dumain.

"And I," came in a chorus from the loungers, who had remained to support Dougherty.

The young man whistled expressively.

"So many! She is a lucky woman. And surely she could use one more."

"Zee next time," Dumain observed significantly, "there will be five of us, or seex. I imagine you will have rather a lively time of it. And be good enough to refrain from remarks such as zee one you have just made. They displease us."

"But what the deuce!" the young man exclaimed.

Then he hesitated and appeared to consider.

"Now, listen here," he continued finally; "you can't frighten me. I'd take you all on in a minute. But I'm a good fellow. I would rather walk on my own feet than somebody else's toes.

"As far as your Miss Williams is concerned, I'm interested in her. But if you chaps have any reason, philosophical, domestic, or amatory, which might cause me to smother my inclinations, I'm willing to hear it. I put it up to you."

"Indeed!" said Dumain contemptuously. "And who are you?"

"Let him alone," said Dougherty. "I like him. Moreover, I'll talk to him."

The young man smiled.

"My name is Driscoll—Bub Driscoll," he said, holding out his hand to Dougherty.

"Tom Dougherty," said that gentleman, taking the hand.

They found chairs in a corner of the billiard room, and Dougherty began his tale. Some of the others gathered round—for Dougherty's tongue was famous—and divided their attention between the narration and a game of billiards begun by Harry Jennings and Billy Sherman.

Driscoll, during the readjustment, found opportunity for the first time to take note of his surroundings.

Filled with stale tobacco smoke, poorly ventilated, and receiving constantly the heterogeneous fumes from the bar adjoining, the most noticeable thing about the room was the odor which pervaded it. To an ordinary human being this atmosphere is vitiating: but the sport and the tenderloin loafer thrive and grow fat on it. They breathe it as the salamander does the flame.

The room, long and narrow, was lined along either side with chairs with raised seats, the better to overlook the five or six billiard tables which ranged along the center from end to end. On the walls were hung pictures of racehorses and actresses, and copies of the rules of the National Billiard Association; at intervals a cue rack. A wide arch at one end led into the main half of the hotel; a small door at an opposite corner connected with the bar.

Here and there were small tables ready to hold whatever might be deposited on them by the white-coated attendants, at the request of those made thirsty by the exercise and mental strain occasioned by the classic and subtle game of billiards.

The occupants were few. This was not the result of any lack of popularity for the Lamartine, being on the Madison Square section, in the Nineties, was at the height of its career. The fact is, it was only ten o'clock; an hour when any sensible man—according to the view of the Broadway sport—should be trying to decide whether to turn over for another snatch of sleep or to get up and give his serious consideration to the question of breakfast. Therefore was the billiard room by no means filled.

The game just begun by Harry Jennings and Billy Sherman was the only one in progress, and the spectators were few in number.

In the farthest corner the white-coated attendant was replacing some chairs that had been overturned during the late unpleasantness. Driscoll, observing this, smiled at some inward recollection and turned to Dougherty who was seated at his side.

"Really," said Dougherty, "there's nothing to it. We're Miss Williams's friends, and we don't intend to let anyone annoy her. That's all."

"But it's not enough," declared Driscoll. "We've agreed to argue this out as man to man. Very well. Now, I'll leave it to you: If, in my wanderings through the highways and byways of existence, I suddenly find a young woman who causes my heart to jump from side to side like the pendulum of an eight-day clock, what is there to keep me from telling her so? The mere fact that she possesses friends? Hardly."

Dougherty observed him with a new interest.

"That was exactly how I felt," he observed.

"How? What?"

"Like the pendulum of an eight-day clock."

"Oh! Well?"

"Well"—Dougherty hesitated—"it's like this: I suppose I must begin at the beginning. If I didn't you wouldn't understand how we feel. Anyway, there's not much to tell.

"It was about two months ago that we first saw Miss Williams. We all hang out here in the Lamartine—that is, Dumain, Booth, Sherman, Jennings, myself, and one or two others. Well, one day, coming in the lobby, what do I see? I see what I call the Queen of Egypt sitting at the telegraph desk.

" 'Aha!' says I, 'a new one.' Without loss of time I proceed to skirmish. The enemy ignores me. I advance right up to the fortifications.

Still no sign. I prepare to turn loose with my artillery, and at that point am interrupted by Dumain and Jennings entering the lobby.

"As soon as they observe me they hasten up with reenforcements. 'Who is it?' says Jennings. 'The Queen of Egypt,' says I, 'and no time to be lost.' Then we begin in earnest.

"Dumain had a roll—some rich guy wanted to find out who to give it to (you know, Dumain's a palmist)—and that day we must have sent something like five million telegrams, having found her silent on all other topics. It wasn't easy. Did you ever try to write a telegram when you had nothing to say and nobody to say it to? And still we never got across the trenches. It went something like this:

" 'How much?' says I, handing over for the ninth time a telegram to my brother in Trenton, telling him I was well and hoping he was the same.

" 'Sixty cents,' says the Queen of Egypt.

" 'Now,' says I, 'that's what I don't like. I don't mind paying out five for a dinner or tickets to a show, but I do hate to spend money on telegrams. But as I say, I'd just as soon buy tickets to a show as not—any show.'

" 'Sixty cents,' says the Queen of Egypt.

" 'And so far as dinner is concerned—why, I hardly consider ten dollars too much for a good dinner,' says I.

" 'Sixty cents, please,' says she.

"And that was the way it went all day. Not a word could we get. It appeared to be hopeless. Jennings got disgusted.

" 'You've made a mistake, Dougherty,' says he. 'She belongs to Egypt all right, but she's not the queen. She's the Sphinx.' I was inclined to agree with him.

"The time passed quicker than we thought. We were sitting over in the corner, trying to think up one more telegram, when we heard somebody stop right in front of us. It was the Queen of Egypt, with her hat and coat on, ready to go home. Before we could say a word she spoke.

" 'Gentlemen,' she says, 'you must pardon me for speaking to you. I do it because I believe you are gentlemen. I suppose you have been trying to joke with me today; and I am sure that when I tell you it disturbs me and makes me unhappy, you will promise not to do it any more. For if you continue, I must give up my position.'

"You can imagine—maybe—how we felt. Dumain stammered something, and I choked, and the next minute we saw the door close behind her. I guess she realized our condition.

"Well, the next day we had to catch Booth and train him. And the day after that, Sherman. He was the hardest of all. About every day it happens that some stranger suddenly finds himself de trop, though we don't usually interfere unless he insists. And now you get us. She is no longer the Queen of Egypt. She is Miss Lila Williams— which is to say, she's better than any queen."

"But still," persisted Driscoll, "by what right do you interfere with me?"

"Well," Dougherty appeared to reflect, "perhaps none. But there's one or two things we've found out that I haven't told you. One is that she has no father or mother. She's all alone.

"Very well. One thing a mother does is this: if some guy comes round with a meaning eye, she hauls him up short. She says to him: 'Who are you, and what are you good for, and what are your intentions?' Well, that's us. As far as that part of it's con-cerned, we're mama."

"But I have no intentions," said Driscoll.

"That's just the point. You have no intentions. Then hands off."

Dougherty at this point glanced aside at a shout from the bil-liard players. When he turned back he found Driscoll standing before him with outstretched hand.

"You're on," said Driscoll briefly. "Shake."

"You're a gentleman," said Dougherty, grasping the hand.

"And now—will you introduce me to Miss Williams?"

Dougherty looked somewhat taken aback.

"I want to apologize to her," Driscoll explained.

"Why, sure," said Dougherty. "Of course. I forgot. Come on."

Halfway to the door they were intercepted by Dumain.

"Well?" said he.

"Oh, it's all right," said Dougherty. "Driscoll's a gentleman."

"Mon Dieu!" exclaimed the little Frenchman. "Eet ees not surprising. For zee little Miss Williams—she ees irresistible."

He returned to the game, and Driscoll and Dougherty passed down the hall and thence into the lobby.

The lobby, more ornate and pretentious than the billiard room, was at the same time more typical. With Driscoll, we shall pause to observe it in detail.

There were two entrances: the main one on Broadway, and a side door leading to a crosstown street not far from Madison Square. On the right, entering, were the hotel desk and the cigar stand; beyond, the hall leading to the bar and billiard room. Further on came the telegraph desk and the elevators. Along the whole length of the opposite side was a line of leather-covered lounges and chairs, broken only by the side entrance.

At one time the Lamartine had been quiet, fashionable, and exclusive. Now it was noisy, sporty, and popular; for fashion had moved north.

The marble pillars stood in lofty indifference to the ever-changing aspect and character of the human creatures who moved about on the patterned floor; subtly time had imprinted the mark of his fingers on the carvings, frescoes, and furniture. From magnificent the lobby had become presentable; it was now all but dingy.

With its appearance and character, its employees had changed also. The clerks were noisy and assertive, the bell boys worldly-wise to the point of impudence, and the Venus at the cigar stand needs no further description than the phrase itself.

But what of the girl at the telegraph desk? Here, indeed, we find an anomaly. And it is here that Driscoll and Dougherty stop on their way from the billiard room.

As Lila Williams looked up and found the two men standing before her, her face turned a delicious pink and her eyes fell with embarrassment. Before Dougherty spoke Driscoll found time to regard her even more closely than he had before, in the light of the new and interesting information he had received concerning her.

Her figure was slender and of medium height; exactly of the proper mold and strength for her small, birdlike head, that seemed to have fluttered and settled of itself on the white and delicate neck. Her lips, partly open, seemed ever to tremble with a sweet consciousness of the mystery she held within her—the mystery of the eternal feminine.

Her hands, lying before her on the desk, were very white, and perhaps a little too thin; her hair a fluffy, tangled mass of glorious brown.

"Altogether," thought Driscoll, "I was not mistaken. She is absolutely a peach."

"Miss Williams," Dougherty was saying, "allow me to introduce a friend. Mr. Driscoll—Miss Williams."

Lila extended a friendly hand.

"A little while ago," said Driscoll, "I was presumptuous and foolish. I want to ask you to forgive me. I know there was no excuse for it—and yet there was—"

He stopped short, perceiving that Lila was not listening to him. She was gazing at Dougherty with what seemed to Driscoll an expression of tender alarm.

"Oh!" she exclaimed suddenly. "Mr. Dougherty!"

That gentleman appeared startled.

"What is it?"

"Your—your—why, what has happened to your nose?"

"My nose?" he repeated, puzzled.

"Yes. What has happened?"

Dougherty raised his hand and roughly grasped that rather prominent feature of his face; then his hand suddenly fell and he made a grimace of pain. Then he remembered.

"Oh," he said, as carelessly as possible, "a mere nothing. I fell. Struck it against a billiard table."

Driscoll was doing his best to keep a straight face.

"Mr. Dougherty," said Lila, shaking a finger at him solemnly, "tell me the truth. You have been fighting."

The ex-prizefighter and Broadway loafer, blushing like a schoolboy, gathered himself together as though about to attack the entire heavyweight division.

"Well," he demanded with assumed bravado, "and what if I have been fighting?"

"You promised me you wouldn't," said Lila. "That is, you said you wouldn't—anyone—who annoyed—about me."

"It wasn't his fault, Miss Williams," said Driscoll, coming to his friend's assistance. "The blame is mine. It is for that I want to apologize. I can't say how sorry I am, and I hope you'll forgive me, and if there's any—I mean—"

Driscoll, too, found himself hopelessly confused by the frank gaze of those brown eyes.

"Anyway," he ended lamely, "I'll renew his promise for him. He'll never do it again."

"No, you won't do anything of the kind!" exclaimed Dougherty, who, during the period of relief offered by Driscoll, had fully recovered himself—"nobody shall promise anything for me. And, Miss Williams, I am very sorry I ever made that promise to you.

I take it back. What has happened today is proof that I would never be able to keep it, anyway."

"But you must keep it," said Lila.

"I can't."

"Mr. Dougherty!"

"Well, I'll try," Dougherty agreed. "I promise to try. But there are some things I can't stand for; and we all feel the same way about it. You leave it to us. We know you don't like us much, and we don't blame you. But any guy that tries to get into informal communication with your eyes is going to see stars—and that's no pretty speech, either."

Lila opened her mouth to renew her protest, but someone approached to send a telegram, and she contented herself with a disapproving shake of the head.

Driscoll touched the ex-prizefighter on the arm.

"Dougherty," he said, "you're enough to frighten a chorus girl; and that's going some. Come on, for Heaven's sake, and do something to that nose!"

Dougherty allowed himself to be led away.

CHAPTER II

⌐⌐

The Recruit

*I*T WAS three or four days later, about one o'clock in the afternoon, that Pierre Dumain and Bub Driscoll, seated in the lobby of the Lamartine, beheld a sight that left them speechless with astonishment.

They saw Tom Dougherty enter the hotel by the Broadway door, carrying a bouquet of roses—red roses. They were unwrapped, and he bore them openly, flamboyantly, without shame. An ex-prizefighter carrying roses on Broadway in the light of day!

" 'Mother, Mother, Mother, pin a rose on me!' " they sang in unison.

Dougherty ignored them. He scowled darkly at the hotel clerk, who grinned at him delightedly, and walked boldly down the center of the lobby, past a score of curious eyes. At the telegraph desk he halted and accosted the messenger boy. Lila had gone to lunch.

"Got a vase?" Dougherty demanded.

The boy gaped in complete bewilderment.

"Don't you know what a vase is?" said Dougherty sarcastically. "V-a-s, vase. Get one."

"They ain't any," said the boy.

"Then get one!" Dougherty roared, producing a dollar bill. "Here, run around to Adler's. They keep all kinds of 'em. Get a pretty one."

The boy disappeared. In a few minutes he returned, bearing a huge, showy, glass vase, the color of dead leaves. During his absence Dougherty had kept his back resolutely turned on Dumain and Driscoll, who received only silence in return for their witty and cutting remarks.

"Fill it with water," commanded Dougherty.

The boy obeyed.

"Now," said Dougherty, arranging the roses in the vase and placing it on the top of Lila's desk, "see that you leave 'em alone. And don't say anything to Miss Williams. If she asks where they came from, you don't know. Understand?"

The boy nodded an affirmative. Dougherty stepped back a pace or two, eyed the roses with evident satisfaction, and proceeded to the corner where the others were seated.

"Do you know who that is?" said Driscoll in a loud whisper as the ex-prizefighter approached.

"No," said Dumain. "Who ees eet?"

"Bertha, the flower girl," Driscoll replied solemnly.

"Oh, shut up!" growled Dougherty. "You fellows have no sentiment."

Dumain lay back in his chair and laughed boisterously.

"Sentiment!" he gasped. "Dougherty talking of sentiment!"

Then suddenly he became sober.

"All the same, you are right," he said. "Miss Williams should get zee roses. They seem made for her. Only, you know, eet is not—what you say—correct. We can't allow it."

"How?" said Dougherty. "Can't allow it?"

"Positively not," put in Driscoll. "Too much of a liberty, my dear fellow. 'Tis presumptuous. You know your own views on the subject."

This staggered Dougherty. Without a word he seated himself, and appeared to ponder. Dumain and Driscoll, after trying vainly to rouse him by sarcastic observations and comments, finally tired of the sport and wandered over to throw Indian dice for cigars with Miss Hughes. That lady, being wise in her manner, separated them from two or three dollars in as many minutes with ease, complacency, and despatch.

They were rescued by Dougherty, who came bounding over to them with the grace of a rhinoceros.

"I have it!" he exclaimed triumphantly.

"Then hold onto it," said Driscoll, setting the dice box far back on the counter with an emphatic bang. "You have what?"

"About the roses. See here, Miss Williams ought to have 'em. Dumain said so. Well, why can't we take turns at it? Say, every day we fill up the vase, each one in his turn. She'll never know where they come from. Are you on?"

"Wiz pleasure," said Dumain. "And I'll tell Booth and Sherman and the others. We'll have to let them in."

"Ordinarily," said Driscoll, "I would be compelled to refuse. Being an actor, and, I think I may add, an artist, my normal condition is that of flatness. But at the present time I have a job. I'm on."

Thus it was that Lila, on her return from lunch, was surprised by the sight of a floral offering which flamed like a beacon on the top of her desk. She regarded it in wonder while taking off her coat and hat, and glanced up in time to receive a knowing smirk from the hotel clerk. Then she saw the three conspirators observing her furtively with self-conscious indifference. She smiled at them pleasantly, reached up for the vase, and buried her face in the velvet petals. Then, replacing the vase, she seated herself at her desk and picked up a book.

"Gad!" exclaimed Dougherty in high delight. "She kissed 'em! D'ye see that? And say, d'ye notice how they match the pink on her cheeks?"

"My dear fellow," said Driscoll, "that won't do. It's absolutely poetical."

"Well, and what if it is?" Dougherty was lighting a cigarette at the taper at the cigar stand. "Can't a prizefighter be a poet?"

"If you are talking of the poetry of motion, yes. But this is the poetry of e-motion."

Miss Hughes, the Venus at the cigar stand, tittered.

"You Erring Knights are funny," she observed. "Who bought the roses?"

"Us what?" said Dougherty, ignoring the question. "What kind of knights did you say?"

"Erring Knights."

"She means knights errant," put in Driscoll.

"I do not," denied Miss Hughes.

"It's a pun. Erring Knights."

"Well," said Dougherty, "and why not? I like the title."

And the title stuck. The lobby loungers of the Hotel Lamartine, purveyors of roses and protectors of beauty in distress, shall henceforth be designated by it.

They formed a curious community. What any one of them might have attempted but for the restraining presence of the others may only be conjectured. Collectively, they became the bulwark of innocence; individually, they were—almost anything.

There was Pierre Dumain, palmist and clairvoyant, with offices just around the corner on Twenty-third Street, a little garrulous Frenchman who always had money.

Tom Dougherty, ex-prizefighter, bookmaker, and sport, who was generally understood to be living under the shadow of a secret.

Bub Driscoll, actor and philosopher, about whom there was known just one fact: he had floored Tom Dougherty.

Billy Sherman, newspaper reporter (at intervals), who was always broke and always thirsty.

Sam Booth, typewriter salesman, who was regarded as somewhat inferior because he rose every morning at nine o'clock to go to work.

Harry Jennings, actor, who was always just going to sign a contract to play leads for Charles Frohman.

What a collection of Broadway butterflies for a young girl to accept as protectors and friends! And yet—you shall see what came of it.

For something over a month the roll of membership remained as given above; then, on a day in October, a candidate presented himself for election.

The corner of the lobby preempted by the Erring Knights was that farthest from the Broadway entrance, opposite the telegraph desk. It was partially hidden from the front by two massive marble pillars, and contained an old worn leather lounge, three or four chairs, and a wide window seat.

This corner had been so long occupied by a dozen or so of the oldest habitués that the advent of a stranger within its sacred precincts was held to be an unwarranted intrusion. This opinion was usually communicated to the stranger with speed and emphasis.

Here it was, at about two o'clock in the afternoon, that Driscoll, Sherman, and Dougherty were seated, discoursing amiably.

Sherman, a tall, dark man, with a general air of assertiveness, was explaining the deficiencies and general inutility of the New York press.

The door opened; Dumain approached. At his side was a stranger, whom he introduced to the others as Mr. Knowlton.

"I believe I've met Mr. Knowlton before," said Sherman, extending a hand.

"You have the advantage of me," said the newcomer politely.

Sherman was silent, but gazed at him curiously as he turned to Driscoll.

They conversed. Knowlton appeared to be educated, well informed, and a good fellow. He also possessed an indefinable air of good breeding—lacking in the others.

Driscoll proposed a game of billiards.

"You're on," the others agreed.

"As for me," said Knowlton. "I'll be with you in a minute. Want to send a telegram."

They nodded and proceeded to the billiard room, while Knowlton approached Lila's desk.

Lila was reading a book, and handed him a pad of blanks absently, without looking up; and when he pushed the telegram across the counter she took it and counted the words, still without looking at him. It was signed "John Knowlton."

"Eighty cents, please," said Lila.

As she raised her head and met the eyes of the stranger she was conscious of a distinct and undeniable shock.

Why, she could not have told. There was nothing alarming in the young man's appearance; he had a very ordinary face and figure, though the former was marked by an unusually genial and pleasing pair of gray eyes, and bore an expression of uncommon frank good nature. Lila, feeling that she was staring at him, flushed and turned aside, and the gray eyes twinkled with an amused smile as their owner took a ten-dollar bill from his wallet and held it out to her.

"Is this the smallest you have?" asked Lila, opening the cash drawer.

"I believe it is," said Knowlton. "Sorry; but you see, being a millionaire, I never care to be bothered with anything smaller. Can you make it?"

Lila examined the contents of the drawer.

"If you'll take some silver."

"Anything," Knowlton smiled.

Lila handed him his change.

"You will send it at once?" asked Knowlton.

She nodded. Knowlton appeared to be in no hurry to leave.

"I suppose that since my business is over I should make my bow and depart," he said finally. "But I like to talk and I hate billiards."

"Then why do you play?" Lila asked.

"Why? Oh, why do we do anything? I suppose merely to kill time."

"But that is wrong. A man ought to do something—something worth while. He should never want to kill time, but to use it."

"A sermon?" Knowlton smiled.

"I beg your pardon," said Lila, coloring.

"But I was joking."

"I know—of course—and it was very silly of me. Only I do believe that what I said is true. I have always wished to be a man."

"Motion denied," said Knowlton.

"And that means?"

"That it is impossible. That is to say, my guess is that you are thoroughly a woman. Am I right?"

"Do I look so old?"

"Oh, I didn't mean that! Then we'll say girl. You are—let's see—nineteen."

"Twenty," Lila declared.

"Well, that leaves one for safety. It really wasn't a bad guess. It's always best to—"

"Are you coming, Knowlton?" came a voice.

Billy Sherman was standing in the hall leading to the billiard room, regarding them with a sinister frown.

"Right away," Knowlton answered. "Didn't know you were waiting."

He lifted his hat to Lila and joined Sherman. The two disappeared within.

Lila began humming a tune softly under her breath. She picked up her book and turned to the page she had marked, then suddenly let it fall to the desk, gasping with amazement. She had been conversing familiarly, even intimately, with a man she had never before seen—an utter stranger! And at first she had not even realized it! What had she been thinking of? It was incredible.

"Of course," she thought, "there was really nothing wrong about it. I suppose I am silly. And yet—how did it happen? He is certainly different from other men. And, oh, what will he think of me? I hope he will understand that I don't talk to everybody."

Again she picked up the book and tried to read, but the printed words were blurred and meaningless to her eyes. She was saying to herself over and over: "I wonder what he is thinking of me?"

The truth is, that just at that moment Knowlton was not only thinking of her, but was also talking about her.

On entering the billiard room with Sherman he had found the others waiting. Two or three other games were in progress, and the room was filled with men and smoke, the clicking of balls, and the clinking of glasses. Dumain was sitting on a billiard table to preserve their claim to its use.

"Come on!" called Dougherty; "get a cue!"

Knowlton took one from a rack, tested its weight, and chalked it.

"How do we play?" he asked.

"You and Dougherty, Dumain and I," said Driscoll. "Sherman's out."

The game proceeded. They had run through the first frame and begun on the second before Knowlton found opportunity to put his question.

"Who is she?" he said to Dougherty.

Dougherty stared at him.

"Who?"

"The girl at the telegraph desk."

"None of your business," said the ex-prizefighter.

"Why," said Knowlton, surprised at his bruskness, "I meant no offense, I'm sure."

"That's all right," said Dougherty, "but we don't allow anybody to talk about Miss Williams who doesn't know her. Perhaps you'll have that honor—some day."

"Your shot, Knowlton!" called Driscoll.

Knowlton made a try at a cushion-carrom and missed badly. Dumain, who followed, nursed the balls into a corner and seemed in for a run.

"So her name is Miss Williams?" said Knowlton, returning to Dougherty.

Dougherty turned on him sharply.

"See here," he said, "I told you not to talk about her."

"Who's talking about her? I merely asked her name. Is that an insult?"

"Perhaps not," Dougherty admitted. "But it's too familiar. And I don't like your tone."

Knowlton assured him that if he read anything but the deepest respect in his tone he was mistaken. This somewhat mollified Dougherty, and he ended by reciting the tale of the Erring Knights.

"I fancied it was something like that," said Knowlton when he had finished. "And she appears to be all you say she is. But it is really rather amusing. A Broadway gang acting chaperon for a pretty girl! Who would believe it?"

"It's the hardest job I ever had," said Dougherty. "See this nose?

I got that from a guy that was making eyes at her just the other day—Driscoll yonder. He's one of us now."

"And how may one be elected a member of this club?"

"Nothing doing. We're full up."

"But I want to join. Really—I'm serious about it. To tell the truth"—Knowlton hesitated—"it's been such a deuce of a time since I've done anything really decent that the idea appeals to me. How about it?"

"Oh, stick round if you want to," said Dougherty. "If you feel that way about it, I have no objections. And anytime you want to know—"

"Your shot, Dougherty," called Dumain. "I just ran thirty-two. Zat win zee game. You haven't got a chance."

And they hadn't. Driscoll completed the frame in the next inning, and the game was ended.

"Enough!" said Dougherty. "Dumain ought to be ashamed of himself. He's a blooming professional. It's time to eat, anyway. Come on."

The others trooped out in a body, while Knowlton remained behind to pay for the game. He had just pocketed his change and was turning to follow, when he heard his name called. At his elbow was Billy Sherman, who had remained seated in a corner while the others were playing.

"Did you call me?" asked Knowlton.

"Yes," said Sherman. "I want a word with you—alone."

His eyes glittered with hostility and with a certain air of command as he turned to leave the room with a gesture to Knowlton to follow.

Knowlton appeared surprised, but obeyed with a shrug of the shoulders. "Another of Miss Williams's chaperons," he thought. "Jove, they're worse than a pack of women!"

Sherman led the way down the hall, round a corner, and into

a small room containing a table or two, some chairs, and a sofa—evidently a private parlor. When Knowlton had followed him inside he locked the door. Then, motioning Knowlton to a chair, he stood before him with his hands in his pockets, looking down on him with an insolent leer.

But Knowlton refused to be impressed. "This air of mystery appeals to me," he smiled. "Is it murder or merely a sermon? Now that you have aroused my expectations, I shall expect you to satisfy them."

Sherman, disregarding him, came directly to the point. "You were talking with Miss Williams," he said abruptly.

Knowlton, with a smile of amusement, admitted it.

"Well, you'll have to cut it," said Sherman calmly.

"But why?"

"No questions. I say cut it."

"Mr. Sherman"—Knowlton's voice remained calm—"you are impudent. This thing is no longer amusing. It is decidedly tiresome. I shall talk to whomever I please."

Sherman nodded.

"I expected you to say that. Very well. In that case, I have a story to tell you." He leaned forward, and continued in a tone of sneering insult: "I lived for ten years in a little town called Warton. Does that interest you?"

Knowlton turned suddenly pale, and appeared to control himself with an effort.

"Well?" he said finally.

"Well," repeated Sherman, with a smile of satisfaction at having touched his man, "isn't that enough? If it isn't, listen to this. You don't need to talk; I'll spare you the trouble.

"In the first place, there's the Warton National Bank. I know they're done with you; but it shows I know what I'm talking about.

"I know why you left Warton. I know why you came to New

York, and I know who brought you. I know why you call yourself
John Knowlton instead of—you know what. I know why you
choose a new hangout every week, and I know where you get the
coin. Is that enough?"

"I haven't the slightest idea what you are driving at," said
Knowlton, with a light laugh. If it was acting, it was cleverly done. "I
do come from Warton, and my name is not John Knowlton; but anybody is welcome to that information. As for the rest—is it a puzzle?"

Sherman grinned.

"You do it very well," he admitted. "But it's no go. I'm on. That's
what I know. Now, here's what I want:

"Today I saw you talking to Miss Williams; and, frankly, I don't
like the way she looked at you. These other guys are dubs. They don't
bother me. They can buy roses forever if they want to. But that little Williams girl looks good to me, and it's me for her.

"If I can't get her one way, I'll take her another. But I'll get her.
As I said, these other guys don't count. But you do. I don't like the
way she looked at you. And it's your move."

"You mean?"

"I mean just this—beat it."

"And if I don't?"

"The cops."

Knowlton rose to his feet, smiling.

"Stand away," he said pleasantly. Sherman, unsuspecting and
wondering a little at the request, obeyed it.

Then, like a leaping flame, Knowlton's fist shot forth straight
from the shoulder. With terrific force it caught Sherman full in the
face. He staggered, fell against a table, then dropped to the floor in
a heap.

Knowlton, with the light of battle in his eyes, stood above him
with clenched fists. Then, without a word, he turned, unlocked the
door, and disappeared into the hall.

Sherman sat up, lifted his hand gingerly to his face, and let out a volley of curses.

"Well," he muttered, "I made a bad guess. And yet—I can't be wrong. He's crooked and I'll get him. And when I do I'll pay him for this."

He rose to his feet painfully and made his way unobserved to the street.

CHAPTER III

~~~

Hidden Wire

O N THE following morning Knowlton was formally enrolled as a member of the Erring Knights.

"The qualifications," said Tom Dougherty, "are a good pair of biceps and a boundless esteem for Miss Lila Williams. The dues are two dozen roses each week. A fresh bouquet every morning. Your day will be Saturday."

Dumain was really not quite easy about it. He himself had introduced Knowlton to the Lamartine, and he knew nothing whatever about him, having picked him up in a Broadway café by accident. But, as was quite right for a palmist and clairvoyant, he trusted to Providence for justification of his action.

From that day forth Knowlton took his place and held it. In spite of his superior education and breeding, he seemed exactly to fit, and within a week had earned quite a reputation as a good fellow. He always had money, and leisure and willingness to spend it.

Nothing came of the encounter with Sherman. A day or two afterward they had met in the billiard room. Dumain and Knowlton were playing.

"Take a cue, Sherman?" Dumain had said.

"If Knowlton doesn't object," Sherman replied.

"Not I," laughed Knowlton. "You can't bluff in billiards, you know. It's either hit or miss."

The significance of this remark was not lost on Sherman.

No one knew anything of the nature of Knowlton's occupation, or even if he had any. He was in the Lamartine at all hours of the day, and he always had leisure to perform any favor or meet any engagement.

He had one habit that aroused some comment. Two or three times each week he sent a telegram at Lila's desk. It always bore the same address.

Laughingly alluding to their first meeting, he always insisted on paying with a ten-dollar bill, and the state of Lila's cash drawer became a standing joke between them. Lila wondered a little about the mysterious telegrams; in fact, she wondered about everything connected with him—and knew nothing.

She even wondered why she was interested in him; why she looked forward to the sight of his face and the sound of his voice. For her innocence was that of inexperience and ignorance—the purest if not the best. It led her into a score of charming deceptions, of which, however, she herself was always the victim.

One of these had to do with the bouquet of roses.

In the first place, no girl likes to receive flowers unless she knows who gives them to her. So, on the first appearance of the glorious vase, Lila had set about discovering its source.

Let us not be too harsh on the poor little messenger boy. It is true that he had promised Dougherty not to tell, but if you blame him severely for his betrayal of the confidence it merely proves that you know nothing of the charm of Lila's smile.

It would have coaxed a secret from the Sphinx herself. Thus she became aware that the roses were the gift of the Erring Knights, furnished by each in his turn.

Then one morning, about a week after the first appearance of Knowlton, she decided that her information was not sufficiently definite. Observe the effect of love! Ordinarily Lila was the most open and straightforward creature in the world. But see the cunning of her procedure!

"Jimmie," she said to the messenger boy, "the roses yesterday were the most beautiful shade I have ever seen. Do you know who got them?"

"What's today—Saturday?" Jimmie asked.

"Yes. Yesterday was Friday."

"Then it was Mr. Driscoll."

"Oh!" Lila hesitated. "And who—who gets them on Thursday?"

"Mr. Dumain—Frenchy."

"And on Wednesday?"

Jimmie remained silent and eyed her keenly.

"Mr. Knowlton's day is Saturday," he said finally. "That's today." Lila blushed a rosy pink.

"Jimmie!" she exclaimed.

"Aw, come off! Don't you think I know nothin'?" said the boy. Only a boy—or a woman—could have guessed it.

Lila was silent. But that evening she took the bouquet of roses home with her. As to what she did with them after she got them there, you must guess for yourself. Unlike Jimmie, I can keep a secret.

A month passed uneventfully.

Dumain improved his play at billiards till he threatened to take part in a tournament; Jennings reported daily concerning his contract with Charles Frohman; Knowlton continued to spend his ten-dollar bills on telegrams at Lila's desk, and Driscoll spouted the classics on all occasions. Dougherty and Booth held down their chairs and talked philosophy.

Since the day of Knowlton's introduction, Sherman, who had

always been barely tolerated by the others, had increased his attentions to Lila to a point where they were noticed by several of the others. But, as Driscoll said, they regarded him as harmless.

Had Lila cared to speak she could have told them that which would have caused them to think differently; but she bore his troublesome attentions in silence. And if she had but known the depth of his treachery and the strength of his passion for her, she would have feared him, instead of merely despising him, and avoided many a poignant hour of sorrow and anxiety.

But Sherman cleverly concealed his real nature and treacherous designs under an appearance of blunt frankness. It must be admitted that the others were easily deceived. But then what cause had they for suspicion? We learn of the presence of the deadly rattlesnake only when we hear his warning rattle, and Sherman, like the serpent, was waiting silently for the time to spring.

It was Dumain who first noticed that Lila carried home the bouquet of roses on Saturday evening. These Frenchmen have an eye for such things. He watched and discovered that this compliment was paid on Saturdays only.

Now Dumain was not exactly jealous. The mere fact that Lila exhibited a preference for Knowlton's roses did not disturb him; but the question was, what had Knowlton done to bring about such a state of affairs? For it was evident to Dumain that Knowlton must have done or said something thus to have installed himself in the first place in Lila's affections.

Of course, Dumain was mistaken. A girl gives her heart not to a man's actions or words, but to the man himself. Knowlton was innocent of any treachery to the Erring Knights. He was not to blame for the vagaries of Dan Cupid.

But when, for the fourth Saturday in succession, he saw Lila carefully place the roses in a large paper-bag and leave the hotel with the bag under her arm, he could contain himself no longer.

He called to Knowlton, who was talking with the Venus at the cigar stand.

Knowlton walked over to him in a secluded corner of the lobby.

"I want to talk to you," said Dumain.

"Fire away!" said Knowlton.

"It is about zee roses."

"Roses?"

"Yes. Zee roses you gave to Miss Williams."

"What about them?"

Dumain pointed toward Lila's desk.

"You see. Zee vase is empty."

"Why, so it is," said Knowlton. "I wonder—that's funny."

"Very funny," said Dumain sarcastically. "Now, where are they?"

"I have no idea."

"Do you mean to say you don't know?"

"I don't know."

Dumain eyed him incredulously.

"Well, zen, I tell you," fie said finally. "Miss Williams took zem home."

Knowlton seemed surprised.

"Miss Williams took them home?" he repeated.

"Yes."

"Well, they are hers, aren't they? Hasn't she a right to do as she pleases with them? Why do you trouble me about it?"

"Because she pay zat compliment to no one but you," said Dumain impressively.

"What? How—only to me?"

"She never take any roses home but yours. She does it now for—oh, a month. And what does zat mean? It means you're a traitor. It means you've deceived us. It means you are trying to make zee impression on Mees Williams, and I am afraid you succeed."

Knowlton appeared to be touched. His face colored, and he

seemed to be at a loss for words. Was it possible that this evidence of an interest in him on the part of Miss Williams found a corresponding thrill in his own breast?

Suddenly he smiled—a smile of genuine amusement.

"Dumain," he said, "you fellows are the limit. You're not only amusing—you're extremely dense. I would be very happy indeed if I could believe that Miss Williams had singled me out for the distinction you mention; but the real cause of her seeming preference is only too evident."

"Well?"

"Every evening," Knowlton continued, "Miss Williams's roses are left to adorn the lobby of this hotel. It is by her order, as you know. But as she is at home on Sunday she wants them on that day for herself.

"So every Saturday evening she takes them home. That must be the correct explanation. She can't even know that I bought them."

Dumain's little round face was filled with light.

"Of course!" he exclaimed. "What an ass am I! Forgive me, Knowlton. Zen she doesn't care for you?"

"I'm afraid not." Knowlton smiled. But the smile was not an easy one.

"And you haven't been trying to—"

"My good fellow," Knowlton interrupted him, "as long as I am an Erring Knight I shall act only in the role of protector."

At that moment Driscoll approached and the interview was ended. Knowlton wandered over to the cigar stand, bought a packet of cigarettes, and, lighting one, transferred the remainder to a silver-mounted leather case. Then strolling past Lila's desk with a nod, he stopped in front of the lounge in the corner and exchanged the time of day with Harry Jennings and Billy Sherman.

After a few minutes of desultory conversation with Jennings, during which Sherman sat noticeably silent, Knowlton, glancing at

his watch and observing that he had an engagement, left the lobby
of the hotel, and started up Broadway.

He had no sooner disappeared than Sherman sprang up from
the lounge, left by the side door, and followed him some twenty
paces in the rear.

Broadway was crowded and Sherman was forced to keep close
to his quarry in order not to lose sight of him. Knowlton walked
with a swinging, athletic stride, looking neither to right nor left—
ordinarily the gait of a man who has nothing to fear and nothing to
be ashamed of. Now and then the pressure of the crowd caused him
to make a detour, and Sherman dodged in and out behind him.

At Madison Square Knowlton stopped abruptly and looked first
to one side, then the other. On account of the congested traffic at
that point the action was perfectly natural, and Sherman, who had
darted quickly behind a standing cab, was convinced that he had not
been seen. After a short wait Knowlton stepped off the curb, crossed
the square, and proceeded up Broadway.

At Twenty-eighth Street he turned suddenly and disappeared
through the swinging doors of a café.

Sherman approached, and halted a foot from the door.

"Now," he muttered, "if I only dared go in! I'd give a ten-spot
to know who he's with in there. That would settle it. But they'll
probably come out together, anyway." He retired to a doorway nearby and waited.

In a few minutes Knowlton emerged alone. Sherman, cursing
under his breath, hesitated and appeared ready to give it up; then,
with a gesture of decision, he resumed the chase with an air of determined resolve. Knowlton had quickened his step, and Sherman had
to move swiftly to overtake him.

At Thirtieth Street Knowlton turned westward. At once the pur-
suer's task became more difficult. There was no crowd of pedestrians
here, as on Broadway, and there was imminent danger of discovery.

Twice when Knowlton halted he was forced to dodge aside into a doorway.

At Sixth Avenue Sherman found his passage obstructed by a passing cab. It was empty. Struck by a sudden thought, he sprang inside and, thinking thus to lessen the chances of detection, pointed to Knowlton and instructed the driver to follow him.

The driver grinned, wheeled his cab sharply, and turned down Thirtieth Street.

They crossed Seventh Avenue and Eighth, past rows of five-story apartment houses, with their narrow brass-railed stoops and air of dingy respectability. Straight ahead at a distance the Hudson could be seen shimmering in the light of the winter sun; from the rear came the sounding rumble and rattle of an Elevated train above the low, never-ceasing hum of the great city.

Knowlton continued his rapid stride to Ninth Avenue, and beyond, while the cab followed cautiously. Then suddenly he turned in at the entrance of one of a row of apartment houses. By the time the cab approached he had disappeared within.

Sherman ordered the driver to halt in front of the entrance, while a look of disappointment and chagrin covered his face. "Well, I'll be hanged," he said finally. "I thought sure I had him this time. And here he comes home to take a nap!"

He sat undecided in a corner of the cab.

"Hello, Sherman!" came a voice from above.

Sherman, startled, leaned out through the cab door and looked up. Knowlton was leaning out of an open window on the second story of the apartment house he had entered, looking down with an amused grin.

"Won't you come up and have some tea?" he sang out pleasantly.

Sherman's face colored with rage.

"No, thank you, *Mr. John Norton,*" he called. Then he turned and shouted at the driver to go on, while his brain whirled with the thousand wild schemes of a baffled and enraged man.

He, too, had noticed Lila's preference for Knowlton. And he understood it, as Dumain did not; for the eyes of love are keen. He saw the uselessness of trying to combat that preference, for he recognized Knowlton's superiority; but he hoped to acquire the power to force Knowlton to remove himself.

He believed that he possessed the key to that power, and he had sought in many ways to verify his suspicions, but so far without success. He had begun by attempting a bluff. But Knowlton had called it, and it had failed.

He had started a correspondence with friends in Warton. The information he obtained from them encouraged him; his suspicions were strengthened, but not confirmed. And he required evidence.

Then he had shadowed Knowlton, and seemed ever on the verge of a discovery. But the proof he sought, though ever within his grasp, forever eluded him. He was at last almost persuaded to give it up as hopeless.

He was filled with chagrin, disappointment, and despair, while the sight of Lila's face and his desire for her spurred him on to renewed effort.

Now, as he made his way back to the Lamartine, he resolved on a stroke in the open. He would enlist the services of the Erring Knights, at the same time blinding them as to his own designs.

"They're a bunch of fools, anyway," he thought. "I think I'll tackle the little Frenchman."

Accordingly, when he reached the Lamartine he called Dumain aside.

"What do you want?" Dumain asked shortly.

"I want to talk to you about Knowlton," said Sherman.

"What ees eet?"

"I've discovered something about him that I think you ought to know—something not exactly to his credit."

Dumain stiffened.

"Knowlton ees my friend," he observed meaningly. "Go slow, Sherman."

"If that's the way you feel about it I have nothing more to say," said Sherman, turning to go. "Only I thought you were a friend of Miss Williams."

Dumain looked up quickly.

"And so I am," he declared. "But what is zee connection?"

"Only this: That no one who is a real friend of Miss Williams can possibly be a friend of John Knowlton."

"And why?"

"Because—well, I don't think he intends to marry her."

"Mon Dieu!" Dumain gasped. "Has he been—"

"No—not yet. But he will be. And she likes him too well already. Have you noticed what she does with the roses he gives her? And do you know how her eyes follow him all over the lobby?"

"Well?"

"Well, you know what that means. It means that Knowlton can do just about what he likes with her. If not now, it'll come soon. And he'll ruin her. Do you know anything about Knowlton? Listen:

"His real name is Norton. One year ago he was cashier in a bank in a little town in Ohio. One morning they find the safe robbed—dynamited. They couldn't prove Norton was implicated, but everybody knew he was. He beat it to New York. That explains where he got his coin. Now you have it. Should a guy like that be allowed to hang around Lila Williams?"

Dumain sighed.

"We are none of us pairfect," he observed.

"Oh, the devil!" exclaimed Sherman, exasperated. "Perhaps not.

I guess neither you nor me is going to publish our diaries. But that isn't the point. To put it plainly, I happen to know that Miss Williams is in love with this Knowlton, and that he fully intends to take advantage of it. You know what that means."

Dumain appeared to be lost in thought.

"But what can we do?" he said finally.

"The same as we've done to a dozen others."

"But zis Knowlton—he is no coward."

"There are six of us," said Sherman meaningly.

Dumain rose from his chair with a gesture of decision.

"I speak to Dougherty and Driscoll," he said as he turned to go.

Sherman watched him cross the lobby.

"The little idiot!" he muttered contemptuously. Then he turned his eyes toward Lila's desk.

As he gazed at her his face burned with desire and his eyes glittered like the eyes of the serpent. Slowly they filled with evil exultation. Then, subduing this outward betrayal of his thoughts, he crossed to her desk, halted uncertainly, and finally reached for a telegram blank.

"You have decided to give me some of your patronage?" Lila smiled.

"Yes," Sherman replied. "Only it won't be in code."

A tinge of color appeared in Lila's cheeks, and a pang of jealousy that stung Sherman's heart made him regret the observation. He placed the telegram blank on the top of the desk and after a minute's thought wrote on it as follows:

Mr. Gerald Hamilton,
President of the Warton National Bank, Warton, Ohio.
In case you wish to find John Norton, try the Hotel Lamartine, New York.

                                                        W. S.

Lila smiled as she read it.

"You newspaper men are so mysterious," she observed. Then suddenly she turned slightly pale and glanced up quickly.

"She's noticed the similarity in the names," thought Sherman.

"Why?" he said aloud. "Is there anything so mysterious about that?"

"It sounds like a missing heir or a—an embezzler," said Lila.

"I'm sorry I can't enlighten you."

"Oh, I wouldn't expect you to. I suppose you're full of important and terrible secrets."

"Perhaps." Sherman hesitated a moment, then added: "But there's only one that I regard as important."

Lila was silent.

"It is about you," Sherman continued.

"About me?" Lila's tone was incredulous.

"About you," Sherman repeated. His tone was low and significant as he added, "and me."

His meaning was too clear to admit of any pretense that it was not understood. For a moment Lila's face was lowered, then she raised it and said firmly: "Mr. Sherman, I do not wish you to talk to me—like—that."

"I can't help it. You know it, anyway. I love you." Sherman's voice trembled with desire.

"Must I tell you that you annoy me?" she said, rising to her feet.

Sherman lost control of himself.

"You wouldn't say that to Mr. John Knowlton," he sneered. "And the time will come when you can't say it to me. I want you. Look at me. Do I look like a man who wouldn't take what he wants? You will—you must be mine."

The unexpectedness of it caused Lila's face to turn a fiery red. Then she as suddenly became pale. For a moment neither spoke. They had no words; for Sherman had no sooner spoken than he regretted the rashness of his premature avowal. Lila was the first to recover herself.

"Mr. Sherman," she said calmly, "if you ever speak to me in this way again I shall tell Mr. Dougherty and Mr. Driscoll that you are annoying me. Now go."

And Sherman went.

—w—

Danger

D UMAIN PONDERED long over the information Sherman had given him concerning Knowlton before he decided to act on it.

The fact is that Dumain was strongly opposed to the revealing of a man's past. He may have had a personal reason for this; but let us be charitable. Broadway is not the only place in the world where they act on the belief that a man's past is his own and should not be held against him.

Besides, Sherman had admitted that Knowlton had merely been suspected. There had been no evidence; he had been allowed to go free. And Dumain was not inclined to strike a blow at an innocent man who suffered under the blasting stigma of an unproved accusation.

Still, there was Lila. She must be protected at any cost. And had not Dumain himself noticed her interest in Knowlton? What if she really loved him?

And what if Knowlton was the sort of man Sherman had declared him to be? Clearly it meant Lila's ruin. For it is the belief of all Broadway cynics that any woman will do anything for the man she loves. So, early the next morning (that is, early for him), Dumain made his decision on the side of prudence.

He spoke first to Dougherty. The ex-prizefighter was greatly surprised.

"I like Knowlton," he said, "and I believe you're wrong to suspect him. But you know what I think of Miss Williams; and where she's concerned we can't leave any room for doubt. Knowlton must be informed that he is absolutely not wanted."

"Zat ees zee way eet looks to me," said Dumain.

He had met Dougherty on Broadway, and as they talked they strolled to the hotel and entered the lobby. The hotel clerk threw them a familiar nod. Miss Hughes sang out a cheery "Good morning," and Lila smiled pleasantly as they passed her desk. Except for two or three strangers, probably commercial buyers, reading their morning newspapers, the place was empty.

"Sure," said Dougherty, continuing. "When are you going to tell him?"

Dumain looked aghast.

"Tom! Surely you don't expect me to tell heem?"

"Why not?"

"What! How could I? Here are zee facts: Knowlton weighs one hundred and eighty pounds. I weigh a hundred and twentee. It would be absurd. I don't think I am a coward; but I would like to leeve anozzer year or two."

Dougherty laughed.

"All right. Leave it to me. I'll tell him. It's too bad," he added regretfully. "I liked Knowlton."

A few minutes later Knowlton entered the lobby. He walked straight to Lila's desk and wrote out a telegram. Dumain and Dougherty, who were only a few feet away, overheard the conversation.

"You're early this morning," said Lila, as Knowlton handed her a bill from a bulging wallet.

Knowlton glanced at his watch. "Early? It's past eleven."

"I know. But that's early for you."

"Perhaps. A little," Knowlton admitted. "And how are you this fine wintry morning?"

"Well, thank you," Lila smiled.

Knowlton turned away.

"In the name of Heaven, is there anything wrong with that?" Dougherty growled.

"No," Dumain admitted. "But zee die is cast. Never retract a deleeberate decision. There's your man; go after heem."

The ex-prizefighter started across the lobby. Knowlton turned.

"Hello, Tom!"

"Good morning," said Dougherty, visibly ill at ease.

"Are you on for a game of billiards?"

"No," Dougherty hesitated. "The fact is, Knowlton, there's something I have to say to you."

"Is it much?" Knowlton smiled.

"It's enough."

"Then come over to the corner. It's more comfortable. Hello, Dumain. How's the world?" Knowlton continued chattering as they walked to the leather lounge sacred to the Erring Knights. Then he produced some cigars, offering one to Dougherty.

"No, thanks," said Dougherty stiffly.

"What! Won't take a cigar? What's happened?"

Dougherty coughed and cleared his throat.

"Well," he stammered, "the truth is we—that is, they—they think you ought to go—that is, leave—Oh, darn it all!"

"Easy, Tom," said Knowlton. "Give it to me a word at a time."

Dougherty recommenced his stammering, but a word here and there gave Knowlton an idea of what he was trying to say.

"I believe," he interrupted, "you are trying to tell me that I have become *persona non grata*. In other words, the Erring Knights have seen fit to expel their youngest member."

"Right," said Dougherty, inexpressibly relieved. "If I could have said it like that I would have had no trouble."

Knowlton cut off the end of a cigar and lit it.

"And now," he said between puffs, "what is it—*puff*—you want?"

"That's not the question. It's what we don't want."

"All right." Knowlton waved aside the distinction. "Go on."

"In the first place," Dougherty began, "there's Miss Williams."

"I see her," said Knowlton gravely. "She's sending a telegram. Probably mine. See how the light plays on her hair? Well, what about her?"

"You are not to go near her," said Dougherty with emphasis.

"Ever?"

"Never."

Knowlton blew a cloud of smoke toward the ceiling.

"I see. And what else?"

"You are to stay away from the Lamartine."

"M–m–m. Anything else?"

"That is all."

Knowlton rose, walked to a cuspidor and knocked the ashes from his cigar, then returned to his seat. For another minute he smoked in silence.

"And if I refuse?" he said finally.

"There are six of us," said Dougherty with meaning.

"Then, if I enter the doors of the Lamartine I displease the Erring Knights?"

"You do."

"In that case," Knowlton again rose, "I have to announce that in the future the Erring Knights will be displeased on an average of fourteen times a week. It pains me to cause my old friends so much displeasure, but you leave me no choice." He hesitated a moment, then added: "You should have known better than to try to frighten me, Dougherty." With that he walked away.

Dougherty saw him go to the cigar stand, relight his cigar, start toward Lila's desk, suddenly change his direction, and leave the hotel by the Broadway door. Then the ex-prizefighter hurried over to Dumain.

"I told you so," he said gloomily.

"What deed he say?" asked Dumain.

"Just what I said he'd say."

"Well?" Dumain passed over the fact that Dougherty had said nothing whatever about it.

"He ignores us. He intends to do just as he pleases. We're in for it."

"It seems to me," Dumain retorted, "eet would be better to say he's in for it. We'll have to show him we are not to be trifled wiz. Come on; I have zee idea."

They seated themselves on the lounge in the corner and proceeded to a discussion of the plan of battle.

In the meantime Knowlton was striding swiftly toward his rooms on Thirtieth Street. His face wore a worried frown, and every now and then he glanced nervously to the rear. Occasionally, too, his lips parted in an amused smile; possibly whenever he thought of the quixotic chivalry of the Erring Knights.

The streets and sidewalks were covered with snow—the first of the season. Surface cars clanged noisily; voices sounded in the crisp, bracing air with the sharp clarity of bell tones; faces glowed with the healthful exhilaration of quickened steps and the rush of inward warmth to meet the frosty attack of old winter.

The vigor of the north and the restlessness of the great city combined to supply the deficiencies of the November sun, ineffectual against the stern attack of his annual enemy.

Knowlton turned in at the same door on Thirtieth Street we have seen him enter before, and mounted the stairs to an apartment on the second floor.

Once inside he locked the door carefully behind him, then walked to a wardrobe in a corner of the adjoining room and took from it a small black bag. His hand trembled a little as he placed the bag on a table in the center of the room.

"My good friend," he said aloud, "I am inclined to believe that they are trying to separate us. The little comedy just performed at the hotel must have resulted from the good offices of a certain Mr. Sherman.

"Now, the question is, shall I remain true to you or not? You must admit that you're dangerous; still, I'm willing to give you another chance. We'll leave it to fate. Heads you stay; tails you go."

He took a coin from his vest pocket and flipped it high in the air. It struck the table, bounced off onto the floor and rolled halfway across the room.

Knowlton stooped over and looked at it curiously, picked it up and returned it to his pocket. Then he carried the bag back to the wardrobe and replaced it on the shelf.

As he turned and seated himself in a chair by the table, his face wore an expression of gravity and anxiety that belied the lightness of his tone and words.

To the most casual observer it would have been apparent that John Knowlton was approaching, or passing through, a crisis. But suddenly he smiled; sweetly, almost tenderly.

We follow his thought, and it brings us to the lobby of the Lamartine.

Besides the usual crowd of transient guests and midday idlers, we find the Erring Knights assembled in full force. Sherman and Booth, with two or three strangers, are conversing amiably with the Venus at the cigar stand, Driscoll and Jennings are at a game of billiards down the hall, and Dumain and Dougherty are completing their discussion of the ways and means of war. Lila is putting on her hat and coat to go to lunch.

Sherman detached himself from the group at the cigar stand and walked over to the lounge where Dumain and Dougherty were seated.

"Well?" he said significantly, stopping in front of them.

They looked up at him inquiringly.

"Knowlton didn't show up yet," he continued.

"Yes, he deed," said the little Frenchman.

"What?"

"I say, he deed."

"Then, where is he?"

"I don't know."

"Oh!" A light of evil satisfaction appeared in Sherman's eyes. "Then you spoke to him?"

"Yes."

"Then he's gone."

"So eet seems; but he'll probably be back."

"Ah! And what did he say?"

"In effect, he advised us to go to zee devil."

Sherman seemed taken aback.

"But didn't you tell him we'd get him?" he demanded.

But Dumain and Dougherty rose and went to join Driscoll and Jennings in the billiard room without answering him. Sherman's face colored slightly, but he remained silent, gazing after them with a contemptuous sneer.

"My turn next," he muttered after they had gone.

Within the next hour Dumain spoke to each of the Erring

Knights concerning Knowlton; and he was somewhat surprised at the unanimity with which they favored his proposal. Driscoll was the only one who had a good word for Knowlton. But he was easily persuaded.

Then Dumain decided on a little strategy of his own. The result was unfortunate; but he could not have foreseen that. The little Frenchman was well acquainted with woman's weakness; but he knew little of her strength. On that day he was destined to acquire knowledge.

When the others wandered out in search of lunch, leaving the lobby all but deserted, he remained behind. For the sake of moral support he communicated his design to Dougherty, who expressed a fear that something was about to be started which it would be difficult to finish.

"Bah!" said Dumain. "You shall see. Sit here to wait. It will be easy."

When Lila returned from lunch he hurried to her desk and helped her off with her coat.

"Have you been taking lessons in gallantry, Mr. Dumain?" Lila smiled.

"Such a question as zat is insult to zee Frenchman," said Dumain, assuming an injured air. "We do not learn gallantry; we are born wiz eet. I insist on an apology."

"But that is not gallant," Lila protested.

Dumain laughed.

"*Eh bien!* We all have our lapses. And, too, you should not have offended me. I am very sensiteeve. Eet ees not fair. Only today I have rendered you a very great sairvice. Not zat I expect any reward—or even gratitude. But I think you should know of eet."

Lila looked up quickly.

"You mustn't talk like that, Mr. Dumain. You have been good

and kind to me—all of you; and you know I am grateful. I can never thank you enough."

Dumain was silent.

"But what is the service you have rendered me?" Lila said presently.

"One zat you may not thank me for," said Dumain.

"But what was it?"

"Killing anozzer dragon—of zee human species."

She frowned.

"I'm afraid I don't understand you."

Dumain stammered something about "men" and "danger," and "the need of a protector." He was finding it harder than he had thought.

"But what do you mean?" Lila insisted.

The little Frenchman gathered himself together and plunged in.

"I mean," he said impressively, "zat we have dropped Knowlton and told heem to stay away from you."

The unexpectedness of it made Lila catch her breath in surprise. Then her face colored gloriously, treacherously. A little tremulous, uncertain laugh came from between her lips.

"That was hardly necessary, was it?" she inquired with a brave attempt at indifference.

"We thought so," Dumain answered, admiring her courage. He was thinking to himself: "She's a thoroughbred. *Mon Dieu!* What a woman!"

"You see," he added aloud, "we found out something about heem that was not exactly to his credit. So, of course, we cut heem. What does that mean?" noticing a curious smile on Lila's face.

"I was just thinking," said Lila slowly, "that it must be a very good man who could afford to say to another man: 'You are not fit to associate with me.' Don't you think so?"

Dumain winced.

"But that wasn't it," he protested. "We were thinking of you. None of us pretend to be angels. But we know you are one."

"But why should you have singled out Mr. Knowlton?" Lila insisted, ignoring the compliment. "He acted just as the rest of you. He is kind to me—so are you, so is Mr. Dougherty. He has never offended me."

Dumain opened his mouth as though to answer; but was silent.

"Why?" Lila persisted.

Dumain stammered something about roses.

"Roses!" exclaimed Lila in amazement. "What do you mean?"

"I mean zat you take hees roses home," said Dumain desperately, "and no one else's."

He should have known better. No one can get a secret from a woman in that manner; provided, of course, that it is her own secret. Lila leaned back in her chair and laughed delightedly. The little Frenchman regarded her with a comical expression of wounded vanity.

"Oh!" Lila cried, as soon as she could speak. "Mr. Dumain, you are positively childish! You must forgive me; but it is so funny!"

It was too much for Dumain; he gave it up.

"Tom!" he called in the tone of a drowning man crying for help.

Dougherty rose from the seat Dumain had assigned to him and came over to them. In as few words as possible Dumain explained his dilemma, telling him that Lila was aggrieved at their attitude toward Knowlton.

Lila interrupted him.

"Not aggrieved," she said. "It does not especially interest me; only it seems unjust. And I see no reason for it."

Dougherty turned to Dumain.

"Why did you say anything about it to her?" he growled.

Dumain, having nothing to say, was silent.

Dougherty turned to Lila.

"And you think we are unjust?"

"Yes," she replied.

"Well, you are wrong."

"I believe I am right."

Dougherty reflected for a moment, sighed for courage, cleared his throat, and said:

"Miss Williams, it is time we understand each other. Now is as good a time as any."

"I don't understand you," said Lila.

"You will before I get through. I only ask you to remember what I—what we think of you.

"You know what we've done—not much, perhaps, but all we could—to show you how we feel. We've been glad enough for the chance. There's not much good in any of us, but we're always anxious to use what we've got.

"Now about Knowlton. As long as he was merely one of us, we asked no questions. He was good enough for us. And I guess he always treated you all right. But that's not the point. We have an idea you're beginning to think too much of him.

"And that won't do. Knowlton's all right to buy you roses, and look after you, like the rest of us. But we ain't fit to touch you, and neither is he.

"That's all there is to it. If you'll tell us you don't think any more of Knowlton than you do of any of the rest of us, we'll admit we're wrong and apologize.

"We have some rights, you know. You've let us stand by you and do things for you. All we ask you to do is this: say you don't love this Knowlton."

During this speech Lila lost her courage. Was everyone in on her secret? Her color rose and fell, her face was lowered, and her hand trembled as she raised it to adjust a stray lock of hair behind her ear. Still, she found sufficient strength to answer:

"I know—I know you have rights, Mr. Dougherty. I know what you have done for me. If it were not for that I would be very angry. You may treat Mr. Knowlton just as you like; the subject does not interest me. And now—go, please."

"But you ought to tell us—"

"Go!" Lila exclaimed. "Please!"

They turned and left her without another word.

And Lila knew she had done right not to be angry with them. Perhaps they had been impertinent; but she knew they had not meant to be.

And she was frightened; rather, vaguely anxious. For she felt that they would never have presumed so far unless they knew more of Knowlton than they had told her.

What could it be? Her heart said, he is worthy. But she had not spent months in the Hotel Lamartine without learning something of the unsightly mess that lies concealed beneath the crust; and she feared.

But after all, why should she trouble herself with thoughts of Knowlton? *He* had shown no interest in *her*. He had treated her with courtesy, of course; he was obviously a gentleman. But he had given her no reason to suppose that he would ever be the instrument either of her pleasure or her sorrow.

The afternoon passed slowly. The telegraph desk at the Lamartine was never overworked; but today it seemed to Lila duller than usual. She tried to read, but found it impossible to settle her mind.

At five o'clock she began to fill in her daily report, and prolonged the task as far as possible in the effort to remain occupied. At half past five she prepared the cash for the collector of the telegraph company, who called every evening.

A few minutes later he arrived.

"Not much for you today," Lila smiled.

The collector, a short, plump man with an air of importance, counted the cash, wrote out a receipt and handed it to Lila. Then he took an envelope from his pocket and drew from it a crisp, new ten-dollar bill, which he laid on the desk in front of her.

He leaned toward her with a mysterious air as he said:

"Miss Williams, do you know who gave you that?"

Lila looked at the bill, wondering.

"In the past month," continued the collector, "you have turned in something like a dozen of these. We want to know where they come from."

The oddity of the question had taken Lila by surprise, and she had remained silent, gathering her wits; but now she remembered.

Of course, the bills were Knowlton's. Did he not always pay for his telegrams with new bills? And her receipts were not so large but that she would have remembered any others.

"But why?" she stammered, to gain time.

The collector ignored the question.

"Do you know who gave them to you?" he repeated.

"No," replied Lila distinctly.

"No recollection whatever?"

"None."

He reached in another pocket and drew forth another bill exactly similar to the one he had shown her, saying:

"I just got this out of your cash drawer. You took it in today. Surely you remember who gave you this?"

Lila repeated "No."

For a minute the collector eyed her keenly in silence. Then, returning the bills to the envelope, he said slowly:

"That's odd. Very odd—in a little office like this. I don't see how you could help remembering. Anyway, be sure you keep a lookout from now on. They're counterfeit."

"Counterfeit!" Ltla gasped.

The collector nodded, repeated his injunction to "keep a lookout," and departed.

Counterfeit!

Lila buried her face in her hands and sat quivering, horrified.

—∿—

CHAPTER V

Two Escorts

THAT NIGHT was an unpleasant one for Lila. She perceived clearly for the first time whither her heart was leading her, and recoiled in terror from the dangerous path on which she had already set her foot.

She had lied, and she had been faithless to her trust—which, though a small one, was felt by her to be none the less inviolable. She had lied instinctively, naturally, as a matter of course—the heart commands the brain, if at all, with an awful authority.

And for whom had she made the sacrifice? she asked herself. For a man about whom she knew one thing, and that thing was: she loved him. Perhaps, after all, the Broadway cynic is partly right.

Alone in her room that night she attempted to subject herself to a strict and sincere examination. She asked herself: "Why have you done this thing?" and her heart fluttered painfully, endeavoring by silence to keep its secret; but she felt the answer.

She crept, shivering, from her bed, and buried her face in a tray of withered rose leaves on the table.

Love is no snob. He forces the princess to deceive a court, defy a king, and renounce her royalty, that she may fly to the open arms

of her despised lover; he forces the working girl to laugh at justice
and law, and sacrifice her dearest possession—even herself. And the
one triumph is to him fully as sweet as the other. Love is no snob.

His struggle with Lila was a hard one. She fought with the
strength of despair, having forced herself to realize the significance
of the battle. Nothing is more horrible to a woman than the fear that
she has bestowed her heart on one unworthy; I say, the fear, for when
the bestowal is once consummated and admitted, she is more apt to
glory in it than to be ashamed of it.

Lila ended by saying to herself: "I have done right to shield
him. He is good—I know it—surely my heart would not deceive
me? What am I to do? I do not know. But I do not regret what I
have done."

And she smiled, and slept.

The following day, at her desk in the Lamartine, she felt her
doubts and fears return. She chafed under an indefinable sensation
of restlessness and expectancy; she performed her duties absent-
mindedly and perfunctorily; there was a marked absence of the
usual pleasant cheerfulness in her manner; her eyes constantly wandered to the door, and returned again to her desk, filled with disappointment. The lobby of the Lamartine did not see Knowlton
that day.

To the Erring Knights this meant a triumph. They believed that
after all Knowlton had heeded their warning and decided to obey
their dictum. They allowed themselves to become unduly excited
over the matter, and as the afternoon wore away their faces took on
an expression of jubilant satisfaction. Partly was this owing to their
genuinely tender interest in Miss Williams; partly to the inherent
vanity of man.

At four o'clock in the afternoon Dougherty was pacing up and
down the lobby, past the lofty marble pillars, through clouds of

tobacco smoke, with the air of a pitcher strolling to the bench after a victorious inning.

He was superbly indifferent to the amused glances of the loungers seated and standing here and there about the lobby, and was even undisturbed by the biting remarks of the Venus at the cigar stand. Finally he strolled over to the leather lounge where two or three of the others were seated.

"You see," said he, waving his hand grandly, "he does not come. And who was it that told him to stay away? I."

"Wait," said Driscoll darkly. "It's early yet. And then—what will you do?"

"Bah!" said Dumain explosively. "As for me, I theenk he is no coward. He will come. And zen—well, we have our program."

But Knowlton did not arrive. Five o'clock came, and six. At the approach of dinnertime the crowd in the lobby thinned perceptibly, and the Erring Knights disappeared by ones and twos.

Jennings, on his way out from the billiard room, stopped at the corner in search of a dinner companion. He found Sherman seated there alone.

"Thanks," said Sherman in response to his invitation. "I'd like to go, but I have a date. See you tonight."

Jennings nodded and left the lobby.

Lila was still at her desk. It was nearly an hour past her period of duty, and there was nothing, apparently, to detain her; still she lingered. She sat with her eyes fixed on the door, hoping that the figure she longed to see would appear at the last minute.

Finally, she arose and slowly put on her coat and hat. On her way out she stopped at the cigar stand and chatted for a moment with Miss Hughes, who expressed some concern at her pallor and appearance of fatigue.

"It's no wonder you're sick," said the Venus sympathetically. "A dump like this is enough to kill you. I can stand it. I'm used to it. But sometimes it gives even me the willies."

"It's nothing," Lila smiled. "I think I have a headache. Thank you for asking. Good night."

She left the lobby by the main entrance, walked up Broadway to Twenty-third Street, then turned west. The rush hour was past, and the sidewalks were nearly deserted. A few belated pedestrians hurried along as rapidly as the slippery condition of the pavement would permit.

The lighted shop windows shone in the frosty air with a sharp brilliancy. Taxicabs and hansoms picked their way cautiously through the ice and snow, and the crosstown cars clanged noisily on their way to either river.

Lila had got nearly to Sixth Avenue, and was hastening her step at the urging of the cold east wind at her back, when she heard her name called behind her. Turning, she saw Billy Sherman, who advanced smiling, with lifted hat.

Half frightened, she nodded and turned to go, but Sherman stopped her with a gesture. There was a conciliatory smile on his dark, handsome face as he looked down at her.

"Do you take the Sixth Avenue 'L'?" he asked.

Lila nodded.

"Then we can ride together. I am going uptown. You are ill, and you need some one to look after you. If you would only—"

Lila broke in with a protest, but Sherman paid no attention to it, and walked by her side to the Elevated station and up the steps. He stopped at the window to buy tickets, but Lila took one from her purse and dropped it in the box as she passed to the platform. In a moment he joined her.

"Are you unwilling that I should do even so little for you?" he asked reproachfully.

Lila was silent. A train pulled in, and they boarded it together.

On account of the late hour, they had no difficulty to find seats. As the train started Sherman turned in his seat to look at her, and repeated his question.

His manner was respectful, and his solicitude appeared to be genuine; and Lila, wearied and worn by anxiety, was touched by it. After all, she asked herself bitterly, who was she, to despise anybody?

"I don't know," she said doubtfully in answer to his question, which he repeated for the third time. "You must remember—what you have said to me—and how you have acted. I wish—I think it would be best for you to leave me at the next station. You were not going uptown, were you?"

"I beg you to forget how I have acted," said Sherman earnestly. "I know that twice I have forgotten myself, but not without reason. You must know that I am and want to be, your friend.

"I shall not pretend that it is all my desire. But if you will not allow me to be more than a friend, I will be satisfied with that. I couldn't let you come home alone tonight. You were so weak you could hardly stand."

He continued in this strain for many minutes, while the train rumbled northward, and Lila sat back in her seat with her eyes half closed, scarcely listening.

His voice came to her in a gruff monotone above the rattle of the train, and against her will filled her with a sense of protection and comfort. The words came to her vaguely, unintelligible; but the tone was that of sympathy and friendship—and how she needed them!

Thus she allowed him to continue, while she remained silent, dimly conscious of the danger she had once felt in his glance and voice.

At the One Hundred and Fourth Street station he rose, and she saw with a sense of surprise that she had reached her destination. At the train gate she turned to thank him, but he assisted her down the steps of the station and started west on One Hundred and Fourth Street at her side.

"You are surprised that I know the way?" he smiled. "You should not be. How many times have I stood in this street looking up at your window, when you thought I was far away—or, rather, when you were not thinking of me at all!"

"Mr. Sherman!" exclaimed Lila warningly.

They had halted at the stoop of an old-fashioned brownstone apartment house, and Lila had mounted the three or four steps and stood looking down at him.

"Forgive me," said Sherman in a tone of contrition. "But you have not answered me—I mean, what I said on the train. There could be nothing offensive in what I proposed, unless you hate me."

"No. I think I do not hate you," said Lila slowly.

She was tired, and longed to be alone, and was forcing herself to be polite to him.

"Then you are my friend?"

"I—think—so."

"Will you shake hands on it?"

Lila appeared to hesitate, and shivered—possibly from the cold. Finally she extended a reluctant hand a few inches in front of her.

Then, as soon as Sherman touched it with his fingers, she withdrew it hastily, and, with a hurried "Good night, and thank you," disappeared within the house.

For a long minute Sherman stood gazing at the door which had closed behind her; then, turning sharply, he started off down the street. At Columbus Avenue he entered a saloon and ordered a brandy.

"God knows I need it," he muttered to himself. "The little devil! Well, I can't play that game. It's too hard to hold myself in. The other way is more dangerous, perhaps, but it's easier. Friendship! I'll show you a new kind of friendship!"

He beckoned to the bartender and ordered another brandy, with a knowing leer at his reflection in the mirror opposite. Then, having drained his second glass, he left the saloon and, crossing the street to the Elevated station, boarded a downtown train. In thirty minutes he was back at the Lamartine.

The lobby was almost deserted; it was too early for the evening throng. Sherman wandered about in search of one of the Erring Knights, but in vain; and he finally asked the Venus at the cigar stand if she had seen Knowlton. She replied that he had not been in the lobby, and Sherman departed for dinner, well satisfied with the events of the day.

He was destined, on the following day, to have that feeling of satisfaction rudely shattered and converted into despair.

––––––

The next morning the Erring Knights were openly and frankly jubilant. Knowlton had obeyed their warning; clearly, he was afraid of them. They felt an increased sense of proprietary right in Miss Williams.

Dougherty, entering the lobby about eleven o'clock, stopped at Lila's desk to say good morning, and stared in anxious surprise at her pale cheeks and red, tear-stained eyes.

"Are you ill?" he asked bluntly.

"Not I," she answered, trying to smile. "I had a headache, but it is all right now."

Dougherty grumbled something unintelligible, and proceeded to the corner where the Erring Knights were assembled. He was the last to arrive. Dumain, Jennings, and Driscoll were seated on the leather lounge, and Sherman and Booth were leaning against the marble pillars in front of it. They greeted Dougherty in a chorus.

"*Bone jore,*" said Dougherty, with an elaborate bow. "How's that Dumain?"

"Pairfect," smiled the little Frenchman.

"Really," the ex-prizefighter asserted, "I think I'll learn French. I like the way it sounds. *'Monseere'* is much more classy than 'mister,' for instance."

"If you do," put in Driscoll, "you'd better speak it better than Dumain speaks English. If a man could be electrocuted for murdering a language he'd be a storage battery by this time."

"Have your fun," said Dumain, rising to his feet and shrugging his shoulders good-naturedly. "Eet ees a treeck—zat Angleesh. I have eet not."

"Hardly," laughed Jennings. "You don't speak it with the finish of our late friend Mr. Knowlton, for instance. By the way, have you seen him?" he added, turning to Dougherty.

"Who? Knowlton?"

"Yes."

"Well, I should say not." Dougherty grinned as though the idea were absurd. "And, believe me, I won't see him—at least, not in the Lamartine. When I tell a guy he's not wanted, that ends it."

"Don't be too sure," Booth advised. "Just because he didn't come yesterday—you know today is another day."

Dougherty turned on the speaker scornfully. "Listen," he said with emphasis. "If that Knowlton shows his face in this lobby— which he won't—but if he does, we'll eat him up."

"Diable! Mon Dieu!"

The exclamation came from Dumain, in an undertone of surprise and alarm. The others turned to him in wonder, and, following his fixed gaze toward the main entrance, saw Knowlton walk down the center of the lobby and stop at Lila's desk!

The action and facial expression of each of the Erring Knights at this juncture was curiously indicative of their different characters.

Driscoll and Dougherty moved forward and glared belligerently;

Booth and Jennings glanced from one side to the other as though in search of reenforcements; Dumain sputtered with wrath and indignation, and Sherman's face darkened with a menacing scowl. None of them, however, appeared to be particularly anxious to cross the lobby.

Knowlton had not cast a single glance in their direction. His back was turned to them as he stood talking with Lila, and their conversation was in so low a tone that the Erring Knights heard not a word of it.

For perhaps two minutes this scene, half farcical, remained unchanged. The Erring Knights muttered to each other in undertones and glared fiercely, but they made no move.

Suddenly they saw Knowlton lift his hat and bow to Lila, turn sharply, and leave the lobby even more hurriedly than he had entered it.

Each of the Erring Knights glanced round the circle of his companions; some questioning, others assertive. "It's up to us," declared Dougherty. "We've got to show him."

They gathered themselves closely about the lounge, and all began talking at once.

In the meantime, what of Lila?

When Knowlton entered the lobby she was busied with some papers on her desk, and therefore did not see him. She became aware of his presence only when he stopped at her side and spoke to her.

For a moment she was speechless with surprise and gladness and confusion. She stared at him strangely, unseeing.

"What's the matter?" smiled Knowlton. "I hope I don't look as fierce as that."

Then, as Lila did not answer, he reached for a telegraph blank, wrote on it, and handed it to her, together with a ten-dollar bill which he took from his wallet.

Lila's dismay and confusion were doubled. The bill was exactly similar to the others he had given her, and to those which the collector had declared to be counterfeit.

What could she say? Finding no words, and feeling that she must do something, she extended her hand to take the bill, then drew it back, shivering involuntarily. Summoning her courage by a violent effort, she faltered:

"Mr. Knowlton, that bill—I—I cannot take it."

And as Knowlton's face filled with surprise and something else that resembled uneasiness, and before he could speak she continued:

"The other day our collector showed me one of the bills you had given me, and asked where I got it. He said they were counterfeit. I thought you would want to know."

Knowlton had turned pale and was staring at her fixedly.

"Well?" he said.

"Shall I tell him?"

"Why—didn't you?" the young man stammered eagerly.

"No. I thought I had better speak to you first. You see—" Lila's voice faltered and ceased, her face reddening to the tips of her ears with shame.

Knowlton picked up the bill he had laid on the counter and returned it to his pocket. His hand trembled nervously, and his voice was low and uncertain as he said:

"If it's all the same to you, I—it would be better not to tell him. I shall not bother you with more of them. And I—I thank you," he added, as he turned away. That was all.

Lila turned to her desk, sick at heart; and when little Dumain bustled over a few minutes later with the intention of learning something of what Knowlton had said to her, he found her in tears.

"*Mon Dieu!*" he gasped. The sight of Miss Williams crying was unprecedented and, to Dumain, extremely painful. "What is zee mattaire?"

"Nothing," said Lila. "I have a headache. For goodness' sake, don't stand and stare at me!"

Whereupon Dumain retreated to the corner where he had left the others in secret session. He decided not to tell them about Lila's tears, being convinced that if he did so they would proceed to murder Knowlton on Broadway at high noon.

Besides, he had an idea that the tears were caused by Knowlton's having said farewell, in which case there would be no necessity for action on the part of the Erring Knights. Dumain was certainly not a coward; but he was—let us say—discreet.

Lila was overwhelmed with shame and humiliation. She had told Knowlton that she had lied for his sake, which amounted to a confession of her interest in him and regard for him. He must have understood. And he had muttered a perfunctory thank you, and walked away.

But perhaps he took it as a matter of course. Perhaps he regarded her as one of those creatures to whom deception is natural—of loose morals and conscience—whose aid may be depended upon by any stray enemy of society and morality.

This thought was unbearable. Lila clenched her fists tightly till the little pink nails bit sharp rings in the white palms of her hands.

Why had he not explained? It could have been but for one of two reasons: either he was guilty and could not, or he regarded her opinion as unimportant and did not care to.

And if he were guilty; but that was impossible. John Knowlton, the man to whom she had given her heart unreservedly, and forever, a counterfeiter—a criminal? It could not be.

There remained only the supposition that he cared so little about her that her good opinion was a matter of indifference to him. And this, though mortifying, was bearable. Still was she filled with shame, for he had heard her confession, and had made no sign.

Most probably she would never know, for she felt convinced

that she would never see Knowlton again. She had been unable to avoid overhearing a great deal of the conversation of the Erring Knights concerning him, and Dumain himself had told her that they had warned him to stay away from the Lamartine.

She smiled bitterly as she thought of that warning. If her anxious protectors only knew how little likelihood there was of Knowlton's taking the trouble either to harm her or to make her happy!

For hours these thoughts filled her mind, confusedly, without beginning or end. It seemed that the afternoon would never pass.

Gradually the lobby filled, and for a time business at the telegraph desk was almost brisk. The Erring Knights strolled in and out aimlessly. From the billiard room down the hall came the sound of clicking balls and banging cues.

Now and then the strident voice of the Venus at the cigar stand rose above all other sounds as she gave a pointed retort to an intimate or jocular remark of a customer. At intervals the bell on the hotel desk gave forth its jarring jingle.

At five o'clock the crowd in the lobby began to disappear. There came intervals in the confused hum of voices and steps. Half past five arrived; and six. Lila put on her hat and coat and arranged the papers on her deck.

She would not linger tonight; that was over, she told herself. Henceforth she would be sensible, and—and forget.

The lobby was nearly empty except for the Erring Knights, who were gathered in the corner, seemingly engaged in a hot discussion. Lila noticed that Sherman, while apparently attentive to his companions, was watching her covertly, and she surmised that he intended to follow her as he had the evening before, and escort her home.

Why not? she asked herself bitterly. At least he cared.

She stooped to put on her rubbers, and, having some difficulty with one of them, remained for some time with her head lowered.

When she sat up, with flushed face and hair disarranged, she found herself looking into the eyes of John Knowlton.

He stood by her desk, hat in hand, with an air of embarrassment and hesitation. Evidently he was waiting for her to speak; but, overcome with surprise, she found no words.

A glance over his shoulder showed her the Erring Knights standing across the lobby, regarding Knowlton with open hostility.

Finally he spoke.

"I feel I owe you an explanation," he said with an apparent effort. "I hope you don't think there was anything wrong about—what you told me this morning."

Lila's wounded pride came to her assistance and gave her strength. This was the man to whom she had given so much, and from whom she had received so little. Worse, he was aware of her weakness. Yet must he learn that she was worthy of his respect, and her own. And yet—why had he returned? She hesitated.

"I don't know what to think," she said doubtfully.

"It will take some time to explain," said Knowlton. "And I want you—if you can—to think well of me. I wonder if you'd be angry if I asked you to go to dinner with me. Will you go?"

Lila caught her breath, while her heart contracted with a joy so keen as to be painful. Of course she ought not to accept his invitation. She felt that that would somehow be wrong.

Besides, he must not be allowed to believe that her favors could be had for the asking. But how her heart was beating! And she said:

"I—I am not dressed for it, Mr. Knowlton."

"We could go to some quiet little place," he urged. "I know you have been thinking horrible things of me today, and with reason. And of course, if you think I am not—not worthy"—

"Oh, it is not that!" Lila exclaimed.

"Then, will you go?"

And though Lila was silent, he must have read her answer in her eyes, for he picked up her umbrella and opened the gate of the railing for her, and they started down the lobby side by side.

Halfway to the door Lila halted and turned to face the Erring Knights, who had neither stirred nor spoken since the entrance of Knowlton.

"Good night!" she called cheerily.

But there was no response. The six gallant protectors returned her gaze in grim and frigid silence.

A little back of the others Lila saw Sherman's dark face, with his lips parted in a snarl of hate. She shivered slightly and turned to her companion.

"Come!" she said, and in spite of her effort to control it her voice trembled a little.

Knowlton opened the door and they passed out together.

~~~

CHAPTER IV

The Transformation

A WAITING taxicab stood outside the hotel. Knowlton helped Lila inside and got in after her.

"Now," he asked, "where shall we go?"

Lila murmured something about her dress, and left the decision to him. Knowlton leaned forward and spoke to the driver.

"Restaurant Lucia, Thirty-seventh Street, near Sixth Avenue."

The driver nodded and started the cab north on Broadway.

Knowlton sat upright in his corner, intuitively divining Lila's wish for a period of silence to adjust her thoughts. The cab went forward by fits and starts owing to the heavy traffic.

Light and shadow came and went through the windows as they passed glaring cafés and theaters, or darkened shops and office buildings. The air was crisp and tingling.

Lila felt herself transported to a scene in the *Arabian Nights*. Not the gorgeous palaces, or the tricks of magicians, or the dark and mysterious passages, but the spirit of wonder.

This lies not ever in mere things, but in the heart. To ride up Broadway in a taxicab at half past six of a December evening may mean anything, or nothing. To the tired businessman it means a convenient but expensive method of getting home to dinner. To the painted woman it means one of the advantages to be derived from an easy con-science. To Lila it meant love and romance and youth and hope.

She did not stop to analyze her feelings; they surged through her heart and brain tumultuously with a glorious gladness. She was dis-covering for herself what a great philosopher has called "the sweet-ness of facts."

She was with Knowlton. He was able to explain the counterfeit bills. He did care about what she thought of him.

She was grateful to him for his silence. Certainly her mind needed readjustment. For two days she had been miserable and unhappy to the verge of despair.

A few minutes ago she had actually been ready to allow Sherman to accompany her home. The smile which this thought brought to her lips was not very complimentary to Mr. Sherman.

And then, with the suddenness of an impetuous Jove, the prince of her dreams had arrived and carried her off in his chariot! Was it not enough to make a girl wish for time to get her breath?

She was so deep in her contemplation of "the sweetness of facts" that she was positively startled by the sound of Knowlton's voice announcing that they had reached their destination.

He helped her from the cab and paid the driver, and they entered the restaurant.

The Restaurant Lucia was one of those places to be found, by the initiated, here and there from the Battery to Harlem, where one may obtain excellent food, well cooked and well served, without the fuss and glitter and ostentation of the "lobster palaces." It does not pretend to Bohemianism, and is therefore truly Bohemian.

As Knowlton and Lila entered the dining room by a door set two or three steps lower than the sidewalk, the orchestra, consisting of a pianist, a 'cellist, and two violinists, was finishing a Spanish melody. They walked down the aisle to the right to the clapping of hands, and Lila turned to observe the little orchestra leader, who was bowing right and left with the air, and the appearance, of an Italian duke.

Knowlton halted at a table near the wall toward the rear, and they seated themselves opposite each other. It was a little early for dinner in the Restaurant Lucia; it was not yet half filled. Lila glanced about curiously as she took off her gloves and gave the inevitable tug to her hat.

Knowlton, being a man, immediately proceeded to business.

"Will you have oysters, or clams?" he asked. "And will you have a cocktail?"

Lila made a grimace.

"I couldn't possibly decide what to eat," she declared. "You select. And I—I don't care to drink anything."

Knowlton regarded her with the usual mild surprise of a man at a woman's lack of interest in the sublime topic of food, and entered into a serious conversation on that subject with the waiter, while Lila amused herself by a survey of the dining room. She was seated facing the door, to which Knowlton's back was turned.

Knowlton, having completed his order, tossed the menu aside and looked across at his companion. Her elbow was resting on the table, with her chin in her cupped hand.

Her eyelids drooped as though reluctant to leave unveiled the stars they guarded, and a tiny spot of pink glowed on either cheek.

Suddenly, as Knowlton sat watching her silently, her hand dropped to the table and she gave a startled movement, while her face filled with unmistakable alarm. She glanced at Knowlton and met his questioning gaze.

"Mr. Sherman," she whispered excitedly. "He just entered the restaurant, and is sitting at a table near the door. He saw us."

Knowlton started to turn round to see for himself, but thought better of it and remained facing his companion.

"The Erring Knights," he said easily, with an indifferent shrug of the shoulders. "Assuredly, they protect you with a vengeance. But I can hardly compliment them on their choice of an emissary."

"But surely it must be—he is here by accident," said Lila. "They would not have sent him."

"Perhaps he sent himself," Knowlton suggested. "I happen to know that he is an adept at the gentle art of shadowing."

Lila's face flushed with annoyance.

"He has no right"—she began impetuously. "I hate him. He has spoiled my dinner—I mean, our dinner."

At this Knowlton, who was hiding his own annoyance, protested with a laugh that it would take more than Sherman to spoil it for him. His enjoyment, he declared, rested only with his companion. Lila sighed and poised her fork daintily over her plate of clams.

"Does the creature eat?" asked Knowlton presently.

Lila glanced toward the door.

"No," she replied. "He drinks."

Knowlton chuckled at her tone of disgust and declared that he felt a certain pity for Mr. Sherman.

But gradually, as the dinner progressed, they forgot his presence. Knowlton exerted himself to that end, and soon had Lila laughing delightedly at a recital of his boyhood experiences in the country.

Under the influence of his sparkling gaiety her cheeks resumed the healthy flush of youth and health, and her eyes glowed with pleasure and animation.

"Not so much—please!" she protested, as Knowlton heaped her plate high with asparagus tips. "You know, I am not a poor, over-worked farmer, as you seem to have been. Though, to tell the truth, I don't believe half of it."

"I don't blame you," said Knowlton cheerfully. "In fact, I don't believe it all myself."

For a time there was silence, while Lila listened dreamily to the orchestra, and her companion frowned portentously over the delicate and stupendous task of apportioning the salad.

"And now," Knowlton said presently, placing the spoon in the empty bowl with a sigh of relief, "what about yourself? I shall expect you to be just as frank as I have been. I already know your age, so you may leave that out."

Lila felt a little thrill find its way to her heart. Was it possible he remembered their first meeting so well? Of course, she did, but that was different. She decided to find out.

"And pray, what is my age?" she asked.

"Twenty," said Knowlton promptly. "Did you think I had forgotten? I guessed nineteen. You said twenty."

Then he did remember! Lila paused a moment to keep a tremor from her voice as she said:

"Then there is little to tell. I get up in the morning and go to work. I go home at night and go to bed. That's all."

"Fair play!" Knowlton protested. "Now that I have a chance to learn something I shan't let you escape. So far I've been able to learn just one thing about you."

"And that is?"

"That you're an angel."

Lila did not know whether to be angry or amused. The smile on her companion's face added to her uncertainty; but Knowlton hastened to relieve her of her embarrassment.

"I had it from Dougherty," he continued. "On the morning of my admission to the charmed circle of the Erring Knights I asserted my right to information. Tom gave it to me something like this."

Knowlton curled his upper lip and puffed out his cheeks, in imitation of the ex-prizefighter.

" 'Listen here, Knowlton. All we know is that she's an angel. And that's all you need to know.' And," Knowlton finished, "as he seemed to know what he was talking about, I believed him."

Lila opened her mouth to reply, then stopped short and gazed at the door. Then she turned to her companion with a sigh of relief.

"He's gone," she announced.

"Who?" asked Knowlton.

"Mr. Sherman."

"Oh! I had forgotten all about him." Knowlton beckoned to the waiter and asked for his check before he continued: "Well, this time we shall follow him—at least, out of the restaurant."

"Oh!" cried Lila. "Must we go?"

"Unless we are willing to be late," Knowlton smiled, glancing at his watch. "It is 8:15. It will take us ten minutes to get to the theater."

"To the theater!"

Lila's eyes were round with surprise.

On his part, Knowlton pretended surprise.

"Surely you wouldn't think of sending me away so early?" he exclaimed. "I supposed that was understood."

Lila shook her head firmly.

"I couldn't possibly," she declared.

"Have you anything else to do?"

Lila did not answer.

"Do you mean you don't want to go?"

Lila said: "I mean I can't."

"Say you don't want to go."

She was silent.

Knowlton looked at her.

"Is there any reason?"

"Dozens," Lila declared. "For one, my dress. I have been work-ing in it all day. Look at it."

Knowlton did so. It was of dark-blue ratine, with white lace col-lar and cuffs, and its simple delicacy appeared to him to leave noth-ing to be desired. After a scrutiny of some seconds, during which a flush of embarrassment appeared on Lila's cheeks, he looked up at her face and smiled.

"Is that all?" he demanded.

Lila, after some faltering and hesitation, admitted that it was.

"Then you must go," Knowlton declared. "I won't take a refusal. Your dress is perfectly all right. You look a thousand times more—I mean—I would rather be—"

He covered his confusion by rising from his chair to help Lila with her coat. She, still protesting, drew on her gloves and accompanied him to the door. There Knowlton halted to ask if she would choose the theater. She replied that she had no preference.

"But you will go?"

Lila nodded. Knowlton thanked her with a look as they left the restaurant and started toward Broadway.

At the corner he hailed a taxicab and ordered the driver to drive them to the Stuyvesant Theater, having wrapped Lila snugly in the laprobe, for the night was freezing.

"Are you tired or cold?" he asked, bending toward her solicitously.

"Neither," Lila answered, "but very comfortable. I wish you would take your share of the robe."

Knowlton protested that he was really too warm already, while he bit his tongue to keep his teeth from chattering.

Broadway was sprinkled with cabs and limousines, but the sidewalks were almost deserted. Your New Yorker is no cold-weather man. On moderate days he wears an overcoat, and on cold ones he stays indoors.

Knowlton and Lila arrived at the theater barely in time to be seated before the raising of the curtain, and Lila had not even time to note the name of the play. She looked at her program; the lights were down and it was too dark to read. She leaned over to Knowlton.

"The name of the play?" she whispered.

He whispered back: "It hasn't any."

She looked at the stage, and, in her wonder at what she saw, forgot to wonder at the oddity of his reply.

I shall not attempt to describe the scene. It was the ambitious attempt of a daring manager to stage Gautier's famous fantasy in the eleventh chapter of *Mlle. de Maupin.*

He had succeeded, if not perfectly, at least admirably. There were the glowworms and the pea blossoms and the eyes of dwarfs and gnomes and the distance of apple-green. The characters, with their pointed steeple-shaped hats and swollen hose, wandered aimlessly about with an infinite grace and talked of this and that and nothing in soft, musical tones of carelessness.

To Lila, who had certainly not read *Mlle. de Maupin,* the scene was inexplicable, but wonderful. Throughout the entire act she held her breath in amazed delight, expecting every minute that something would happen. Nothing happened, of course; but she was not disappointed. When the curtain fell she sighed deeply and turned to her companion.

He was smiling at her curiously.

"What do you think of it?" he asked.

Lila answered him with a series of "Oh!" and "Ahs!" and exclamations of delight.

"But," she managed to say finally, "I don't understand it a bit."

Knowlton told her of the origin of the fantasy, and explained that she couldn't very well be expected to understand it, since it had neither beginning nor end, nor cause nor reason.

"It wasn't made to be understood," he finished. "It was made to enjoy."

The two following acts were similar to the first, with a change of setting and costumes. Throughout Lila sat in breathless delight, with now and then a glance at Knowlton to see if he were sharing her enjoyment.

Always as she looked at him his eyes turned to meet hers, and they exchanged a smile of sympathy and understanding. When the curtain fell for the last time Lila turned to him with a sigh of regret.

"Oh," she said, "if the world were only like that!"

"It would be amusing," Knowlton agreed "But we would die of *ennui*. It would be too easy. No struggle, no passion, no hate, no love."

Lila was silent as they made their way out of the theater. The audience had been small, and they had no difficulty to find a cab at the door. As Knowlton seated himself at her side he leaned forward and told the driver to drive to the Manton.

Lila laid a hand on his arm.

"Please," she protested earnestly. "I must go home, really. I couldn't eat a bite, anyway; and it would spoil the play. I want to stay in fairyland."

Knowlton felt the earnestness of her tone and forbore to insist. He gave Lila's address to the driver, and they started uptown.

"And now to come to the point," said Knowlton suddenly, after several minutes of silence, during which the cab had sped swiftly northward.

His tone, Lila thought, was constrained and forced. It gave her a vague uneasiness and she asked what he meant.

"About the counterfeit bills," Knowlton explained.

He appeared to be speaking with difficulty, like a man who forces himself to mention an unpleasant subject.

Lila realized with a feeling of surprise that she had forgotten entirely the events that had caused her such great anxiety and pain but a day before.

His words came to her with a distinct shock. She looked at him and wondered at herself for having supposed, under any circumstances, that such a man as John Knowlton could do anything wrong.

"Of course, I must explain—" the young man was continuing, when Lila interrupted him.

"Please, Mr. Knowlton, don't! There is nothing to explain—or rather there is nothing which needs to be explained. I was silly ever to imagine that you could be—I mean, please don't talk about it."

Knowlton tried to insist, but without eagerness.

"But that is what we are here for. It was my excuse for asking you to come. I admit the subject is painful and embarrassing to me, but I promised to explain and I ought to."

"But why?"

"Because I want you to believe in me and be my friend. I—I want you to think well of me."

"Well, I do," said Lila. The protecting darkness hid the glowing color that mounted to her face. "I am your friend. There!" She held out a tiny gloved hand.

Knowlton took it and held it for a moment in his own. But he did not smile, and his manner was uneasy and constrained.

"Please let's forget it," Lila begged. "Do you want to spoil my whole evening?"

Knowlton said "No" without enthusiasm.

"Well, you are doing it," Lila declared with pretended severity. "And if you don't improve within one minute I shall complain of you to Mr. Dumain and Mr. Dougherty and Mr. Driscoll."

This brought a smile.

"I imagine that will be unnecessary," Knowlton observed.

"But I can goad them on."

"That would be unfair. They are already six to one. I had counted on having you on my side."

"And so I would be if you weren't so gloomy."

"Then from now on I shall be Momus himself," laughed Knowlton. "We are already at Ninety-sixth Street, and surely I can wear the mask for three minutes."

He began with an imitation of Pierre Dumain expounding the scientific value of the game of billiards, and soon had Lila laughing unrestrainedly. By the time the cab stopped at her door he was as gay as she.

As the driver opened the door of the taxi Knowlton sprang out and assisted Lila up the steps of the apartment-house stoop. At the door Lila stopped and held out her hand.

"Have you your key?" asked Knowlton.

Lila produced it from a pocket in her coat. He unlocked the door and she passed within. She thanked him and gave him her hand, and fluttered up the stairs. At the top of the first flight she halted. She had not heard the door close.

"Good night!" she called softly, and up to her came Knowlton's voice in return:

"Good night!" Then the sound of the closing door.

Lila entered her room and lit the gas. It seemed strangely unfamiliar. Here she had wept and read and slept and prayed. But here she had never been happy. For two years—since her mother's death—it had been her home. Home! Rather it had been her cage.

But now, as she sat on the edge of the bed without having removed her hat or coat or gloves, the room seemed transformed. The dingy little dressing table, the chairs, the pictures, seemed to have assumed a new form of beauty.

The ticking of the little marble clock on the mantel, that had been mournful and melancholy and disconsolate, sounded a cheerful note of sympathy. For Lila was happy!

Half an hour later she was standing in front of her mirror, gazing at the reflection of a rosy, flushed face and deep, liquid, lustrous eyes. "Why," she said aloud, "that can't be me! I never saw anything so beautiful in my life!"

Then, laughing happily at her own foolishness, she got into bed and snuggled cozily beneath the covers.

CHAPTER VII

—⁓—

The Enemy's Roof

KNOWLTON, HAVING bid Lila good night, stood irresolutely for a moment with his foot on the step of the taxicab. He thought of walking downtown and mentally calculated the distance—seventy blocks—three miles and a half. He looked at his watch; it was a quarter to twelve, and the cold had increased with the deepening of the night.

Drawing his coat closer round him and stepping into the cab, he gave the driver the number of his rooms on Thirtieth Street.

As the vehicle started forward the face of the man inside was set sternly, almost painfully. His eyes stared straight ahead, his lips formed a thin, straight line, and now and then the muscles of the cheek quivered from the tensity of the jaws.

Thus he remained, motionless, for many minutes; evidence of a conflict of no common strength and importance. He was insensible to the movement of the cab, to the streets through which they passed, even to the nipping cold. He gave a start of surprise when the cab stopped and looked up to find himself arrived at his destination.

He sprang out, handed the driver a bill, and started toward the entrance of the apartment house.

"Wait a minute, mister!" came the driver's voice. "This is a ten-spot."

"All right; keep it," replied Knowlton.

He halted and turned to observe the curious phenomenon—a New York taxicab driver who announced that he had been paid too much! He heard his cry of "Thank ye sir!" and saw him mount his seat and send his taxi off at a speed that carried him out of sight in three seconds.

As Knowlton turned again to mount the stoop he noticed a big red limousine approaching from the east slowly. He glanced at it in idle curiosity as it stopped directly in front of his own door, then began to move up the steps, feeling in his pocket for his key.

Suddenly he was halted by a shout from the street:

"Is that you, Knowlton?"

The voice was Tom Dougherty's.

Knowlton, mastering his surprise, with his hand on his key in the door, turned and sang out:

"Yes. What do you want?"

Three men had got out of the limousine and were standing on the edge of the sidewalk. In front was Dougherty; Knowlton recognized him by his slouch hat. Dougherty made a step forward as he called in a lower tone:

"Come here."

Knowlton understood, of course, what was up. That is, he knew why they wanted him—but what did they want? And, being curious and by no means a coward he decided to find out. He stepped back to the sidewalk and across to the three men.

"Well?" he inquired coolly.

Dougherty pointed to the limousine.

"Get in!" he commanded.

The other two men, whom Knowlton saw to be Sherman and Jennings, made a cautious step forward, evidently with the intention of getting between him and the door.

"Take it easy," advised Knowlton, smiling at them composedly. "If I want to go in," he nodded toward the door of the apartment house, "I'll go. And now, Dougherty, what is it you want? I'd advise you not to try any tricks."

"To Hades with your advice!" put in Sherman. "This is our game."

"Shut up!" growled Dougherty. Then he turned to Knowlton. "You know why we're after you. Dumain and Driscoll and Booth are waiting at Dumain's rooms. We'll give you a fair chance in ten-round go with Driscoll. But, believe me, he'll beat you up right. And if he don't, I will."

Knowlton gazed at the ex-prizefighter for a second in silence, then started toward the limousine.

"You say this is a square deal, Dougherty?" he asked, turning suddenly.

Dougherty, amazed at his coolness, replied that it was.

Knowlton continued:

"I'm willing to take you on one at a time, but I don't care to walk into a trap."

He looked at Dougherty for another minute, appeared to hesitate, then jumped up on the seat in front beside the chauffeur.

"You'll freeze, man!" exclaimed Dougherty, while Sherman and Jennings got in the limousine. "Get inside with us."

"No thanks," said Knowlton dryly. "I prefer the cold."

Dumain's rooms were only a few blocks away, and within five minutes the limousine had stopped in front of them. The cold wind rushing against Knowlton with stinging force had set every nerve in his body tingling and filled him with a glow of exhilaration.

Dumain's rooms—on Twenty-first Street a little west of Sixth Avenue—were on the first floor of a four-story apartment house, with an old-fashioned high stoop leading to the door. Up the steps of this went Dougherty, with Knowlton at his side, followed by Sherman and Jennings. In answer to their ring Dumain himself opened the door.

"Did you get heem?" he asked.

"I came," Knowlton answered before Dougherty could speak.

Dumain led them down a long hall and into a room on the right.

Evidently this room—a large one—had been arranged for the expected encounter. It was bare of furniture save for a row of chairs along the further wall. The floor was partly covered with a coarse Wilton rug.

At one end, in the center, was a high mantel loaded down with vases, bronzes, trays, and pasteboard boxes—these latter evidently containing some of the paraphernalia of the palmist. The two windows at the opposite end were closed and the shades drawn.

Driscoll and Booth were seated on two of the chairs along the wall when the newcomers entered.

"All ready, eh?" Knowlton observed, standing in the middle of the room and looking around with an amused smile.

Dougherty regarded him with undisguised admiration.

"By gad, you're a cool one!" he remarked.

Knowlton walked over to a chair and sat down without answering him.

The others were gathered together in a group by the door, consulting in undertones, with occasional glances at Knowlton. Finally, with nods of satisfaction and at a word from Dumain, they crossed the room and seated themselves.

The little Frenchman stood in front of them and spoke:

"We deed not come here to talk. I will say very leetle. I will mention no names. Zat is, I will not mention her name. Eet ees to be a fight for ten rounds by Meester Dreescoll and Meester Knowlton. Meester Dougherty will referee. Meester Knowlton must have what you call a second. Will you be heem, Sherman?"

"No!" Knowlton interposed. "I want no second. I shan't need any."

Dougherty sprang to his feet impatiently.

"Strip, then!" he shouted.

The combatants lost no time. Driscoll carried a chair to the corner of the room near the door; Knowlton carried one to the opposite corner. Then, stripping bare to the waist, each seated himself to await the call of the referee. Booth stood by Driscoll's chair, holding his overcoat. The others were seated in the chairs along the wall.

"Two-minute rounds," announced Dougherty from the middle of the room. He was in his shirtsleeves and was holding a watch in his hand. Then, stepping to one side, he called:

"Time!"

The fighters, as they advanced to the center of the room, appeared to be evenly matched in weight and build. Their white bodies, trim and supple, glowed from the sudden contact with the air, for even within the room it was chilly.

But a closer inspection revealed a difference. Driscoll was a little too fat; his arms too plump and smooth. And his step to the practised eye lacked elasticity and lightness. His eyes gleamed with a wariness and alertness which it was impossible to communicate to the body, handicapped as it was.

A little murmur of astonishment ran along the quartet of spectators as they turned their eyes on Knowlton, and the referee, in his surprise, nearly dropped his watch.

Here was a man worth looking at. His flesh, white and smooth as his opponent's, showed little muscular ripples as he bent forward in a posture of defense, and his arms, firm and of goodly length, displayed magnificent knots on the inner forearm and from the elbow to the shoulder. His waist was small, and under the skin on the back of the shoulders appeared tightly drawn, steel-like bands of muscle.

Exclamations in undertones came from the row of chairs:

"Heavens! The man's a white hope!"

"I'd hate to be in Driscoll's place!"

"Where d'ye suppose he got it?"

On the face of Sherman, who was silent, appeared a curious expression of mingled fear and hatred.

Really, there was no mystery about it. The athletic records of a certain Western university could have explained all in five minutes. This was the man who had made it necessary for that university to add another cabinet to their trophy and medal room.

But, feeling as they did that their man was hopelessly beaten on form, the Erring Knights nevertheless urged him on with cheering words as the fighters squared off.

"Go to it, Driscoll!"

"Eat him up, Bub!"

"Soak the big dub!"

And Driscoll did his best. He began by trying to outbox his opponent. But within the first twenty seconds Knowlton pulled down his guard with a clever feint and staggered him with a straight punch to the face.

Driscoll came back with a cheerful grin and by fast footwork and taking the fullest advantage of his longer reach, went to the end of the round without further damage. Knowlton went to his corner smiling.

The next three rounds were slow. Driscoll, afraid of his wind, tried once or twice to rush the fighting, but was unable to reach his

man. Knowlton, always smiling; took it easy. His breath came as regularly as though he were sitting still.

The smile got on Driscoll's nerves. He knew he was being
played with, and that aroused his anger. Time and again he aimed a
blow at those lightly parted lips, only to find them a foot out of his
reach.

He began to pant heavily and was unsteady on his feet as he
walked to his corner at the end of the fourth round. Helpless rage
possessed him as he looked across the room and saw Knowlton sitting in his chair with easy unconcern.

At the cry of "Time!" he gathered himself together and rushed
at Knowlton with set teeth and glaring eyes. Knowlton, unprepared
for the sudden onslaught, was caught off his guard and carried to the
floor.

Shouts of encouragement came from the excited spectators.
Knowlton sprang to his feet. The smile was gone.

"Kill him, Driscoll!"

"You've got him going!"

"Put him to sleep!"

Again Driscoll rushed madly. But this time Knowlton was prepared. He stepped aside nimbly as a cat, and Driscoll stumbled and
nearly fell. As he recovered his balance Knowlton turned and swung
with his right.

It caught Driscoll on the ear and he went down like a shot. He
was up at the count of three and, sobbing with rage, rushed again.
The onlookers sprang to their feet in excitement.

This time Knowlton met the assault squarely and stopped it
with a stiff punch.

"Time!" called Dougherty.

Everybody began to talk at once. Booth helped Driscoll to his
corner. Blood was on his face and he breathed in quick, short gasps.

"Cut it, Bub," said Jennings, running over to him. "The big slob'll kill you."

Driscoll tried to grin, but wasted no breath on speech. He leaned back in his chair while Booth waved a towel wildly up and down in front of him. When he heard Dougherty call "Time!" for the sixth round he would have sworn that he had rested not more than ten seconds.

Cries came from the onlookers to "take it easy" and "watch him," but Driscoll heeded them not. His blood was boiling and the face of his opponent appeared to him in a dim and wavering haze.

Toward it he rushed in blind fury. Knowlton stepped back and there was a dull thud as his fist landed on Driscoll's shoulder.

Driscoll staggered, but kept his feet. Again and again he rushed, and again and again he was stopped by Knowlton's fist. It was evident that Knowlton was putting no force in his blows, but was merely stopping the rushes with extended arm.

This enraged the spectators.

"End it, darn you!" howled Booth.

Knowlton smiled—and ended it. Not waiting for Driscoll's rush, he leaped forward and swung with his right. Driscoll, receiving the blow on his left side, staggered and swayed, then sank to the floor, a limp, helpless heap.

Knowlton gave the prostrate form a single glance, then walked to his corner and sang out coolly: "Next!"

"I'll next you, you bruiser!" The voice, filled with tears of rage, was Dougherty's. He had sprung to Driscoll's corner and was removing his vest and shirt.

The others lifted Driscoll, assisted him to the side of the room, and, wrapping his overcoat closely about him, seated him in a chair. His eyes were closed, and Booth stood at his side to support him.

Jennings ran over to help Dougherty. Sherman sat silent, the muscles of his face twitching queerly. Little Dumain was jumping up and down in the intensity of his excitement.

"I hope he keels you!" he screamed, shaking a fist at Knowlton.

"Chacun tire de son côte," said Knowlton calmly.

"Mon Dieu! Français!" shrieked Dumain. "Eetees degradation!"

Knowlton laughed at him.

Dougherty, stripped to the waist, advanced to the middle of the room and pushed the little Frenchman aside.

"Come on," he said grimly to Knowlton. "We don't need a referee. This is no boxing match. It's a fight, and you'll soon find it out.

Dumain retreated to the side of Booth. Sherman rose from his chair and stood in front of it. Driscoll opened his eyes for the first time, and kept them open.

The battle that followed was worth the price of a ringside seat at Madison Square Garden.

Within the first minute Knowlton discovered that the man he was facing was by no means a tyro. He had thought that Dougherty, completely out of condition, would be unable to withstand even the crudest kind of attack and had led with a double swing. Dougherty stepped back cleverly, waited the exact fraction of a second necessary, and then lunged forward like a panther.

Knowlton found himself on the floor with blood streaming from his nose, while the onlookers shrieked with ecstasy. He regained his feet warily, and, changing his mind as to the capabilities of his opponent, altered his tactics to suit.

Dougherty was fighting with all the cunning at his command. He realized that he was handicapped by the shortness of his wind, but figured that this was nearly, if not quite, equalized by the fact that Knowlton was not fresh. He did not throw himself away, as he had done in the encounter with Driscoll in the billiard room of the Lamartine. Instead, he called into play all his old-time ring knowledge and relied on superior tactics and skill. He waited for another break on the part of Knowlton.

But Knowlton was not to be caught napping again. He fought cautiously and warily, watching for an opening. He was not a pleasant sight to look at. The blood from his nose covered the lower half of his face and one side of his neck. His hair was matted with sweat, and his damp body glistened as he bent, now, forward, now to one side or the other, dodging, feinting, waiting.

For upward of five minutes they sparred and shifted, neither one gaining any advantage or landing a punishing blow. Then it began to get warmer.

Dougherty's foot happened to alight on an upturned corner of the rug, and as he glanced downward for the merest fraction of a second Knowlton closed in and landed a stinging jab on his face, turning him half round.

Instead of returning, he completed the circle, and, catching Knowlton unaware, staggered him with a left swing. They exchanged blows at close quarters, then clinched for a rest.

Knowlton was beginning to weaken under the prolonged strain. He had played with Driscoll longer than was good for his wind, and by now he was breathing heavily, while Dougherty was comparatively fresh. He tried to hold the clinch to get his wind, but Dougherty broke away.

Then, urged on by the exited and encouraging cries of the Erring Knights, Dougherty started in to finish it. By using his feet cleverly Knowlton avoided close fighting, but he received two body blows that made him grunt.

In recovering from the second of these he opened his guard, and a clean uppercut on the point of the jaw bent him backward and left him dazed.

Dougherty followed it up savagely, landing on the body at will, while Knowlton retreated blindly, covering his face with his hands. The onlookers howled with delight.

"Now get him, Tom!"

"It's all yours, old boy!"

"Keel heem!"

But they did not know Knowlton. Driven into a corner, apparently a beaten man, he felt within himself that stirring of the spirit that comes only on the boundary line of despair.

He had felt it before on the gridiron when, with his body a mass of bruises, he had hurled himself savagely forward and caught in a viselike grip and held the flying figure that sought to reach the sacred white line but a few feet away—on the track when, with aching legs and painful, gasping breath, he had by one last supreme effort passed the streak of white that seemed to his blurred eyes to have been there before him since the beginning of time. It is the spirit of the true fighting man.

He pushed Dougherty away from the corner, merely shaking his head slightly as he received a swinging blow full in the face. Then he fought back stubbornly, desperately, irresistibly.

Dougherty gave ground. It was by inches, but he retreated. Knowlton made no pretense at guarding. He simply fought.

The tide began to turn. Dougherty fell back more rapidly. His breath came heavily.

Perspiration ran in little rivulets down his cheeks and neck and body and stood out in large beads on his forehead. His face became fixed in a sort of unseeing stare, and his blows were wild and purposeless. He seemed unable to see his opponent.

"My God, Tom! Hit him! Can't you hit him?" cried Driscoll.

Knowlton pressed on unwaveringly. He landed blow after blow on his opponent's unprotected body. Dougherty attempted to swing, took a step forward, stumbled, and fell to his knees. It appeared to be the end.

But the end came from an unexpected quarter. As Dougherty fell, Sherman ran to the mantel at the end of the room, took from it a figure of bronze, and, before any one could guess his purpose, hurled it straight at Knowlton. Knowlton turned, threw up his arms, and sank to the floor with the blood streaming from a deep gash on his head just back of the temple.

For a moment there was dead silence, while all eyes were turned on Sherman. He stood motionless by the mantel, his face very white.

Then all was confusion. Dumain and Booth ran and bent over Knowlton, crying to Jennings to watch Sherman. Driscoll, by this time fully recovered, ran to Dougherty. Sherman started for the door, but was stopped by Jennings, whose eyes were filled with a dangerous light.

"Stay there, you——coward!" he bellowed.

Dougherty had pushed Driscoll aside and was kneeling by the side of Knowlton, and he at once took command of the situation.

Dumain was sent off for bandages and returned with a white linen shirt, tearing it into strips. Booth brought water and some towels, and Driscoll sought the telephone in the next room to call up a doctor. Jennings was assisting Dougherty in his attempt to stop the flow of blood.

Thus busied, they entirely overlooked Sherman.

Intercepted by Driscoll in his attempt to get away, he had returned to the farther corner of the room and had looked on at the scene of activity with an assumed indifference which did not entirely conceal his fear.

Moving suddenly, he felt his foot meet with an obstruction, and, looking down, saw Knowlton's clothing lying in a heap on the floor.

Quick as thought, and glancing at the others to see if he were observed, he stooped down and searched the pockets of the coat and vest. A shade of disappointment crossed his face at the result.

All that he was able to find was a long, black wallet in the inside pocket of the coat.

This he transferred to his own pocket and then assumed his former position of indifference.

In a few minutes the doctor arrived. He viewed the curious scene that greeted his eyes with professional stolidity and proceeded to examine his patient, who remained lying on the floor in the position in which he had fallen.

Without a word, save now and then a grunted command for water or other assistance, the doctor examined the wound and washed, stitched, and bandaged it.

At the commencement of the operation of stitching Knowlton opened his eyes, raised a hand to his head, and struggled to rise.

"Easy—easy. Lie still," said the doctor.

"What is it?" demanded Knowlton.

"They opened up your head," answered the doctor, still busily engaged with the bandage. "I'm putting it together again. Can you stand it?"

Knowlton smiled and closed his eyes.

"How about it?" asked Dougherty when the doctor finally arose.

"Very simple. Merely stunned. No danger. Twenty-five dollars," said the doctor.

"Can he go home?" asked Dumain, handing him the money.

The doctor shook his head.

"Bad—very bad. Too cold. Good night."

He opened the door, bowed, and departed.

"He's a talkative devil," observed Dougherty. "But how about Knowlton?"

"I have plenty of room. He can stay here," said Dumain.

Thus it was arranged, and John Knowlton, perforce, slept under the roof of the enemy.

Dougherty offered to stay with Dumain also, and the offer was eagerly accepted. The others departed at once in a body.

No one had anything to say to Sherman; they thought it hardly worthwhile. All's well that ends without the police.

Knowlton walked to his bed, supported by Dougherty. He was barely conscious and very weak.

They rubbed him down with witchhazel and put woolen pajamas on him and tucked him in like a baby. Then they went into the next room and sat down for a smoke.

Fifteen minutes later, thinking they heard a voice, they returned to their patient.

The voice was his own. He was talking in his sleep half deliriously.

"Lila!" he muttered. "Good-by, Lila! You know you are to live in fairyland and—hang you, Dougherty—no, I don't mean that—Lila—"

Dumain looked at Dougherty and said: "Zat is not for us, my friend."

Together they tiptoed silently out of the room.

—⁓—

CHAPTER VIII

Until Tomorrow

WHEN YOU throw a heavy lump of hard metal at a man and hit him on the side of the head you make an impression on him. I am not assuming artlessness or naïveté—I do not mean a physical impression.

What I wish to say is that his attitude and conduct toward you will undergo a sudden and notable change. He will be filled either with fear or with a desire for vengeance.

He will either betake himself to a distance where there is little possibility that you will present him with any more lumps of metal, or he will take firm and decided steps to return the one you have given him.

Of this rule of life the Erring Knights were perfectly aware, and they wondered much as to which of the two courses would be adopted by John Knowlton. As a matter of fact, he adopted neither— but let us not anticipate.

Knowlton's injury had proved even less serious than the doctor had declared it to be. On the morning after the fight Dumain and Dougherty had been amazed on awakening to find him fully dressed and holding his hat and overcoat, standing by the side of their bed.

"Sorry to disturb you," he had said, "but I am going. Thanks for your hospitality, Dumain. And for your—square deal—Dougherty."

Then, before they had time to recover from their surprise or utter a word, he had turned and disappeared.

For three days the Erring Knights had neither seen him nor heard from him, and they had about concluded that he had seen the wisdom of discretion and decided to practise it.

There was a general disposition to overlook Sherman's contribution to the little entertainment at Dumain's rooms. To be sure, they condemned his cowardice and violence. Since, however, it appeared to have had the desired effect on Knowlton without having inflicted any permanent injury, they were inclined to pardon it. Of course they despised him, as the law does its stool pigeon; but still they tolerated him.

It was with mingled feelings of anxiety and quiet joy that Lila lived through the three days during which Knowlton did not appear at the Lamartine. She had heard nothing of what had happened after Knowlton had left her at the door that evening, but she had not forgotten the appearance of Sherman at the Restaurant Lucia; hence her anxiety. She hugged her memory and waited.

On the morning of the fourth day her patience was rewarded by the following note, handed to her at her desk in the hotel by a messenger boy:

Dear Miss Williams:
I had expected to see you before this, but it has been impossible, owing to an accident I encountered.

I have been—let us say incapacitated.

But will you dine with me this evening? I shall call at the hotel for you at six.

John Knowlton.

Lila flushed with happiness as she folded the note and placed it in the bosom of her dress, at the same time looking round for the messenger boy to take her answer. But the boy had disappeared. What difference? She was to be with him again!

As she glanced up and happened to meet the eye of the Venus at the cigar stand she smiled involuntarily, so brightly that Miss Hughes fairly grinned in sympathy.

This little incident did not pass unnoticed. Dumain and Dougherty, seated on the leather lounge in the corner, saw the messenger boy hand her the note and her change of color as she read it, and they glanced at each other significantly.

"I wonder!" Dougherty observed.

"Yes," said Dumain positively. "Eet was from heem. Zat expression of zee face—I know eet. He ees a what you call eet comeback."

And when they saw Lila place the note in her bosom they were sure of it. Dumain sighed. Dougherty swore. They departed for the billiard room to communicate the sad intelligence.

Thus were they not wholly surprised when, at six o'clock that evening, they saw Knowlton enter the lobby and walk to Lila's desk.

There was a small, ugly, black patch over his right ear; otherwise no indication of the injury he had received at Dumain's rooms.

He escorted Lila from the hotel, while the Erring Knights looked on in helpless silence.

Forthwith they entered into a warm discussion. Dougherty and Driscoll were for immediate and drastic action, though they were unable to suggest any particular method; Dumain, Jennings, and Booth advised delay and caution; Sherman grunted unintelligibly and left the hotel. They argued till seven o'clock, then dispersed and went their several ways without having decided on anything definitely.

Meanwhile Sherman, who had seen Knowlton and Lila enter a

taxicab and followed them in another, was acting on his own account. He had his trouble for his pains.

They stopped at a restaurant for dinner, and Sherman shivered for an hour on the outside, waiting for them to reappear. He then followed them to a concert at Carnegie Hall, and kicked his heels in the foyer for two hours and a half—only to find at the end that they had left by another door, or that he had missed them in the crowd.

He swore violently under his breath, dismissed his cab, and walked at a furious pace to his room downtown, consumed by the fires of jealousy and hate.

Thenceforth the pursuit was one of relentless malignity. Sherman saw clearly that he was playing a losing game, and he redoubled his vigilance and activity with the energy of despair.

To see the woman he coveted thus smiling on another man appeared to him to justify any treachery or baseness, however vile; if, indeed, his evil mind were in need of any impetus.

He felt that he had some evidence of the correctness of his suspicions concerning Knowlton—for instance, the contents of the wallet he had taken from his coat at Domain's rooms; but he knew that was not enough.

There was not a day during the month that followed but found him on the heels of his quarry. He followed him to cafés, restaurants, theaters, and concert halls, often in company with Lila. He followed him home and to the Lamartine, and on endless walks along the drive and through the park. And all without result.

Then there came a sudden change in Knowlton's habits. One weary morning he began calling at real-estate offices.

By the time they had reached the fifth of these, Sherman, who was following him, disguised with a blond wig and mustache, began to suspect that he had been discovered and was being played with. But he continued the chase.

Knowlton stopped in another real-estate office, and another. Here he remained for over an hour, while Sherman lurked in a nearby doorway. Then he emerged with a companion. Sherman will not soon forget what followed.

They led him to the downtown subway.

At Brooklyn Bridge they boarded a Coney Island Elevated train. On this they rode two or three stations past Bath Beach, then left it for a trolleycar, landing finally at a dreary, swamp-like tract of land, with but one or two houses in sight.

The inevitable cheap saloon was on the corner.

Here they remained for three hours—it was a cold, windy day in January—walking up and down the newly laid eighteen-inch sidewalks while Sherman sat in the saloon, trying to warm himself with cheap brandy and watching them through a window. They gave no sign of preparation to depart. Sherman could bear it no longer.

"I wonder what the fool is up to?" he muttered as he boarded a trolley car. "Is he going to buy a home?"

And that brought with it a thought which caused him to squirm with pain.

He resumed his muttering: "By Heavens, he'll never get her! If I have to I'll see Colly. He can get the gang, and that means—"

A sinister smile overspread his face.

The fact about Knowlton was, he had got a job.

That evening at the Restaurant Lucia he surprised Lila by telling her of the day's occurrences. They were dining together nearly every evening now, though Knowlton was seldom seen at the Lamartine. He called for Lila at her room.

They had discovered a common love for music and books, and spent half of their evenings at concert halls and theaters. And when Lila felt indisposed or too tired to go out, or the weather was inclement, they remained in her room and Knowlton read stories and poems to her in his deep, well-modulated voice. Lila could never decide which she liked the more—the quiet, happy evenings at home or the more exciting pleasures to be found downtown.

But one thing she knew: never before had she tasted life. For the first time she saw its colors and scented its perfumes. Each day was a new delight; each look and word of Knowlton's a new sensation.

Knowlton spoke no word of love, and Lila wondered a little at it in her innocent way. He was attentive and solicitous even to the point of tenderness, and he was certainly not timid; but he never gave voice to any expression of sentiment.

Lila did not allow herself to be disturbed by this, nor did she employ any artifices—knowing none. She merely waited.

"Perhaps," she would whisper to herself at night when he had gone—"perhaps he will—will tell me—when—"

Then she would flush at the half-formed thought, innocent as it was, and brush it aside.

Nor did Knowlton ever talk of himself. Long since he had heard the story of Lila's life—how she had been left alone and penniless at the age of eighteen, and of the resulting struggle, courageous and at times almost desperate, to keep her head above the alluring and deadly waves of the metropolis. But he had given no confidence in return. He seemed forever entrenched behind an impenetrable barrier of reserve, and Lila never presumed to storm it.

Then, on the evening mentioned above, at the Restaurant Lucia, he suddenly lowered one of the gates of his barrier. They had been seated for some thirty minutes and were waiting for the roast, when, after a period of unusual taciturnity, he had suddenly burst forth:

"I got a job today."

Lila stared at him. At her frank surprise he seemed for a moment amused, then embarrassed. He continued, trying to speak lightly.

"Yes, at last I'm going to work. Real work. Something I've never tried before, but I think I'll like it."

"What—what is it?"

"Real estate. Selling a nice wet swamp in lots of twenty-five hundred square feet each to build houses on. Though I believe they are going to drain it." Then, as Lila remained silent, "But you aren't interested."

"I am," Lila contradicted. "But—as a young lady is supposed to say when she is asked a certain question—'this is so sudden.' I know so little about you."

This was almost a challenge, and it was Knowlton's turn for silence. Then he found his tongue and soon had Lila laughing merrily at his description of the "lots" he was supposed to sell.

"But who will ever buy them?" she demanded.

"Anybody," Knowlton declared. "There are two million people living in Manhattan. Of these exactly one million nine hundred and sixty-nine thousand five hundred and forty-two think they want to live where they can have a vegetable garden and three chickens."

"And how about the other thirty thousand?"

"Oh, they're the real-estate agents. They know better."

But when Lila had finished laughing she became suddenly serious, saying:

"But that is shameful—to take such an advantage of ignorance."

Whereupon Knowlton spent a half hour defending the ethics of his new profession, with only fair success. Lila insisted that the customers were being duped and held to her belief with such tenacity that Knowlton finally became genuinely concerned.

Lila stopped suddenly.

"But, of course, it doesn't matter what I think," she said, and could have bitten her tongue off the moment afterward.

Knowlton colored slightly and opened his mouth as though to protest, then was silent. This increased Lila's embarrassment, and the waiter, approaching with their coffee, relieved an awkward situation by overturning one of the cups on the tablecloth.

From the restaurant they went to a concert.

"Some day, after they're filled in, I'll take you down and show you my swamps," said Knowlton as they parted three hours later at Lila's door. "And it does matter what you think. You know it does. Good night."

They shook hands gravely, as was their custom.

Thereafter their meetings were less frequent. Knowlton explained that his new position took more time than he had expect- ed and complained considerably of his trials and tribulations in the disposal of swamp lots.

But his appearance and manner contradicted him. There was a new light in his eyes, a new spring in his step, a new note of freedom in his voice. Lila wondered at it.

But he still managed to see her two or three evenings a week, and in one particular it would have seemed to the ordinary mind that he had lost a job instead of getting one.

Instead of taxicabs, they patronized the elevated and subway. Instead of orchids, he sent Lila roses and violets. Instead of *de luxe,* expensive editions his book presents were dressed in ordinary cloth and leather.

"To be perfectly frank, I must economize," he had explained one evening.

Lila had exclaimed:

"I am glad!"

Though he attempted all the way downtown to get her reason for this peculiar sentiment, she obstinately refused to give it. The truth was she hardly knew her reason herself, but she felt vaguely that both the fact and his frank confession of it brought them closer together.

This, she admitted to herself, meant happiness—the only happiness she could ever have.

As for Knowlton—well, the troubles of a salesman of real estate belong properly to comedy. That is a fact. But it would be unsafe to declare it in the presence of a real-estate salesman.

Knowlton was having his full share of the usual troubles, plus a few that were peculiar to himself. He will not soon forget that month.

In the first place he was perfectly well aware that he was being shadowed by Sherman. At times he was inclined to regard it as a joke; at others it caused him serious anxiety.

More than once he started for the Lamartine to discover whether he was acting for the Erring Knights or on his own account, but something held him back—perhaps a remembrance of Sherman's attempted bluff on the day of their first meeting. How much did Sherman know?

Then, as nothing resulted from the long-continued mysterious activities of the amateur detective, Knowlton gave him less and less thought.

Besides, he had no time for mysteries or Erring Knights. He was selling real estate. Not trying to—he was really selling it.

One evening when he called for Lila she found a taxicab waiting at the door as they descended the stoop.

"You see," Knowlton explained after they had settled themselves comfortably on the cushions and the cab had started forward, "I am getting to be quite a businessman. Really, I didn't think I had it in me. I'm fast becoming a bloated plutocrat. Someday you'll be proud of me."

"Not for that reason," said Lila.

"Then there's my last chance gone," Knowlton laughed. "For Heaven knows I've nothing else to be proud of—except that you are my friend," he added, suddenly serious.

But Lila, being in a gay mood, refused to humor him.

"Am I your friend?" she said thoughtfully.

"Aren't you?"

"I'm just trying to decide. I do like parts of you. When you are gay you're very jolly company. When you are serious you are impossible. It seems to me that I could get the most out of your friendship by taking a scientific course in the art of titillation."

"Who would you practise on?"

"Oh—my cat. Goodness knows she's grave enough—she needs it. And if it will work with her—"

"Cats never laugh," Knowlton declared solemnly.

"What frightful ignorance!" exclaimed Lila, with immeasurable scorn. "Did you never hear of the Cheshire?"

"Cheese?"

"No. Cat."

"But that was a grin. She didn't laugh. The distinction is subtle, but important."

"Well, anyway," Lila sighed, "it ought to be effective with you."

"But why do I need it?"

And thus they pretended to wrangle, with neither sense nor intention, till the cab stopped in front of the restaurant.

After dinner they attended a concert of one of the metropolitan string quartets. The program was short, and they arrived at Lila's room before half past ten, their hearts filled with the singing magic of Haydn.

"It's early," said Lila at the door. "Won't you come up and read to me—or talk?"

Knowlton replied that he had an engagement downtown at midnight, which left him an empty hour, and that he would rather spend it with her than anywhere else, and if she were sure he wouldn't annoy her—

"Come," Lila smiled, starting toward the stairs. Knowlton followed.

They talked of the concert. Then Knowlton read a portion of *Otho the Great,* while Lila lay back in an easy chair with closed eyes.

Now and then he would stop, asking softly, "Are you asleep?" and Lila would slowly open her eyes and smile at him and shake her head.

The tones of his voice, though lowered, filled the room with the musical cadences of the Poet of Beauty.

At the end of the second act he looked at his watch and closed the book suddenly, observing that he had only twenty minutes to get downtown.

"I suppose you are going to sell a swamp," said Lila, rising from her chair. "But what an hour!"

Knowlton did not answer. He found his coat and hat and said good night. At the door he turned and there was a new note in his voice—of seriousness and deep feeling—as he said:

"Tomorrow I shall have something to say to you. It has been hard to keep from telling you before, but I felt I had no right. Then—thank God—I shall be free. And I don't want to wait till evening. Will you lunch with me?"

Lila said "Yes," and before she could speak further Knowlton continued:

"I will call for you at the Lamartine at twelve o'clock, if that isn't too early. Tomorrow—at noon."

He turned and departed hurriedly, without giving her time to answer.

At the door he glanced at his watch—a quarter to twelve. He had dismissed the cab. He started at a rapid pace for the Elevated station on Columbus Avenue and barely caught a downtown train.

During the ride he kept glancing impatiently at his watch. Beside him on the seat was a late evening newspaper and he picked it up and tried to read, but was unable to compose himself. His midnight engagement was evidently not with a prospective customer.

At Twenty-eighth Street he left the train, walked east to Broadway, and entered a café on the corner.

The café was very similar to a thousand others on that street and in that neighborhood. It was half filled with men and completely filled with tobacco smoke. On the right was the bar; to the rear a series of partitions and doors leading to the inner rooms; on the left, a few tables and chairs and a row of stalls with leather seats surrounding wooden tables.

Knowlton glanced quickly round, noted that the hands of the clock above the bar pointed to a quarter past twelve, then walked slowly down the room in front of the stalls, glancing in at the occupants of each as he passed.

At the fifth stall he halted. The man seated there looked up quickly, and at sight of Knowlton rose to his feet and held out his hand.

"You're late," he said gruffly.

Knowlton, without replying, edged his way into the corner and sat down.

The man gazed at him curiously.

"What's the matter?" he asked. "You look pale."

"Don't talk so loud," said Knowlton, glancing at a group of three men who had halted within a few feet of the stall.

"All right," the other agreed good-naturedly. "Anyway, there's not much to say."

Reaching in his inside overcoat pocket, he drew forth a small flat package about the size of a cigar-box, wrapped in brown paper.

"Here's the stuff," he continued, placing the package on the seat beside Knowlton. "Shove it away quick. The usual amount—two hundred at one-tenth."

"I don't want it."

The words came from Knowlton in a whisper and with an apparent effort; but his manner was calm and unruffled.

The other half rose from his seat.

"Don't want it!" he cried; but at a warning glance from Knowlton he dropped back and continued in a whisper:

"What's up now? Cold feet? I always thought you was a baby. You've got to take it."

Knowlton repeated with calm decision:

"I don't want it. I'm through."

There ensued a controversy lasting a quarter of an hour. Knowlton was quiet but determined; the other, insistent and nervously excited. Several times Knowlton cautioned him to speak lower, as the same group of men remained standing near the stall, and others were constantly passing within earshot.

Finally, finding Knowlton utterly immovable, the man sighed resignedly and picked up the package and replaced it in his pocket.

"If you won't, you won't," he said. "And now, pal, let me tell you something: you're a wiser guy than I thought you was. They're after us. I beat it on the one-thirty tonight for Montreal."

"And yet—" Knowlton began indignantly.

"No, I wasn't," the other interrupted. "I wouldn't have let you sow it here. All I wanted was the two hundred, then I'd put you next. But you was next already."

Knowlton smiled, knowing the uselessness of any attempt to explain his own motives, and rose to depart, when the other, remarking that he was about due at the station, rose also, and they left the café together. In front they parted, with a smile and a good word. Knowlton walked home with a singing heart, thinking and dreaming of the morrow.

Twenty minutes later, in a room not twenty blocks away from the one where Knowlton was sleeping peacefully, two men were conversing in low, eager tones.

One, a tall, dark man with an evil countenance, was sitting on the edge of the bed dressed in pajamas; the other, with overcoat and hat, was standing in front of him.

"He spent twenty minutes at a café on Twenty-eighth and Broadway, talking with Red Tim," one was saying.

"And who is Red Tim?" asked the man on the bed.

"Number something-or-other in the gallery down at headquarters. Known from Frisco to the Battery. Just now he seems to be shoving the queer. He tried to give a bundle to your man, but he said he was through, and wouldn't take it.

"Evidently, though, he has some of it—your man, I mean. I could have taken Red Tim with the goods on, but I was looking out for you. It might have wised your man to the game."

The man on the bed was calm and thoughtful.

He asked some questions, and his eyes lit up with satisfaction at the answers.

"You've done well, Harden," he said finally. "I suspected this, and now I guess we've got him. It's too late to try to do anything tonight. Come round early in the morning; I may need you. Here's a ten. Good night."

The other, who had turned to go, stopped at the door to call back:

"Good night, Mr. Sherman."

~~~

CHAPTER IX

Betrayed

THE ERRING Knights had for two months been divided into hostile camps, in support of two widely differing doctrines.

One division, consisting of Dumain, Driscoll, and Jennings, advanced the argument that it was no part of their duty to protect Lila against herself, and that if she chose to disregard their solemn warnings against Knowlton it was up to her.

The other division, to which Dougherty, Booth, and Sherman belonged, declared that they owed it to Miss Williams and to themselves to throw Knowlton from the top of the Flatiron Building, or cut him up into very small pieces, or tie him to a rock at the bottom of New York Bay.

They were all pretty good talkers, and they had many wordy discussions, renewed every time they saw Knowlton enter the lobby and take Lila out with him. They concocted many schemes, and at one time even went so far as to consider an offer from Sherman to procure the services of an East Side gang.

But they never did anything. They talked too much.

This was not without its utility. It furnished any amount of amusement to the Venus at the cigar stand.

If Dougherty approached to buy a cigar, or light one, she would whisper mysteriously, "Is he dead?" and pretend unbounded amazement when informed that Knowlton had been allowed to live a day longer. And all that was needed to start Dumain off on a frenzied oration was for her to observe scornfully: "Gee, I thought a Frenchman had some nerve!"

But most successful of all was her conundrum: "Why are the Erring Knights like the Republican party?" The answer, wrung from her after several days of entreaties and threats, was: "Because their protective system is on the fritz."

But to the Erring Knights themselves the thing was no joke. They talked and schemed and discussed and argued. Dumain and Driscoll were strong for moderation, and succeeded in holding the others in check, sometimes even going so far as to threaten to support Knowlton when the others became unusually reckless in their suggestions. But the attacks of Booth and Dougherty, and especially Sherman, were persistent, and they began to weaken.

On the morning following the events narrated in the preceding chapter Dougherty entered the lobby earlier than usual and found Dumain and Jennings talking to Miss Hughes. Walking over to the cigar stand, he grunted, nodded to the Venus, and pointed with his finger to his particular brand.

"A little off-color?" said Miss Hughes, setting the box in front of him on the counter.

"Best you've got?" Dougherty grunted, selecting a cigar.

"Oh, I meant you!" she grinned. "The cigars are all right. You look like you'd been playing the title role at a leather wedding."

"Huh!" Dougherty grunted.

"Let heem alone," Dumain smiled. "He has zee temperament. He ees veree dangerous."

This awakened Dougherty.

"Shut up!" he exploded. "When I'm like I am now I'm bad."

Whereupon Dumain giggled and Jennings roared. Dougherty started for them, and they retreated to the leather lounge in the corner.

Soon Driscoll arrived, and, finding Dougherty gazing moodily out of the window, took him over to join the others, stopping on the way to say good morning to Lila.

"Pipe the gown!" said Dougherty, with a backward motion of the head as they halted in front of Dumain and Jennings.

"Where?"

"Miss Williams. She's lit up like a cathedral. You know what that means."

The others protested ignorance, and he went on to explain:

"She's expecting Knowlton. Don't tell me. I can *see* it. And if that guy comes around here today I'll act up. Believe me, he's through."

That started them. The word "Knowlton" was enough. When Booth entered ten minutes later he found Dougherty holding his own valiantly against Dumain, Driscoll, and Jennings.

Booth brought fuel for the flame. His first words were: "I saw Knowlton last night." Then, seeing that he had their attention, he added: "With Miss Williams."

They stared at him and demanded particulars.

"It was by accident," he went on. "A friend of mine said he had tickets to a show, and asked me to go. I went. Great jumping frogs! He said it was a show. Well, it was in a hall—the hall was all right— on Forty-second Street.

"Four little dagoes came out with violins. For two solid hours they sat there, looking kinda sick. What did they play? Search me. It sounded like a—"

"But what about Knowlton?"

"Oh, yes! Well, when I went in who did I see two rows ahead? Mr. John Knowlton and Miss Lila Williams, side by side. When the dagoes pulled off anything particularly awful they'd turn and look at each other as much as to say: 'I heard that tune the last time I was in Heaven.' And he called it a show!"

"That proves I was right," said Dougherty, rising to his feet and glaring down at Dumain. "He's been going up to her house maybe every night, and we've been sitting here like boobs. Just because he came to the hotel only once a month you thought that was all he saw her. And here he's been—Do what you please. I'm going to get him."

Dumain and Driscoll were genuinely shocked. They had really thought that Knowlton had not seen Lila except the few times he had called at the hotel; Booth's tale was a revelation. Besides, they had already begun to weaken in their support of Knowlton. And perhaps now they were too late.

"Where's Sherman?" Dougherty was saying. "I can count on him."

"And us," chorused the others.

"Wait a minute," said Dumain. "I tell you. We owe something to her. Well, I go and ask her—never mind what I ask her. Anyway, you wait. Eet weel take me only a minute. Go to zee billiard room."

"That's nonsense," Dougherty protested.

But the others persuaded him that Dumain was right and led him off to the billiard room, while the little Frenchman took his courage between his teeth and crossed to Lila's desk.

Lila was indeed, as Dougherty had expressed it, "lit up." She wore a dress of very soft and very dark brown, relieved at the cuffs and throat and down the front of the waist by bits of cream lace.

Her eyes glowed, too, and her lips were parted as though in happy expectancy. It will be remembered that at twelve o'clock she was to lunch with Knowlton.

As Dumain approached her desk she looked up and smiled brightly.

"You are veree *chic*," said Dumain, surveying her with admiration.

"What is French for 'blarney'?" Lila demanded.

"No," said Dumain; "really, you are." Then: "Were you at home last night?" he blurted out.

Lila showed her surprise at the question, answering:

"Why—no. I attended a concert."

Then Dumain plunged in.

"I know," he said. "Wiz zat Knowlton."

Lila was silent. It had been many days since they had spoken to her of Knowlton.

"Were you not?" Dumain demanded.

She said: "Yes."

The little Frenchman continued:

"You must excuse me eef I speak frankly. Long ago we said he was not good, yet you continue to see heem. Dear lady, do you not theenk we know? Eet ees for you we care."

"But why?" Lila demanded. "You know, Mr. Dumain, if anyone else spoke to me like this I should be angry. But I know you mean to be kind, and I cannot offend you. But I must if you speak this way about Mr. Knowlton. He, too, is my friend."

"Only zat?" Dumain demanded.

"Only—what do you mean?"

"Only a friend?"

"What—what else should he be?"

"Mon Dieu!" Dumain exploded, angry at what he thought her assumption of ignorance. "What else? What do you theenk a man like Knowlton wants with a prettee girl like you? Friendship! Ha! Zee kind of friendship zat—"

But the sight of Lila's pale cheeks and flashing eyes stopped him. She did not speak, nor was it necessary. Dumain withstood the fire of her glance for a short second, then fled precipitately.

He found the others waiting for him in the billiard room, which at this early hour—eleven o'clock—was empty. They gathered around him, demanding an account of his success.

"Zee only theeng to do," said Dumain, "ees to finish Knowlton. She ees veree angry. For two months I have thought it best to wait, and now—she loves heem. Eet ees een her eyes. He ees one big scoundrel!"

"That's the first sensible thing I've heard you say for a long time," observed Dougherty.

"I guess I'm with you," said Driscoll.

"I'm on," came from Jennings.

"What did she say?" asked Booth.

"Nozzing," said Dumain. "She just looked. Eet made a hole through me. Eet ees no good to talk to her."

At that moment Sherman entered the billiard room.

"No need to convert you," shouted Jennings, hailing him.

"What's that?" asked Sherman, stopping beside the group.

"Why, about Knowlton. We've decided to fix him. He was with Miss Williams last night."

"Do you call that news?" asked Sherman scornfully.

"Why, how did you know?"

"I saw them. Do you think because you're blind everyone else is? Also, he was with her Wednesday night and Monday."

"Where?" Dougherty demanded.

"Never mind where. Anyway, they were together. I suppose you're ready to listen to me now," Sherman sneered. "After I've done all the work and set the trap for him, you're quite willing to spring it."

"Don't get heady," Dougherty advised. "What is this trap stuff? And what do you mean by 'work'? If you were so Johnnie Wise, why didn't you put us next?"

"And have Dumain or Driscoll running off to slip the information to Mr. Knowlton?" sneered Sherman. "Hardly. I'm not that kind. At last I've got Knowlton where I want him. I'll make him look like a monkey—all I've got to do is pull the string. You guys that love him so much had better hurry around and tell him good-by." As he said this last, Sherman, glancing keenly around, could observe no sign of sympathy or pity for Knowlton on the faces that were eagerly surrounding him.

"But what are you talking about?" they demanded.

"Do you think I'll tell you?" asked Sherman scornfully.

They protested that they were fully as hostile toward Knowlton as he could possibly be, and suggested that he might find their assistance useful. Sherman admitted that they were possibly correct.

"Well, then, what is it?" they demanded. "Where's the trap?"

Still Sherman hesitated. He knew perfectly well that he could easily perfect his plans and carry them out without assistance; but he had a reason, and a strong one, for letting the Erring Knights in on it. The question was, would anyone of them warn Knowlton? He glanced again keenly around the circle of faces, and said for a feeler:

"I know enough to put him behind the bars."

"What's the dope?" asked Dougherty, frowning.

"Counterfeiting," replied Sherman, evidently satisfied with his scrutiny.

"Round ones?"

"No. Paper."

He was immediately besieged with questions:

"Was it tens? He always had 'em."

"How do you know?"

"Is he in with the aristocrats?"

"Does he make it or sow it?"

"He gets it from a Western gang, through a guy called Red Tim," said Sherman. "They've been closing in on 'em for two months, and Red Tim beat it last night. He can't be found this morning, though he was seen on Broadway at midnight. That makes it harder for us."

"How?" inquired Dougherty.

"It makes it harder to get anything on him," Sherman explained. "Red Tim was probably the only one that ever saw Knowlton. He would have peached in a minute; but now he's gone, and the only way to get anything on Knowlton is to catch him with the goods on. And you'd be taking a chance. If you grabbed him he might happen to be clean."

"But that has nothing to do with us," Dougherty objected. "We don't want to grab him."

"No, I suppose you want him to make his getaway," Sherman sneered.

Dougherty stared at him.

"What else would we want?" he demanded. "Do you think we want to peach? No, thank you. We may be none too good, but we won't hang a guy up, no matter who he is. Anyway, we want him to beat it. Ain't that what we've been after all along—to get him away from here? All we've got to do is to see that he does make his getaway."

Sherman's face was a study. Filled with chagrin at having miscalculated and with rage at the possible frustration of his designs, he controlled himself with difficulty.

"And you think that will work?" he demanded, while his voice trembled. "How would you go about it?"

"Easee," put in Dumain. "We tell heem either he goes or we what you call eet report. We tell heem what we know. We prove eet to heem. Zen he goes. No more Knowlton."

"Sure," Sherman sneered. "How easy! No more Knowlton, eh? Do you know what he'd do? He'd go home, burn up all his nice little paper, come back, and tell us to go to the deuce."

"Veree well," Dumain agreed. "Zen we make heem go. We would no longer what you call fool wiz heem. Because now we know he ees no fit for her."

"You tried that once before. Did he go? If it hadn't been for me bringing him down with a piece of bronze he'd have gone out laughing at us," Sherman retorted. "I tell you, the only thing to do is to lock him up."

But at this there was a general clamor. On this point the Erring Knights, with the exception of Sherman, seemed to be all of one mind. They would not "peach."

What they contemplated doing was perhaps a species of black-mail—but we are getting into deep water. With them it was no subtle question of ethics; it was simply an instinctive belief that one was excusable and the other was not.

Sherman found himself the sole member of a helpless minority. He argued and pleaded and threatened, but they were immovable. Too late he realized his mistake in having taken the others into his confidence, and, while prolonging the discussion as far as possible, his brain was busily working to discover a way to retrieve his error.

If he persisted he saw plainly that the others would turn against him and warn Knowlton. Craftily he sought to recover the lost ground.

He began slowly to yield to the others' arguments, and he perceived that they were swallowing the bait.

"I owe him no more than you do," he said in answer to a question from Dumain.

"Then why are you so anxious to see him jugged?" Dougherty demanded.

"I'm not," replied Sherman with a show of exasperation. "All I want is to get him away from here. My way is sure and yours isn't."

"But it is," put in Driscoll. "Dumain and I have been responsible for letting it go as far as it has, but do you think we'll do it again? Anyway, what does it matter what you want? We'll do as we please."

"That's right," said Sherman bitterly. "I do all the work and furnish the information, and this is what I get. Sure, what does it matter what I want?"

"Well, you're right about that," Dougherty admitted. "But we can't see this other thing—we simply can't do it. And our way is just as good if we stick."

"But you won't stick."

"What about it, boys?" Dougherty queried.

There came a chorus of oaths and protestations to the effect that John Knowlton would now, then, and forever find the lobby of the Lamartine extremely uninhabitable.

Sherman appeared to weaken.

"Go slow, go slow, or they'll suspect," he was saying to himself.

The others pressed harder and assaulted him from all sides at once. Finally, "Well, have it your own way," he said with a shrug of the shoulders.

The others applauded.

"But there's one thing I want to say," Sherman continued, "and that is, don't say anything to Knowlton till tomorrow."

"And why?" said Dougherty.

"Because I've got a private detective on his trail, and I want to call him off. And there's another reason, which you don't need to know. What are you going to do—wait till he shows up here?"

"What do you think?"

"I'd wait for him here till tomorrow night, and then, if he hasn't come, go to his rooms. But remember, not a word till tomorrow."

"All right," Dougherty agreed. "And now, who'll be spokesman?"

Sherman rose to his feet, glancing at his watch.

"Count me out," he said, turning to go. "That's your job. Dougherty. See you later."

He sauntered carelessly into the lobby, spoke to Lila and the Venus at the cigar stand, then wandered out into the street.

For a block he strolled along slowly, glancing in at the shop windows, and now and then to the rear. But as soon as he had rounded a corner, out of sight of the hotel, he broke into long, rapid strides.

He had made one mistake, he told himself; he would not make another.

His first thought, after the visit of his detective the night before, was to immediately betray Knowlton to the police. But it was certain that whoever betrayed Knowlton would earn the undying hatred of Lila Williams, and Sherman had therefore sought to bestow that office on one of the Erring Knights.

And they—fools, he said scornfully—had decided to speak to Knowlton instead.

But there was still a chance. He had gotten Dougherty to agree to wait until the following day, and before that time he hoped to have the game in his own hands, if only Dougherty would stick to his agreement, and there was no reason to think otherwise.

He hastened his step. At the subway station on Twenty-third Street he boarded a downtown train.

Fifteen minutes later he was seated in the outer office of a dingy suite whose windows looked out on that curious labyrinth south of the Brooklyn Bridge, and beyond, the East River.

An attendant approached.

"He will see you now, sir."

Sherman rose and followed him to an inner room.

The room was uncarpeted and bare save for two wooden chairs, a massive steel safe, and a roll-top desk. On one of the chairs, placed in front of the desk, was seated a heavy, red-faced man with carroty hair. He dismissed the attendant with a curt nod before he spoke to Sherman.

"What's up now, Billy?"

Sherman, knowing that he had to deal with a busy man, told him in as few words as possible what the reader already knows concerning Knowlton. The other listened to the end with an impassive face.

"You say he was seen with Red Tim last night?" he asked, when Sherman had finished.

"Yes. At Manx's café on Twenty-eighth Street and Broadway."

"And Red Tim had a bundle! Who was the idiot that saw him? Why didn't he arrest him?"

"Private. He was working for me. He didn't want to put Knowlton next."

"Ah! This is personal, then?"

"What if it is?" Sherman returned. "Does that make any difference?"

"No-o," said the other slowly. "But I don't see how we can get him. What evidence have we got? Red Tim can't be found. You say Knowlton refused a bundle last night. Of course, if he had taken that, and had it on him—"

"That isn't necessary," Sherman interrupted. "Why didn't he take that last night? Because he already had all he could handle. He's stuffed with it. Look here." He drew forth a wallet and took from it a stack of bills. "This was his. I got it—never mind how."

"All tens, eh?" said the other, taking the bills. "And beauties!" He examined them curiously. "But how can we prove they were found on him?"

"I can swear to it," said Sherman. "And that isn't all. He's sure to have more on him now. And he's sure to have a bunch stowed away in his rooms. If you get him there, unexpected, you'll have all the evidence you need and more, too."

The man at the desk appeared to be lost in thought.

"What is the address of his rooms?" he asked finally.

Sherman gave him the number of the house on West Thirtieth Street.

"What floor?"

"Second."

"Do you know anything of his habits? When will he be there?"

"Between seven o'clock and a quarter to eight in the evening."

"Anyone living with him?"

"No."

"Flat in his name?"

"Yes. John Knowlton."

The man at the desk had taken a fountain pen from his pocket and was writing on a pad of paper. He tore off the sheet he had written on, placed it in a drawer of the desk, returned the pen to his pocket, and gazed thoughtfully out of the window for some time.

Then he turned to Sherman, saying:

"We'll get Mr. Knowlton tonight."

—〜〜—

CHAPTER X

The End of the Rope

SHERMAN HAD left the Erring Knights in the billiard room of the Lamartine in a state of unrestrained delight.

At last they were to triumph over Knowlton. And it would be, so Jennings declared, a bloodless and well-deserved victory. Dougherty alone appeared to wear an expression of dissatisfaction, and he was urged to explain it.

"I don't like it," declared the ex-prizefighter. "That's no way to fight a guy. Oh, I'll stick, all right, and I'll hand it to him straight, but I don't like it."

"Nobody expects to see you satisfied," Booth observed.

Dougherty, disregarding him, continued:

"And another thing. Why does Sherman want us to hold off till tomorrow? It looks funny. You can't tell what that guy will do."

Dumain put in:

"He said something about zee defective."

"Well, and what about that? He said he wanted time to call off his detective. What sense is there in that? I don't see how it could make any difference when we tell him. It looks funny."

"But what other motive could Sherman have?" Booth demanded.

Dougherty looked at him.

"You know a lot," he observed contemptuously. "You know how wrong Sherman was to have us peach. Well, when he found out we wouldn't, what if he decided to do it himself? And then, to give him time for action, he gets us to promise not to put Knowlton next till tomorrow.

"I don't say that's his game, but it looks suspicious. That guff about his detective is silly. He probably knew it himself, but he didn't have time to think up a better reason."

"Well," put in Driscoll, "it's easy enough to fix it. All you have to do is to see Knowlton today."

"And the sooner the better," said Jennings. "Beat Mr. Sherman at his own game, if that is his game."

"I agree," said little Dumain pompously.

Dougherty slid down from the billiard table on which he was sitting and glanced at his watch, saying:

"Ten minutes to twelve. I wonder if he'd be at home now."

"Probably he's in bed," said Driscoll.

Dougherty appeared to consider.

"I'll go right after lunch," he said finally. "That's settled."

They wandered into the lobby, which by this time was pretty well filled. Dougherty and Jennings stopped in front of a racing bulletin and sighed for the good old days at Sheepshead Bay and Brighton; Driscoll strolled over to the leather lounge in the corner with a morning paper.

Dumain and Booth, joined a group at the cigar stand who were politely but firmly endeavoring to make the Venus admit that she had attempted to improve on nature in the matter of hair. She took it all in fun and good humor and kept them off with a flow of witty evasions. And, incidentally, they bought many cigars.

Driscoll, seated in the corner with his paper, was reading a certain article for the sixth time with an angry frown. The night before he had substituted for the leading man, who had suddenly been taken ill. And this article was not exactly complimentary to the substitute.

He told himself, also for the sixth time, that it was written by an idiot, a Philistine, a man who had no appreciation of true art. Then he threw down the paper, yawning, and glanced round the lobby.

Suddenly he sat bolt upright, staring in the direction of the telegraph desk. Then he looked round the lobby, saw Dougherty standing by the racing bulletin, and ran over to him.

"Look!" he said, laying one hand on Dougherty's shoulder and pointing with the other.

The ex-prizefighter, turning and gazing in the direction indicated, saw Knowlton standing by Lila's desk, helping her on with her coat.

"Now's your chance," said Driscoll.

When Knowlton heard his name called, and, turning, found Dougherty at his side, he uttered an involuntary exclamation of impatience, while Lila looked up in uneasy surprise.

She feared a scene, remembering what Dumain had said to her an hour or so before. But Dougherty seemed calm enough as he said:

"I want a word with you. Will you step aside a minute?"

Knowlton was inclined to refuse, and would have done so had the request come from any other than Dougherty.

After a moment of hesitation he excused himself to Lila, telling her he would return in a moment, and accompanied Dougherty over to the leather lounge in the corner.

The ex-prizefighter began with a recapitulation of the events of the preceding three months, while Knowlton restrained his impatience with difficulty.

They were seated side by side on the lounge. Across the lobby Lila was seen seated at her desk, drumming on it absently with her fingers. Driscoll and Jennings had joined Dumain and Booth at the cigar stand, and the four were pretending to talk, with occasional furtive glances of ill-concealed curiosity at the two men seated in the corner.

The lobby was full of men smoking and laughing and talking, oblivious of the fact that a near tragedy was being enacted scarcely a dozen feet away.

"And then," Dougherty was saying, "we let you alone. It wasn't my fault, but Dumain and Driscoll wouldn't stand with us. Now they've got to. We've got you marked, and the game's up."

"What is it—another prize-ring entertainment?" asked Knowlton.

"No. I wish it was. I don't like this thing any better than you do. It ain't the right kind of a deal."

Dougherty spoke slowly and with some hesitation as he continued:

"But I promised to stick, so here goes. It's this way: you leave New York today and give us your word to let Miss Williams alone, or in you go. We're on. You're shoving the queer."

Knowlton didn't blink an eyelash. He sat gazing across the lobby at Lila's profile in silence, without a sign even that he had heard. Then he turned his head and met Dougherty's eyes, saying in an even tone:

"That's pretty bad, Tom. Couldn't you think up anything better? You've been having bad dreams."

But Dougherty shook his head.

"It's no use, Knowlton. We know. No matter how, but it ought to be enough to tell you that you shouldn't have trusted Red Tim. We've got enough on you right now to hold you tight. The game's up."

Knowlton was regarding his companion keenly, and he saw the truth in his unwavering gaze and air of half commiseration. Subterfuge was useless. The game was up.

For a long minute he sat trying to collect his thoughts. Dougherty's untroubled calmness, the careless attitude of Lila seated but a few feet away, the gaiety of the lobby, all combined to give the thing an appearance of triviality. He could hardly realize the fact that the earth was falling away under his feet.

He turned to Dougherty:

"All right, then. You've got it on me. But you can't do this, Tom. It's not like you. Do you mean to say you'd actually peach on me?"

"Perhaps not," the ex-prizefighter admitted. "But I'm not the only one. There's no use talking, you're up against it, and the only way out is to beat it.

"It's a dirty trick, and I don't like it any better than you do, but the fact is I'm doing you a favor. The others all know about it, and they're dead sore, and they'd do it anyway if I didn't."

Knowlton's face was expressionless. His eyes stared straight into his companion's, and they held no anger nor resentment nor appeal. But his hand held the arm of the lounge with a grip of steel and the muscles of his jaw were set tensely in his effort to control himself.

Dougherty continued to speak. He explained the conditions under which they would leave Knowlton unmolested—he must leave New York at once and give them his word not to communicate with Miss Williams. And the sooner he left the better, since there was one member of the gang who could not be trusted. It was unnecessary, said the ex-prizefighter, to mention his name.

In the end Knowlton agreed, observing calmly that he was at the end of his rope and had no alternative. In spite of his effort at control, a lifelessness and despair crept into his tone that made Dougherty curse the part he had played. Knowlton gave his promise not to see Lila and said that he would leave New York at once.

He finished:

"Of course, she will know. That's the worst of it, Dougherty. I don't hold any grudge against you; I suppose you couldn't help it. But you were all blithering idiots to imagine that she could ever do anything wrong. She never did and never will.

"I was going to lunch with her today. When I think of—but that's useless, I suppose if I wanted to see her—but I don't want to. It would do no good.

"There's a lot I could tell you, Dougherty, but that, too, would be useless. You've called the turn on me, and I certainly don't intend to whine. Tell Dumain good-by; he was all right. He's a good fellow, that little Frenchman."

Knowlton rose to his feet.

"Is—is she waiting for you now?" stammered Dougherty, glancing across at Lila.

"Yes. When I'm gone, tell her not to wait any longer."

Knowlton hesitated as though about to speak further, then, changing his mind, turned abruptly and without another word passed down the lobby and out into the street. As he passed the cigar stand he heard his name called. He recognized Dumain's voice, but did not halt.

On the sidewalk he stopped and glanced to either side as though undecided which way to turn. Then he started at a rapid stride uptown.

His mind was still a chaos of mingled thoughts. Curiously enough, he felt little surprise.

"I am paying," he kept muttering to himself over and over. "I am paying."

For two hours he walked the streets, unconscious of direction or surroundings, his brain in a turmoil of regret and despair.

Rarely had he so given way to his emotions, but fate had struck him a blow that left him weak and helpless in their grasp. He called it fate. So do we all.

At the end of the two hours he found himself far uptown, on the Drive. It was a clear, crisp February day. Up from the Hudson came a damp, chilling breeze, with the faintest subtle suggestion of the spring about to come; it brought with it the shrieks of tugs and the more resonant calls of ferryboats. Above the factories and piers across the river slanted the descending sun, disclosing the melancholy barrenness of the slope below the Drive.

Knowlton faced about suddenly and retraced his steps downtown. He was fighting the hardest of all fights, and he had had no time for preparation.

He tried to clear his brain of feeling, to think connectedly; he caught himself trying to conduct a mental operation in mathematics in order to prove to himself that he could think, and he laughed aloud. That was a good sign, he told himself: he could still laugh.

He found himself, without knowing how he had come there, at the entrance of the house on Thirtieth Street. He looked at the door for a moment irresolutely, then entered and mounted the stairs to his rooms on the second floor.

He glanced at a little bronze clock on the mantel; it was half past four. His train for the West was to leave Grand Central Station at seven-thirty.

He sat down on a chair by the window, trying once more to collect his thoughts, but in vain. One picture filled his brain to the exclusion of all else.

Remorse, which comes only after suffering, had not yet touched him; he knew only that his every sense, his very reason, had been dulled and obscured by an all-pervading pain.

But if he could not think, he could act, he told himself. As to the course to be followed he had no choice. He had promised

Dougherty that he would leave New York, and since his future was decided by that promise there was really no necessity for thought.

He pulled his trunk to the middle of the floor and began to pack, throwing in suits and shirts indiscriminately. From a shelf in the wardrobe he took a package wrapped in brown paper, about a foot square, and stood for some minutes regarding it uncertainly.

"That won't do," he muttered, glancing at the fireplace, long disused, "and I don't dare take it to the furnace." Then, still undecided and placing the package on a table, he resumed his packing.

Finally the trunk was filled and there remained only to place his toilet articles and a change of linen in his suitcase, together with the contents of a lower drawer in the wardrobe. These items were somewhat curious.

There was a small white glove, two tiny handkerchiefs, a dozen or more letters, two photographs, and several books. These he wrapped carefully and placed in the suitcase, with the exception of one of the books and a photograph.

Glancing at his watch, he saw that it was six o'clock. The cab which he had ordered would arrive in three-quarters of an hour.

The early winter night had long since fallen; the room was dark. He sat down on the trunk to wait.

—※—

In the meantime Lila had spent a long and weary afternoon at her desk in the Lamartine.

When she had seen Knowlton, after he had left her for a moment to speak with Dougherty, turn and leave the lobby without so much as looking in her direction, she had been overcome with amazement.

That he, of all men, should be thus openly discourteous, was unbelievable. Well, she thought, of course he would soon return, and when they were at lunch together—

But as the minutes passed by with no sign of his return she grew uneasy. Was it possible he had forgotten his engagement with her? For that he could have deliberately disregarded it was impossible.

Could his conversation with Dougherty have had anything to do with it? She wondered what the ex-prizefighter had said to him; for she knew that Knowlton had scorned the threats of the Erring Knights.

The minutes flew; a half-hour passed. She told herself that she would wait five minutes more, and then if he had not come, go without him. The five minutes passed, it seemed, as so many seconds; she decided to wait five more. She was glad that Dougherty was not to be seen; she knew that she would have been unable to refrain from asking him to explain.

At one o'clock she forced herself to go.

When she returned from lunch she half expected to find Knowlton in the lobby, and, not seeing him, she burned to ask Miss Hughes or the hotel clerk if he had been there. But she could not bring herself to it, and she proceeded to her desk with a heavy heart.

She was mortified and half angry; but above all, she was uneasy. She told herself that Knowlton would never have thus humiliated her but for some cogent and powerful reason, and she could imagine none, unless—

When Dougherty entered the lobby and joined Dumain and Driscoll in the corner Lila kept herself from calling to him only by an extreme exertion of the will. And, after all, she thought, it might all amount to a mere nothing that could easily be explained and forgiven by a word.

The afternoon dragged slowly by.

You may be sure Dougherty had lost no time in telling the others of his success with Knowlton. They were in high glee.

"But weel he keep zee promise about Mees Williams?" said Dumain.

"As well as you would, my friend." Dougherty was in ill humor. "I'd like to hear you ask him that."

"And now, thank the Lord, we're rid of him," said Driscoll in a tone of finality.

It voiced the general feeling and it was supposed to be Knowlton's epitaph.

They wandered into the billiard room—it was the middle of the afternoon—and began a four-handed game; Driscoll and Booth against Jennings and Dougherty.

Sherman had not been seen since he had left earlier in the day. Dumain, barred from the game on account of his superior skill, took a chair nearby and after each miss explained to the player how easy the shot would have been for him.

But Dumain's mind was only half on the billiard game.

With all due respect to a great people, the fact remains that Frenchmen are as a rule "gabby" little fellows, and Dumain was a true son of his country. They can talk about anything, and at all times with pleasure, and when they really have something to say and somebody to say it to, silence becomes for them a positive pain.

Thus it was that Dumain squirmed in his chair.

Not fifty feet away Lila was seated at her desk, and how he longed to tell her of Knowlton!

The reason he did not run to her at once with the news may be summed up in one word: Dougherty. He knew that the ex-prizefighter would not approve, and he was half afraid of him. Dumain was a little man.

The billiard game lasted until five o'clock, when Booth suddenly ended it by announcing that he had to see a customer and departed in haste.

"That's what comes of having a job," said Dougherty in disgust, as they wandered into the lobby. "How anybody can be a typewriter salesman I don't understand. Why can't he live like a gentleman?"

This seemed to be an unanswerable question, as no one responded. They strolled up and down the lobby, then over to the leather lounge and loafed and smoked like gentlemen. Dumain kept one eye—an eye of impatience—on Lila.

At a quarter to six Jennings and Driscoll rose and announced that it was time for them to depart. They were due at the theater at seven-thirty, and they had yet to dine.

"Where are you going?" Dougherty demanded.

They replied that they intended to eat at Tony's and invited him and Dumain to accompany them.

"Eel ees too early for me," said the little Frenchman.

Dougherty hesitated, giving the matter due consideration, and finally decided to accept. They left Dumain alone in the corner. He watched them through the window till they had disappeared up Broadway, then turned quickly. Now was his chance.

Lila, with her hat and coat on, was arranging her desk, preparing to go home. At Dumain's approach she looked up quickly. Her face wore a tired and listless expression that caused the little Frenchman to hesitate. But only for a moment; then he said:

"So your friend deed not even stop to say good-by! You see I was right about heem. Of course you could not know—but when we told you! And now you see."

Lila looked at him.

"What are you talking about?" she said shortly.

Dumain was undisturbed:

"I mean zat Knowlton—you know eet. Bah! Deed you not see heem run like a dog wiz hees tail between hees feet? Do you know why? We found out about heem. He ees what you call eet a counterfeiter. And when we tell heem he runs."

Lila had clenched her fists on the desk before her and was leaning on them heavily.

"That is not true," she said calmly.

Ignoring her, Dumain went on:

"We made heem to leave New York today. Most probable he ees already gone. Perhaps now you will admit I know something when I tol' you two, three months ago about zis Knowlton? Bah! You were veree angry. You said I am impertinent." He nodded his head sagely: "I am wise."

Lila's face was very white. But her voice, though little above a whisper, was fairly under control as she said:

"You say Mr. Knowlton is going away?"

Dumain said "Yes," while his eyes gleamed with satisfaction at the impression he was making.

"Has he gone?"

Dumain supposed so, but wasn't sure.

Lila straightened herself firmly and a new light appeared in her eyes, of resolve, while she calmly buttoned her coat.

"I thought you ought to know about eet," said Dumain a trifle lamely.

Lila appeared to be little moved. She made no comment on Dumain's observation, but thanked him and turned to go, leaving him staring at her in profound amazement.

"Zee devil!" he ejaculated, snapping his fingers. "She cares not zat much!"

But once outside the lobby Lila's courage forsook her. She grasped at a railing and seemed about to fall.

Then, pressing her lips together tightly and forcing back the tears that sought to blind her, she started up Broadway at a walk that was almost a run. She stopped suddenly. Should she call a cab? But, no, she felt it would be impossible to sit still. Again she started forward.

Darkness had fallen nearly an hour before, and the yellow glare of Broadway lighted her steps. The lull following the close of business and preceding the theater hour was evidenced by the quietness of the street; and the few pedestrians to be seen were hurrying to get home to a late dinner.

But Lila was aware of nothing save a fearful anxiety. Would she be too late? Would she find him gone—forever?

This thought occupied her brain to the exclusion of all else. She did not consider whether Dumain had spoken the truth, nor why she was going, nor what she would do: nor was she conscious of any feeling, one way or the other, concerning the revelation that the man she loved was a criminal. She only knew that she must see him.

At Thirtieth Street she turned westward. In another ten minutes of breathless, rapid steps she found herself at the address to which she had sent his letters.

She ascended the stoop and searched on the letterboxes for his name. There it was—the second on the left—John Knowlton.

For a moment she hesitated, half conscious for the first time of the recklessness and immodesty of what she was doing.

Then she pressed the bell button firmly.

—ᴠᴠ—

The Voice of the Law

*T*HE LATCH clicked; she entered and ascended the stairs.

In an open door to the left, peering at her curiously in the dim light of the hall, stood a man. It was Knowlton. Back of him the room inside was dark.

Lila's anxiety dropped from her as a cloak and gave way to a sudden and overwhelming embarrassment. She stood at the top of the stairs looking at him, unable to speak or move.

Knowlton advanced a step from the door, saying:

"Who is it?"

And then, as Lila did not answer, "Who is it?" he repeated, advancing toward her. "Did you want—why—not—Miss Williams! What does this mean? Why did you come? Speak—tell me—"

"I—I don't know—" Lila stammered in confusion. "I thought—they told me—you had gone—"

She stood with one hand resting on the baluster, her breath coming in quick gasps.

Knowlton jerked himself together with an effort.

"But this will not do. You must go home at once." He took her arm.

Lila shook her head.

"I want to talk to you. I must. You mean that I should not come to your rooms? Well—I trust you, and what else matters?"

Knowlton, taken by surprise and at his wits' end, tried to insist, but Lila refused to listen. Finally, in despair, he led the way into his rooms. He lighted the gas and brought a chair for her, then seated himself on the trunk which he had just finished packing.

Lila looked at it.

"So what they said is true. You are going away."

He attempted playfulness.

"Yes, I am taking some of my swamps out West to sell to some of my old friends. You must admit, though, I never tried to sell you one."

"And you were going—without saying good-by?"

"I—I had to," he stammered. "It was on very short notice. There was no time."

Lila's face colored, then grew very white. She could not know the effort it was costing Knowlton to play his role; to her his lightness seemed sincere. She rose to her feet uncertainly.

"I do not know why I came," she said breathlessly. "But, yes, I do know. And now I am sorry. I cannot tell you how ashamed and sorry I am."

Her lip was quivering, but her eyes were firm and her voice even.

"Mr. Dumain told me you were in trouble—but I have been very bold—and—and I am sorry—"

She was moving toward the door.

At such times and under such circumstances men forget promises and danger, and throw prudence to the winds. Knowlton sprang to his feet and turned to her.

"Lila!"

She stopped, trembling from head to foot. All that she had longed to hear was in his voice—anguish and entreaty and love.

And now that the gates were broken the flood burst forth.

"Lila! For God's sake don't leave me like this! I can't bear it—I won't! Oh, what a miserable coward I am!"

In another moment she was at his side and in his arms, laughing and crying at once, and placing her hands over his mouth to keep him from calling himself a coward.

"No, no, no!" she kept saying, while he held her closer and closer and covered her hands and wrists with kisses.

"Lila! Tell me—my darling—do you love me?"

She nodded.

"You do love me?"

"Yes."

"Say it."

"I—love—you."

"And I—oh, my dear little girl, I worship you. You have known—you must have known, but I want to tell you. And you love me! It can't be true. Tell me."

"I love you," said Lila. And, oh, the curve of her lips and the light in her eyes and the clinging warmth of her arms!

Knowlton kissed her hair, saying:

"And see! You are my little girl." He picked her up in his arms and carried her to a chair, then knelt before her, muttering, "My little girl!" over and over. He was intoxicated.

Lila's eyes were swimming in tears of happiness. She stroked his hair and pronounced his name with a delightful shyness and made him tell her how long he had loved her.

He said, "Always," and got his reward at once.

There was a long silence, while they gazed into each other's eyes. Then Lila, happening to glance up, sighed and pointed to the trunk.

"And now, what about that?"

Knowlton turned sharply—and awoke. He sprang to his feet.

"My God! I had forgotten! And this—this is madness! Ah! You do not know—and I am a coward."

Lila said simply:

"I know everything."

Knowlton stared at her.

"Mr. Dumain told me why you were going away," she continued. "Did you think I did not know? And I—I have been waiting for you to tell me—" She stopped, coloring.

Knowlton suppressed a groan of anguish and forced himself to speak. The words choked him.

"I am a counterfeiter."

"I know it," Lila smiled.

Still Knowlton could not believe, or would not accept. His hands opened and closed convulsively, his breath came in quick gasps, and his eyes were narrowed with misery. Again he forced himself to speak, and the words came with a painful pause between them.

"But—you don't—understand. I am—a criminal. I am running away."

Lila shivered involuntarily at the word, but the smile did not leave her face as she said:

"I love you."

Then Knowlton burst forth:

"But, Lila, you do not know all! Ever since the day—the first time I was with you, I have been straight. And Heaven knows I have tried to make it up. But you humiliate me—you ask me nothing! Do you think there is no explanation? You do not even ask me why!"

"I guess there is no 'why' in love," said Lila.

"But there is in—the other thing." Knowlton drew nearer to her and spoke slowly and earnestly. "Do you remember I told you last night that I wanted to ask you something today? Well—I was going to ask you to marry me. I would have done that, and I would have kept my secret. But now that you know some of it you must know all."

"No," said Lila, "not that. Of the future, perhaps, but not of the past. What does it all matter now?"

But Knowlton insisted.

"Yes, I must. I want you to know it. It is not that I would give excuses; there can be none. But you must know my weakness and folly, and then if you can trust me—"

He paced the floor nervously as he continued:

"In the first place, my name is not Knowlton. It is John Norton. My father is the wealthiest citizen of a town named Warton, in Ohio. I am his only child. My mother died ten years ago.

"My father made his money in the manufacturing business, and he earned every cent of it. All his life he has worked like a slave. I can remember, when I was a little chap, how he used to come home late at night completely exhausted, and come to my room to kiss me good night. He would always reply to my mother's expostulations with the words, 'It is for him.'

"He wanted me to be a gentleman—in a certain sense of the word—and I was perfectly willing. Still I was not lazy. I studied hard at college, and made as good a showing in the classroom as I did on the athletic field.

"After graduation I made a two years' tour of the world, and at the age of twenty-four returned to Warton with a somewhat exaggerated idea of my attainments and accomplishments and a varied assortment of opinions and theories."

Lila was bending forward to listen, with parted lips and glowing eyes. Knowlton stopped pacing the floor and stood in front of her.

"But my father was by no means a fool. Although it was his dearest wish that his wealth should prevent my toiling and laboring as he had done, he did not intend that I should live a life of idleness.

He had at first been desirous that I should enter a profession, but, seeing that I was unsuited for either the law or medicine, he left it to my own choice.

"I chose banking, and he was delighted, declaring that nothing could please him better. He owned a portion of the stock of the Warton National Bank, and I was at once placed in its offices. At the end of six months I was made cashier, and at the end of the year a vice president.

"Of course I deserved no credit for my success, for the work was pleasing to me and everything was made easy for me. But my father was highly gratified, and, saying that my future was assured, began to press me on a point which had for some months been a bone of contention between us."

"He wanted you to marry some one," Lila said abruptly.

Knowlton gazed at her in amazement. "How in the name of—"

"I don't know," Lila smiled. "I seemed to feel it. You see now that you have no chance to keep anything from me. Who—who was she?"

Knowlton's eyes were still filled with surprise as he continued:

"A Miss Sherman. She was the daughter of a very old friend of my father's, and our parents had decided long before that we should marry when we had reached a proper age. But, though I had no particular objection to her, still I did not care for her, and was certainly anything but an ardent wooer. My father had often complained to me on account of my lack of appreciation of her charms."

"What was she like?" Lila demanded.

"Oh, like any girl! She had hair, and eyes—"

"Like me?"

"There is no one in the world like you," Knowlton declared, but as Lila started to rise he protested:

"No—please—let me finish. When I was elected vice president of the bank my father began to insist that I should marry at once. I demurred. We had many hot discussions on the subject, and it ended by my refusing pointblank to marry Miss Sherman at all.

"Naturally, he was disappointed and angry, but if it had not been for Miss Sherman herself the thing would have soon blown over. She developed an unexpected obstinacy, and declared that I was bound by the agreement made with her father, who had been dead for several years.

"To make matters worse, about this time she received a visit from her brother. This brother had some years before been driven out of Warton on account of some youthful indiscretion, and he had left behind him an exceedingly unsavory reputation. He had gone East—it was said to New York—and had not been heard of for some time until he suddenly put in an appearance at the time I mention.

"He immediately began to threaten me with all sorts of calamities and disasters if I did not marry Miss Sherman. I don't know whether this was with his sister's cognizance and approval or not; I doubt it, for she would hardly have so demeaned herself.

"Sherman acted like a sneak. I never once saw him, but he pestered me with letters and messages until I had about decided either to thrash him soundly or have recourse to the courts."

Lila interrupted eagerly:

"This man—Mr. Sherman—her brother—was he—"

"The same as Mr. Sherman of the Erring Knights? I think so; in fact, I am pretty positive of it, though, as I say, I never saw him in Warton. But he recognized me the first time he saw me at the Lamartine, so there is little doubt of it."

He resumed his narrative, while Lila's interest was so intense that she scarcely breathed.

"This went on for two or three months. My father had come over to my side unconditionally. Miss Sherman had prepared to

enter a suit for breach of promise, and her brother was making himself as obnoxious as possible. He spread stories concerning me all
over the town, and did everything that could suggest itself to his
mind—in the dark.

"One night—I shall never forget it—one Wednesday night I was
at work in the bank alone. I had been away for the two or three days
previous, and a great deal of work had accumulated during my
absence. Also, we had that very day received a large shipment of cur-
rency from the East, and I had to check that and stow it away in the
vault.

"I had just completed this task, and had not yet closed the
vault—it was about eleven o'clock—when I heard some one
pounding on the outer door. I called out, asking who it was, and
heard in a woman's voice a name which astonished me: 'Alma
Sherman.'

"Not knowing what else to do, I opened the door, drawing the
heavy steel bolts, and she entered. Before I had time to speak or
move she seized me by the arm and drew me over to a private room
on the left. 'Wait,' I said, 'I must close the door.'

"But she would not let me go. She seemed half insane, clinging
to me and entreating—well, I can't tell you what she said. In fact,
the whole thing is in my memory as a nightmare, indistinct and
horrible.

"I don't know what I was thinking of, not to have insisted on
going back to close the door, but she must have carried me completely off my feet.

"Gradually she became calmer, but still was unable to tell me
what she had come for or indeed to speak intelligently at all. I had
begun to think she was really out of her mind, when she suddenly
sprang to the door and disappeared as mysteriously as she had come.

"I looked for her through the window, but the night was very dark and I could see nothing. She had been with me, I think, about twenty minutes.

"I was roused and curious, of course, but I finished my work nevertheless, locked the vault and the outer doors, and went home.

"The next morning the cashier ran in to me with a face of terror and announced that there was twenty thousand dollars missing from the vault."

Lila gasped involuntarily, and Knowlton answered the question in her eyes:

"No, I don't think Alma Sherman had anything to do with it intentionally. But I think her brother did, and that she was an unconscious accomplice. I don't know. I thought at the time that someone happening to pass by had seen the open door and taken advantage of it.

"There is no use in giving you the details of what followed. I shall come to the end as rapidly as possible.

"Of course, all was confusion and speculation in the bank—and as soon as the news got around in the town. At first I was not suspected; I was considered above it. But it was inevitable.

"I had been left in the bank alone, I had locked the vault myself after it had been checked up by the cashier, and there was no evidence of any kind that it had been tampered with. I made no mention to anyone of Alma Sherman's visit; I did not see how it could do any possible good, and I thought the least I could do was to shield her name.

"Even then I did not know that I was suspected. I discovered later that I had been followed and investigated by detectives. A week after the robbery ten thousand dollars of the missing money was found hidden in a closet in my room in my father's house."

Lila sprang to her feet with a cry of astonishment; but Knowlton, not heeding her, continued:

"Of course, that settled it. What need to tell of the terrible scene with my father—his grief and anger, and my protestations of innocence? I stood convicted by facts, delusive and stubborn.

"Now, when it was too late, I told of the visit paid me by Alma Sherman, being convinced that her brother was at the bottom of the plot against me. I was jeered at for my pains. They asked why I had not mentioned it before, and reminded me that I had declared that no one had been with me at the bank on the night of the robbery.

"I insisted that they search for William Sherman. His sister told them that he had returned to New York, and declared that my statement that she had called on me at the bank was false!

"My father paid the shortage, arranged that I should not be prosecuted, and then—disowned me and drove me from his house."

As he said this Knowlton's voice trembled for the first time. He hesitated, then conquered his emotion with a visible effort, and resumed:

"Well, there I was. For a time I stayed in Warton, determined to prove my innocence, or, if that were impossible, live down the accusation. But everyone was against me.

"By my youthful assumption of superiority I had made many enemies, unknown to myself, and they were implacable. It was unbearable, horrible! I stood it as long as I could, then came to New York embittered, cynical, and penniless.

"I had one or two friends here, but as soon as I told them of my troubles—and I concealed nothing—they promptly forgot me. Getting a position in my own line—in a bank—was of course out of the question. They require references. At the end of a week I was about ready to go down to the sea by way of the Hudson, when I accidentally met Red Tim.

"It doesn't matter who Red Tim is. There are thousands of him. He is everywhere. We talked for an hour, and met again the following day. I was still well-dressed, and I had a fairly good appearance. At our third meeting he showed me a stack of counterfeit ten-dollar bills.

"You know the rest. I don't want you to think it was all weakness. It was partly bitterness and partly despair, and I think I was even so far gone as to repeat, 'I have the name, I'll have the game.' I think I was temporarily insane; no one can feel more horror at it now than I feel.

"When I met Sherman at the Lamartine I began to devise schemes for revenge and for clearing my name. But what could I do? I had no friends, nor evidence, nor much hope of getting either. Perhaps some day—

"I had been passing counterfeit money for a month when I met you. During the two months that followed my feelings were indescribable. Whenever I looked at you I felt unspeakable self-contempt. But I said bitterly that I wanted to get even with the world.

"Then—do you remember the first evening we dined together? And the play? Well, after that I despised myself indeed. I felt that I was not worthy to speak to you, to breathe the same air with you. But—you know—I could not stay away.

"For another month I wavered and hesitated, then got a position that was at least honorable, though you hardly seemed to think so. You didn't know how happy I was in it, and how I worked to earn the right to ask you—to tell you my love! I—really, I am proud of it!

"One thing more, and I am done. I had met Red Tim once each month. That was my own arrangement—I didn't care to see him oftener. Well, I saw him for the last time last night, and told him I was through.

"But there is still something." He pointed to a package wrapped in brown paper lying on the trunk. "That is—I had that left. I should have destroyed it long ago. I am going to tonight."

Lila gazed at the package curiously.

"Is it—how much is there?"

"About ten thousand dollars."

She rose and walked over to him and laid her hand on his arm.

"Destroy it now—at once," she said in a tone half frightened.

Knowlton objected:

"But there is no way. It is best to be safe, and I shall take it to the river. Never fear! But you have not told me what I want to know."

Lila questioned him with her eyes, and he continued:

"I have told you my story. And now?"

At first Lila did not understand; then her eyes filled with light and she raised herself on tiptoe, placing her arms around his neck, and kissed him.

"I love you," she said.

"Will you marry me?"

Her head was on his shoulder. She nodded.

"My darling Lila! I—really, I can't believe it."

"Pooh!" said she scornfully. "You have known it all the time."

"No. I have hoped—and feared. But, ah, I could never have lived without you!"

"And yet"—Lila looked up at him quickly—"you were going away."

Whereupon Knowlton protested that she was unkind, and she admitted it and begged his forgiveness with a kiss. There was a long silence. Finally Knowlton gave a deep sigh and spoke of the future.

He began by saying that he would go away somewhere—anywhere—and make a place and a home for Lila. She interrupted him at once:

"No, no! I will go with you. Why should you go alone? Will we not be stronger together? You think I will be in the way? You do not know me, then."

He tried to argue with her, but she would not listen. He pleaded; there were hardships to be endured which he could not ask her to share; it would cost him his newly regained self-respect. He was crushed, he must have time to get on his feet, he was practically penniless.

Lila replied:

"I have saved a little—enough to last until—until you get—"

"Good Heaven!" he cried in utter humiliation. "And you think that I—no, you do not know me. Can't you understand? Call it pride, if you will, and if you think I have a right to any. There are some things I must do myself. Do you think the confession I have just made has not been painful to me? If you only knew!"

Lila murmured:

"I do not want to hurt you, but I want to be happy, and if you leave me I shall not be."

"Dearest, do I not know?" Knowlton forced himself to be more calm. "And without you every minute will seem a year to me. That is why I shall work all the harder and send for you as soon as I can. And then—"

"And then—" Lila repeated.

"And then I will be the happiest man in the world—happier far than I deserve. And as soon as I can get—"

At that moment a bell in the next room rang violently.

Lila glanced round, startled, and Knowlton turned with an expression of alarm, which speedily gave way to one of relief.

He reassured Lila:

"It is nothing. I ordered a cab to take me to the station."

He ran to the front and looked out on the street below.

"Yes," he said, returning, "it is the cab. It is in front. And that's lucky, for it is dinnertime. Shall we go—"

He was interrupted by a loud knocking on the hall door a few feet away.

He thought it was the cabdriver, and wondered how he had gotten in the outer door below.

He called sharply:

"Who is it?"

There was no answer, but after an interval the knocking was repeated.

"Who is it?" he repeated angrily.

Another short pause, during which Knowlton fancied he heard whispering in the hall outside; then came the reply in a peremptory tone:

"Open in the name of the law!"

—⁓—

CHAPTER XII

The Long Night

*L*ILA GAVE a gasp of terror and seized Knowlton's arm convulsively, while the young man stood speechless with surprise and alarm.

What did he see in that one flash of horror and regret? He saw Lila accused, arrested, dishonored—and all for him. The thought petrified him; he was unable to move.

No care for himself or concern for his own danger could have moved him to anything save reckless courage or stoical acceptance; but it stunned his every sense to think that Lila would be caught in the net he had spread for himself.

But Lila, seeing his helplessness, acted for herself. For a second only she stood rooted to the spot with terror; then she glanced with a flashing eye round the room, while her brain worked with the rapidity of lightning.

She saw, a few feet to the right, a curtained alcove; then, as she turned, her eye fell on the package of counterfeit money lying on the trunk. With silent swiftness she crossed the room and picked up the package, and as swiftly sped back to the side of Knowlton.

She held her mouth close, very close against his ear, that no sound might reach the other side of the door, and whispered:

"Get them into the other room—all of them—as far away as possible."

She saw that he did not comprehend her meaning, but there was no time to explain further. She must trust to his sagacity as soon as he recovered his wits.

With one last glance about the room to make sure that there was nothing in it to reveal her presence, she pressed his hand swiftly and disappeared behind the curtain of the alcove. All this had taken but three or four seconds.

The knocking on the door and the command to open were repeated. Knowlton turned the knob of the catch-lock and the door flew open.

Three men burst into the room, the foremost exclaiming, "Here he is!" as he ran to Knowlton, who had fallen back several steps from the door.

And then Knowlton understood Lila's plan, simple and admirable. In an instant his brain cleared, and, realizing that Lila had taken the package of counterfeit money—the evidence—with her into the alcove, he decided on his own plan of action.

Turning suddenly, just as the man nearest him was about to grasp him by the shoulder, he sprang aside with the swiftness and agility of a panther and disappeared into the room beyond, toward the rear. As he had foreseen, the three men, all of them, rushed after him and found him standing by a window looking out on the rear court, laughing gaily.

"Why all the excitement?" he queried pleasantly. "Did you think I was trying to run away?"

The leader of the detectives, a heavy, red-faced man with carroty hair, grunted.

"Get him!" he said to his companions.

Then Knowlton had need of all his composure. But he was not thinking of himself. As the two detectives grasped him roughly and handcuffed his wrists and led him back into the room in front, he was saying to himself. "She had plenty of time. But was that what she meant? It must have been. But where did she go?"

He dared not glance at the alcove; he felt that his eyes would have burned a hole through the curtain.

Then the detectives began a search of the rooms.

"I'm sure the stuff is here," said the red-faced man, "and we've got to find it. You might save us the trouble," he added, turning to Knowlton. "What's the use? The game's up. Where is it?"

Knowlton did not answer. He was leaning forward in an agony of anxiety, watching one of the detectives, who had just approached the alcove and grasped the curtain.

He pulled the curtain aside, letting the gaslight stream into the alcove, and Knowlton barely suppressed a cry of joy. It was empty.

Then he replied to the man who had spoken to him:

"If you'll tell me what you want I may be of some assistance. Everything I own is in that trunk and suitcase," pointing to them.

"Huh!" the red-faced man grunted. "Going to beat it, eh? Open 'em up, boys, while I look him over. Got a key for the trunk?"

Knowlton drew a bunch of keys from his pocket and tossed it to one of the men, then submitted himself to be searched. The detective took several miscellaneous articles from the young man's pockets, then a pocketbook. This he opened expectantly; but as he examined its contents there appeared on his face an expression of keen disappointment.

"What the deuce!" he exclaimed. "Where do you keep it?"

"I have said," Knowlton replied, "that I have no idea what you are looking for. If you will tell me—"

"Cut it!" said the other roughly. "I guess you're a wise one, all right, but what's the use? I tell you we've got enough on you already to send you up. You might as well talk straight."

Knowlton was silent. The red-faced man glared at him for a

moment, then walked over to aid the others in their search of the trunk and suitcase.

They pulled out clothing and toilet articles and books, and heaped them indiscriminately on the floor, while Knowlton looked on with a grim smile. Now and then oaths of disappointment came from the lips of the searchers.

Suddenly one of them uttered a cry of triumph and drew forth a neatly wrapped brown paper parcel. The leader took a knife from his pocket, cut the string of the parcel, and tore away the wrapper with eager fingers, disclosing to view—a stack of real-estate contracts.

"The deuce!" he ejaculated. "You're a boob, Evans."

Again they set to work.

Soon they finished with the trunk and suitcase and began on the rooms themselves. Nothing escaped them. They took the covers and mattress from the bed and shook each separately.

The couch was turned upside down and examined with probes. The drawers in the bureaus and tables and wardrobes were removed, and the interiors of the articles subjected to a close scrutiny. They raked out the dust and rubbish from the fireplace, and lifted the bricks.

The search lasted nearly an hour. They found nothing.

The red-faced man, muttering an oath, turned to Knowlton:

"Well, we've got you, anyway, my boy. I guess you'll find out you can't play with Uncle Sam."

Then he turned to his men:

"Come on, Evans, we'll take him down. You stay here, Corliss, and look the place over again and keep an eye out. Try the fire escape—we didn't look out there—and the dumbwaiter. The stuff ought to be here somewhere. If you find anything let me know; if not, report at the office in the morning as usual. Come along, Knowlton."

"But where?" Knowlton stood up. "And on what authority? And for what?"

"To the Ritz, for dinner," said the red-faced man sarcastically, while the others grinned delightedly at the keen wit of their superior. "Where d'ye suppose? To the Tombs. I suppose next you'll want to see the paper. Here it is."

He drew a stamped, official-looking document from his pocket and waved it about in front of Knowlton's face.

The young man said nothing further, but allowed himself to be led out of the rooms into the hall.

"Is it necessary—must I wear these on the street?" he stammered, holding up his shackled hands.

The red-faced man eyed him grimly.

"I guess two of us can take care of you," he said finally. "Take off the irons, Evans."

The other removed the handcuffs from Knowlton's wrists, and they descended the stairs and passed out to the street, one on either side of the prisoner.

Half an hour later Knowlton was pacing the floor of a narrow cell in the Tombs prison, with a heart full of remorse and bitterness and despair.

Yet he had no thought of his own danger, but was possessed of a fearful anxiety for Lila. Where had she gone? What had she done? Alone on the street at night, and with such a burden—the burden of his own crime! He felt that the thought would drive him mad, and he bit his lips to keep himself from crying out.

He thought of her magnificent courage in the awful scene at his rooms, and his eyes filled with tears. How brave and daring she had been! And how it must have hurt her innocence and proud womanhood to have been driven to such extremities for him—a criminal!

He told himself that she would despise him.

"She loves you," said his heart; "do not insult her by doubting it." Yes, but women sometimes despise the man they love. What a weak, blind fool he had been!

He groaned aloud in unutterable anguish. Piercing, overpowering emotion caused him to tremble and shake as a man with the palsy. He threw himself on the floor of the cell by the prison cot and buried his face in his hands.

He remained thus for an hour. Then he rose and seated himself on the edge of the cot.

"After all," he thought, "this, too, is weakness, and I must fight it. She has said that she loves me. Very well. I shall get out of this, and I have a lifetime to prove myself worthy of her. It is useless to waste time on vain regrets. Oh! She has given me strength. Every minute of my life belongs to her. And I said I didn't want to lose my self-respect! If I ever regain it, it will be through her."

Finally, after many hours of alternate despair and anxiety and resolution, he threw himself face downward on the cot, utterly exhausted, and slept.

We shall leave him there and return to Lila.

Her plan, swiftly conceived and perfectly executed, had worked admirably.

Her hiding place behind the curtain in the alcove exactly suited her purpose, for the curtain was flimsy and transparent, and, placed as it was between herself and the light, she was able to observe what took place in the room without any danger of being seen herself.

She had trusted to Knowlton's wit, and he had not failed her. As soon as the detectives had rushed to the rear of the apartment in pursuit of him she had quietly stepped forth from her hiding place and gained the outer hall, closing the door softly behind her.

There she hesitated. Her first impulse was to descend at once to the street. But what if some one had been left on guard below? Was it not likely that she would be stopped and questioned; and the tell-tale parcel examined?

She stood for a few seconds trying to decide what to do; then, at the sound of returning footsteps in the room she had just left, fled in a sudden panic up the stairs to the landing above.

She realized the thousand dangers of her position. What if a detective had been sent up to guard the roof and should return and find her? What if some tenant of the house, entering or leaving, should question her? What if one of the detectives below should happen to ascend the stairs?

And yet, what could she do? Nothing. She must remain where she was and wait. To go either up or down might be fatal.

She tried to think of some way to get rid of the parcel, which weighed on her arm with all the heaviness of fear. She hated it as though it were a human being. Fantastic schemes raced into her brain.

Should she ring the bell of one of the apartments and hand in the parcel as though it were a delivery from some tradesman? Should she place it on the floor of the hall and set it afire?

Suddenly the street door opened two flights below, and she heard footsteps entering and ascending the stairs. She quivered with terror, and felt a wild impulse to rush madly down and hurl the parcel into the street.

Then, just in time to prevent her crying out, the footsteps halted on the landing below, and there came the sound of a key turning in a lock and a door opening and closing. Evidently the person who had entered had been the tenant on the same floor with Knowlton, across the hall. She sighed with unutterable relief.

Many minutes passed, and each seemed to Lila an hour. What could the detectives be doing? Why did they not go, since they could have found nothing? For she thought, in her ignorance, that by her removal of the counterfeit money she had saved Knowlton from arrest. Her ideas of the manner of procedure of the law and its minions were extremely hazy, as those of a young girl should be. She was soon to be undeceived.

She waited, it seemed to her, for years. She felt faint and dizzy from fatigue and anxiety, her body was limp and nerveless, and she was telling herself that she must soon succumb, when she heard a door open in the hall below. At last!

There were footsteps, and Knowlton's voice came up to her:

"Is it necessary—must I wear these on the street?"

Then came the reply of the detective, and the sound of clinking steel, and steps descending the stairs, and the opening and closing of the street door.

Lila stood dumb with amazement. The meaning of what she had heard was clear to her: they had arrested him and were taking him to prison! But why? Was there something else of which she did not know? But she tossed that thought aside impatiently.

Knowlton had told her his story in detail, and she trusted him. But—prison! She shuddered with horror, and felt herself unable to stand, grasping at the baluster for support.

It was the necessity for action alone that sustained and roused her. To meet this new crisis she forgot her weakness of a moment before, and became again the courageous and daring woman she had been at the arrival of the detectives. She no longer hesitated or feared. She had something to do that must be done.

Holding the parcel tightly under her arm, she descended the stairs. As she passed through the hall in front of Knowlton's rooms the detective who had been left behind to complete the search for evidence looked out at her through the open door. Her heart beat madly, but she forced herself not to hasten her step as she descended the first flight of stairs to the outer door.

Another moment and she was in the street—free.

She glanced to the right and left, uncertain which way to turn.

What should she do with the parcel? She wondered why it seemed so difficult to get rid of the thing. Surely nothing could be simpler than to dispose of an ordinary-looking parcel, a foot square.

One could drop it in an ash can, or leave it on a bench in the park, or merely place it on a stoop—any stoop—anywhere. But somehow to do any of these things seemed fraught with horrible danger. She could have cried with exasperation at her hesitation over a difficulty apparently so simple.

Suddenly she remembered what Knowlton had said: "It is best to be safe, and I shall take it to the river." Of course! Why had she not thought of it before?

She turned sharply, and as she turned noticed a man standing directly across the street gazing curiously at the house she had just left. At sight of him she started violently, and looked again. It was Sherman. There could be no doubt of it; the light from a streetlamp shone full on his face.

The spot where Lila was standing was comparatively dark, and as Sherman remained motionless she was convinced that she had not been recognized. But she was seized with terror, and, fearing every moment to hear his footsteps behind her, but not daring to look round, she turned and moved rapidly in the direction of the Hudson.

Ten minutes later she entered the ferry-house at the foot of West Twenty-third Street. A boat was in the slip and she boarded it and walked to the farther end.

She leaned on the rail, gazing toward the bay, as the boat glided away from the shore, and almost forgot her anxiety and her errand in contemplating the fairyland before her eyes.

The myriads of tiny twinkling lights with their background of mysterious half darkness, the skeletonlike forms of the massive build-ings, barely revealed, and farther south, the towering outlines of the palaces of industry, were combined in a fantastic dream-picture of a modern monster.

Lila looked up, startled to find that the ferryboat had already reached the middle of the river. She glanced round to make sure she was not observed—there were few passengers on the boat—then quickly lifted the parcel over the rail and let it fall into the dark water below.

She could hardly realize that it was gone. Her arm was numb where it had been tightly pressed against the parcel, and it felt as though it still held its burden. She felt tired, and faint, and walked inside and seated herself.

When the boat arrived at the Jersey City slip she did not land. A half hour later she left it at Twenty-third Street. Another half hour and she was ascending the stairs to her room uptown.

Entering, she removed her hat and coat and threw them on a chair. She was tired, dead tired, in brain and body. She wanted to think: she told herself she had so much to think about.

The face of her world had changed utterly in the past few hours. But thought was impossible. She felt only a dull, listless sense of despair.

She had gained love, but what had she lost? Everything else had been given up in exchange for it. But how she loved him!

But even that thought was torture. Her head seemed ready to burst. Tears would have been a relief, but they would not come.

She dropped into a chair by the window, and, pressing her hands tightly against her throbbing temples, gazed out unseeing at the night.

When the dawn came, eight hours later, she had not moved.

CHAPTER XIII

———

The End of the Day

WHEN BILLY Sherman had visited detective Barrett—the red-faced man with carroty hair—and had heard him say, "We will get Mr. Knowlton tonight," he knew that the thing was as good as done. Detective Barrett was a man to be depended upon.

But Billy Sherman never depended upon anybody. He made the rather common mistake of judging humanity from the inside—of himself—and the result was that he had acquired a distorted opinion of human nature. His topsyturvy logic went something like this, though not exactly in this form: "I am a man. I am bad. Therefore, all men are bad."

And there is more of that sort of reasoning in the world than we are willing to admit.

Sherman did not go so far as to distrust Detective Barrett, but he had an idea that he wanted to see the thing for himself. Accordingly, shortly after six o'clock in the evening he posted himself in a doorway opposite Knowlton's rooms on Thirtieth Street.

He had been there but a few minutes when he was startled by the sight of Lila approaching and entering the house. This led to a long consideration of probabilities which ended in a grim smile. He thought: "If they get her, too, all the better. Barrett's a good fellow, and I can do whatever I want with her."

Soon a light appeared in the windows of Knowlton's rooms. The shades were drawn, but the man in the street could see two shadows thrown on them as the occupants moved about inside.

Suddenly the two shadows melted into one, and Sherman found the thing no longer amusing. Cursing the detectives for their tardiness, he repaired to the corner for a bracer.

He soon returned and resumed his position in the doorway.

After another interminable wait he saw Detective Barrett arrive with his men, and with fierce exultation watched them enter.

Another wait—this time nearly an hour—before two of the detectives emerged with Knowlton. This puzzled Sherman. "Where the deuce is Lila?" he muttered. Then he reflected that the other detective was probably waiting with her for a conveyance.

And then, to his astonishment, he beheld Lila descending the stoop alone.

She was half a block away before he recovered his wits sufficiently to follow her.

On the ferryboat he mounted to the upper deck to escape observation, completely at a loss to account for Lila's freedom, or for this night trip across the Hudson. Looking cautiously over the upper railing, he had observed her every movement as she stood almost directly beneath him.

And then, as he saw her lift the parcel and drop it in the river, he had comprehended all in a flash. Stifling the exclamation that rose to his lips, he shrank back from the rail, muttering an imprecation.

Somehow she had obtained possession of the evidence—the chief evidence—against Knowlton, and destroyed it! And he had calmly looked on, like a weak fool! Why had he not had sense enough to stop her when she had first left the house? These were the thoughts that whipped him into a frenzy of rage.

But Sherman was not the man to waste time crying over spilled milk. After all, he reflected, the damage was not irreparable, since his knowledge gave him a power over her that should prove irresistible. By the time the boat had returned to Twenty-third Street he was once more fiercely exultant.

But he took the precaution of following Lila uptown; nor was he satisfied until he saw her white face dimly outlined at her own window.

Then he turned, muttering: "I guess she'll do no more mischief tonight."

He was determined that he would not make a second mistake. The first thing was to make sure of Knowlton. Perhaps early in the morning— He glanced at his watch; it was a quarter past nine.

At the corner he turned into a saloon and telephoned the office of Detective Barrett, and, finding him in, made an appointment to call on him in three-quarters of an hour.

He was there five minutes ahead of time. The detective was alone in the office and opened the door himself in response to his visitor's knock.

He was in ill humor.

"You've got us in a pretty mess," he began, placing a chair for Sherman and seating himself at his desk. "We got Knowlton all right, but there wasn't a scrap of stuff in the whole place. Unless we can dig up something, what he can do to us won't be a little. That was a beautiful tip-off of yours—I don't think. I don't say it wasn't on the square, but it looks like—"

Sherman cut him short.

"Wait a minute, Barrett. You shut your eyes and go to sleep, and then when you don't see anything you blame it on me. The stuff was there, and it's your own fault you didn't get it."

"Then you'd better go up there and show it to Corliss. He's probably looking for it yet."

"Oh, he won't find it now." Sherman leaned forward in his chair and held up a finger impressively. "When you went in that house Knowlton wasn't alone. There was a woman in his rooms with him, and a big bundle of the queer. And you politely closed your eyes and let her walk out with it."

The other stared at him.

"What sort of a game is this?" he demanded.

"This is straight," said Sherman, "and I can prove it. I know who the woman was, and I know what she did with the stuff. What I can't understand is how she ever got away."

"Do you mean to say she was inside when we got there?"

Sherman nodded emphatically.

The detective looked puzzled:

"Then how in the name of—" He stopped short, while his face was suddenly filled with the light of understanding—and chagrin.

"Well, I'm jiggered," he said finally. Then he explained Knowlton's ruse—or rather Lila's—to Sherman. "It's an old trick," he ended, "but we weren't looking for it. We thought he was alone. But where did she go? What did she do with it? Who is she?"

"She took a ride on a ferryboat and dropped it in the middle of the Hudson."

"Then it's gone."

"Thanks to you, yes."

"But where did you get all this? Of course, she's a—"

"Back up!" Sherman interrupted. "She's a friend of mine."

"She seems not exactly to hate Knowlton," the detective observed dryly. "Who is she?"

Sherman winced.

"What does that matter? She knows enough to send him higher than a kite, and she'll have to come through with it."

The other became impatient.

"But who is she? We ought to get her tonight."

There was a pause; then Sherman said slowly:

"You won't get her at all."

At the look of inquiry and surprise on the detective's face he proceeded to explain:

"I told you she's a friend of mine. Maybe it would be better to say I'm a friend of hers. Put it however you please, but she's not to be locked up. Serve her as a witness, and she'll give you all you need against Knowlton, and more, too.

"I'll see to that. She can't get out of it. Anyway, if you arrested her, what would happen? You couldn't make them testify against each other, and they'd both get off."

"But as soon as we serve her she'll beat it," the other objected.

"Leave that to me. Of course, I've got a personal interest in this, and you ought to consider it. I don't have to remind you—"

"No," the detective interrupted hastily, "you don't. I have a memory, Billy."

"Well, then it's up to you."

The detective finally capitulated and agreed to do as Sherman wished. Sherman gave him Lila's name and address, and advised him to postpone serving the subpoena as long as possible.

"I want to prepare her for it," he explained as the detective accompanied him to the door. "I'll see her first thing in the morning. If possible, we want to prevent Knowlton from knowing that she is to appear against him, and I think I can manage it. You'll hear from me tomorrow. Going uptown?"

The other replied that he had work to do in the office that would keep him till midnight, and wished him good night.

Sherman was well satisfied with the day's work. With Knowlton in the Tombs and Lila completely in his power, he felt that there was nothing left to be desired. As he sat in an uptown subway local he reviewed his position with the eye of a general, and, discovering no possible loophole for the enemy, sighed with satisfaction.

At Twenty-third Street he left the train and made his way to the lobby of the Lamartine.

He was led there more by force of habit than by any particular purpose. At first he had thought of going to see Lila at once, but had decided that it would serve his ends better to allow her to have a night for reflection over the day's events. She would be less able to resist his demands.

It was but little past ten o'clock, and he found the lobby almost deserted. Night at the Lamartine began late and ended early—in the morning.

One or two nondescripts loitered about the entrance inside, the hotel clerk yawned behind his desk, and the weary-looking female who took Miss Hughes's place during the hours of darkness was drumming on the counter with her fingers, chewing gum, and reading a newspaper, thus exercising three different sets of muscles at the same time.

Sherman approached her:

"Have any of the boys been in?"

She looked up from her newspaper and regarded him chillingly:

"Huh?"

It was this young girl's habit never to understand questions addressed to her till they had been repeated at least once. It argued a superiority over the questioner; an indifference to common and sublunary affairs.

She condescended finally to inform Sherman that Driscoll and Booth had been seen in the lobby some two hours before. While talking she contrived somehow to lose not a single stroke on the gum.

Sherman wandered about for half an hour, tried to find someone to take a cue at billiards without success, and had about decided to go home when Dumain and Dougherty entered arm-in-arm.

Dumain called to Sherman, and the three proceeded to the bar.

Sherman ordered a whisky, Dougherty a gin rickey, and Dumain an absinth frappé. This is for the benefit of those who judge a man by what he drinks. You see what it amounts to.

The ex-prizefighter was a little ill at ease. He felt that he had treated Sherman a little shabbily by breaking his promise not to speak to Knowlton till the following day; perhaps, after all, he thought, Sherman had acted in good faith.

"I suppose you called off your sleuth," he observed.

Sherman looked up quickly.

"What? Oh, yes. I saw him this afternoon. Good thing, too. He was costing me more than a prima donna. Fill 'em up, bartender."

"Then it's all right to speak to Knowlton now?"

"As far as I'm concerned, yes."

"The reason I wanted to know," Dougherty hesitated, "is because I already spoke to him. It wasn't because I wanted to put anything over on you—don't think that. He came in here about noon, and it was too good a chance to pass up.

"Besides, Miss Williams was going out with him, and I had to head him off somehow. I was a little uneasy about it, but since you say it's all right, I'll forget it. And, thank Heaven, we've seen the last of Knowlton. By this time he's probably so far away from little old New York you couldn't see him with a telescope from the top of the Singer Building."

"Well, you didn't do any harm." Sherman was picking up his change on the bar.

"Eet was best," put in Dumain. "Zee sooner zee bettaire. He was a quiet scoundrel. You should have seen heem when Dougherty told heem! He had not a word. He walked out wiz a frown."

Each man lifted his glass in silence. Each had his own thoughts.

"I'm a little worried about Miss Williams," said Dougherty presently. "I wonder what she thought when she saw him walk out without speaking to her? Knowlton asked me to tell her, but I didn't have the nerve. I think they had a date to go to lunch. And all afternoon she kept watching for him. I saw her."

"She'll soon forget him," said Sherman.

"I doubt it," declared Dougherty. "You know yourself he was different from us. And from the way she looked this afternoon—I doubt it."

"Bah!" Dumain snapped his fingers. "She care not zat much for heem. If she did would she not have been—ah, grief—*distrait*— when she hear he was a what you call eet counterfeiter?"

There was a sudden pause, while Dougherty turned and gazed at Dumain keenly.

"When did you tell her?" he demanded finally.

Dumain was silent, while his face reddened in confusion, and Sherman raised his hand to his mouth to conceal a smile.

"When did you tell her?" repeated the ex-prizefighter, more sternly than before.

"Tonight," Dumain stammered. "You see, Knowlton had left so sudden, and I thought she ought to know. You see—"

"Yes, I see!" Dougherty roared. "You're a darn Frenchman. That's what you are; you're a darn Frenchman! You can't keep your mouth shut. You ought to be muzzled. If you wasn't such a human shrimp I'd—Bartender, for the love of Mike, give us a drink."

He drained a highball with two prodigious gulps.

Dumain took courage.

"But eet was best. She had to know sometime. So tell her at once, zat is what I theenk. Zen I tell her."

"What did she say?" Dougherty demanded.

"Nozzing." The little Frenchman shrugged his shoulders expressively. "I tell you she care leetle for heem. She lifted her eyes upward in surprise"—he rolled his own toward heaven—"and say, 'Has he gone?' like zat. Zen she say good night like any other time and went home."

Dougherty grunted in disbelief.

Sherman had for some minutes been meditating on the question whether he should tell his companions what he knew—or, rather, what he had done. It would be in the nature of a triumph over them, but would it not be dangerous? He reflected, and could not resist the temptation.

He took up Dumain's last words:

"And what makes you think she went home?"

The others stared at him—a stare that plainly meant:

"Where else should she go?"

"You evidently don't know the lady very well," Sherman continued. "You think she's as innocent as she looks. She went straight from here to Knowlton's rooms, and she seemed to know pretty well how to get there. You can guess as well as I can what she went after. And how many times—"

He stopped suddenly, though not of his own volition. The compelling cause was Dougherty's fingers about his throat, in a grip of steel.

Dumain had hurriedly stepped aside, and the bartender was loudly expostulating in a tone of alarm, while three or four men who were standing at the bar a few feet away looked on with pleasurable expectations. They knew Dougherty.

The ex-prizefighter spoke no word—he never talked and acted at the same time. He pressed his fingers tighter and tighter, till the face of the man who had insulted Lila began to assume a hue of purple as he pawed helplessly at the wrists that seemed to be made of iron.

"You keel heem," said Dumain quietly. "Let heem go, Tom."

Dougherty did so, and Sherman stood erect. Then, with a single glance charged with malevolence and hatred, he turned to go.

"No, you don't," said the ex-prizefighter grimly, stepping in front of him. "You've said too much. Tell us what you meant."

Sherman opened his lips to speak, but the words would not pass his throat. He gulped spasmodically.

"Here," said the bartender, handing him a drink of brandy. "This'll fix you."

Sherman drained the glass at one swallow, with a grimace of pain.

"Now," said Dougherty, "speak up."

Sherman wanted to defy him, but dared not. He, too, knew Dougherty.

He began:

"I'll even up for this, Dougherty. What I said was the truth."

"Go on. I'll take care of myself."

Sherman spoke with difficulty, but in a tone of sneering satisfaction:

"Immediately after Dumain spoke to her tonight she went to Knowlton's rooms. She was there when the cops came for Knowlton, and she crawled out somehow with a bundle of the queer and threw it in the middle of the Hudson. Knowlton's in the Tombs, where he ought to be."

The others were gazing at him speechless with surprise.

"That's what your innocent Miss Williams has come to." Sherman continued with a sneer. "And it's your own fault. You wouldn't listen to me. And now——"

The look in Dougherty's eyes stopped him.

The ex-prizefighter's tone was threatening:

"Who put them onto Knowlton?"

"How do I know?" Sherman retorted with an assumption of bravado.

"Maybe you don't," said Dougherty grimly, "but I do. Sherman, you're a skunk. I don't want to touch you. You're too rotten. But I want to ask you some questions—and look here! No—look in my eyes. Now talk straight. Who peached on Knowlton?"

The answer was low but distinct:

"I did."

"You say he's in the Tombs?"

"Yes."

"What's the charge against him?"

"Passing counterfeit money."

"Where is Miss Williams?"

"How do I know?"

"Answer!" Dougherty advanced a step. "You know, all right, you sneak. Where is she?"

"At home."

"Who arrested Knowlton?"

"Detective Barrett, of the Secret Service."

"Does he know anything about Miss Williams?"

Sherman opened his mouth to speak, then closed it again and was silent.

"Answer!" Dougherty's voice trembled with his effort to control it. "And look at me! Don't try to lie!"

There was no escape.

"He—he knows all about her," Sherman stammered.

Then, at the look of uncontrollable fury that appeared on his questioner's face, he sprang to one side, bounded to the door, and fled through the lobby and madly down the street.

Dougherty had started to pursue him, but thought better of it and halted.

He turned to Dumain and said shortly:

"Come on; get home and go to bed. We have work to do in the morning."

—ᴍ—

The Morning After

*M*RS. AMANDA Berry paused at the head of the stairs and looked curiously at a closed door to the right.

"Now, I call that funny," she remarked to herself. "I ain't seen her go out, and it's past nine o'clock. Surely she ain't sick."

She hesitated, glanced again at the door, and started to descend the stairs, then turned suddenly and reascended them, and knocked sharply on the door at which she had aimed her remark.

Mrs. Berry was a curious phenomenon—a *rara avis*. She owned and operated a rooming house on One Hundred and Fourth Street, New York, and she took a personal interest in her roomers. Not that she was inquisitive or—to put it vulgarly—nosy; she merely had a heart. This was so far from being resented by the roomers that they were all a little jealous of one of their number for whom Mrs. Berry had more than once betrayed a decided preference—Lila Williams.

Receiving no response to her knock, Mrs. Berry knocked again. After a long pause there was a faint "Come in."

She entered.

Lila was sitting in a chair by the window. Her hat and coat lay on another chair near the door. The bed had not been slept in.

"Now what's the matter?" Mrs. Berry sang out cheerily, crossing the room. "Another headache, I'll bet a dollar. If you don't—
why, what's the matter? Goodness sakes alive, just look at the girl's
face! No wonder you didn't go to work! You just wait—"

"Now, please, Mrs. Berry," Lila interrupted, rising to her feet and
trying to smile, "don't bother about me. I—I want to be alone.
Really."

Her face was deadly white, giving her eyes and cheeks a sunken
appearance, and as she stood with one hand resting heavily on the
back of the chair she was quivering from head to foot. Mrs. Berry
stared at her in wrathful amazement.

"You want to be alone! Look at you! You get right in that
bed—and look at it! You ain't been in bed at all—and I know you
come in early, because I heard you. So you ain't sick. Then you're in
trouble."

She looked at Lila keenly to confirm her diagnosis, and nodded
her head. She knew the signs, and she knew the one thing that
would help.

Mrs. Berry was a good-sized woman. She walked over to Lila,
picked her up in her arms as though she were a baby, and seated herself in a chair. Then she spoke grimly:

"You're a little fool. If you keep on like this you'll die. Don't you
know what tears is good for? Now go on and cry as hard as you can,
and hurry up about it."

Lila was motionless and silent. Mrs. Berry folded her arms
tighter around her and continued:

"You know, if it's any real trouble I'll help you. Of course I ain't
like a mother, but I'll do all I can. Look, dearie, look at me! What is
it? Tell me. Tell me all about it. I'm your mother now, you know.
Here, put your arm round my neck—that's right. Now what is it,
dearie; won't you tell me?"

She felt the slender body tremble in her arms and something hot and wet on her hand that touched Lila's cheek, but she pretended not to notice, and went on:

"You don't need to be afraid to tell me, no matter what it is, because I can stand anything. Lord! I've been through it all. Of course it's a man—it always is. There! That's right. Now! There, dearie—never you mind me—"

Lila was sobbing, with great sighs and shakings of her frame, the sobs that come from the heart. Mrs. Berry held her in her arms, patting and soothing her, while the storm raged. Presently she rose and laid her, all bathed in tears, on the bed.

"There! That'll do you good. You just keep it up as long as you can. Lord! To think you've had that in you all night!"

She moved busily about the room, hanging Lila's hat and coat in the wardrobe, adjusting the window-shades, and moving chairs that were better off where they were. Finally she moved to the door. She started to speak, but thought better of it, and went out softly, closing the door behind her.

Lila remained on the bed for many minutes, while the tempest gradually calmed, and at length left her with only an occasional long, quivering sigh. Then she arose and bathed her face in cold water and arranged her hair. When Mrs. Berry entered a minute later she was putting on her hat, with fingers that trembled.

"Now what?" Mrs. Berry demanded, stopping in the doorway.

Lila answered:

"I am going to work."

"You are, eh?" Mrs. Berry snorted. "Not if I know it! You take off that hat and set right down in that chair—or, better still, go to bed."

"But I must," protested Lila. "I'm all right now, Mrs. Berry; really I am."

"All right, then you're all right. I don't say you ain't. But you ain't goin' to work."

This was said in a tone which had been only too well known by the late Mr. Berry. He had never been able to resist it, nor was Lila. It forbore all opposition; and without knowing exactly how or why, some minutes later she found herself in the chair by the window eating an excellent breakfast brought up on a tray by Mrs. Berry.

During the morning Lila received several visits from the good woman. She came to remove the tray, she came to fetch the morning papers, and she came to "tidy up the room." On her sixth visit she entered somewhat precipitately and announced that there was a gentleman below to see Lila.

"Who is it?" asked Lila, turning quickly.

"He didn't give his name," said Mrs. Berry. "He's a tall, sporty-lookin', mean-lookin' man."

Lila reflected a moment, then asked Mrs. Berry to show him up. She grunted, and departed.

A minute later Billy Sherman entered the room.

Lila sprang to her feet with an involuntary exclamation of surprise and dismay.

"You!" she breathed.

Sherman nodded, laid his hat and gloves on a table near the door, and crossed the room to her side.

"Yes," he said calmly, "I. Aren't you glad to see me?"

Then, as Lila, unable to speak, pointed to the door with a shaking finger, he continued:

"Well, I'm glad to see you. No, I won't go. And when you hear what I have to tell you, you won't want me to go. I've played with you long enough, and it's about time for us to understand each other. Sit down."

Lila was trembling with indignation and fear. She remembered Knowlton's story: this was the man who had caused all her suffering and Knowlton's misfortune. Sherman's person had always impressed her disagreeably; she now shrank from him as from a snake.

She forced herself to look at him.

"Mr. Sherman, if I had known it was you asking for me I would not have seen you. Go—at once—or I'll call Mrs. Berry."

"So you wouldn't have seen me?" Sherman sneered. "Well, you'd have been sorry for it. If it wasn't for me, do you know where you'd be now? You'd be in the Tombs. That trip of yours across the Hudson last night was a little indiscreet."

He smiled grimly at her gasp of surprise and horror as he went on:

"You wouldn't believe I was your friend, but maybe you will now. Couldn't I have turned you over to the detectives last night? Remember, all I have to do is walk to a telephone—it's not too late."

Lila could only repeat:

"Go—go!"

"But that's not what I want," he continued, ignoring her cry. "I'm fool enough to want to protect you. I love you. For months you've laughed at me; now it's my turn. You can't look at me any more with your darned pious air of superiority. A girl that goes to visit a man in his rooms at night had better take what she can get. Wait! Wait till I finish!"

Lila, her eyes ablaze, had sprung to the door and begun to open it. But at the tone of Sherman's last words, menacing and significant, she halted.

"I thought so," said Sherman meaningly. "You're not the one to break your own neck. Now do as I tell you, and you can save both Knowlton and yourself."

Lila stared at him in surprise, incredulous.

"Oh, not for you," he continued, reading her thought. "I'm not that kind of a fool. I put it to you straight: do you want to save Knowlton?"

"What—what has that to do with you?" stammered Lila, removing her hand from the door and turning to face him.

"Just this: I can save him, and I will—on one condition."

"And the—one condition?"

"That you marry me."

"I—marry—you!" The words choked her.

"Yes. The day that you become my wife John Knowlton is a free man. Otherwise—you know the alternative. And, my dear, you could make a worse bargain. As I said, you are not in a position to choose. And I love you; I will try to make you happy—"

"You—make me happy!"

The stinging scorn of the tone was indescribable. Sherman winced, and was moved to a sudden fury:

"Well, and if I don't? I'll have you! At last! And be careful—I may decide not to marry you. After all, why should I marry you? Knowlton didn't. That touches you, does it? And what do you think of your lover now? Why don't you go down to the Tombs and tell him—tell him—"

He sputtered and paused, overcome with jealous rage. Then, recovering himself with difficulty, he said calmly:

"And now I want your answer. You're at the end of your rope, and you may as well talk sense. None of your high-flown, touch-me-if-you-dare stuff will go now—you're up against a stiff proposition and you've got to make good.

"I've got you. Do you understand that? I've got you. You'd do anything for this Knowlton, would you? All right. When will you marry me?"

Lila wanted to cry out, to run from the room, to close her ears and eyes against his insults and his leering face. But she stood glued to the spot, unable either to speak or move.

The man, advancing a threatening step, repeated his question:

"When will you marry me?"

Her lips moved, but there was no sound.

"By Heaven, you will answer me!" said Sherman through

clenched teeth. He reached her side in two long strides and grasped her arm fiercely. "Speak!" he hissed. "You little black-eyed devil—speak—tell me—"

At that moment there came three sharp knocks on the door—barely in time.

Sherman, muttering an oath, released Lila's arm and turned quickly about. Lila placed her hand on the back of a chair for support, and, between quick, short, breaths, managed to murmur:

"Come in."

The door opened. Mrs. Berry entered.

"More visitors," she announced shortly, from the doorway. She seemed not to notice Lila's agitation, and Sherman's back was turned. "Mr. Dumain and Mr. Dougherty is down below and asks to see you."

Then she ran over to Lila, and, placing her mouth close to her ear, whispered:

"I don't know what this is all about, dearie, but if I can help you—"

Lila threw her arms around the good woman's neck and kissed her.

"You can help me," she murmured. "Send them up—Mr. Dumain and Mr. Dougherty—send them up at once! Dear Mrs. Berry, hurry!"

Whereupon Mrs. Berry sped from the room and down the stairs with flying skirts.

Lila stood by the open door. Sherman turned, his face livid with rage—or was it fear? His lips moved, but no words came from them. He stared straight at the door, as though stunned by surprise at the sudden check to his plans, and remained so as Lila advanced eagerly to meet the two men who came puffing up the stairs.

"I am glad to see you," she declared, taking a hand of each.

Dumain bowed grandly, in silence. Dougherty gripped her hand with awkward roughness and stammered an unintelligible "Good morning!"

But he soon found his tongue. Lila moved aside, and at the same instant the newcomers caught sight of Sherman.

Dougherty's eyes were filled with surprise for a moment, then they became alight with an unholy joy. He had spent half the night regretting what he considered the leniency of his treatment of Sherman, and here he was delivered unto his hand!

He pointed a finger at him and spoke to Lila.

"What is he doing here?"

But Lila was so relieved by the unexpected succor that she was scarcely able to speak.

"I don't know," she stammered. "I mean—it doesn't matter, since you have come. Only, send him away—please—at once!"

Then at sight of the look on Dougherty's face she grasped his arm.

"No—not that! Don't hurt him! I mean—just send him away."

But the ex-prizefighter shook off her detaining hand.

"Hurt him? Oh, no. No, I won't exactly hurt him. I'll just shake hands with him. Only I'm so glad to see him that I may be a little rough."

His tone was sharp and clear as the ring of steel, and the touch of sarcasm made it only the more deadly. He started toward Sherman, who retreated with his back against the window, crouched halfway to the floor with his teeth showing in an ugly snarl of fear. The sight struck Lila dumb with terror.

It was Dumain who averted the catastrophe. Dougherty had nearly reached the window when he felt the little Frenchman's hand on his arm, and tried to shake it off.

But Dumain only tightened his grip.

"But, Tom! *Mon Dieu!* Look at her! She weel scream—she weel faint. You can't keel heem in zee presence of zee lady. Eet ees not what you call eet polite. Come! Beeg eediot!"

"Do you mean I ought to let him go?" demanded Dougherty, amazed.

"For now—yes. We keel heem later. Come—look at her!"

Lila added her voice:

"Please, Mr. Dougherty, just send him away. I think he won't bother any more."

Dougherty sighed. Such conduct as this was entirely beyond his comprehension. Since the fellow was there, why not give him what was coming to him?

However, he felt that he must bend to the wishes of the lady. Perhaps, after all, it would be a breach of decorum. But he was unable to speak; he merely stepped to one side as a sign that he obeyed the will of the majority against his own.

Sherman attempted to make his exit with dignity. But his step was considerably hurried as he crossed the room, and it degenerated into a run at the head of the stairs; and he forgot his hat and gloves. Dumain saw them on the table and threw them down the stairs after him.

Then Lila sank into a chair and burst into tears.

This rattled Dumain and Dougherty more than the presence of a dozen Shermans would have done. The little Frenchman walked about as though in search of a means of escape, and finally began examining a vase on the mantel with minute care.

The ex-prizefighter was seized with a fit of coughing and went over to close the door, banging it with a force that shook the house. They avoided meeting each other's eyes and kept their backs turned toward Lila.

Dougherty watched Dumain fingering the vase till he could stand it no longer, then burst forth:

"You fool, can't you do anything?"

Whereupon Lila smiled through her tears, and Dumain, turning, saw her, and sighed with immense relief.

"It's I that am a fool," said Lila, dabbing at her eyes with her handkerchief, "but I just couldn't help it. Oh, I am so glad you came! I thank you—thank you, with all my heart. And now he—Mr. Dougherty, why is he so afraid of you?"

"Him!" the ex-prizefighter snorted. "He's afraid of everyone on earth, including himself. What was he doing here?"

Lila stammered, coloring.

"He—he wanted me to do something. It would do no good to tell you. I hope I shall never see him again. He frightens me. I am so glad you came!"

Then she forgot her confusion when she realized that she had not offered them chairs, and begged them to be seated. They obeyed her, Dumain with a flourish, Dougherty awkwardly.

There was a silence. Each of the men was waiting for the other to speak, and Lila gazed at each in turn.

Finally she said:

"Did you come from the hotel?"

"Yes," echoed the two men.

Another silence. Dougherty moved about uneasily in his chair. Dumain twirled his mustache. Lila tried to think of something to say, but found her tongue tied by their embarrassment.

It was Dougherty who finally burst forth with a prodigious effort:

"I suppose you know why we came?"

Lila shook her head and invited an explanation.

"Well, we saw you wasn't at the hotel, and we thought maybe you was at home, so we came up to see."

"We thought perhaps eet was eelness."

"You are very kind," Lila murmured.

"And," Dougherty continued, swallowing hard and forcing the words between his lips, "we wanted to talk to you about Knowlton."

Lila turned her eyes full on the speaker, and Dumain threw him a nod of applause and encouragement.

"You see, we saw Sherman last night, and he told us all about it. I don't want you to think we had anything to do with it. We wouldn't peach on a guy, no matter who he was."

"I didn't think you would," said Lila.

"But," continued Dougherty, now fully started, "we ain't sorry he got it. We're glad he's put away where he can't do any more harm. We don't like the way—"

"Did Mr. Sherman say—anything—about me?" Lila interrupted.

The ex-prizefighter looked away from her.

"Yes," he said finally. "We know everything."

"Then why did you come—"

"That's what I'm going to tell you. And that's why I started like I did. I want you to understand that we're dead against Knowlton.

"Now, there's no use talking about what's past. We don't care what you've done; we ain't even going to say, 'I told you so.' What we want is to help you now.

"Knowlton's done for, so there's no use worrying about him, but from what Sherman said last night we was afraid you might get tangled up so you might have some trouble to get loose, and we want to let you know we're right on the job to help you out of it. I guess that's about all."

Lila leaned forward in her chair.

"But you say—you are 'dead against' Mr. Knowlton?"

Dougherty said "Yes" with emphasis, and Dumain nodded vigorously.

"Then—I thank you," said Lila.

Her tone caused the ex-prizefighter to look at her quickly.

"You mean—"

Lila rose to her feet. Tears were in her eyes, and her hands were clasped together so that little spots of red and white showed on them. Her voice, when she spoke, was low and quavering, but it held that depth of tone which is heard only when the words come from the heart.

"I mean—it is useless to talk to me longer, Mr. Dougherty. I am a very wretched girl. And now I shall offend you—I know it, but cannot help it. I can't take your help, because I won't desert Mr. Knowlton."

Dougherty swore, and immediately was on his feet, stammering an apology, while Dumain glared at him fiercely.

Lila paid no attention to the interruption.

"You see—I can't. Oh, don't think me an ingrate—I know how kind you have been—but you don't know as much about him as I do. And I can't leave him without—I can't think of him as you do"—she tried to smile—"because I am going to be his wife."

"Mon Dieu!" gasped Dumain. Dougherty was speechless.

"Yes," said Lila—and there was a note of pride in her voice— "we are to be married. So, of course, you know how I feel about it, and I couldn't very well expect you to help me—us. I am sorry, because I do care for you, but you would never understand—"

She paused. The ex-prizefighter and the little Frenchman each heaved a prodigious sigh. They looked at each other, and each read in the other's eyes his own thought. The Frenchman nodded significantly and Dougherty turned to Lila.

He said:

"We're friends of yours, ain't we, Miss Williams?"

She nodded, wondering.

"Old friends—pals?"

"Yes."

"Well, I want to ask you a question. If you don't want to answer it, all right. What I mean is, maybe I've got no right to ask it, but I want to know. Do you love this guy Knowlton?"

Lila's face colored, she hesitated, and then answered simply: "Yes."

"How well do you love him?"

"As well"—the answer came as promptly as though it were printed in a catechism—as indeed it is—"as he loves me."

Dumain cried *"Bravo!"* and Dougherty grinned. Then they rose, and each extended a hand to Lila, as a "pal."

She understood, but could not speak, and took the outstretched hands, one in each of her own. Then she found her tongue and started to stammer her gratitude.

"Cut it!" said Dougherty rudely. He was unused to emotion of the tender sort, and this had been a trying scene. "The thing to do now is to get him out. And, little pal, leave it to us. It's a cinch. But, believe me, you'll have to pay for it. There's one thing we've got to have."

"A kees from zee bride?" Dumain suggested.

"No, you darned Frenchman. An invitation to the wedding!"

—⁓—

CHAPTER XV

Number Thirty-two

AFTER A night in his cell at the Tombs Knowlton rose from his cot early in the morning with a racking headache and a poignant sense of desolation and despair.

But his breakfast, which he forced himself to swallow, and his bath, such as it was, considerably refreshed him, and he found that the night had, at least, cleared his brain and left him able to think. He sat on the edge of his cot and considered his calamity, if not calmly, with fortitude and a supply of the dry light of reason.

He tried to keep his mind off of Lila; he could not think of her with fortitude; it filled him with an overwhelming sense of her loyalty and bravery and sweet compassion.

He reviewed in his mind the probable evidence against himself, turning it over and over, trying to discover its value, but it was like groping blindly in the dark. He knew nothing of what was known.

Had Red Tim been captured? Did they have any direct evidence of any of his—he sought a word—transactions? Or had they counted on catching him "with the goods on"—and been foiled by Lila?

All the morning he sat and pondered on these questions when

he was not thinking of Lila. He felt little anxiety concerning her; she had given, before him, so convincing an instance of her wit and courage that he felt assured of her safety. He knew she had escaped from the rooms, and though she had carried a dangerous burden she could have found no serious difficulty in disposing of it.

He remembered her embarrassed timidity as she had entered his rooms, her flash of anger at his seeming indifference, the light of awakening gladness in her eyes as he had told her his love—and then, her arms clasped about his neck, her lips pressed to his, her frank, sweet words of surrender.

And now—he glanced at the bare prison walls—this! He shuddered and groaned.

At that moment there came a voice from the grated door—the rasping voice of the turnkey:

"Knowlton! Someone to see you!"

The man on the cot sprang to his feet in surprise. Could it be— But no, surely it could not be Lila, he thought, and, hesitating, stammered:

"Who is it?"

Then he crossed to the door and peered through the grating.

"Dougherty!" he cried, astonished. "What in the name of Heaven brings you here?"

The ex-prizefighter, who was standing in the middle of the corridor, approached the door.

"Hello, Knowlton! You seem to be on the wrong side this time. How's the world?"

Knowlton stood staring at him stiffly, without speaking. Why had he come? Had anything happened to Lila? Had she been arrested?

"What do you want?" he demanded, in a voice hoarse with anxiety.

Dougherty laughed.

"That's a devil of a way to talk to a friend. But I can see you've got the Willies, so I'll excuse you."

"A—a friend?" Knowlton stammered.

"Sure." Dougherty laughed again, possibly to hide a certain embarrassment. "Do you think I'd be here if I wasn't? Among other things, I've got a little note here for you from Miss Williams."

"Where is she?"

"At home."

"Is she all right? Is she well?"

"Yes—both."

"Thank God! And the note?"

"Not so loud." Dougherty came closer to the door. "I'll have to slip it to you on the quiet. And talk lower—you never can tell in this little hotel who's around. Wait a minute—here—quick!"

A tiny roll of paper showed itself through the bars of the door. Knowlton grasped it with anxious fingers and placed it in his pocket.

His voice was tremulous with feeling.

"Thanks, old man. A thousand thanks. You're sure she's all right?"

"Absolutely."

"Thank God!" Knowlton's fingers closed convulsively over the paper in his pocket. "That's really all I cared about. It doesn't matter much what happens to me—anyway, I deserve it. But if she had been—"

"Well, she wasn't," Dougherty interrupted. "And now to get down to business, for I haven't got any too much time. You're going to get out of this thing, Knowlton, and we're going to help you."

"But why—"

"Never mind why. Of course we're doing it mostly for *her*, but she told us some stuff about you this morning that we didn't know, and we feel we gave you kind of a dirty deal, and we want to square up. But mostly it's for her. You are on the square with her, ain't you? That's all we want to know."

The question was humiliating, but Knowlton swallowed it. He felt that he deserved it, and he realized that Dougherty had a right to ask it.

He said simply:

"You know I am. Didn't she tell you?"

"Yes. I know. And say—you're a lucky devil, Knowlton."

Then they proceeded to a discussion of the steps to be taken for Knowlton's defense. Dougherty was surprised to discover that he knew nothing of the nature of the evidence against him, and declared that it greatly increased their difficulties.

He ended:

"But leave that to the lawyer. Dumain has gone after him now—I left him over at the subway—and they'll probably be here this afternoon."

"But—" Knowlton hesitated.

"Well?"

"Why, about the lawyer. I had thought of conducting my own defense. I don't believe he can help us any."

"What's the matter? Broke?" said Dougherty bluntly.

"The fact is—yes. Or nearly so. And I certainly can't take any more favors—"

"Go to the deuce with your favors! Didn't I say we're going to help you out of this? Don't be a fool, Knowlton! But I can't quite understand how you can be broke. I supposed you had a nice little pile stowed away somewhere. You don't mean to tell me you shoved the queer for that gang and got nothing out of it?"

Knowlton almost smiled.

"But I stopped that a month ago."

"I know that. She told us all about it. But didn't you have sense enough to dig a fat little hole somewhere?"

Instead of answering the question Knowlton asked one of his own:

"Didn't you ask me a little while ago if I was on the square with Miss Williams?"

Dougherty nodded, wondering what that had to do with the accumulation of a "pile."

"Well, I'll show you how square I was. I had two thousand dollars put away. After I got to know her, I—disposed of it."

Dougherty stared at him incredulously.

"Do you mean to say you threw away two thousand dollars in real money?"

"Yes."

It took the ex-prizefighter a full minute to recover from his astonishment and find his tongue, after which he stated it as his settled and firm opinion that Knowlton was hopelessly insane.

He added:

"But don't you worry about the lawyer—leave it to us. And everything else. And now"—he glanced at his watch—"I've got to leave you. It's nearly noon, and I want to catch the boys before they go out to lunch. Dumain will be here this afternoon."

They talked a few minutes longer before the ex-prizefighter finally departed.

Knowlton listened to his footsteps and those of the turnkey as they passed down the corridor, then he crossed to the little barred window and drew forth the note from Lila. It was short:

Dear: I have nothing to say, except that I love you, and are you sure you want to hear that? You see, I am cheerful. Mr. Dougherty and Mr. Dumain are very, very kind to me, and to you. We can never repay them. You must be cheerful, too, if you love me.

Lila.

Knowlton read it over many times and pressed it to his lips. And such is the heart of man that the tears of gratitude which filled his eyes were not for Dougherty's offer of practical and valuable assistance, but for this little inconsequential note, which said nothing except, "I love you!"

———

Dougherty, on his way uptown, was facing a new difficulty—a little matter of cash. He was reflecting on the fact that it takes money to prove a man's innocence, especially when he happens to be guilty. And where was the money to come from?

He considered all possible sources of revenue, and found the total sadly deficient. He counted his own purse three times—it amounted to sixty-two dollars and forty-five cents. And this was a matter, not of a hundred or so, but of two or three thousands.

A thousand for the lawyer, a thousand for a "stake" for Knowlton and Lila, and a thousand for miscellaneous expenses. The ex-prizefighter was determined not to do the thing by halves. But where to get the three thousand?

He had been headed straight for the Lamartine; but instead of leaving the subway at Twenty-third Street he continued to Columbus Circle, and went for a walk in the park to think it over. One idea he had had from the first he dismissed as too hazardous; but as his field of speculation narrowed and revealed the entire lack of anything better, or even so good, he returned to it again and considered it seriously.

It was by no means sure, but it appealed to him—and there was nothing else. He left the park at Ninety-sixth Street and boarded a downtown Elevated.

It was a quarter past three by the solemn-faced clock above the hotel desk when Dougherty entered the lobby of the Lamartine. All of the men he sought—the Erring Knights—were there, except, of course, Sherman.

Dumain greeted the newcomer.

"Deed you see Knowlton?"

"Yes. Did you?"

The little Frenchman nodded.

"Wiz a lawyer. And I gave heem—zee—lawyer—two hundred dollars. Knowlton ees—ees—"

"Broke?"

"Yes."

"I know it. That puts it up to us, and we've got to make good. Have you said anything to the boys?"

For reply Dumain began to give him an account of what had happened in the Lamartine during the preceding hour.

The other interrupted him impatiently.

"I don't care what they thought. The point is, are they with us?"

"Yes. Positeevely. But they don't understand—"

"I don't care whether they understand or not. Where are they? There's work to do. Come on!"

Five minutes later the five were gathered together on the leather lounge in the corner. Dumain arrived last, having gone to fetch Driscoll from the barber shop in the basement.

Dougherty, leaning against a marble pillar in front of the lounge, began:

"Now, is there anything you guys want to know? Did Dumain explain everything to you? Talk fast!"

There being no response he continued:

"All right. You all know the hole Knowlton's in, and that we've promised Miss Williams to get him out. Well, we need three thousand dollars."

There were exclamations of astonishment, and Booth, who was seated on the arm of the lounge puffing a cigarette, was so profoundly shocked that he fell off onto the floor.

"What do you want to do—buy up a jury?" came from Driscoll.

"Never mind what I want to do," returned Dougherty. "I say we need three thousand. Ask Dumain how much the lawyer wants."

They turned to the little Frenchman, who informed them that the attorney's fee would hardly be less than a thousand, and might be more.

"And another thousand for a stake for Knowlton," said Dougherty, "and the rest for—"

"But why should we stake Knowlton?"

"Shut up! I'm not asking you what to do—I'm telling you!" Dougherty roared. "Are we pikers? That's what I want to know, are we pikers?"

The opinion of the majority, expressed somewhat forcibly, appeared to be that they were not "pikers."

"Then listen to me. First, I say that we need that thousand dollars, and I don't want to have to say it again. We're lucky if we've got three hundred among us, except Dumain, and he's no millionaire. The question is—where'll we get it?"

"And that is what I would call quite some question," remarked Driscoll.

"It is," Dougherty admitted, "but I've got a plan. It requires a little capital. I have here fifty dollars. Everybody shell."

They hesitated for a moment, but Dougherty's tone was one not to be withstood—and they "shelled." The ex-prizefighter tabulated this result:

Dougherty $50

Driscoll 32

Jennings 13

Booth 65

Said he:

"That's a hundred and sixty. I need two hundred and fifty. Dumain, give me ninety dollars."

The little Frenchman handed it over without a word. He had already given the lawyer two hundred, and it left his purse pretty slim.

"Now," said Dougherty, "my plan is short and sweet, and make or break. I'm going to divide this into five parts. Each of us gets fifty dollars. You can take your choice of anything in town—go wherever you please and play any game you like.

"No two are to go together. We'll meet at Dumain's rooms at midnight, and if one or two of us hasn't scared up a killing somewhere, you can shoot me for a fool. We've got five chances."

The faces of the Erring Knights were alight with joy. They had not expected anything like this. With vociferous applause they proclaimed the greatness of Dougherty, while that gentleman divided the two hundred and fifty among them evenly and gave them sundry advice.

Driscoll and Jennings protested that they had not an even chance with the others, since they had to work from eight till eleven in the evening, whereupon Booth remarked that it was only four o'clock, and that you could lose fifty dollars in fifty seconds if you only went about it right.

They were all optimistic. Dougherty's scheme was an excellent one, they declared—perfect, certain to win. Knowlton was as good as free. Three thousand? It would be nearer ten.

"Wait," said the ex-prizefighter as they left the lobby together, "wait till tonight. It'll be time enough to crow then. I never yet saw a referee count a guy out when he was still on his feet. Remember, midnight, at Dumain's rooms."

They parted on the sidewalk in front of the hotel, each going his own way and sending back a "Good luck!" over his shoulder to the others.

It would have appeared to the casual observer that Knowlton's chance for freedom, if it depended on the success of this hare-brained, desperate scheme of Dougherty's, was a slim one. But yet it was a chance.

There were five of them—they were anything but inexperienced—and they were at concert pitch. True knighthood finds its brightest glory when pitted against seemingly overwhelming odds; and though the ribbon of their lady fluttered not from their button-holes, yet did they fight valiantly for her.

The hour of midnight found them—all five—reassembled at Dumain's apartments on Twenty-first Street, in the room which, some two months previous, had seen the triumph of Knowlton and the treacherous blow of Sherman.

The room was not bare, as it had been then. In the center stood a table littered with books and magazines, above which a massive reading globe cast its circle of light downward, leaving the upper half of the room in darkness.

A piano stood in one corner; by the mantel a chess table with the pieces arranged, apparently, at the crisis of an unfinished game; and there were half a dozen easy chairs, of various shapes and sizes. Altogether, a very pleasant spot—Booth declared he was about per-suaded to become a palmist himself.

Driscoll, who arrived last, entered on the stroke of twelve. He found the others waiting impatiently—for Dougherty had insisted that each man should keep the story of his success or failure to him-self until all were present. Judging from the expression on their faces, there was little to tell.

The little Frenchman waved Driscoll to a chair on the other side of the table and seated himself on the piano stool. Booth threw down a book he had been pretending to read, and Jennings yawned ostentatiously. All looked expectantly at Dougherty as he pounded on the arm of his chair for attention.

"I guess it's time to kill the cat," said the ex-prizefighter gloomily. "For your benefit," he turned to Driscoll, "we've held off on the dope. I will now tell the sad story of my life. Heaven knows I wish it was different. Maybe I was wrong, but we've only lost two hundred—"

"Come on, cut your mutton," Driscoll interrupted.

Dougherty glared at him, sighed, and began:

"I hate to tell it. There's not much to tell. At exactly four-fifteen this afternoon I took a seat at a table of five at Webster's on Thirty-sixth Street and bought a stack of blues. For an hour I fed the kitty, then it began to come.

"I helped every pair I drew to. I couldn't lose. At about seven o'clock I'd cashed in four hundred and had a stack about the size of the Flatiron Building in front of me.

"If I've ever played poker I played it then. But it began to turn. They wouldn't come. I couldn't get better than a pair, and they were never good enough. I boosted twice on a one-card draw to four pink ones, but couldn't get the filler.

"I prayed for 'em and tore 'em up and tried to run away with one or two, but they called me. And then—I had four ladies topped by a little guy on his first pot!"

A universal groan came from the audience.

"That finished me. I fought back as hard as I could, but they rushed me off my feet. At a quarter past eleven I cashed in exactly fifty dollars. Here it is."

There was complete silence as Dougherty held up five ten-dollar bills and sorrowfully returned them to his pocket. Then everybody began talking at once.

"Anyway, you kept your fifty."

"It could have been worse."

"Zat pokaire is zee devil of a game."

"Come on—who's next? Go on with the story!"

This last from Driscoll.

Dougherty motioned to the little Frenchman.

"Me?" said Dumain. "I am worse yet than Dougherty. I got nozzing. I lost zee fifty."

"But how?"

"Zee race ponies," answered Dumain, with a fling at the jargon. "I play nozzing but *écarté*, and there is not zat here. I had a good what you call eet teep for Peemlico. Zee fourth race—zee name of zee horse was Parcel-Post."

"How did you play him?"

"Straight. To win. A friend of mine got a telegram from zee owner. It was certain he should win."

"And I suppose he got the place?" asked Booth.

"What does zat mean?"

"It means he came in second."

The little Frenchman shook his head sorrowfully.

"Oh, no. He came een last."

There was a shout of laughter from the others, but it was soon stopped by Dougherty, who turned to Jennings with a gesture. He wanted to get the thing finished.

"I'm in the same class with Dumain," said Jennings. "I tried your game, Dougherty, and I thought I was some poker player—but good night! They took my fifty so quick I didn't have time to tell it good-by."

"Where'd you go?"

"Pearly's, on Sixth Avenue. I've sat in there once or twice before, and about six months ago I made a clean-up. But tonight—don't make me talk about it."

"We're a bunch of boobs," Dougherty groaned. "We'd better all go out in the morning and sell lead pencils. Your turn, Driscoll."

But Driscoll said that he would prefer to follow Booth, and since Dougherty was not inclined to argue the matter, he turned to the typewriter salesman instead.

"I'm willing," said that gentleman, "though my tale contains but little joy. Still, I guess we're about even.

"It doesn't matter exactly where I went. It's downtown, and it's in the rear of a two-by-four billiard hall. At any hour of any afternoon you may find there a number of gentlemen engaged in the ancient and honorable game of craps.

"I'll spare you the details—at least, most of 'em. The game is a big one: there's lots of real money there for the man that knows how to get it, and I figured it out that I was just about the man.

"I rolled the bones till my fingers ached and my knees were stiff, and my voice sounded like a Staten Island ferryboat in a fog—I have a little habit of talking to the ivories.

"Well, to cut it short, I played in all directions. At one time I had six hundred dollars. At another time I had fifteen dollars. At half past eleven tonight I had an even hundred, and it was time to go.

"I had the dice, and I decided on one more throw. My hundred— I played it all—was faded before I put it down, and I threw a natural— a seven. I stuck the two hundred in my pocket and said good night."

"Well, we've got our two hundred and fifty back, anyway," observed Jennings.

"And what good will that do?" growled Dougherty.

"You never can tell. Tomorrow's another day."

"It seems to me," put in Driscoll, "that I remain to be heard from."

"Shoot your head off," said the ex-prizefighter, "and hurry up about it. This is awful!"

Driscoll blew his nose with care and deliberation, cleared his throat three times, and arose to his feet. There was something in his manner that caused the others to sit up straighter in their chairs with an air of expectancy. Noticing this flattering increase of attention, he smiled grandly and surveyed them with a leisurely eye.

"In the first place, gentlemen," he began, "I wish to say that I do not regard myself as a genius, in any sense of the word. At poker I am worse than helpless. The race ponies, as Dumain calls them, are a mystery to me. Nor have I that deft and subtle touch required to roll dice successfully."

There came a chorus of cries:

"Cut it!"

"Cheese the guff!"

"Talk sense!"

"Go on with the story!"

Driscoll waited for them to finish, then resumed calmly:

"Do not be impatient, gentlemen. As I say, I am well aware of the fact that I am no genius. Therefore, I realized that if my fifty dollars grew to the desired proportions it would be only by the aid of miraculous chance. I made my plans accordingly.

"When I left you in front of the Lamartine at four o'clock I went straight to my own room. There I procured a piece of paper, and marked on it with a pen the figures from one to thirty-five, about an inch apart.

"I then tore the paper into thirty-five pieces, so that I had each figure on a piece by itself. I placed these in my hat, mixed them around, and drew one forth. It was the figure thirty-two."

Again there came cries of impatience from the audience, who began to perceive that this lengthy preamble meant an interesting conclusion, and again the speaker ignored them and continued:

"That operation completed, I threw myself on my bed for a nap. At six o'clock I rose, went to a restaurant for dinner, and from there to my work at the theater. My first action there was to borrow fifty dollars, thereby doubling my capital.

"At the end of the play I dressed as hurriedly as possible, leaving the theater at exactly a quarter past eleven, and made my way to a certain establishment on Fiftieth Street, conducted by a Mr. Merrifield.

"It is, I believe, the largest and finest of its kind in New York. They have there a contrivance commonly known as a roulette wheel, which has numbers and colors arranged on it in an unique fashion. I stood before it and placed my hundred dollars on the number thirty-two."

The speaker paused, turned, and took his overcoat from the back of the chair on which he had been sitting, while his audience looked on in breathless silence.

Then he finished:

"The result, gentlemen, can be easier shown than told. Here it is."

He drew forth from a pocket of the overcoat a stack of bills and tossed them on the table, crying:

"There she is, boys! Thirty-five nice, crisp hundreds on one spin of the wheel!"

Then and there was pandemonium. They shouted and danced about, and clapped Driscoll on the back till he sought a corner for refuge, and spread the bills over the table to gloat over, and generally raised the devil. Dumain was sitting down at the piano to play a triumphal march when Dougherty suddenly rushed over to him and clasped his shoulder.

"Did you notice that number?" he asked excitedly.

The little Frenchman looked up at Dougherty.

"What number?"

"The one that Driscoll played on the wheel."

"Yes—thirty-two. Why?"

"Sure," said Dougherty. "Number thirty-two. Don't you remember?—you was down there this afternoon. That's the number of Knowlton's cell in the Tombs!"

~m~

All Together

WHEN LILA reached the lobby of the Lamartine at nine o'clock on the following morning she found the Erring Knights already assembled in their corner.

For a moment she forgot everything else in her surprise; she had thought that nothing less than the end of the world could possibly have roused these gentlemen of leisure from their beds at so early an hour.

Dougherty hastened over to her desk and demanded to know why she had left her room.

"Why not?" Lila smiled. "I feel all right, really. And, anyway, I had rather be down here than up there alone. Did you see him?"

The ex-prizefighter grunted an affirmative and proceeded to give her a detailed account of his conversation with Knowlton on the previous morning. He ended by saying that they had engaged a lawyer, and that the sinews of war in the sum of three thousand dollars had been entrusted to Dumain as treasurer.

"But Mr. Dougherty," Lila exclaimed, "we can't possibly use that! I thought—you see, I have saved a little—"

Dougherty interrupted her:

"Now see here. We're doing this, and you've got to let us alone. Anyway, it's not really costing us a cent. I won't explain how, but you can take my word for it.

"Everything's all right, and you don't need to worry, and for Heaven's sake don't begin any of that stuff about you won't take this and you won't take that. If we're going to help you we've got to help you. What did you think I meant yesterday morning—that I was going to carry a note to Knowlton and then go home and sit down with my fingers crossed?"

Whereupon, giving her no time to answer, Dougherty turned and rejoined the others across the lobby.

This was the beginning of a campaign which lasted a little over a month.

The duties of the Erring Knights were varied and arduous. Each morning one of them conducted Lila to the hotel, and took her home each evening, this escort being necessitated by the fact that Sherman had twice accosted her on the street. He had also called at her home, but there was no necessity for a male guardian there. Mrs. Amanda Berry was a legion in herself.

Dougherty was the official messenger between the Lamartine and the Tombs. At first Lila had insisted on going to see Knowlton herself, but he had begged her to spare him this final humiliation.

The prisoner wrote:

I long to see you; you know it; but it is enough to have the picture of this place imprinted on my own memory—I can't bear that you should see me here.

Whatever your imagination shows you it cannot be as dreadful as the reality. If I obtain my freedom I shall not feel that I have cheated justice. Heaven knows I could not pay more dearly for my crime than I have already paid.

Knowlton stubbornly refused to allow his lawyer to procure his release on bail. The lawyer said he was quixotic; Dougherty used a stronger and commoner term, but they could not change his decision. He gave no reasons, but they understood; and the lawyer, who was at least as scrupulous as the average of his profession, declared to Dumain that for the first time in ten years' practise he was defending a guilty man with a clear conscience.

As for the case itself, it appeared to be by no means simple. The fact that they had no knowledge of the evidence held by the prosecution made them uneasy, and they bent their efforts mainly to attempts to discover its nature.

There was no danger, they found, from Red Tim, who had got away safely the night before Knowlton's arrest. And he was the only one of the gang whom Knowlton had ever seen or dealt with.

The evidence which the lawyer feared most was that concerning any specific operations, and in relation to the wallet which Knowlton had missed the day following the fight in Dumain's rooms. Knowlton suspected Sherman, but thought it possible that he had lost it on the street.

"Well," said the attorney, "the best we can say is that we're on our guard. We must keep our wits about us and fight it out in the courtroom. We won't know much about what they know before the day of the trial. It's a fight in the dark for us; but remember, they have to furnish the proof."

Dougherty was openly optimistic. After winning a one to thirty-five shot on the number of Knowlton's cell—he had recited the tale to the prisoner with great gusto—he refused to believe that their efforts could possibly culminate in anything short of glorious victory.

"Think of it; just think of it," he would say to Knowlton in a tone which partook of awe. "He drew the blooming number out of

his hat—that was the first shot. Then he plays it single, and wins—
that was the second. Why, we can't lose. We'll beat 'em both ways
from the middle."

"Thanks, old man; I hope so," Knowlton would reply.

Thus three weeks passed by and found them marking time,
waiting for the day of the trial. Dougherty spent the better part of
two days seeking for Sherman, but without success. They had heard
nothing from him, save the times he had accosted Lila on the street,
nor seen him since the morning in Lila's room.

"He's surely round somewhere," said Dougherty to Dumain as
they met in the lobby one morning. "In fact, I know he's in town,
because he's still got that room on Thirty-fourth Street. But I can't
get in, and I can't get him either going or coming."

The little Frenchman shrugged his shoulders and glanced across
the lobby where Lila sat at her desk talking to a man who had just
approached—probably a customer.

"Bah! Let heem alone. So long as he ees not bother Mees
Williams that ees all we want."

"It's not all I want," said Dougherty. "I want to punch his face,
and I will. He's a low-down, dirty—"

He was interrupted by a call:

"Mr. Dumain!"

The voice was Lila's. They turned. She was standing in front
of her desk, her face very white, holding in her hand a sheet of
printed paper. Dumain hurried over to her, gave one look at the
paper which she thrust at him with a trembling hand, and called to
Dougherty.

The ex-prizefighter crossed the lobby:

"What is it?"

"Look!" Dumain held the paper before him. "A what you call
eet—subpoena—for Mees Williams! *Mon Dieu!* Eet is all up!"

"Shut up," growled Dougherty, taking the subpoena. "Do you want the whole lobby to know about it? You get excited too easy."

"But what am I to do?" faltered Lila.

"Be a sport. Don't let 'em floor you with a little thing like this. They want you for a witness, do they? It's a good job. I'd advise you to take it."

Lila gazed at him, amazed at his levity concerning what appeared to her to be the destruction of all their plans.

Dougherty read over the subpoena with a smile.

"The fact is," said he, "that I'm surprised they didn't spring this before. I've expected it all the time.

"Sherman knew all about your being at Knowlton's rooms—he told me and Dumain—and what's more, he told us that he'd told the Secret Service about you. Now, why did they hold off so long? That's the only part I don't like."

"But what am I to do?" Lila repeated.

"There's only one thing you can do—go on the stand."

"But Mr. Dougherty! Don't you see? They will ask me about that night, and about the—the money. And he will be convicted."

Dougherty appeared to be greatly surprised.

"And how so? Let 'em question you from now till doomsday and what will they find out? Simply that you went straight home from the hotel and spent the evening in your room reading *Pilgrim's Progress*. The only one they'll have against you is Sherman, and if a jury wouldn't rather believe you than him I'm a liar."

Still Lila did not understand. She protested:

"But I didn't spend the evening in my room."

"Don't you think I know it? I'm talking about evidence, not facts. As far as the jury's concerned you did."

Lila gazed at him in horror.

"Do you mean I'd have to lie?"

"Well, that's a pretty strong word," said Dougherty, "but you can call it that if you want to."

"But I couldn't—I couldn't!"

"You'll have to."

Lila looked at him:

"No. I know I couldn't. If I am a witness, and they ask me about—that evening, I couldn't tell them anything but the truth."

It was the tone rather than the words that caused Dougherty to force back the protest that came to his lips and convinced him of its uselessness.

Here was an obstacle, indeed! And utterly unexpected. Dougherty was not up on feminine psychology, and he couldn't understand how a girl could do for a man what Lila had done on the night of Knowlton's arrest, and then refuse to lie for him.

"Besides, it would be useless," Lila was saying. "I think it was Mr. Sherman who saw me, but it may not have been. Some of the others may have seen me also. And now I remember: the man they left in the room did see me as I passed the door. He might not recognize me, but how can we know? And if he did—"

"All right," Dougherty interrupted; "then there's no use talking about it. We're in a he—we're in a mess; but we'll find a way out, somehow. Dumain, find Driscoll and Booth. I'll get Jennings. Leave it to us, Miss Williams. Don't you worry about that thing"—pointing to the subpoena—"for a minute. Hurry up, Dumain!"

And ten minutes later the Erring Knights, five strong, were assembled in their corner, holding a council of war over this new and dangerous complication.

Booth was ready to throw up the sponge.

"What's the use?" he demanded. "They've got him fifty ways from breakfast. And this thing finishes it. If Miss Williams goes on the stand and tells what she knows, he doesn't stand a chance."

"You don't say!" observed Dougherty ironically. "What's the matter—cold feet? And what do you think we're here for? It's up to us to fix it so that she don't go on the stand."

"Tell me one thing," said Driscoll. "Why haven't they arrested her?"

"Easy enough." This from Jennings. "Because if they did they couldn't force her to testify against Knowlton, and they couldn't force Knowlton to testify against her. They figure that one is better than none."

"Come on, boys; talk business." Dougherty pulled Jennings down on the lounge and glared at Booth. "We have enough trouble as it is, without trying to figure out why we haven't got more."

But their wits refused to work. No one had anything to suggest that was worth listening to, unless it was Driscoll, who was strongly in favor of avoiding the subpoena by the simple expedient of running away from it.

"The trial is only four days off," said he. "Convey Miss Williams to some safe and sheltered spot till it's over, and let Knowlton join her there."

"But then there'd be a warrant out for her for contempt," Jennings objected.

"Well, you can't have everything," retorted Driscoll.

Dougherty told them to wait a moment and crossed the lobby to Lila's desk. Soon he returned, shaking his head negatively.

"She won't do it," he announced.

"She's darned particular," growled Booth. "What *will* she do?"

But the ex-prizefighter stood up for Lila:

"No, you can't blame her. She looks at it different from us. We'll have to think up something else."

There was a silence. Driscoll lighted a cigarette, offering one to each of the others, and soon the corner was decorated with spirals of smoke. Finally Dumain spoke, for the first time.

"I tell you," said he, "as soon as you feenish this foolishness, what I will do. You know nozzing. I weel ask Siegel."

"And what can he do?" demanded Driscoll. "He'll want to fix up an alibi for her, and she won't stand for it, and then he'll try to bully her."

But the others signified their approval of Dumain's suggestion, especially Dougherty, and the little Frenchman was soon on his way downtown to the attorney's office, while Dougherty left for his daily visit to the Tombs.

Driscoll strolled over to Lila's desk and told her that Dumain had gone to consult their lawyer.

"But he cannot help us," she faltered. "There is nothing I can do, is there, Mr. Driscoll? Tell me."

"You can keep up your courage," returned the young man. "As Tom would say, be a sport. And this Siegel is a shrewd man; he'll get us through safely, never fear. Dumain ought to be back before noon."

But Lila was completely terrified, and refused to be reassured. The formal phraseology of the subpoena had impressed her with the power of the law; it seemed to her to smell of courts and prisons; and her woman's mind was affected more by the document itself than by the very real danger it threatened.

Throughout the remainder of the morning she sat with her eyes glued on the entrance to the lobby. At eleven o'clock Dougherty returned from the Tombs with a note from Knowlton, but an hour later the little Frenchman had not arrived. Lila put on her hat and coat to go to lunch with a heavy heart.

The day was one of brilliant sunshine, with a saucy, freshening breeze coming in from the bay. Lila ate little and hurriedly, then strolled along the walks of Madison Square.

The grass plots were beginning to turn green, and the trees were covered with brown, damp buds, and in the center of the square a gardener was raking the newly turned earth. The gladness of the approaching spring was in the air.

Lila found it intolerable. She returned to the Lamartine.

Dumain rushed to meet her as she entered the door.

"Mees Williams! I've been waiting for you. Such a plan! Zat lawyer ees a genius!"

The lobby was accustomed to Dumain, and paid little attention to his gesticulations and shrill, high-pitched tones; but Lila flushed with embarrassment as they walked to her desk. She felt that everyone was in on her secret, wherein she was unjust to the loyalty and discretion of the Erring Knights.

But this was nothing to the deep, rich crimson that flooded her cheeks as the little Frenchman, in low, excited tones, unfolded to her the plan of Lawyer Siegel. And with it came a smile, curiously tender, as Dumain expressed a doubt as to her willingness to act upon it.

He finished:

"You see, he don't know if you will do eet, and I am to telephone heem at one o'clock; so eef he must—"

"But I will," said Lila. "Oh, I will! But are you sure I won't have to testify? Are you sure?"

"Positeevely."

"Then—couldn't we do it today instead of tomorrow?"

"No," Dumain smiled. "Eet weel take till tomorrow morning to get zee bail for Knowlton. Dougherty ees down to see heem now. Tomorrow afternoon eet will be—remember. I must go to see Siegel for zee bondsman."

And he trotted off, leaving Lila with face still flushed and the shadow of a doubt in her eyes, but with her lips parted in a trembling, wistful smile.

But the plan of Lawyer Siegel, clever and effective as it was, nearly caused a disruption in the ranks of the Erring Knights.

For Dumain and Dougherty alone were in the secret, which they refused to divulge; and the three others strenuously objected. Booth and Jennings threatened, half in earnest, to go over to the prosecution and tell all they knew, while Driscoll made many pointed and cutting remarks concerning the source of the money they were using. But the little Frenchman and the ex-prizefighter were as adamant.

"It's Miss Williams's secret," said they, "and it wouldn't be fair to her to tell it. The fact is, she asked us not to."

This last was not true, but Dougherty knew they wouldn't ask Lila.

"And all we're good for, I suppose, is to sit round with our hands in our pockets," said Driscoll bitterly. This was on the day after the plan had been consummated. "You get Knowlton out on bail and don't show up in the lobby for a day at a time, and when you come back expect us to clap you on the back and tell you how well we like you. It's not a square deal."

"Now, listen here," said Dougherty; "don't be a sorehead. The trial is day after tomorrow; can't you wait that long? Besides, you fellows have had your share. You've been bringing her to work every morning and taking her home every evening, and, believe me, that's some job.

"And here's another. If Knowlton gets out—and he will—there's going to be a little dinner for him and Lila in Dumain's rooms Friday evening. The trial can't last more than one day. We'll leave that dinner to you and Booth and Jennings. When Dumain comes in this afternoon he'll give you the keys to his flat and all the money you need. Go as far as you like."

"For how many?"

"Seven. Us five and them two."

Driscoll grunted, and departed to consult with Booth and Jennings.

On Thursday evening, the day before the trial, Miss Williams was escorted to her home by Dougherty himself. She was depressed and nervous, and his repeated attempts to rally her spirit were unsuccessful. They dined at a little restaurant on Columbus Avenue, and from there walked to One Hundred and Fourth Street.

"Brace up," said Dougherty, as they stopped at her door. "This time tomorrow night you'll be ready to start on your honeymoon. Don't you like the idea?"

"What do you think he is doing now?" asked Lila, with apparent irrelevance. She had learned to talk to Dougherty as to a chum.

"Reading your letters," said the ex-prizefighter with conviction. "He always is. And now you go up and get to bed and sleep. None of this endless night business."

Lila was standing in the open door.

"I'll try," she promised, smiling. "Good night, and thank you. I'll be waiting for you in the morning."

CHAPTER XVII

—〰—

The Trial

M AY IT please your honor, Mr. Foreman, and gentlemen of the jury—"

The speaker was a United States assistant district attorney; the scene, a Federal courtroom in the post office building on Park Row. John Knowlton, alleged counterfeiter, was on trial before twelve of his peers.

The room was old and dingy—the building itself has been called the ugliest in New York. The jurybox, the benches, the railings, were blackened by time and use; the clerk appeared to have been fastened to his desk for many years. A dreary, melancholy room.

The spectators' benches are by no means filled; most of the faces are familiar ones. In a group at the right are Detective Barrett and his two men, with Billy Sherman. Seated side by side on the front row of benches are Driscoll, Booth, Dumain, Jennings, and Dougherty. Toward the rear of the room Lila is seen, and by her side— Mrs. Amanda Berry! There are some dozen others—hangers-on, sensation-seekers, and young lawyers.

Knowlton, who was seated by the side of his attorney and engaged in a whispered consultation with him, looked up quickly as the prosecuting attorney rose to address the court and jury. The clock on the wall pointed to half past eleven; ninety minutes had sufficed for the preliminaries, including the selection of the jury. Lawyer Siegel had proven extraordinarily easy to please, thereby earning the gratitude of the judge.

"May it please your honor, Mr. Foreman, and gentlemen of the jury—"

The assistant district attorney proceeded with his opening speech. He was a young fellow—perhaps eight and twenty—and he spoke with the earnest enthusiasm of youth, with forceful, sounding phrases.

The prisoner felt his cheeks burn more than once at their sting. He wound up with the assertion that he would produce sufficient evidence to convict ten times over.

Lawyer Siegel turned and whispered to his client:

"He didn't let anything out—he's a slick one."

Before Knowlton could do more than nod in response Siegel had risen to his feet and begun the opening speech for the defense. It was surprisingly short; it entered not at all into details, or even the nature of his evidence, and amounted, in fact, to little more than a general denial. But as he stated that the accused would not be called to the stand in his own defense Knowlton perceived a swift, almost imperceptible, expression of doubt and disapproval flit across the faces of the jurors.

As Siegel sat down the prisoner turned for a fleeting glance at Lila; she smiled at him brightly.

The prosecuting attorney called his first witness:

"James Barrett!"

The detective had little to tell. He identified Knowlton and gave an account of his arrest, dwelling pointedly on his flight to the rear of the flat as they entered.

Siegel, for the defense, did not cross-examine.

The second witness for the prosecution was Billy Sherman.

"What is your name?"

"William Sherman."

"Your business?"

"Journalist."

"Your address?"

He gave a number on West Thirty-fourth Street.

There followed some questions concerning the length of Sherman's acquaintance with the prisoner and the amount of time he had spent in his company; then the prosecuting attorney asked:

"Did you ever see Knowlton pass, or offer to pass, counterfeit money?"

Instantly Siegel was on his feet with an objection.

"Sustained," said the judge.

This was the beginning of a battle royal between the two lawyers. Time and again the prosecuting attorney tried to make his point, approaching it from every possible angle; and time and again Siegel objected that the witness was incompetent to answer.

Finally the judge himself became impatient and addressed the assistant district attorney with some severity:

"Mr. Brant, this witness has not qualified as an expert. You must give up this line of questioning or dismiss him."

Siegel seated himself with a triumphant smile. The prosecuting attorney frowned and cleared his throat. Knowlton cast a glance over his shoulder at the spectators' benches and sent a smile to Lila.

Dougherty leaned over and whispered to Driscoll:

"I don't know what the deuce they're talking about, but that cagey little guy looks like he'd just stopped a swing on the jaw and was hanging over the ropes."

But young Mr. Brant had another cartridge in his belt. He asked that an exception be noted on the ruling of the court, then turned to the witness:

"Mr. Sherman, where were you on the evening of the 11th of December last?"

"At the rooms of Pierre Dumain, a palmist."

"Where are those rooms?"

"In West Twenty-first Street."

"What is the number?"

"I don't know."

"Who was there with you?"

"The defendant, Knowlton, and four or five others."

"What are the names of the others?"

"Tom Dougherty, Pierre Dumain, Bub Driscoll, Sam Booth, and Harry Jennings."

"What were you doing there?"

The witness hesitated a moment before he answered:

"Having a fight. You see—"

"No; answer my questions," interrupted the lawyer. "Were you fighting?"

"No, sir."

"Who was?"

"Knowlton and Driscoll. Knowlton knocked him out."

"And then?"

"Then Knowlton and Dougherty fought. It lasted ten or fifteen minutes and—"

"Now tell the court and the jury exactly what happened."

"Well, Knowlton was getting the better of Dougherty and had him up against the wall, when all of a sudden somebody threw a piece of bronze or something at Knowlton and hit him on the head. He dropped like a shot."

"Then what did you do?"

"I ran over toward the door, where Knowlton was lying on the floor, and so did the others. As I was standing near him I saw a wallet sticking out of his hip pocket, and I knew they—"

"You mean Knowlton's pocket?"

"Yes. And I was afraid one of the guys might take it, so I stooped down when no one was looking and pulled it out of his pocket—it was nearly out already—and put it in my own, thinking to keep it for him. Dumain had sent somebody—"

Mr. Brand interrupted.

"Never mind the others. What did you do?"

"I waited till the doctor came, and when he said Knowlton's injury was not serious I went home. I believe Knowlton stayed at Dumain's rooms all night. When I got home I put his wallet away—"

"Why didn't you return it to him before you left Dumain's rooms?"

"Because he was still half unconscious. He was in no condition to talk to. Then the next afternoon, I think it was—"

"Aren't you sure?"

"Yes," said the witness, after a moment's hesitation, "it was the next afternoon. I took the wallet out of the drawer where I had put it away, thinking to take it round to Knowlton's rooms, and as I put it in my pocket I happened to look into it, just out of curiosity, and I nearly fell over when I saw it was full of counterfeit—"

Lawyer Siegel sprang to his feet:

"I object, on the ground that the witness is incompetent."

"Sustained," said the judge.

"Exception," said Mr. Brant.

The judge turned to the witness:

"Confine yourself to a recital of your own actions."

"Did you return the wallet to Knowlton?" asked the prosecuting attorney.

Sherman answered: "No, sir."

"What did you do with it?"

"I kept it awhile, then I took it to Detective Barrett, of the secret service."

The prosecuting attorney took something from a leather case on the desk before him and, handing it to the witness, asked:

"Do you recognize that?"

"Yes," said Sherman. "It's the wallet I've been talking about."

"Is it the one you took from Knowlton's pocket?"

"Yes, sir."

"Inspect the contents. Are they the same as when you first saw it?"

There was a pause while the witness examined each of the compartments of the wallet, then he answered:

"Yes, sir."

"Everything the same?"

"Yes, sir."

Mr. Brant stepped forward and took the wallet from Sherman and handed it to the clerk of the court:

"Your honor," said he, "I wish to introduce this wallet as evidence, with its contents. I shall call an expert later to prove that they are counterfeit."

This was a blow to the defense which, though not entirely unexpected, appeared to be serious. The Erring Knights looked gloomily at each other, but forbore to speak.

Lila was scarcely breathing in the intensity of her anxiety, while Mrs. Berry patted her hand soothingly. The accused was whispering excitedly to his attorney, who listened with keen interest, nodding his head with satisfaction at intervals. The result of this conference was to appear later.

The prosecuting attorney asked his witness a few more questions, for the most part unimportant, then turned him over for cross-examination.

Lawyer Siegel rose to his feet. He had not an impressive appearance, but as he stepped directly in front of Sherman he shot at him a glance so severe and terrifying that the witness involuntarily recoiled.

The tone was no less severe:

"How long did you keep this wallet before you turned it over to Detective Barrett?"

Sherman's answer was low:

"About two months."

"Why?"

But Mr. Brant objected to the question, and was sustained.

Siegel resumed:

"You say somebody hit Knowlton on the head with 'a piece of bronze or something.' Who was it that threw that bronze?"

The witness was silent.

"Who was it?" repeated the lawyer.

Sherman stammered:

"I did."

"I see. Had you been fighting with him?"

"No."

The attorney was shouting his questions with great rapidity, giving the witness barely time to answer, and no time at all to think. Sherman was nervously grasping the arm of his chair.

"Were you standing very close to Knowlton when you threw the bronze at him?"

"No, sir."

"Across the room, weren't you?"

"Yes, sir."

"And as soon as he fell Dumain and Dougherty ran over and knelt down by him, didn't they?"

"Yes, sir."

"And Jennings stopped you when you started to leave the room, didn't he?"

"Yes, sir."

The questions were coming like the rattle of a Gatling gun.

"And he forced you back to the corner?"

"Yes, sir."

"Then he went to help the others with Knowlton?"

"Yes, sir."

"You were over in the opposite corner alone?"

"Yes, sir."

"And when you found the wallet, was it in the coat or the vest?"

"The coat."

"Which pocket?"

"The insi—" Sherman began; then, realizing suddenly what he was saying, stopped short with a look of horror.

He was trapped.

The reason for his previous story of having taken the wallet from Knowlton's hip pocket as he lay on the floor could be found only in the tortuous channels of Sherman's treacherous brain.

Undoubtedly, he had thought to make his evidence stronger by making it appear that the thing had actually been taken from the person of the accused, and had anticipated the difficulty of proving that the coat was Knowlton's. And now he was fairly caught.

Siegel pursued his advantage relentlessly. He hammered the witness with questions, and Sherman stammered and grew red in the face with helpless anger, and finally admitted that his first story had been false. That was all Siegel wanted; he sat down with a smile of triumph; his forehead was covered with beads of sweat.

On redirect examination the prosecuting attorney made a valiant attempt to bring his witness out of the hole he had dug for himself, but in vain. Sherman was hopelessly confused; he made matters worse instead of better, and ended by refusing to answer at all. He was dismissed by the court with a reprimand, and at a sign from Mr. Brant seated himself on the front row of benches.

For a few moments the progress of the trial was halted by a conference between the prosecuting attorney and Detective Barrett, while Knowlton whispered animatedly to his counsel and the faces of the Erring Knights beamed with joy.

"What did I tell you?" said Dougherty to Driscoll *sotto voce.* "Didn't I say he was a slick guy?"

Then the prosecuting attorney turned to face the courtroom:

"Miss Williams, please take the stand."

There was a silence. No one moved. Knowlton kept his eyes fastened on the desk before him. Three of the Erring Knights glanced accusingly at the other two.

Mr. Brant, whose temper had not been improved by the discrediting of Sherman's testimony, looked directly at Lila, who had remained in her seat, and repeated his question.

"Will you please take the stand?"

Lila rose and faced him.

"Do you mean me?" she asked.

"Yes. I called your name. Take the stand."

Lila did not move.

"I beg your pardon, but you did not call my name."

"Aren't you Miss Williams?" said Mr. Brant testily.

Lila answered clearly:

"No."

The attorney started with incredulous surprise. Driscoll, Booth, and Jennings looked around at her in amazement, while Dougherty and Dumain smiled in their superior knowledge. Knowlton did not move.

Sherman sprang from his seat and, crossing to the side of Attorney Brant, whispered excitedly:

"That's her, all right. They're up to some trick. Call her up. She won't lie on the stand."

But Mr. Brant shook him off, and after a moment's hesitation again spoke to Lila:

"Then what is your name?"

Lila sent a single fleeting glance to the prisoner, who had turned in his chair to face her; then looked directly at the questioner. Her answer was low, but distinct and half triumphant:

"Mrs. John Knowlton."

Then she sat down and buried her face in her hands; and, as everybody stared at her in consternation, surprise, or wonder, Lawyer Siegel rose to his feet and addressed the listening judge:

"Your honor, this woman is the wife of the accused; and, therefore, may not be called as a witness by the prosecution. Your honor sees that she is in distress. May I ask that counsel be instructed not to question her further in court?"

But Mr. Brant turned on him angrily:

"Your proof! Show us your proof!"

"Of course," said the other, taking a paper from his portfolio, "I expected you would demand it; I do not expect courtesy from you, sir." He handed the paper to the judge. "That is the marriage certificate, your honor."

There was a breathless silence throughout the room while the judge adjusted his eyeglasses and inspected the large, stamped document. He looked at the date and the signatures, and glanced at Attorney Siegel searchingly; then turned to Lila and asked her to step to the witness stand.

"I object, your honor—" began Lawyer Siegel, but the judge stopped him with a gesture.

Lila was in the witness chair. The clerk of the court administered the oath. The judge turned to her.

"Are you the 'Lila Williams' mentioned in this certificate?"

Lila barely glanced at it before answering:

"Yes, sir."

"Are you the wife of the accused, John Knowlton?"

"Yes, sir."

"Do you wish to testify for the people in this action?"

"Yes, sir."

"That is all," said the judge; "you may go."

Then, as Lila glanced at him gratefully and rose to return to her seat, he handed the certificate back to Lawyer Siegel and turned to speak to the prosecuting attorney with judicial calmness:

"Call your next witness, Mr. Brant."

But the trial had become a farce; a huge joke—on the prosecution. Of his two chief witnesses, one had been discredited and the other disqualified; and Attorney Brant stammered in angry confusion that he had no others.

He recalled Sherman to the stand to give a recital of Lila's movements, as observed by him, on the evening of Knowlton's arrest; but Sherman could tell little, and it was easy to perceive by the expression on the faces of the jurors that the little he could tell was not believed.

Mr. Brant also called an expert, who testified that the bills in the wallet in evidence for the prosecution were counterfeit; then the prosecution rested.

The defense rested without calling a witness.

Then came the closing speeches.

Young Mr. Brant stammered and hesitated for a quarter of an hour, and, considering the paucity of his material, made a very creditable effort; but it was thrown completely in the shade by that of Lawyer Siegel, which may be given in full:

"May it please your honor, Mr. Foreman, and gentlemen of the jury: Without any desire to be flippant, I can only state that since I am confined to the evidence, and since there has been no evidence worth speaking of, I have nothing to say."

And five minutes later, without leaving their box, the jury returned a verdict of "Not guilty," and John Knowlton was a free man.

It was Lila who reached his side first, but the Erring Knights were not far behind; and Knowlton found himself the center of an excited, laughing group of faces filled with goodwill and friendship and—one of them—with love.

In one of his hands he held both of Lila's, and gave the other to each of the Erring Knights in turn; but his lips were silent. Before all these faces, at that moment, he could not trust himself to speak.

"But I was so frightened," Lila was saying. "Oh, I was *so* frightened!"

"Bah!" said Dumain. "At what, madam?"

Lila's cheek flushed at the title, and Driscoll, observing it, put in mischievously:

"Yes; that really isn't very complimentary to us, Mrs. Knowlton."

"Oh!" said Lila helplessly, while the flush deepened.

"And now," said Dougherty, "where's that guy, Siegel? I want to ask him to come up to the dinner tonight. I wonder where—What? Look at that!"

He was pointing excitedly across the room. The others turned and saw Billy Sherman being escorted to the door of the courtroom by two police officers in uniform.

"Probably some of his friends," observed Booth.

"No," said Driscoll; "it's more likely that little slip-up in his testimony. I believe they call it perjury."

At that moment Siegel approached the group.

"Come on," he called gaily; "they're going to clear the room. And I guess we'll be glad enough to go, since we don't have to leave anyone behind. And, by the way, did you notice our friend,

Sherman? He seems to be having a little trouble of his own. They just arrested him."

"What is it?" asked Booth. "Perjury? They certainly didn't lose much time."

"No. It isn't that. That was merely a lapse of memory. They came from the outside. I didn't hear what they said, but from the expression on Mr. Sherman's face I wouldn't be surprised if it was murder. We caught him prettily, didn't we?"

They had left the courtroom and were standing at the head of the stairs in the corridor.

"Well, let's forget him," said Driscoll. "He was bound to hang himself sooner or later. Maybe he's done it already. Come on—everybody."

They moved down the stairs and out to the sidewalk, chattering and laughing, still nervous and ill at ease from the restraint and anxiety of the courtroom.

Lined up along the curb were three big gray limousines.

"Now," said Dougherty, stopping in front of them, in the tone of a general marshaling his forces, "here's where we separate."

He pointed to the first of the limousines. "Dumain, you take this car with Knowlton and take him to your rooms. He'll find there what he needs.

"Can't help it, Mrs. Knowlton; it's only for an hour or two. Driscoll, you are to take Mrs. Knowlton to One Hundred and Fourth Street, and get her trunk and bags. The rest of you come with me. And remember: six o'clock at Dumain's rooms. No later. Come on, boys!"

"But what—" Knowlton began.

"Listen here," Dougherty interrupted sternly; "are you going to obey orders or not? Hereafter Mrs. Knowlton can boss you. It's our turn today."

In pretended fright Knowlton turned to Lila and bade her *au revoir* with a pressure of the hand, then sprang into the automobile beside Dumain.

"That's right," said Dougherty. "Here you go, Mrs. Knowlton. Help the lady in, Driscoll. Come on, Siegel, with us. What's that? Yes, you will—come on! All ready, boys? Let 'er go! So long! Remember, six o'clock!"

—※—

CHAPTER XVIII

Westward Ho!

*E*IGHT GILT chairs with embroidered seats and backs surrounding a table covered with snowy linen and shining silver; four diminutive Swiss waiters with quick eyes and silent feet; roses everywhere—on the mantel, in vases on the table, clustered over the door, red and white; candles—hundreds of them—placed wherever there was an inch of space to hold them; such was the scene prepared by Bub Driscoll and his aids for the joy dinner in honor of Mr. and Mrs. John Knowlton, in that apartment on West Twenty-first Street which we have seen twice before.

Lila was escorted to the dining room on the arm of Lawyer Siegel, after an extended and heated controversy among the Erring Knights as to which of them should have that honor.

When it appeared that the matter was apt to be argued till the dinner was ruined, Siegel stepped in and settled the question by offering his services, which were gladly accepted.

Pierre Dumain, as host, sat at one end of the table; Knowlton at the other. On one side was Lila, between Dougherty and Driscoll; opposite them Booth, Jennings, and Siegel.

"What a shame!" said Lila. "I'm so excited I can't eat."

Driscoll observed:

"Now, that's just like a woman. For two months you've been as cool and collected as a cake of ice, while you've had enough trouble to scare an army; and now that everything's over, and you're just at the beginning of a lifelong siege of matrimonial boredom, you're so excited you can't eat!"

"I never did a harder day's work in my life," declared Dougherty, "and I'm hungry like a bear. What do you call this, Driscoll? I'm no bridegroom—I can't eat roses."

But he was promptly squelched by the master of ceremonies, and everybody talked at once till the soup arrived.

Never was gayer company. Lila was at first a little embarrassed at finding herself the eighth at a table with seven men, but that did not last long; no longer, in fact, than when Dougherty, at the finish of the fish, arose to his feet to give an imitation of Miss Hughes chewing gum, powdering her face, and waiting on three customers at the same time.

"She never did," declared Lila, when she could speak for laughing. "That's a slander, Mr. Dougherty."

"What?" exclaimed the ex-prizefighter. "I'll admit it's not true to life; it's too delicate and refined. Not that I don't like her; the Venus is a good sport. And if there's any—What's this?"

"Sweetbreads in tambo shell, *m'sieu'*," murmured the waiter.

After which Dougherty was silent—and busy—for ten minutes.

Then Lawyer Siegel related some of his court experiences, both humorous and tragical, and Dumain described the mysteries and secrets of the gentle art of reading palms, and Jennings explained that his contract with Mr. Frohman would probably not be signed till the following day, and Dougherty described his first prizefight with an animation and picturesqueness of language that left the others in a condition bordering on hysteria.

"There's one thing," said Driscoll, turning to Lila, "for which I shall never forgive you—that you didn't invite me to the wedding."

"Here, too," put in Jennings. "I call it snobbish."

"Where was it, anyway?" Booth wanted to know. "How did you manage it?"

Dougherty explained:

"Easy. You know we got Knowlton out on bail for one day. Well, he got a license and I got a preacher, and Dumain let us use his French parlor, and stuff was all off in fifteen minutes, But you may get to see a wedding, after all."

Dougherty glanced at Knowlton. Knowlton nodded. Then the ex-prizefighter continued:

"We all know that our friend Mr. Knowlton is traveling sort of incog. His real name is Norton, and that fact demands what you might call supplementary proceedings. The big show is on tomorrow, and if you treat Mrs. Knowlton right she's very apt to give you a bid."

"Hurrah!" shouted Driscoll. "In at the death is all I ask."

"What an expression!" said Lila. "Mr. Driscoll, I'm offended."

"I beg your pardon," said the gentleman gallantly. "I didn't mean it, I assure you. Waiter!"

"Yes, sir."

"If I order another bottle of white wine—"

"Yes, sir."

"I say, if I order more white wine—"

"Yes, sir."

"Don't bring it."

"Yes, sir. No, sir."

The table grinned, and made a concerted and valiant attack on the dessert, while Jennings and Booth accused each other with some heat of being the cause of Driscoll's order.

Presently Driscoll rapped on the table for attention, and glared fiercely at the disputants till he got it.

"Lady and gentlemen," said he, "I must ask your kind favor and indulgence. Unlike the rest of this proud assembly, Mr. Jennings and myself are workingmen. We earn our bread by toil."

Cries of "Hear, hear!" came from Jennings, while the others jeered.

"Howbeit," continued the speaker, silencing the interruptions with an imperious gesture, "we must be at our tasks by eight o'clock. It is now seven-twenty.

"I understand that Mr. Dumain has a surprise in store for us, and that Mr. Knowlton has kindly consented to make a speech. In the interests of equality and justice I demand that these ceremonies begin at once."

Applause, continued and vociferous, from Jennings. Booth and Siegel each grasped one of his arms and held him quiet. Driscoll turned to Dumain and demanded an answer.

"All right," said the little Frenchman, "I'm ready."

"What about it?" Driscoll turned to the others.

They signified their approval. Knowlton, who had been silent throughout the dinner, nodded. Dumain rose to his feet, pushed back his chair, and cleared his throat.

"About zee surprise," the little Frenchman began; "eet ees a pleasant surprise. We are here this evening—"

"Hear, hear!" murmured Jennings.

"Silence him!" ordered Driscoll. Booth and Siegel obeyed, and the speaker continued:

"I say we are here this evening because our hearts are glad for our friend Mr. Knowlton and our very dear lady—God bless her!— zee Lady Lila!"

"To her!" shouted Dougherty, springing to his feet and raising his glass on high.

"To Lady Lila!" came in a deafening chorus, while Lila rose to her feet, trembling and confused.

They drank the toast amid cheers and applause.

"And now," continued Dumain, when they had rescated themselves, "for zee surprise. I must go back a leetle, and I do not speak zee Angleesh so well, so you must have zee patience.

"About Knowlton eet ees—only hees name ees Norton. I can only tell what I know. From what Sherman and our very dear lady have say to me I add zis to zat, and I know nearly all.

"I know he was officer in a bank in Warton, Ohio, and zat money was missing, and zat our friend was what you call eet suspicioned. And about zis Sherman tol' me, and from what he look at me I theenk to myself, aha! Sherman know more zan he say.

"Well, I theenk very little about all zat—I nearly forget eet because we are all busy wiz trying to put Knowlton away from all. For many weeks I forget eet."

Dumain paused, glanced at his audience with the assurance of a man who holds a high trump, and continued:

"All zis we all know. Well. Today I take Knowlton here to my rooms where ees hees trunk I brought. But he needs something— we go out. I stop in zee Lamartine to wait for heem—I go to zee telegraph desk, I go to zee cigar stand, I go to zee front desk, and Geebson call me and say, 'Telegram here for a man named John Norton. Do you know heem, Dumain?'

"I say, 'Yes, I will take eet to heem,' and he give eet to me, and I open eet and read eet to make sure. What I theenk, eet ees for Knowlton. Right. Here eet ees."

He took a yellow telegraph form from his pocket and waved it in the air. It was extra size—the telegram was a long one.

They shouted, "Read it!"

But Dumain tossed it to Knowlton, who, after reading it through, let it fall from his hands to the table and turned a white face to Lila.

"What is it?" Lila faltered.

Dougherty snatched up the telegram and read it aloud:

"Mr. John Norton, Hotel Lamartine, New York. Alma Sherman has confessed all. I was a fool not to believe you, but come home. Her brother got the money. They have wired to the New York police. Come home at once. Letter follows, but don't wait for it. Wire me immediately.

Father."

"Oh!" cried Lila. "And now—and now—"

In the confusion that followed, while the others applauded and shouted and clapped Knowlton on the back, Dougherty had to place his mouth close to her ear to make her hear:

"And now what?" he demanded.

"And now," Lila answered, "he—he doesn't need me, after all."

The ex-prizefighter sprang to his feet.

"Ha!" he cried in a tone of thunder. "Silence! Shut up, you! Knowlton, do you know what your wife is saying? She says that now you won't need her!"

Another moment and Knowlton was at her side, holding her in his arms.

"Lila! Dear little girl! We shall go home—home—together. Darling! Not need you? Look at me!"

For the next five minutes the Erring Knights and Lawyer Siegel were occupied in the next room, chased thereto by Dougherty, who commanded them to make as much noise as possible.

Presently Knowlton's voice came:

"Come back here! What are you doing in there? I say, Dumain! Dougherty!"

They came through the door backward, in single file, and Lila was forced to laugh in spite of herself.

"That's better," said Dougherty approvingly. "This is an occasion of joy, Mrs. Knowlton. No tears allowed."

Lila smiled at him.

"But say!" put in Driscoll, as he lit a cigarette—Lila had long since commanded them to smoke—"do you know what? That's what they took Sherman for at the courtroom!"

"They didn't waste any time," Booth observed.

"Oh, I know how he knew that," Lila was saying to Knowlton and Dumain, who had expressed their wonder at his father's knowledge of his address. "It was Mr. Sherman who told him."

"Sherman!" they exclaimed.

"Yes," Lila asserted.

Then she told them of the telegram Sherman had sent to the president of the Warton National Bank concerning John Norton, and Dumain and Knowlton hastened to inform the others of the fact that they owed the receipt of the telegram to the enemy himself, thereby doubling their joyous hilarity.

Then they surrounded Knowlton and demanded a speech. He protested; they insisted. He appealed to Lila for assistance; she commanded him to do his duty.

There was no escape; he motioned them to be seated, and began:

"Boys, I know this is no time to be serious—for you. You're having a good time. But you've asked me to talk, and to tell the truth, I'm glad of the chance to relieve my mind. If you don't like what I say it's your own fault. I know you're good sports, but there are one or two things I have to speak about.

"First, money. You've spent about sixteen hundred dollars on my defense, and you've given me a thousand for a stake. There's been nothing said about it—you've turned it over to me without a word—but I want you to know that the first thing I'll do when I get home—when we get home—is to send you a check for the twenty-six hundred. Now, don't think I'm refusing a favor; it isn't that. The Lord knows I've accepted enough favors from you without your insisting on that one, too."

"Oh, of course, if you're rolling in wealth—" put in Driscoll.

"Then that's settled. I'm not going to try to thank you; if I talked all night I couldn't make it strong enough. Lila and I are going out West where they like to say you find nothing but good, clean Americans, and I've always thought the boast was justified; but wherever we go, and whoever we see, we'll never meet as good men, or as straight sports, or as true friends as the Erring Knights.

"Here's to you, boys! God bless you!"

Knowlton's voice was trembling so that he could scarcely speak, and his eyes shone with tears as he drained the glass and threw it on the floor, where it broke in a thousand fragments.

The following afternoon the bride and groom were escorted to Grand Central Station by the Erring Knights. And there they received their reward if they had felt they needed any. For after Knowlton had shaken hands with each of them and arranged for a grand reunion when he and his wife should next visit New York, as they stood lined up at the entrance to the trackway, Lila approached Dougherty, who happened to be first, with a farewell on her lips.

He held out his hand. She ignored it, and, stretching on tiptoe, placed a hearty uncompromising kiss on his either cheek! And before he could recover she had passed on to Dumain and repeated the operation, and then to the remaining three.

In another moment she was walking down the platform by the side of the train with her arm through that of her husband, preceded by two porters loaded with bags and suitcases and flowers and candy; and every now and then she turned to look back at the Erring Knights, who were waving their handkerchiefs frantically in unrestrained and triumphant glee. And then, throwing a last kiss from the car platform, while Knowlton waved his hat, they disappeared inside, and a minute later the train pulled out.

It happened, by a curious coincidence, that that train held two sets of passengers for the little town of Warton, Ohio.

In a day-coach, seated side by side, were two men. The face of one, dark and evil looking, wore lines of sleeplessness and despair and fear. The other, a small, heavy-set man with a ruddy countenance, was seated next the aisle, and had an appearance of watchfulness as he kept one eye on his companion while he scanned the columns of a newspaper with the other. William Sherman was going home to pay.

But a few feet away, in a Pullman, sat the man he had tried to ruin and the girl he had tried to wrong.

They were looking at each other, they felt, almost for the first time. Between them, on the seat, their hands were closely clasped together.

Thus they sat for many minutes, silent, while the train passed through the city, crossed to the west, and started on its journey northward along the banks of the glorious Hudson.

"Dearest," said the man in a caressing tone.

The girl pressed his hand tighter and sighed happily.

"They're good fellows," the man continued, "every one of them. And to think what we owe them! Everything—everything."

"Yes," said the girl, "everything. We must never forget them."

But the truth was, as was clearly apparent from the tone of her voice and the melting of her eyes into his, that she had forgotten them already!

A
Prize
for
Princes

CHAPTER I

———ᏔᏔ———

The Convent

RICHARD STETTON stopped at the first turn into the main street and gazed down its length, lit by the soft brilliance of the moon.

What he had seen in the last hour made him regret that he had come to Fasilica; he cursed the insatiable and morbid curiosity of youth that had brought him there.

Gutters running with blood; wild-eyed Turks, drunk with victory, striking down men, women, and children and looting their pockets and homes; the pitiful cowardice of the small garrison of soldiers whose duty it was to protect the little town with their lives; all this filled him with a revolting disgust and made him long to flee somewhere, anywhere, away from the sights and sounds of this night of horror.

Suddenly, as he stood wondering which way to turn, surrounded on every side by the terrible din and confusion of the stricken city, he was startled by hearing a new sound that rose above all the others.

It was the ringing of a bell, in wild, irregular strokes that seemed to epitomize the cries of suffering and despair which filled the streets from one end of the town to the other.

Stetton looked up; there could be no doubt of it—the sound of
the bell came from the air directly above; and there, before his eyes,
he saw the form of a belfry in the shape of a cross appearing dimly
in the moonlight, at the top of a low, rambling building of dark
stone, against which he was at that moment leaning.

The significance of the cross did not escape the young man; his
face went white as he murmured: "A convent! God pity them!"

He turned and started to retrace his steps down the little street
through which he had reached the center of the town.

As he turned he was jostled roughly by three or four Turks who
were rushing past with drawn bayonets, and he again sought the
shelter of the wall. Other soldiers came, until a group of thirty or
more were gathered on the street in front of the stone building.

"This is the place," they were calling to one another. "How do
we get in?"

They were searching along the wall for an entrance to the
convent.

From round the corner there came a great shout of triumph and
exultation from many gruff throats.

"Come, they have found it!" called the soldiers, as they disappeared in the direction whence the cries came.

Stetton, following them round the corner, saw in one glance that
the convent and its occupants were doomed. A hundred or more soldiers were banging away with stones and paving-blocks at a little iron
gate set between two pillars at the foot of a short flight of steps.

Others were approaching at a run down the street from either
direction, having left their victims to a short respite at the scent of
this larger and richer prey. The bell above continued to ring in a wild
and vain cry to Heaven for assistance.

The gate trembled, hung crazily on one hinge, and fell. For an
instant the soldiers hung back, then swept toward the opening in a
mad rush.

Stetton saw, just within the door, the figure of a woman, bent and gray-haired, standing in the path of the invaders with uplifted arm. A stone hurled by the foremost soldier struck her in the face, and she sank to the ground, while the soldiers surged through the gateway over her body.

Stetton, feeling himself grow faint, again turned the corner to escape the fearful scene. Then, possessed of a sudden hot anger against these men whom war had turned into wild beasts, he halted and looked round as though for some magic wand or brand from Heaven with which to annihilate them.

His eye, roving about thus in helpless fury, fell on an open window set in the wall of the convent, not three feet above his head. It was protected by iron bars, through which the dim light of a candle escaped to meet that of the moon outside.

Without stopping to consider the reason or rashness of his action, Stetton rushed into the street, picked up a heavy stone and hurled it with all his force at the window. It struck squarely in the center, bending two of the bars aside for a space of a foot or more.

In another second the young man had leaped up and caught one of the bars, and, pulling his body up and squeezing it through the space left by the stone, found himself within the convent.

He stood in a small room with a low ceiling, entirely bare and unoccupied. At one end was a narrow door; he crossed to it, and, stopping on the threshold, stood transfixed with astonishment.

Before him was a room exactly similar to the other. Two wooden chairs were placed against the wall at the right. A closet stood on the opposite side, and in the center was a wooden table holding some scattered papers, a Bible, and a crucifix. Near the left wall was a *prie-dieu;* and before it, on the bare stone floor, knelt the figures of a young woman and a girl.

It was the sight of the young woman that had halted Stetton and rendered him speechless. At the noise of his entrance she had turned her head to face him without moving from her position, and it was not strange that he was startled by the beauty of her face even in that moment of excitement.

Her hair, magnificently golden, flowed over the folds of her gray dress and covered the ground behind; her eyes, whose deep, blue-gray color could be perceived even in the dim candle light, gazed compellingly straight into the face of the intruder. He remained silent, returning the gaze.

The girl who knelt beside the young woman—a small, slender creature with black hair and olive skin—suddenly sprang to her feet and crossed to the center of the room, while her black eyes snapped viciously at the young man in the doorway.

"Coward!" she said in a low tone of hatred and fear. "Strike! Are you afraid, because we are two to one? Strike!"

"Vivi!"

It was the young woman who called. She had risen to her feet and made a step forward.

"You are not—with them?" she continued, as her eyes again found Stetton's and seemed to take in every detail of his face and clothing. "You are of the town—you will save us?"

The young man found his voice.

"I am an American. I came through the window. I will save you if I can. They have already entered the convent—listen!"

From the corridors without came the sound of tramping feet and shouting voices.

"There is no time to be lost."

The girl and the young woman gazed about in terror, crying: "What shall we do? Save us!"

Stetton tried to collect his wits.

"Is there no way out—no secret passage?"

"None."

"The rear entrance?"

"It can be reached only by the main corridor," replied the young woman.

"The roof?"

"There is no way to reach it."

"But where are the others? Surely you are not alone here? Have they escaped?"

The young woman opened her lips to reply, but the answer came from another quarter. As Stetton spoke, the oaths and ejaculations of the soldiers in the corridors without were redoubled, and a series of frightful screams sounded throughout the convent. The shrieks of distress and despair rose even above the hoarse cries of the soldiers; they came evidently from the room on the other side of the wall. The face of the girl was white as she looked at Stetton and stammered:

"They are in the chapel. They were hiding there. God pity them!"

She approached the young man with trembling knees and an eloquent gesture of appeal; he stood as though paralyzed by the cries from beyond.

The cries grew louder. Footsteps and the gruff voices of soldiers were heard approaching down the corridor outside; another moment and they would be discovered.

Feeling a hand on his arm, Stetton turned to find the young woman gazing at him with eyes that held impatience and resolution, but nothing of fear.

"Could we not escape through the window?" Her voice was firm and calm.

"The window?" Stetton repeated stupidly.

Suddenly roused, he turned and ran swiftly into the next room and glanced through the barred window by which he had entered. The street without was deserted.

With a word to the others, who had followed and stood at his side, he squeezed his way through the bars and dropped to the ground below, falling to his knees. He got to his feet in time to catch the girl as she was pushed through the window by her companion. The young woman followed, disdaining any assistance as she came down lightly as a bird, and they stood together in the dimly lighted street.

Knowing that, close as they were to the main thoroughfare, they were apt to be discovered at any moment, Stetton lost no time in discussion of a route.

"Run!" he whispered, pointing down the narrow street by which he had approached the center of the town.

The young woman hesitated.

"But you?"

"I'll follow. Go!"

As they ran the shouts of the drunken soldiers and the cries of their victims assailed their ears from behind, urging them forward. The street which they were following—crooked and narrow, and saved from darkness only by the fading light of the moon—appeared to be completely deserted and the houses on either side were closed and shuttered and without lights.

Here and there a head appeared, thrust through a door or window, but at their approach was hastily withdrawn. It was evident that this street had not yet been invaded: their escape seemed a certainty—but where to find a safe retreat? Stetton overtook his companions and spoke as they ran:

"Do you know the town? Do you know any place to go?"

The young woman shook her head.

"No."

"Then follow this street. We must take to the country. If I could find General Nirzann—I know him—"

This suggestion—a somewhat foolish one under the circumstances—brought no response, and they continued their rapid flight.

They had already passed three or four cross streets, and Stetton was beginning to think they were well beyond danger, when, as they reached the next crossing, they were suddenly confronted by a band of Turks who pounced on them from behind a little wooden build ing on the corner.

At the same moment, glancing to the left, Stetton was dimly aware of a fresh burst of shouts and outcries as the soldiers came rushing into the street from the other end and began a furious assault on the doors and windows of the houses and shops.

As the group of six or seven soldiers stopped directly in the path of the fugitives, they appeared to hesitate momentarily. Stetton heard one of them cry, "Come on, they have nothing! To the stores!"

Then, catching sight of the face of the young woman as she stood clinging to Stetton's arm, the speaker jerked himself forward and stared at her with a drunken leer.

"Allah! A beauty!" he laughed, and grasped her roughly by the shoulder.

Even as he acted, Stetton cursed himself for his folly. He knew that the little slip of paper in his breast-pocket, signed by General Nirzann, would permit him to pass unmolested, though it would be useless to protect his companions.

With a rapid glance he counted the group of soldiers—there were seven of them. Against such odds what could he do? He was a man of caution; he thrust his hand into his pocket and brought forth the slip of paper.

As he did so the leader of the band jerked the young woman violently forward and caught her in his arms.

It was then that Stetton acted, cursing his own folly. Leaping forward, he struck the soldier a savage blow in the face with his fist.

The soldier staggered back with a cry of surprise and pain, releasing his hold on his intended victim.

"Pig!" he screamed, rushing at Stetton. His comrades sprang to his assistance with upraised bayonets and pistols.

Before they could reach him Stetton had thrust the young woman and the girl to one side, calling to them to run. Then he himself leaped aside, barely missing the point of the foremost bayonet. Dashing off to the right he had joined his companions before the soldiers had time to turn, and was racing down the street at the top of his speed.

The girl who had been called Vivi caught his hand as he came up to them, saying, "Are you hurt?" Stetton shook his head and urged them forward.

The sound of pistol shots came from behind, and bullets whistled past their ears. Then the shouts of the soldiers as they started in wild pursuit, shooting as they ran.

There came a sudden, sharp cry from the young woman.

"Are you hurt?" panted Stetton. "In the arm. It is nothing," she answered, without slackening her pace.

Glancing behind, Stetton muttered an oath as he saw that the soldiers were gaining on them. The street ran straight ahead as far as he could see in the moonlight, and he knew that a turn to the right or left would probably land them in the arms of another of the bands of marauding soldiers.

To escape by flight appeared impossible. With a hasty glance toward either side of the narrow street, in search of a possible refuge, he saw, some distance ahead and to the right, a house, through the window of which appeared the feeble light of a candle. It was removed somewhat from the street; reaching it, Stetton dashed suddenly onto the gravel walk in front, pulling his companions after him.

The door was locked; he rattled the knob and pounded frantically on the panels with his fists; the soldiers had turned into the path were now but a short distance away.

"In Heaven's name, open!" shouted the young man.

His companions had crouched against the door, locked in each other's arms. There was the sound of bolts drawn back, the door flew open, and the fugitives tumbled within.

Stetton heard a man's voice calling to the young woman and the girl to go to the rear of the house, to escape the bullets that were coming through the door. He turned to face the speaker—a giant of a man with a bushy black beard who was relocking and bolting the door.

"How many are there?" asked the man with the beard, pulling Stetton aside, out of range from the door.

"Seven."

"Turks?"

"Yes."

The man with the beard muttered an oath and ran to a window. Soon he called out:

"They seem to be out of ammunition. The drunken devils! Come here!"

Stetton joined him and looked through the window. The soldiers had halted a dozen paces from the door, and the one who had felt Stetton's fist appeared to be urging the others to make an attack.

Suddenly the man with the beard pulled a revolver from his pocket, thrust it through the glass of the window, and fired into their midst. One of the soldiers fell; the others, without stopping to look after their comrade, took to their heels and disappeared down the moonlit street.

"Cowards!" the man grunted contemptuously, pocketing his revolver. Then he turned to Stetton:

"You had better look after your companions—I'll stay here."

"But how—I don't know where—"

"You must remain for the night. By morning the officers will get these brutes under control, and you can return home. There are two rooms with beds in the rear. If you need me, you will find me in there," he finished, pointing to a room on the right.

"But, pardon me, are you alone?"

The man with the beard gazed at Stetton with piercing eyes. "Young man, you talk too much. But then—no wonder—it is your confounded English impertinence."

"American," Stetton smiled.

"It is all the same."

"We do not think so."

"Well—leave me." Black eyes flashed above the black beard. "Anyway, all this," he made a circle with his arm to encompass the war-devastated city of Fasilica, "this is all the result of your impudent interference. These mountains were made for us to rest our feet on. And if the Turks did not have your favor to rely upon—if you would leave it to us—"

Stetton had started to leave the room, but turned at the door.

"Us?"

The man with the beard scowled unpleasantly.

"Yes, us. I am a Russian, sir."

The scowl deepened; and Stetton, thinking that this was a strange host indeed, turned without making any reply and went in search of the young woman and the girl. He found them in a room in the rear, crouched on a bed in the corner. At his entrance they sprang to the floor and advanced to meet him with an eager question:

"The soldiers?"

"They have gone," said Stetton. "You are safe."

His eyes were fastened on the face of the young woman; now that they had leisure for the feast, they could not leave it.

Wondrously beautiful she was, indeed; almost supernaturally so; what with the whiteness of her velvet skin, her glorious golden crown of hair, and the bright glitter of her gray-blue eyes. But even in that moment, when Stetton felt for the first time her compelling fascination, he beheld those gray-blue eyes with something like a shudder as they grazed boldly into his own.

"Our host frightened the soldiers away," he said, recovering himself with an effort. "We are safe for the night—we can sleep here—and by morning the trouble will be over."

"Oh, but you are good to us!" cried Vivi, advancing with out-stretched hand.

She was a girl of seventeen or eighteen; while her companion was perhaps five years older. Her modest attractions, though by no means contemptible, were completely eclipsed by the other's bold beauty.

"You are so good to us!" Vivi repeated.

The young woman smiled.

"Indeed, you have earned our gratitude," she said. "If it had not been for you—but it is too horrible to think about. It would be absurd to try to thank you—*monsieur*—"

"My name is Stetton—Richard Stetton."

"And mine is Aline Solini. My little friend is Vivi Janvour—French, as you can see. There is nothing to tell about ourselves; when one has entered a convent the past is dead."

"And the future?" asked Stetton, wondering if he meant anything by the question."

"That, too."

"Still, it seems a shame to bury a flower."

"When it is withered?" Aline Solini smiled.

"I was about to add, when it is yet fresh and beautiful."

"You are bold, M. Stetton."

"Pardon me—I have eyes, and my tongue speaks for them—" Stetton stopped suddenly and cried: "But I forgot! You are wounded and need immediate attention."

Aline shrugged her shoulders.

"It is nothing."

But Stetton insisted, and finally she uncovered her arm for his inspection. The wound was by no means serious—scarcely painful—but the white skin was torn apart for a space of an inch or more, and an ugly red line extended below the elbow. With an exclamation of concern Stetton disappeared, and soon returned with a basin of water and some strips of cloth.

Noting Vivi's smile at his clumsy efforts to bathe and bandage the wound, he allowed her deft fingers to take the place of his awkward ones, watching her in silence from a seat on the edge of the bed.

Now that the danger was past, Stetton was congratulating himself on having met with so interesting an adventure. And, he added complacently, in his thoughts, it was apt to become more interesting still. If it did not, it would be no fault of his.

He looked at Aline, wondering how so glorious a creature had persuaded herself to abjure the world and its pleasures; in the usual total ignorance of the American Protestant concerning the Roman Church, he supposed that no one ever entered a convent without taking the veil.

Well, nun or Ninon, she was perfect, he was reflecting, when he was suddenly startled by the sound of her voice:

"You are staring at me, M. Stetton."

"Forgive me," stammered the young man. "I was thinking."

"I admire boldness," said Aline, and though her tone was playful, her eyes were cold. She turned and spoke to the girl.

"Thank you, Vivi; the bandage is perfect. Do we sleep in this room, *monsieur?*"

"There is another," said Stetton. "Perhaps it is more comfortable. Shall I find it?"

"No; this will do very well. We will leave the other for you."

Stetton shook his head, pointing to the door.

"I shall lie there."

"It is unnecessary."

"But if you will permit me—I should not forgive myself if any harm came to you—"

"Very well." Aline smiled, extending her hand. "Then we will say good night."

Stetton advanced and took the hand in his own. It was white and soft; he could feel the warmth of her blood through the delicate skin. There was a pressure of the fingers—or did he imagine it?

Raising his head, he saw her regarding him with a strange smile at once cold and friendly, and her eyes held an invitation that was at the same a challenge. Stetton felt a thrill run throughout his body—he could not have told whether it was pleasure or fear; still looking into her eyes, he lifted her hand and touched it with his lips deliberately.

Then he turned and left the room without paying any attention to Vivi, who had advanced to his side; nor did he reply to the scarcely audible good night that came from her lips.

Half an hour later, having seen the light of the candle disappear from the transom above their door, he approached and knocked lightly and cautiously.

"Well?" came Aline's voice.

"Do you wish anything?"

"Nothing, thank you."

"All right, good night."

Stetton, having wrapped himself in blankets obtained from the adjoining room, lay down on the floor across the doorway to dream of golden hair and piercing gray-blue eyes.

—⁓—

CHAPTER 11

The Man with the Beard

O N THE following morning the streets of Fasilica bore mute evidence of the havoc wrought by the looting soldiers the night before. Well it was that the commanding officer of the Turkish forces had halted his victorious troops in their career of plunder with sternness and resolution, or the little city would have been leveled to the ground.

Everywhere doors and windows hung in splinters; the streets were strewn with rubbish and articles of clothing or household goods which the soldiers had thrown away in their haste to escape the punishment of their general; great brownish splotches appeared here and there on the pavement, a testimonial to the misfortune or unhappy resistance of some citizen; and in the business section of the town many of the buildings had been destroyed or damaged by fire.

One of these latter was the convent, which had been totally denuded of all its contents. What remained was a mere skeleton of stone, with its empty gloominess accentuated by the rays of the morning sun.

But the sight appeared to strike Richard Stetton as a joyful one rather than a sorrowful. He stood at the corner of the narrow street at the side, exactly opposite the barred window through which he had entered and escaped the night before.

Half an hour previous he had left Aline Solini and Vivi Janvour in the house where they had found refuge from the soldiers, with the object of ascertaining if the convent was in a condition to admit of their return. Obviously, it was not; hence Stetton's smile of satisfaction. His adventure, he was telling himself, was not to end with the excitement of the night.

On his way back to the house he tried to find something to take to his companions for breakfast, but no shops were open; besides, the soldiers had appropriated nearly everything eatable for their own use.

Aline met him at the door of the room in which she said Vivi had slept.

In a few words Stetton told her of the destruction of the convent, and of the impossibility of their finding shelter there. She received the news quite calmly, giving him her hand with a smile and inviting him within the room. Vivi, who had been sitting in a chair by the window, rose as he entered, with a timid nod of greeting.

"The convent is gone," said Aline, turning to her. "We cannot return there."

"Gone!" cried the girl, her face turning pale. "But what—are you sure?"

"I have been there," said Stetton. "It is nothing but an empty ruin."

"Then what are we to do?" faltered Vivi, looking at Aline. "Where can I go? I have no friends, no home—nothing."

"You have me."

Stetton tried, with a sidelong glance, to include Aline in this offer, but felt that the attempt was somehow a failure. She had crossed to the girl and put her arm around her shoulder.

"Don't be alarmed, Vivi," she said. "I shall take care of you."

"And you—have you a home?" asked Stetton.

"I? None." The tone was hard.

"Nor friends?"

"I have never had any."

"Then—if you will permit me—I would be only too happy—"

"Wait a moment." Aline had taken her arm from Vivi's shoulder and crossed half-way to Stetton's side. "You are about to offer us your protection, *monsieur?*"

"I am," Stetton nodded.

"Then before you continue I have something to say. Vivi, leave the room!"

The girl looked up in astonishment, then, as her eyes met those of the speaker, she crossed to the door without a word and disappeared in the hall outside, closing the door behind her. Stetton, left alone with Aline, sat waiting for her to speak.

For a moment the young woman was silent, regarding Stetton with a gaze of speculation, then she said abruptly:

"I thought it best we should be alone."

"But why?" he stammered, frankly puzzled. "What I have to say—"

"I know what you would say, but you think something very different. Let us be frank."

"I have no reason to be otherwise."

"Well, then—what would you say?"

"Merely this, that I place myself at your disposal. You are alone, without friends, with no place to go. I could be of service to you. I will do whatever you say."

"And why?"

"Need I give a reason?" Stetton began to be a little exasperated. "You are a woman, and in trouble. I am a man."

Aline, smiling, came closer to him.

"Do not be angry with me. If I ask questions, it is because my experience has taught me that they are necessary. You are, then, completely disinterested?"

"Yes, I assure you—"

Aline Solini came closer, still smiling. Her eyes looked full into Stetton's, filled, as on the night before, with something that might have been either an invitation or a challenge. There was something in their depths that frightened the young man and made him want to look away from them, but he could not. The woman stood close beside him as she murmured:

"Quite disinterested?"

"No!" Stetton exploded suddenly, and he grasped her hand in his own and held it firmly. "No!"

"Ah! You have spirit, then. I had begun to doubt it. Perhaps, after all— But what do you expect?"

"What you will give," replied Stetton, emboldened by her tone. He still held her hand.

"I do not give," said Aline, still smiling. "I pay—always."

She was quite close to him now; he could almost feel her breath on his face. Her lips were parted in a smile, but the beautiful eyes were cold, and Stetton was conscious of an overmastering desire to see them filled with warm surrender. At the same time, he felt a vague uneasiness; there was something terrifying about that unwavering gaze that seemed to be weighing him in some secret scale.

"You may believe it," he said in answer to her question, while his voice trembled, "for it is so."

He raised her hand to his lips.

She drew away from him and sat down on the edge of the bed.

"Well—we can talk of that later, when you have earned the right. I have something to say to you, Mr. Stetton."

There was a pause. Presently she continued:

"When you offer me your protection, *monsieur*, you invite danger.

You found me in a convent. I had gone there not to escape the world, but a man. No matter why, he is my enemy—and I am his."

The gray-blue eyes flashed, brilliant and merciless.

"If you help me, he will be yours as well, and he is not one to be despised. For more than a year he has been searching for me, and though I fancied myself securely hidden in the convent, I was wrong. In some way he has traced me to Fasilica; two weeks ago, as I looked through the window of my room, I saw him pass below in the street.

"That is why I am willing to accept your aid; I must leave Fasilica at once. If he finds me he will kill me, unless—"

She stopped, looking at the young man significantly.

"But who is this man?" asked Stetton with dry lips. This was rather more than he had bargained for.

"As for that, I cannot tell you. Is it not enough that I hate him?" Aline eyed him narrowly. "If it is not, that is well, you may leave me."

"But who is he?" repeated Stetton, who, like all men except heroes of romance, detested mystery. Besides, his caution was pulling at his coattails. "If he finds us—"

The gray-blue eyes flashed scornfully. "Oh, if I am not worth the trouble—" Then she leaned toward him, softening. "What, *monsieur?* But there, I thought you brave. It was a mistake, then?"

She smiled.

Stetton looked at her and his caution vanished.

"Tell me what to do," he said.

"You will help me?"

"Yes."

"It is dangerous."

"I accept the danger."

"Oh," Aline cried, suddenly, springing to her feet, "if you kill him, Stetton, I will love you! But yet—wait—let us understand each other. I must know what you expect."

"My eyes should tell you that."

"They do—but they say too little."

"It is love that is in them."

"That is not enough."

These words had passed rapidly, and Stetton did not understand them—or would not, had it not been for Aline's significant tone and glance. It was the meaning of these that made him hesitate and bring himself up sharply.

At his decision you will wonder; but not more so than he did himself.

To hear Aline Solini's words—their bluntness, their sharp precision—and to hear and see nothing else, was to lose all the charm of her, which lay in her electric glance, her soft velvety tones, her little movements of arms and shoulders, provocative, alluring, calculated to fire the blood of any man beyond any thought of caution or price.

It was not with words that Cleopatra persuaded Antony to throw away an empire to remain at her side. Words are never the weapon of a beautiful woman, nor should be. Aline Solini understood this—she knew full well the power she held and its source.

Richard Stetton looked at her. Young, vain, impressionable, he met her glance of fire and was lost. It has been said that her meaning was clear to him, and for I a moment, creditable to his caution, he hesitated.

But some few things there are which appear to us, even at a first glance, to be so transcendently priceless that whatever the value set upon them they seem to be cheap indeed; and thus it was with Stetton. Besides, he did not take the time to consider consequences— a habit begun in the cradle. He said:

"It is not enough that I love you?"

"Not—No." This with a smile.

"Not—with all it means?"

"That is what I do not know." Aline raised a hand toward him, then let it fall again. "There can be no double meaning here, *monsieur*. You think I have offered myself to you? Perhaps; but first I must know what you ask."

Stetton looked at her, and thought of nothing but what he saw. He burst forth impetuously:

"I am asking you to marry me, *mademoiselle*."

"Akh!"

This cry, Russian in accent, tender and provocative in tone, was all that was needed to complete the young man's madness. He grasped her hand, standing in front of her, close, and looking into her eyes. Their glances melted into each other like a passionate embrace.

He whispered:

"Say yes—I ask you to marry me—say yes. Anything—anything! Ah! Speak to me!"

"Yes—yes—yes!"

It was a caress and a promise at once, tender and yielding. Sudden tears came to Stetton's eyes as he folded her gently in his arms and held her so for a long time. To look at her was music; to touch her a song of love.

He could not speak; for two minutes he remained silent, feeling himself overwhelmed by a rush of emotion, strange and sweet, but somehow—not satisfying. He moved a little back from her, suddenly demanding:

"When?"

Aline's lips were parted in a little smile at this display of eagerness.

"You must wait," she said.

"Wait?"

"Yes. Have I not said I have an enemy? You have said you love me; you have asked me to marry you; well, we cannot do everything at once. You must realize that I am in danger, that I must first escape—"

"Your fortunes are mine."

Aline flashed a glance at him.

"Thank you for that. Then—we are in danger. But you must make no mistake. I have not said I love you—though—perhaps in time—You have offered me your protection; I have agreed to marry you; that is all—it is a bargain. It must wait; we must first consider our safety."

"Well—" Stetton released her, stepping back a pace—"What are we to do?"

"We must leave Fasilica."

"Where do you want to go?"

"Anywhere—stay—" Aline stopped and appeared to reflect—"To Warsaw. Yes, Warsaw. That is best."

"But how are we to get there?" objected Stetton. "The whole country beyond here is nothing but a battlefield—indeed"—the young man interrupted himself, struck by a sudden thought—"it is most likely that you will not be allowed to leave Fasilica."

"Why should they detain us?"

"The policy of the Turk. Any one who once falls under his authority remains there. But, of course, with the Allies—and yes, by Heaven, that is it! I shall see General Nirzann. He is in command of the Frasars who combined with the Turks in the siege. He will get me passports—I am sure of it."

"Do you know him?"

"Yes—that is, slightly. I came in, you know, with the army."

"Ah! You are a soldier?"

"No."

"A journalist?"

"No. I am merely a curiosity-seeker. I looked for excitement, and I found you. Aline! You will let me call you that?"

"As you please," said the young woman indifferently. "But what of General Nirzann? When will you see him?"

"Today—now—at once."

"That is well. Vivi and I shall wait here."

Stetton turned quickly.

"Ah, I had forgotten her! Who is she? Is she to go with us?"

"She is an orphan. Her parents were French—Janvour was a minor diplomat, I believe, who died somewhere in the Balkans and left Vivi to be cared for by the Church. I met her in the convent. She loves me; we shall take her with us. And now, go."

"Yes."

Stetton hesitated a moment, then bent over Aline to kiss her. But she held him back, saying, "Not yet, you must wait," in so cold a tone that he drew away from her half in anger.

Then, looking into her wonderful eyes and thinking of the future, so rich in promise, he turned without another word and left the room to go in search of General Nirzann. As he passed Vivi in the hall he heard Aline's voice calling to her to return.

On his way to the street Stetton stopped for a moment in the front of the house to look for the man with the beard, their strange host, but he was not to be found.

Once outside, he turned his steps rapidly toward the center of the town, which was gradually resuming its normal appearance as the citizens, reassured by a proclamation of the Turkish commander, came forth to clear away the debris of the night of pillage.

At the first corner, where he turned, Stetton approached a soldier standing on guard and obtained directions to the headquarters of General Nirzann.

As he walked down the narrow sunlit street, his mind was working rapidly, revolving the incidents of the night's adventure and their probable consequences to himself.

He did not know what to think of Aline Solini. What was the truth about this enemy whom she seemed to fear so greatly? Was she an adventuress? A political refugee? Perhaps, even, a fugitive from justice?

He did not know. What he did know was that he was afraid of her. Those eyes, whose beauty was eclipsed by the cold light of some implacable hatred of secret design, were not the eyes of innocence in distress.

"I would do well to be rid of her," muttered Stetton as he turned into the main street. Nevertheless, he continued to follow the route given by the soldier.

Having looked into Aline Solini's face and felt the quick pressure of her velvety fingers, he was held by them in spite of his native caution that amounted at times to cowardice.

"I would do well to be rid of her," he muttered again. Then he remembered the intoxicating promise of her lips and eyes as she had said: "You must wait."

As for time, he had plenty of it for any adventure. His father— a manufacturer of food products, with a plant in Cincinnati and offices in New York—was wealthy and somewhat of a fool, both of which facts were evidenced by his having furnished the necessary funds for a two years' tour of the world by his unpromising son, Richard.

Richard had been sojourning á *la Soudaine* at Budapest, when, on hearing that the mountains to the east were being invaded by the Turks and Frasars, he had betaken himself thither in search of sensation.

At Marisi he had introduced himself into the camp of the Frasars with letters of introduction from Paris and Vienna, and had followed them through their filibustering campaign till they had joined the Turks in the taking of Fasilica.

Then the entry into the town and the adventure of the night before. He was telling himself that he had found the sensation he sought, and, by dint of dwelling on the face and figure of Aline Solini, he became filled with a resolve that amounted almost to heroism.

He would take her away from Fasilica—away from the mysterious enemy whom she so evidently feared, to Moscow, or Berlin, or perhaps even St. Petersburg.

He went up the steps of a large stone building surrounded by a guard of soldiers for the protection and dignity of the general whose temporary headquarters were within.

In the first room off the hall on the right Stetton found General Nirzann seated before a large wooden table on which were spread maps and papers in apparent confusion. Near a window at the farther end stood a small group of young officers, with swords at their sides, conversing together in low tones.

In the rear of the room a telegraph instrument clicked noisily at intervals. The orderly who had conducted Stetton into the room stood at attention, waiting for the general to look up from his papers.

General Nirzann sat with lowered head, evidently lost in thought. He was a medium-sized man of about forty-two or three years. Beneath his bristling brows a long, thin nose extended in a straight line, and under that, in turn, appeared a dark brown mustache, turned up at the ends after the manner of Berlin.

His dark, rather small eyes, as he raised them to address the orderly, were filled with impatience and irritation. At his nod the orderly turned and left the room.

"What can I do for you?" said the general, looking sharply at Stetton.

The young man approached a step nearer the table.

"I have come to ask a favor, sir."

"A little more and you would have been too late. What is it?"

Stetton, who did not understand the remark, but thought he

observed a grin on the face of one of the young officers who had approached, began to tell in as few words as possible of having found the young woman and the girl in the convent, without, however, mentioning the encounter with the soldiers.

The general waited in silence till he had finished; then he said:

"But what do you want of me?"

"Passports, sir, to leave the city."

"Who are these women—residents?"

"No, sir; that is, they were in the convent; one is French, the other, I think, Polish. They wish to go to Warsaw."

For a moment the general was silent, dropping his eyes on the papers before him; then he looked up at Stetton:

"You know, this is none of your affair, *monsieur*. Because you had letters from friends of the prince, you were allowed to accompany us, but only on condition that you would stand on your own responsibility and cause us no trouble. You have annoyed me on several occasions; you are annoying me now. Besides, I do not know that my protection would be of any use; I leave Fasilica tonight. You say you intend to accompany these women to Warsaw. I am sorry for that. I should prefer that you remain here to torment my successor."

"I am sorry, sir—" Stetton began, but the general interrupted him:

"I know, I know; that will do. You shall have your passports. What are their names?"

"Aline Solini and Vivi Janvour," said Stetton.

General Nirzann had picked up a pen and begun to write on a pad of paper, but suddenly threw the pen down and said:

"After all, that will not do. I shall have to see these women and question them. Confound it, Stetton, you are more trouble than a dozen armies! Can you bring them here at once?"

The young man hesitated, thinking rapidly. Aline had said her enemy was in Fasilica; would it not be dangerous for her to appear on the streets in the daytime? But the passports must be obtained; it was necessary to take the risk. Stetton answered:

"Yes, sir; I can bring them."

"Very well, do so." And the general turned again to his papers, indicating that the interview was ended.

On his way out of the building Stetton, meeting a young lieutenant whom he knew, stopped him to ask why General Nirzann was leaving Fasilica.

"You haven't heard?" said the officer, smiling. "The prince has recalled him to Marisi and sent old Norbert in his place. He's in for a picking."

"Well," thought Stetton, "that means that we must get our passports as soon as possible," and he set out down the street at a rapid walk.

He found Aline and Vivi, especially the latter, in a fever of impatience and anxiety. As soon as he told them that it would be necessary for them to go with him to General Nirzann for their passports, this gave way to genuine alarm, in spite of his assurances that no harm would come to them.

"I do not like it," said Aline, frowning. "Besides—you know—it is scarcely safe for me to appear in the streets."

"But what are we to do?" demanded Stetton.

"Are the passports necessary?"

"Positively. Every road out of the city is guarded."

"Then we must make the best of it." The young woman turned to Stetton suddenly: "It is well you returned when you did; Vivi was frightened. Someone has been tramping up and down in the room in front as though he would tear the house down. Where are we? Who was it that let us in last night? I did not see him."

"Russian, he said he was," replied Stetton. "By the way, we must thank him before we leave. I have not seen him this morning. We owe him our lives, perhaps."

They made ready to depart. Vivi was clinging to Aline's arm, evidently completely dazed at her sudden contact with the whirl of life, for she had spent most of her years in the convent. As they passed into the hall and toward the front of the house, she kept muttering a prayer to herself under her breath.

At the end of the hall, Stetton, who was in front, stopped and knocked on a door leading to a room on the left. After a moment's wait a gruff voice sounded:

"Come in."

Stetton looked at Aline. She nodded, and all three of them passed inside.

The man with the beard was seated in a chair by the window, holding in his hand what appeared to be a photograph. As the newcomers entered and he caught sight of the women he rose to his feet and bowed.

"We stopped to give you our thanks and to say good-by," said Stetton. "I assure you, sir—"

"You! *Mon Dieu!*"

The cry came from Aline.

At the same moment that it reached his ears Stetton saw the face of the man with the beard grow livid with violent emotion, and his eyes flashed fire. The next instant, before Stetton had time to move, the man with the beard had leaped past him to the door, which he locked, putting the key in his pocket.

Aline had at first started for the door, but, intercepted in that attempt, had retreated to the other side of the room, where she stood behind a heavy table at a safe distance; and when the man with the beard turned after locking the door he found himself looking straight into the muzzle of a revolver, held firmly in her small, white hand.

Stetton and Vivi stood speechless with astonishment, unable to speak or move.

"Stand where you are, Vasili." It was Aline's voice, calm and terrible. "If you move I shall shoot!"

"Bah!" said the man with the beard, with supreme contempt. Nevertheless, he stood still. "You may shoot if you like; you will not hit me, and you will not escape me. Fate will see to that.

"It has sent you to me, daughter of hell that you are! I am coming; you know my strength, Marie; I am going to choke the life out of your lying throat with these fingers."

As he moved a step forward he extended his hands in a terrible gesture of menace and hate.

"Look out, Vasili—not a step!"

Disregarding the warning, he leaped forward with incredible agility for his ponderous frame.

As he did so the report of the revolver sounded loud and deafening in the small room, and the man with the beard, halted midway in his leap for vengeance, dropped to the floor with a bullet in his side.

Aline stood motionless, with the smoking barrel leveled at the prostrate form. "See if he is dead, Stetton," she said calmly.

The young man jerked himself forward, crying. "Good Heavens! Aline, what have you done?"

"Fool!" she exclaimed, "does the sound of a pistol frighten you?" Then, moving round the table and looking at the form on the floor: "And so, Vasili, you found me. So much the worse for you."

Suddenly the form moved, and, muttering a dreadful curse, the man tried to rise to his knees, but sank back helpless.

"So? You are not dead?" said Aline in a tone indescribable.

She raised the revolver and pointed it at the head of the wounded man. But Stetton sprang across and, snatching the revolver from her hand, threw it out of the window before she could pull the trigger. Then he shrank back before Aline's furious glance.

"Aline! Aline!" Vivi was crying. "Aline!"

"Silence, Vivi!" The young woman turned to Stetton. "We are ready now to go."

"But he may be dying! We cannot leave him—"

"Let us hope so. But for you I would have finished him. Take us to General Nirzann's."

Stetton, completely subdued by the tone of her voice and the imperious look of her eyes, opened the door, taking the key from the pocket of the man with the beard, not without a shudder, and let them pass out before him.

Aline had her arm around the shoulder of Vivi, whose face was deadly pale.

Stetton followed, after a last hasty glance at the prostrate form on the floor, and a moment later they were making their way down the street toward the headquarters of the general.

~

CHAPTER III

Marisi

OFTEN, UNWITTINGLY, the shepherd leads his flock, or a member of it, straight into the jaws of the wolf. Similarly Stetton conducted Aline and Vivi before the gaze of General Paul Nirzann.

If he had been only partially acquainted with the fashionable gossip of Marisi he would have taken them to sleep in the fields in preference.

They found the general in the room where Stetton had had his interview an hour before.

By this time the group of officers had increased to a dozen or more, and the building was filled with an air of bustle and activity, incident, no doubt, to the transfer of the command which was to take place at noon. Orderlies were hurrying to and fro, and the telegraph instrument clicked continuously, while the low hum of voices was heard on every side.

An orderly approached the general:

"Richard Stetton asks to see you, sir."

The general looked up. "Is he alone?"

"No, sir; two women are with him."

"Show them in."

A minute passed, while General Nirzann busied himself with the inventory of ordnance to be handed over to his successor. Then, hearing an ejaculation of astonishment from the officers near the door, he looked up sharply.

Aline Solini had entered the room, followed by Vivi and Stetton.

The eyes of General Paul Nirzann widened in an involuntary stare as they rested on the face of the young woman, while the officers crowded together near the table with murmurs of admiration, which caused a flush of resentment to mount to Stetton's brow, and Vivi shrank closer to him, trembling.

Aline stood perfectly composed, though her face was slightly pale.

"Are these the women who desire the passports?" asked the general, looking at Stetton.

"Yes, sir."

The general regarded them for a moment in silence, then spoke to Aline:

"What is your name?"

"Solini—Aline Solini."

"And yours?"

But Vivi could not utter a syllable, and Aline answered for her:

"Mlle. Vivi Janvour."

"Where do you wish to go?"

"Warsaw."

"You were residing, I believe, in the convent. Are you citizens of Fasilica?"

"No, sir."

"Where do you come from?"

Aline hesitated perceptibly before she answered:

"I am from Odessa."

"And Mlle. Janvour?"

"She is from Paris. Her father, now dead, was Pierre Janvour, a French diplomat."

"You say you are from Odessa?"

"Yes, sir."

"Are you married?"

"No—that is—I am not."

The eyes of the general narrowed.

"You seem to be in doubt on the question," he observed dryly.

"I beg your pardon, sir"—Aline's eyes flashed with resentment—
"I said I am not married."

"Very well, very well," The general was silent for a moment,
then he continued: "I think, *mademoiselle,* I should like to question
you further—alone. Gentlemen, leave us."

The officers went out in a body, with backward glances at Aline;
then the general rang for an orderly and told him to conduct Stetton
and Vivi to another room. Stetton opened his mouth to protest, but
was stopped by a glance from Aline, which said plainly: "Be easy; I
can handle him."

As he waited with Vivi in a room at the further end of the hall,
Stetton was consumed with impatience at the delay. He had before
his eyes a picture of the man with the beard lying wounded on the
floor, and he wanted only one thing now: to get out of Fasilica, and
that as soon as possible.

What if he had been only slightly injured—what if he had followed them and was even now entering the headquarters of the
general? He went to the door of the room and looked down the
hall; no one was to be seen but the guard at the entrance.

"After all, Aline was right; I was a fool to interfere," he muttered.

"I beg your pardon; what did you say?"

It was Vivi's voice; he had forgotten her presence.

"Nothing," he answered, turning. "I was thinking aloud."

Presently the girl spoke again:

"Do you know who that—that man was, M. Stetton?"

"What man?" Stetton affected not to understand.

"The one—we left—back there."

"No." Stetton looked at her. "Do you?"

"No. I know nothing. How could Aline do it? You heard—she would not allow me to speak to her on the way here. She has been so good—I have always loved her so!"

"Did you know her before she came to the convent?" asked Stetton.

"No. I saw her first there. I was not allowed to be with her, and she used to come to my room at night to talk. She was there last night when the soldiers came—and you."

There was something in the last two words that sounded pleasantly in Stetton's ears. He looked at the girl.

"So that was your room?"

"Yes. I have lived there ever since I could remember. It was so pleasant after Aline came, and now—" Vivi shuddered and turned away.

"Now it will be pleasanter still," declared Stetton, "as soon as we get away from Fasilica. You will see. You know nothing of pleasure, child."

He was surprised to hear her cry:

"But I do! And I am not a child!"

"No?" he said, amused. "Pardon me, Mlle. Janvour."

He walked to the door again and looked down the hall. It remained empty.

"What the deuce can they be doing?" he muttered, and took to pacing up and down the room.

Vivi had seated herself in a chair, and her face betrayed an anxiety as keen as his own. For twenty minutes or more they continued to wait thus in silence, and Stetton had about decided to investigate for himself when the orderly appeared at the door to announce that General Nirzann requested his presence.

Vivi accompanied him. They found the general still seated at the

table, while Aline occupied a chair at one end. As they entered, the
general rose to his feet and bowed politely, while Aline sent a reassuring smile to Vivi.

"I beg your pardon, *mademoiselle*," said General Nirzann, "for
having subjected you to an inconvenience that you perhaps regarded as a discourtesy. Believe me, it was not so intended. Mlle. Solini
has explained everything satisfactorily."

Stetton sighed with relief.

"And the passports?"

"They will not be necessary, M. Stetton. Mlle. Solini has
changed her mind—the privilege of every woman. She is going to
Marisi; and, since I myself leave for that place this afternoon, she has
done me the honor to accept the protection of my escort."

Stetton started with anger.

"So that is what—" he began violently, but was interrupted by
Aline's voice:

"We shall expect you to accompany us, M. Stetton. Vivi, too, of
course."

"But I thought you wanted to go to Warsaw!" the young man
protested; then, catching a significant glance from Aline, he checked
himself and said: "Of course, as the general says, you have a right to
change your mind. And, since I have nothing else to do, I shall be
glad to go with you."

This apparently did not please General Nirzann; he frowned at
Stetton with evident hostility, saying: "It is not necessary."
Whereupon the young man smiled provokingly.

"Nevertheless, as Mlle. Solini invites me, I shall go. And now, sir,
we must leave you; the ladies have not breakfasted."

"They can breakfast here," said the general.

"Nor I."

"Well—and you, too."

Stetton hesitated. He wanted to refuse, but caution advised

otherwise. At this moment, he reflected, the man with the beard, breathing vengeance, might be searching the streets for its object; decidedly they were safer where they were, especially under the protection of the general. He ended by accepting.

Breakfast was served to them in a room on the floor above by General Nirzann's personal steward—fruit and eggs and rich, yellow cream from some neighboring farm.

They ate in silence; once or twice Stetton started to speak, but was halted by a glance from Aline, with a nod at the steward. Then, when they were finished and the dishes had been cleared away, she sent Vivi to the other end of the room and turned to him with a smile.

"You look angry, *monsieur*—and full of words. Now you may talk."

"Have I not reason to be?"

"Angry?"

"Yes."

"What is it?"

"Good Heavens!" Stetton burst out. "Have I not seen you mur—"

"Stop!" Aline's eyes flashed. "You are not happy in your choice of terms. It was in self-defense. He would have killed me."

"Not when he was lying on the floor helpless," retorted Stetton. "I cannot help my choice of terms. You would have murdered him."

"I do not deny it," said Aline calmly. "And I do not regret it. He is not fit to live."

"Who is he?"

"Did I not say I had an enemy?"

"Oh," said Stetton slowly, "it was—the one you told me of?" Aline nodded, and he continued: "But I might have guessed it. Then—of course I cannot know—nor can I blame you."

A smile appeared on Aline's lips, and she stretched out her hand and placed it on his as it lay on the arm of his chair.

"You trust me, do you not?" she whispered; and Stetton, gazing into her eyes, forgot to look for a meaning in her words.

Presently he said:

"Still, I failed you. You must laugh at me when you remember that I offered you my protection. It was a sorry bargain you made, *mademoiselle.*"

"I do not think so," said Aline, with her inscrutable smile. "I know why you say that—because I accepted the protection of General Nirzann. But was it not best? Our bargain still holds; I—I do not wish to forget it"—Stetton seized her hand—"and you may still fulfil your part. Did you not say you are an American?"

Stetton nodded, wondering.

"Then," Aline continued, "perhaps it will soon be necessary that you return to your own country?"

"No," said Stetton.

"I suppose you are rich, like all Americans?"

"I am worth ten millions," said the young man impressively. His caution did not extend to his father's money.

"Francs, of course?"

"No, dollars," said Stetton.

"Well, that is not what I wish to talk of," said Aline, who had found out what she wanted to know. "It is this: I have accepted General Nirzann's escort because he declares that without it we would be unable to get ten miles from Fasilica. The country is devastated, and the railroad runs no farther than Tsevor. We must leave Fasilica, so what could I do?"

"It is best, I suppose," muttered Stetton.

"There was another reason," Aline continued, regarding the young man speculatively, "why I accepted General Nirzann's offer. You will be surprised—so was I. He is my cousin."

Stetton turned quickly.

"Your cousin!"

"Yes, a distant one. He is a cousin of my mother. We discovered it quite by accident, while he was questioning me in your absence. I had never seen him before, but he established the fact."

Aline smiled.

"So you see I have a relative, after all."

Stetton looked at her curiously. The truth was, he doubted her, and he was searching for a corroboration of his doubt in her face.

She met his gaze unfalteringly. He ended by believing, and made some remark concerning the strangeness of the coincidence by which she had found this unknown relative.

"Yes," said Aline composedly, "it had been so long since I had heard of him that I had forgotten his very existence.

"But," she added, "notwithstanding the fact that he is my cousin, I do not trust him. He said—it is not necessary to repeat his words, but I want you near me till we arrive safely at Marisi. You see, I trust you."

Stetton, who had not completely lost his reason, tried to tell himself that the timidity of this speech fitted ill with the resolute and terrible action of Aline Solini but two hours before; but what could he do?

Her eyes were now gazing into his with an expression at once tender and appealing, and her hand again sought his and pressed it gently.

"Then it is settled," she said, crossing to the window and looking down into the street. "We leave with General Nirzann this afternoon. Vivi! Come here, child. We must make up a list of things we will need for the journey."

Stetton started up from his chair, exclaiming: "I was a fool not to have thought of that! Of course, you will need—here is my purse. Take what you want."

"Thank you, General Nirzann has already come to our rescue," said Aline. "An orderly is coming at noon for my list."

"And you accepted!" Stetton exclaimed angrily.

"Why not? It was kind of him."

The two women began to write down the names of the articles they desired, and Stetton turned away. A vague sense of uneasiness and danger was within him; he did not know why exactly, but he began to ask himself questions.

This Aline Solini, who and what was she? Why did he feel, as though it were a natural law of his being, that he must follow her and await her pleasure? Young as he was, and cautious, he had not been without affairs of love, but he had always congratulated himself that no woman had ever made a fool of him. And, he had added, never would.

It was evident to him that General Nirzann, too, had been fascinated by her. This increased his uneasiness. Clearly, he would be a fool to have anything more to do with her; he saw before him the form of the man with the beard lying on the floor, with the revolver pointed at his head, and he shuddered.

Then he thought of what she had just said—of her abrupt question concerning his fortune. "She is a schemer, an adventuress," he thought, "and she is too much for me. I will not go to Marisi."

But, looking at Aline, and meeting her eyes, he felt his resolution waver within him. He crossed the room to her side and began to discuss arrangements for the journey.

Three o'clock that afternoon found them ready to depart. They were to travel on horseback to Tsevor, thirty miles away, where they would take train for Marisi. A hundred troopers were to conduct them; a precaution rendered necessary by the wildness of the country and the hostility of its inhabitants to those who had allied themselves with the Turks.

Aline and Vivi, attired in coarse black suits, the best costume obtainable in Fasilica, were mounted on ponies from the mountains— raw, hungry-looking animals, while Stetton had been given an old black troop-horse. General Nirzann rode a magnificent white Arabian.

The formalities were few: a salute from some five hundred soldiers drawn up at attention, and they were off down the main street of Fasilica. As they passed the convent, Stetton saw tears in Vivi's eyes as she gave a last, long look at the ruins of what had sheltered her for so many years.

Aline's face was set straight ahead, without so much as a farewell glance.

Half of the escort of troopers rode ahead as a vanguard, while the remainder brought up the rear, riding in fours. This until they reached the mountains; then they were forced to ride in single file by the narrowness of the trail, which at times hung to the side of a steep precipice, hardly more than a shelf.

Two hours it took them to pass the range, and then they found themselves again in a level, winding valley—the valley of the Schino River, which has so often been the scene of bloody conflicts in that war-infested region.

It was a little past seven o'clock when they clattered on to the pavement of the main street of Tsevor. Vivi, who rode at Stetton's side, was greatly fatigued by the unusual and violent exercise, and was barely able to keep her seat in the saddle.

Stetton himself was angry and in ill humor, for General Nirzann had monopolized Aline's company throughout the journey. As he alighted at the railroad station and helped Vivi to dismount, he tried to persuade himself once more to end the matter by returning with the troopers to Fasilica; but he heard the general's little speech of farewell and saw the men turn and ride off, without hinting at any such intention.

A courier had been sent ahead in the morning to arrange for a private car, and they found everything in readiness. They entered it at once and in haste, for a good-sized crowd had collected on the platform at their arrival, and were amusing themselves by hurling insults and epithets at the head of General Nirzann, who took his seat in his compartment with a scowl, muttering something about "revenge on the scurvy rascals."

Aline and Vivi had a compartment together toward the front of the car; Stetton's was in the rear. A few minutes after they had arrived the train pulled out.

Stetton sank back in the seat of his compartment with a feeling of utter dejection and depression. Something indefinable seemed to weigh upon his heart with a suffocating pressure; something seemed to be saying to him, "Do not go to Marisi."

He tried to shake this feeling off, but it would not leave. He raised the window and allowed the cool night air to rush in against his face, but the desolate blackness without seemed to bring with it a voice that said: "Do not go to Marisi."

He closed the window with a bang, muttering: "This is ridiculous. Am I a weak fool, to allow myself to be afraid of nothing? One might think that Marisi was the home of the devil himself. If it gets too hot for me I can get to Berlin in eighteen hours."

He composed himself with an effort and began to doze, and finally fell sound asleep.

Six hours later he was awakened by some one opening the door of his compartment. It was Vivi. She watched him with a little smile on her face as he opened his eyes.

"What is it—what is it?" asked Stetton, rubbing his eyes.

Vivi replied:

"Aline sent me to wake you. She is the only one who did not sleep. We have reached Marisi."

CHAPTER IV

The Wheel Starts Slowly

*I*T WAS late in the morning of the following day when Stetton awoke after four hours' sleep in a luxurious room of the Hotel Walderin, Marisi, and, rising, walked to an open window which looked out on an open court of the hotel.

All his depression of the night before was gone; he felt buoyant, confident, and he was humming a lively popular tune as he thrust his head into a basin of cold water with a little shiver of pleasure.

At Fasilica and Tsevor he had felt more or less out of the world, away from the safeguards and conventions of civilization; now he was in a fashionable hotel in Walderin Place, as much a part of European life as Hyde Park or the Bois de Boulogne.

This fact drove away his nonsensical fears; he laughed aloud at them. And, he was reflecting, on the floor immediately above was sleeping a young and beautiful woman, as his guest.

He laughed aloud again, in great good humor with himself and the world, and began to dress. What a divine creature! Was she not worth any price? He asked himself this question with an air of bravado to frighten away what doubt remained.

Marry her? Gad! Who would not? Such an opportunity comes only by miraculous luck. This was his thought.

An hour later he presented himself before Aline and Vivi in the drawing-room of their apartment.

"We breakfasted here," said Aline in answer to his question. "How could we go downstairs? We have no clothes."

"I forgot—of course," said Stetton, a little embarrassed. Then he added with a touch of malice: "But what of the general's list?"

Aline laughed at his tone, then said with a smile:

"You are wrong to be angry with me; we needed his help, and it was necessary to humor him."

"Well, as for the clothes—I shall send someone from Morel's. Will that do?"

"That will do excellently."

"And you, *mademoiselle,* is there anything else you require?"

"Nothing," said Vivi quietly.

She was standing by Aline's chair, with her large, dark eyes passing from one to the other as they spoke.

There was an air of watchfulness about her; Stetton had noticed it before, but it appeared to be the result merely of childish and innocent curiosity.

He wished that she would leave the room; he felt constrained in her presence, and there were several questions he wanted to ask Aline. He lingered a while longer, making observations on nothing in particular, then left to perform the errand at Morel's, saying that he would return in the afternoon. As he went out he laid a bank-note on a small pedestal near the door.

As soon as the door had closed behind him Aline crossed the room with quick steps and picked up the bank-note. It was for five thousand francs. Smiling, she placed it in her dress.

"What is that?" asked Vivi curiously.

Aline told her. She looked puzzled.

"But why should he give us so much money? What can we do with it?"

"You little goose," said Aline, and there was genuine affection in her tone; "you are no longer in a convent. Wait; you will see. Luck is with me now; it is all I needed. Ah, Vasili—" her eyes became cold and her tone hardened—"you taught me—others will pay for you."

"All the same, we should not take that money," said the girl stubbornly.

"Listen, Vivi." Aline looked at her speculatively, as though trying to decide what to say. Then she continued: "You know I love you."

"I know," said Vivi, taking her hand.

"You know I would do only what I think best. I am wiser than you."

"I know," Vivi repeated.

"And you do not think I did wrong when—last night."

"No, I no longer think you did wrong; but it was horrible."

"Well, you must trust me." Aline patted the girl's hand gently. "You must not ask me to explain things. As for M. Stetton's money—I will tell you about that. But it is a great secret. You must not mention it."

"How could I? I know no one."

"You know General Nirzann; and you must not speak of it to M. Stetton. He does not wish it to be known. I accept his money because I am going to marry him."

Vivi hastily drew her hand away and looked up with startled eyes.

"You are going to marry him?" she said slowly.

Aline answered: "Yes. Does it surprise you? What is the matter, child?"

Vivi's face had grown pale and she seemed to be trembling. But she soon controlled her emotion and said:

"I am so glad. Aline. Do you love him?"

"Yes," replied the woman with her peculiar, inscrutable smile. "But, remember, you must say nothing of what I told you."

"No; I promise," said Vivi. Her face was still pale and she seemed to be forcing her voice to be calm.

At that moment a servant appeared to announce that a messenger from Morel's asked to see Mlle. Solini. He was admitted at once, and they were soon busily examining samples of dresses, suits, cloaks, and lingerie.

Vivi held back at first, but it was not long before she had entered the performance with as great delight as Aline herself.

In the meantime Stetton, having called at Morel's and performed two or three errands on his own account, was walking along the sunny side of the fashionable drive which stretches away to the north from Walderin Place.

On this side was the park, on the other a long line of sumptuous dwellings, the most important of which was the white marble palace of the Prince of Marisi. It was too early for anyone to be seen; the Drive was practically deserted."

"Hang it all," Stetton was saying to himself as he walked along, "that little Vivi is not at all bad-looking, but she is in the way. Something must be done with her. I wonder if Naumann is in town."

On his way back to the hotel he stopped at the German legation and asked for Frederick Naumann. He was told that his friend would not be in till late in the afternoon, and he resumed his walk along the Drive, now impatient for the time when he should see Aline again.

A little after one o'clock found him in her apartment.

She and Vivi were both quite transformed by their purchases of the morning—so much so that Stetton felt a thrill of joy and pride run through him as he advanced to take the hand of this wondrously beautiful woman who had accept his protection and his money.

He wanted everyone to see her; he wanted to tell people that she belonged to him. Above all, he wanted her; though always he felt a curious sense of uneasiness in her presence.

Instinct was trying to do for him what reason would have done for a wiser man, who, looking at Aline Solini, would have said: "She is that most dangerous thing in the world—a woman with the face of an angel and the heart of a demon. Beware!"

Stetton approached her, saying:

"Now, indeed, you are irresistible."

"The least I could do was my best for you," replied Aline.

"And Vivi, too!" said Stetton. "*Mademoiselle,* allow me to say that you are charming."

The girl bowed without replying as she retreated to a seat at the farther end of the room.

Stetton cast a meaning glance at her, saying to Aline:

"I want to talk with you."

She smiled, reading him with her eyes.

"Yes," she agreed; "it is necessary that we come to an understanding."

She sent Vivi away on some pretext or other and again turned to Stetton:

"Well, *monsieur?*"

But, despite his firm resolution of the morning, the young man could find nothing to say, now that he found himself alone with her. He hesitated, seeming to search for words, and finally ended by stammering out:

"You know—you know—"

Aline laughed outright:

"You are an awkward lover, Stetton!"

This brought Stetton to a standstill and left him without any-thing to say. He burst out brutally:

"Well, you promised to marry me, and I can't wait. You prom-ised me."

Aline said coolly:

"If you can't wait, really I am sorry. I see that you have greatly misjudged me. I will not detain you longer. Good-by, *monsieur.*"

"What do you mean?" cried Stetton, frightened at the thought of losing her.

"You are too impatient. You approach me like a savage with a club; you have no tact, no finesse; in a word, I am disappointed in you, and we had best part while we are friends."

"But that is impossible!"

"Impossible?"

"Yes, it is indeed!" The young man's anxiety made him eloquent—that, and her exquisite face so close to his own. "Good Heavens, I love you! How can I leave you? I see plainly I have made a mistake, but you will forgive me—you must forgive me. I will be patient—I swear it! Tell me you will not send me away!"

"You love me, then?"

"You know it! Devotedly!"

Aline smiled and he seized her hand.

"I may stay?" he cried.

"I don't know," said Aline, assuming a tone of doubt, for she was now sure of him. "I did not wish to forget our bargain—you may believe that, Stetton. But I must have my own time."

"You will see—I shall be patient."

"Then—"

Aline extended her hand, and he pressed it to his lips, kissing the fingers and palm over and over.

She continued slowly, as though picking her words: "It is only fair you should know why I desire a delay. I mean the particular reason—it is Vivi."

"Vivi?"

"Yes. I love her, and I feel that I am responsible for her welfare, which means in the case of a young girl like her, her marriage. I will never have another opportunity like the present.

"General Nirzann"—Stetton started slightly at the name—"has promised to introduce me into the best circles of Marisi, and it will be strange if I cannot find a match for her. Then I shall be ready to leave Marisi—with you, if you still desire it."

"But General Nirzann—why should he do this?" demanded Stetton in astonishment.

"I have made a friend of him. Besides, is he not my cousin? Be easy; you have no reason to be jealous; he is an old fool. I can manage him."

"I don't like it," Stetton muttered.

Aline laughed.

"Surely you have not so poor an opinion of yourself as to fear an old fossil like the general? You should know better—if I did not prefer you to any other—but there, I shall confess too much."

She glanced into his eyes and then quickly away, as though afraid of betraying her thoughts.

"Confess!" cried Stetton. "Ah, tell me!"

"What can I say?" She pretended to hesitate, and actually succeeded in bringing a pink flush to her face.

"Tell me you love me!"

"Well, then—I do—a little."

Stetton clasped her in his arms. She submitted to the embrace for a moment, then drew herself away.

"But there—you know you must be patient."

"I cannot promise that," said Stetton, breathing quickly. "But I

shall not annoy you. You are worth waiting for a lifetime; you will
see if I mean what I say. In the meantime I must see you every day—
you cannot deny me that—and I can help you."

"Yes, you can help, now that you are sensible," said Aline with a
tender and provoking smile.

"No other pleasure is worth a thought," said Stetton, completely bewitched. "Tell me, what can I do?"

Aline had been waiting for that question. She glanced at him
narrowly through her eyelashes, saying:

"There are so many things I don't know where to begin. Of
course, it is all a matter of money."

"Of course," Stetton agreed, kissing her fingers.

"In the first place," Aline continued, "If my plans for Vivi are to
be successful, we cannot live in a hotel, even the Walderin. We must
have a house on the Drive, with a carriage and servants."

Stetton looked up quickly, frowning. He had not thought of
beginning on such a scale. The rent alone would amount to fifty
thousand francs. "But I don't see why—" he began.

"Luckily, that difficulty is settled," Aline interrupted quickly,
noting his frown. "General Nirzann has offered me the use of his
house, since he expects to occupy rooms in Marisi Palace for some
time. He is a bachelor, you know. It is very good of him."

The fact was, General Nirzann was so far from being the owner
of a house on the Drive that he was a pauper, but Stetton did not
know that. What he thought was that under no circumstances should
Aline live in a house belonging to the general. He said sarcastically:

"Yes, I have no doubt it was a very kind offer. But you must not
accept it."

"I have already done so," said Aline.

"Then you must reconsider and decline."

"Stetton, you are positively childish. Besides, I must have the
house."

There was a slight pause before the young man said:

"Then I will rent one."

Aline lowered her eyes, that he might not see the light of triumph in them, saying:

"It will be expensive."

"I can afford it," replied Stetton.

"It must be furnished."

"Of course."

"And we shall need a carriage and servants."

"Certainly."

"Then it is settled?"

For reply, Stetton kissed her hand. They talked a while longer, discussing the details of this new arrangement; then the young man made ready to go. At the door he turned, saying:

"By the way, I have a friend or two in Marisi; you will allow me to introduce them to you?"

Then, as Aline answered in the affirmative, he went away to his room on the floor below. There he sat down to write a letter to his father in New York, containing a request for a fifty-thousand-dollar draft.

An hour later, as Aline sat revolving her plans in her mind, with a smile that meant danger for anyone who got in the way of them, a servant entered with the card of General Paul Nirzann. Aline took the card, while the smile became deeper. Then she said:

"Show him up."

In a few moments the general entered. Though he held himself erect as he walked across the room to bend over Aline's hand, his bearing was more that of a beau than a soldier. His gait was mincing and he wore a smirk on his face.

After greeting him, Aline said:

"Have you made your peace with the prince?"

"Perfectly," replied General Nirzann with a wave of the hand.

"The prince read me a lecture on the brutalities of the campaign, and then opened his arms to me. It is impossible to avoid cruelty when you are allied with the Turks, and I told him so. You may believe he did not like it, but I crammed the truth down his throat."

Aline smiled at the idea of this popinjay cramming anything down another man's throat. She said:

"Why didn't he return you to the command?"

"He preferred to keep me in Marisi," replied the general. "The fact is, he can hardly do without me. When I am not at the palace everything goes wrong. He admits it."

"I see."

"And besides," he continued, "I preferred to stay. He was a little surprised at that, but he has never seen you, *mademoiselle*. He does not know the attraction that Marisi holds for me."

"But he will," thought Aline to herself. She said aloud: "It is good of you to say so, my dear general."

"Tut!" said the general. "There is no sense in that. Nor is there any goodness in me. Ask the ladies of Marisi—they could tell things that would astonish you. You know very well I love you, *mademoiselle*."

"Yes; you have told me so," said Aline, trying not to appear impatient.

This was the general's side of the question, and she wanted to talk on her own. After a short pause she added:

"I suppose you did not mention my name to the prince?"

"Good Heavens, no!"

"I presume that will come later?"

"Much later," said the general emphatically. "We must proceed with caution."

"It is just as well. It will take a week or so, at least, to obtain a house and make the necessary preparations. After that—"

"Have you hooked the American?" the general interrupted.

Aline shrugged her shoulders.

"Of course. And paid him with promises. He is at this moment searching for a house."

The general cackled with amusement.

"The young fool!" he snorted gleefully. "He doesn't know women, that's sure. The way with them is, pay first and maybe afterward. Eh, *mademoiselle?*"

"It is evident that you do know women," said Aline.

She was wondering to herself when the old fool would stop his chatter and allow her to gain some information. After a short pause she said abruptly:

"And now, what of our conspiracy?"

The general looked puzzled as he repeated: "Our conspiracy?"

"Yes. When is my first dinner party?"

"Tomorrow, if you wish." The general bowed gallantly. "You may count on me."

"Thank you," said Aline with a touch of irritation. "But you know very well what I mean."

"Yes, I know what you mean. But are you not pushing things a little, *mademoiselle?*"

"Why delay?"

"Because it is necessary."

"I do not understand that. The season has begun; the sooner we take advantage of it the better."

The general looked at her with something between a simper and a frown; then he said:

"You seem to forget something."

"What is that?"

"My happiness."

"But, my dear general, that is absurd."

The general sighed. *"Chere amie,"* he said, "will you come to dinner with me this evening?"

"I have no clothes."

"That is true. Then I suppose I must wait."

Aline whispered:

"Wait until I am mistress in my own house, and you will see, my brave soldier."

"Divine creature!" the general reiterated, trying to give himself the appearance of one dying for love.

"Still, you try to bargain with me," said Aline.

"Who would not bargain where possible to gain heaven?" exclaimed the general.

"Really, you are in danger of making me think you love me."

"Do I not?"

Aline smiled. "Perhaps."

"But it is certain!" cried General Nirzann fiercely. "You think I bargain with you—well, that is because I love you. Do not think I have been idle in your behalf. As I was coming to the hotel I met Mme. Chébe on the Drive, and I spoke to her of you. You will probably receive her card within the first week at your house, and she is one of the six most important women in Marisi."

"My dear general," cried Aline.

The general was unable to meet her flashing eyes.

"You intoxicate me!" he murmured, half dazzled.

And when five minutes later, General Paul Nirzann left the Hotel Walderin he was hardly able to walk straight for the dizzy exaltation in his brain.

As for Aline, she remained in the chair where the general had left her, with her chin resting on the palm of her hand. Her eyes were narrowed in deep speculation and a peculiar smile appeared on her lips.

But her thoughts were not of Richard Stetton, who at that moment had just finished the last paragraph of a six-page letter to New York, nor of General Nirzann, who was strolling along with an erect figure and a satisfied smile.

No; they had traveled down the fashionable drive to the white marble palace of the Prince of Marisi.

CHAPTER V

Naumann Tells a Tale

THE FOLLOWING morning found Stetton running from one end of Marisi to the other in search of a house suitable as a setting for his jewel. So he phrased it to himself.

Owing to the fact that the fashionable season had begun two weeks before, he found his task by no means an easy one. All day he searched and the better part of the day following; then quite by chance he ran across an old rugged stone structure at one end of the town, in the worst possible repair and filled with musty furniture. He hastened to the hotel to report to Aline.

"But that will not do at all," said she when he told her where the house was. "It would be much better to stay here. We must positively be on the Drive."

Stetton declared that to be impossible, saying that a house on the Drive could not be procured for love or money.

"Nevertheless, we must have it," was her calm reply.

"But I tell you we can't get it!" cried Stetton with pardonable irritation, as he thought of his weary two days' search.

"Then," said Aline, "it will be necessary to accept General Nirzann's offer. It would have been better to do that in the first place."

But Stetton would not hear of it.

"He is too much in evidence already," he muttered angrily, pacing the length of the room. "I don't like it."

"Nevertheless," Aline insisted, "we must have the house."

"Very well," said Stetton, stopping in front of her, "then we'll get it. Give me one more day. If there's no other way, I'll rent the blooming palace itself. I understand the prince is hard up for cash."

"Now, I admire you!" cried Aline. "I could never love a man without spirit."

She allowed him to kiss her hand.

The following morning he set out again. He would have enlisted the services of his friend Frederick Naumann, of the German legation, but for the fact that he had been told the day before that Naumann was spending a week in Berlin. He had inquired at every possible source, and now took to wandering about more or less at random. By noon he had found nothing, and began to fear that he must perforce allow Aline to accept the hospitality of General Nirzann.

Early in the afternoon, at the Hotel Humbert, he was told by some one that there was a possibility of obtaining for the season the house of M. Henri Duroy, at 341 the Drive.

Stetton hastened to the address as fast as a six-cylinder motor-car could take him. He was shown in to M. Duroy himself. Yes, M. Duroy would let his house—he had been called to Paris by the sudden death of his brother. Of course, M. Stetton could furnish the proper references? Very good. The rent would be seventy-five thousand francs.

Stetton made a rapid calculation.

"Fifteen thousand dollars!" he muttered to himself—he was able to think only in dollars. "Good Heavens! It's robbery!"

But he paid it—to keep Aline from accepting an offer that had never been made to live in a house that did not exist.

Four days later—for they had to wait for M. Duroy to depart for
Paris—Stetton took Aline and Vivi to inspect their new home.

It was a three-story structure of blue granite, somewhat imposing,
and in the very best locality. On the ground floor were a reception-
hall, drawing-room, library, and dining-room; the floors above held
the sleeping apartments and servants' quarters.

Aline was frankly delighted, sending Stetton eloquent looks and
words of gratitude that drove all thought of the seventy-five thousand francs from his mind.

"These rooms," he observed—they were in the chambers on the
second floor—"are exactly the thing for you and Vivi. I shall take the
one in the rear. It is not large, but that is of no importance."

Aline looked at him in genuine astonishment.

"But that is impossible!" she cried. "Surely you did not imagine
you are to live here with us!"

It was Stetton's turn to be astonished.

"Not live with you!" he exclaimed. "Where, then, should I
live?"

"I suppose at the hotel."

They began to argue the matter; Stetton with a bluntness that
caused Aline to send Vivi from the room. He was stubborn; Aline was
persistent; finally she declared she would abandon everything.

"Very well," said Stetton sulkily. "There is no good arguing the
matter. I shall live at the hotel."

Frowning, he moved to a window, gazing out on the Drive with
his back turned.

Aline crossed to him, smiling.

"You must not be angry with me," she said in a low voice softly.

Then she placed her arms around his neck and kissed him on
the back of the head.

Turning, Stetton clasped her roughly in his arms and held her
close.

"Would you care?" he demanded.

Aline whispered: "You know I would."

"Do you know something?" said Stetton between his teeth. "It makes me crazy just to look at you—and to feel you—like this—"

"I know—ah, do I not?" Aline drew herself gently away. "But there—I shall confess too much."

"Confess!" cried Stetton. "Tell me you love me!"

There was a noise from behind; Vivi was returning.

"Well, then—I do—a little," Aline whispered. Then, moving away, she went with Vivi to explore the room above.

"Vivi—always Vivi!" Stetton muttered.

Three days later found Aline and Vivi in possession of the house of M. Duroy. Stetton had kept his room at the Hotel Walderin. As for the expenses of the household on the Drive, he had settled that question in what he would have called a businesslike manner.

"I have arranged for a limousine and an open carriage," he told Aline, "and will pay the chauffeur and coachman myself. The other servants will be six hundred francs a month. The table fifteen hundred francs—for you will want good dinners; dress, a thousand; and incidentals, a thousand more. The first of each month I will give you five thousand francs; that will more than cover everything."

Aline thanked him with a kiss; but when he had gone she laughed scornfully. Then she said: "But I suppose I am wrong to blame him; it is the American way, but how detestable!"

She was alone in the library—a tasteful, quiet room, with its low, ebony cases, rich, dark carpets and paintings of the eighteenth century.

"At last," she said to herself, "I have room; I can breathe—and act."

She moved to the dining-room and stood gazing from the doorway with the eye of a general contemplating a field of battle. A smile of anticipatory triumph was on her lips as she walked to the reception-hall and began to mount the stairs to the rooms above.

She had not followed Stetton's suggestion concerning the arrangement of the sleeping chambers. With the exception of the little room in the rear, shut off from the others, which had been given to Vivi, she had taken the entire second floor for herself. A little manipulation of furniture and the result was a bedroom, a dressing-room, and a reception-boudoir. But Vivi had declared herself perfectly satisfied, saying that she had lived so long in the convent that even her one little room appeared frightfully large to her.

Late in the afternoon of the second day at their new home Aline and Vivi went for a drive in the open carriage. Never was toilet more carefully planned and executed than that of Mlle. Solini on this occasion, though she really had little need of it.

Her appearance on the Drive created a sensation that bade fair to become a triumph. Every one was staring at her; every one asked: "Who is she?" Vivi could not have served better as a foil if she had been selected for the purpose.

But the one carriage that Aline was looking for—the carriage of the Prince of Marisi—did not appear; and she ordered the coachman to drive home long before the line had begun to thin.

They had met Stetton, driving alone in his motorcar, and General Nirzann, who was seated by the side of a large, haughty-looking woman with enormous earrings and a wart on her nose.

Aline had returned the general's salutation with the merest inclination of her head; at Stetton's bow she had smiled pleasantly.

That evening General Nirzann called. When the servant entered with his card Aline turned to Vivi and said:

"Remember, Vivi, do not leave the room."

So the general was unable to make much progress in his own interests, and was forced to discuss the plans for Aline's assault on the society of Marisi. She got little satisfaction out of that; the general was cautious, and whenever she asked a leading question he would reply with a knowing smile that seemed to say: "Softly, *mademoiselle,* softly."

Aline said to herself after he had gone:

"Really, that little general is more astute than foolish. Is it possible that he is going to force my hand? Well, if I must, I must; but he shall pay dearly for it after." And her eyes flashed ominously.

In the meantime Stetton, not to be outdone in the business of intrigue, had concocted a little scheme of his own, though an inglorious one. He believed that it was the presence of Vivi that stood in the way of the fulfilment of his desires. His plan led to the removal of this difficulty.

Within an hour after Frederick Naumann's return to Marisi he received a call from Richard Stetton.

Naumann was a young and aspiring diplomat who counted on winning position with his wealth and talents. Stetton had met him a year before in Berlin, and had renewed the acquaintance during his short stay in Marisi previous to the departure of the army.

"But what are you doing here?" asked Naumann, after greetings had been exchanged. "Did the dogs of war bite you?"

"Not exactly," Stetton replied with a laugh. "The fact is, I have found the most beautiful woman in Europe."

"Indeed?" said the other skeptically. "But there is nothing wonderful about that—there are thousands of her. May I ask, has the lady found you?"

"Yes—and no. She is living in a house I have rented—the house of M. Duroy, at 341 the Drive. I have taken it for the season—perhaps longer."

Naumann whistled. "Lucky dog! But is she as beautiful as you say?"

"Ask any one in Marisi. The entire promenade stopped yester-day in confusion when she appeared. And I—well, the fact is, I am going to marry her."

"No."

"Yes. When you see her you will not blame me. She is wonder-ful. Nothing short of it. But it is to remain a secret for the present— our engagement, I mean. No one is to know of it. I count on your discretion."

"You may."

"And, besides that, I count on your help. She has a girl with her—a pretty little thing, about eighteen. Her name is Vivi Janvour. Aline has what she calls plans for Vivi's welfare, and I am supposed to linger in hope till they are accomplished."

Naumann smiled. "But why?"

"On account of General Nirzann. You know him, I believe. He is her cousin; at least, so she says. He is to stand sponsor for her in Marisi, and she is afraid that if he knows of her engagement to me he will decline the office. Besides, she talks some silly rot about not wanting Vivi along on the honeymoon, and that sort of thing. In short, she wants me to wait, and I don't feel like it."

"But what can I do?"

There was a pause while Stetton seemed to be searching for words. Finally he said:

"Well—the fact is—this little Vivi is not bad-looking."

"Ho!" Naumann's eyebrows lifted.

"And you, I believe, are not blind to the charms of the fair. What might come of it I do not pretend to say. Talk to her, drive with her, amuse her; at any rate, I want you to meet her; then we shall see."

"What kind of a girl is she?"

"The quiet, timid sort—lived all her life in a convent. But she is really pretty."

"My dear fellow, I really believe you expect me to marry this creature."

"By no means. I expect nothing. But, at any rate, you can see her—introduce your friends to her, start the ball rolling—I would consider it a great favor."

"I'll see her, of course," replied Naumann.

"That's all I ask of you—now. Dine with me tonight at the Walderin and we'll talk it over."

So much for Stetton's plan, crude and simple indeed, but nevertheless with a fair chance of success. Naumann was a good-looking young fellow, polished and graceful, with an air of cynicism that had made him a great favorite with young ladies under twenty.

The following morning Stetton called at No. 341. Aline received him graciously; she knew that his love must have something to feed on, even if it were only crumbs. Besides, she had an additional favor to obtain from him.

"I have a friend I would like to introduce," said Stetton. "Naumann—Frederick Naumann—secretary of the German legation. He knows every one in Marisi—that is, every one who counts—and he might be of some use to you."

"Bring him to see me," said Aline.

"Tomorrow?"

"Certainly."

They chatted for an hour or so, and Stetton stayed to lunch.

"This is delightful," he said, sitting down with Aline and Vivi; and he felt a thrill of pride and satisfied vanity as he thought that this was his house, these his servants, and that this beautiful woman had promised herself to him.

His was one of those natures that live as much on appearances as on realities. He was so filled with a sense of his royal power and generosity that Aline talked him out of another twenty thousand francs with comparative ease, pleading the poverty of her wardrobe.

On the following day, accordingly, Stetton conducted his friend Naumann to the house on the Drive.

Naumann went with a certain reluctance; but Stetton had befriended him—no matter how—on a certain occasion in Berlin, and for that reason he at least pretended to acquiesce.

After they had waited in the drawing-room for a quarter of an hour the ladies entered.

Aline was ravishing; she was never otherwise; but Stetton himself was struck by the appearance of Vivi, perhaps because he had never before taken the trouble to give her any particular notice.

Her dress was light blue, of some soft material that set off her slender figure to perfection; her face was filled with color and her eyes glowed.

"By Jove," Stetton thought to himself, "Naumann could certainly do worse!"

His friend was thinking the same thing as he heard Vivi's soft voice acknowledging Stetton's introduction.

But within fifteen minutes Stetton was telling himself that he had made a mistake; and, indeed, so it appeared; for as they sat chatting together, Naumann, seeming to forget that the declared object of his attack was Mlle. Janvour, kept his gaze riveted on the face of Mlle. Solini.

"I ought to have known better," said Stetton to himself. "Who could look at any one else when Aline is there?"

He tried to catch Naumann's eye, but the young diplomat took no notice of him.

Aline rang for tea.

"It is too early, I know," she said with a smile; "but we shall be driving at tea-time. Besides, this may be quite correct in Marisi." She turned to Naumann: "You know, I am a stranger here."

"Yes; otherwise I should have seen you," Naumann replied. "Are you to be with us long?"

"For the season, at least."

"And then I suppose you will leave, like everyone else who is worthwhile? You should see Marisi in August! Silent as the grave and hotter than an oven. It is intolerable."

Vivi put in:

"You are here all the year, M. Naumann?"

"Yes, worse luck. For no conceivable reason. The prince invariably goes to Switzerland, and we swelter for nothing."

Tea arrived and Aline poured.

Still Naumann seemed unable to take his eyes from her face, but an acute observer might have thought that it was with an air of intense curiosity, as though he were trying to recall where he had seen her before, rather than one of fascination. This distinction Stetton was incapable of making; he thought only that his friend was succumbing to the irresistible charm of Mlle. Solini, and he grew nervous with fear and displeasure.

"Come," he said to Vivi when tea was finished; "play something."

She walked obediently to the piano.

Naumann left his seat and joined Stetton, who stood near Vivi as she skipped lightly through a tragic piece of Tschaikowsky. It was ludicrous; the girl felt absolutely nothing of the music.

Naumann whispered to Stetton:

"Who is she?"

Stetton looked up.

"I told you. Her father was Pierre Janvour, a Frenchman."

"No; I mean Mlle. Solini. Where is she from?"

"I don't know. Fasilica."

"You don't know?"

"My dear fellow," said Stetton dryly, "I know nothing whatever about her except that you seem to be uncommonly interested in her. Why do you ask?"

"Don't be an ass," said Naumann, moving away and across the room to Aline.

When Stetton and Vivi, tiring of the piano, joined them, a few minutes later, they found them again discussing the disadvantage of being forced to remain in Marisi throughout the summer.

"Really, it is awful," Naumann was saying. "Cheap park concerts, empty hotels, every house on the Drive closed up. Of course, the boss has to stand it with the rest of us, but he is an old elephant with a wife to cool his beer."

"The boss?" Aline looked at him inquiringly.

"Von Krantz, the minister," Naumann explained.

"Oh! Why don't you follow his example and get married yourself?"

"No, thank you," said Naumann with feeling. "I shall never be such a fool."

Aline lifted her eyebrows.

"That is hardly complimentary to us, M. Naumann."

Naumann looked at her.

"I speak from experience, *mademoiselle*. Or, at least, from observation of the experience of others. One thing alone that I have seen was enough to convince me—the experience of a friend of mine, who was also a friend of my father's."

"Indeed?" said Aline. "Tell us about it."

"It is unpleasant."

"That makes it all the more interesting."

Naumann looked at Vivi.

"And you, *mademoiselle*?"

"I should love to hear it," she declared.

The young diplomat seated himself that he might look into Aline's eyes and began:

"This friend of mine—as I say, he was also a friend of my father—was about ten, perhaps fifteen, years older than myself. He was a Russian landowner of noble birth—a man almost without education and yet with a certain strength of intellect that compelled respect and admiration."

"Like all Russians," said Aline contemptuously.

Naumann continued, without noticing the interruption:

"Whenever this man came to Germany on business, which was at least once every year, he paid us a visit. Thus we came to know him well, and to appreciate his finer qualities.

"I used often to have long talks with him. His thoughts were simple and direct as those of a child, and yet his brain was remarkably keen, as was proved by his considerable material success. In my boyhood he was one of my heroes; I used to look forward to his visits with the utmost interest and pleasure."

Naumann paused, glancing round the little circle of his audience. Stetton was listening with ill-concealed irritation, Vivi in frank interest; Aline had on her face the expression of the hostess who wishes to do her duty by her guest.

Naumann kept his eye on her as he resumed:

"One summer—four years ago it was—his first words on entering our house were to the effect that he had found a wife. He gave us all the details; I remember yet with what eager enthusiasm he recounted the incomparable charms and goodness of his wife.

"He had married the daughter of a peasant on one of his neighbor's estates. When my father spoke to him of the danger of a man marrying out of his own class in society, he replied: 'You are right, Herr Naumann; she is not of my class; she is an angel from heaven.'

"Two years passed, during which our friend visited us two or three times. He had, in fact, become rather a bore; he would talk of nothing but his wife. Then—this was about eighteen months ago, and we had not seen our friend for about a year—I was sent on a diplomatic mission to St. Petersburg.

"On my way back, having some leisure at my command, I suddenly decided to pay a visit to our friend's estate, which I had never seen. I felt sure of a welcome, for he had often invited me to visit him.

"If I had been twelve hours later I should not have seen him, for when I arrived he was making the last preparations for a prolonged journey. I was so shocked at the change in his appearance that I could not suppress a cry of amazement at sight of him.

"His face was sunken and deathly pale; his eyes gleamed like two coals of fire, as though he were being consumed by some burning hatred or undying grief. At first he would not tell me the nature of his trouble or the goal of his intended journey; but when I expressed a desire to meet his wife he broke down completely and told me everything."

The narrator paused.

He held the interest of his audience now; Vivi and Stetton moved a little closer that they might not miss a word. But Naumann did not look at them; he kept his eyes fastened on the face of Mlle. Solini, who still listened as though with an effort at politeness.

"Two months before, so our friend told me, he had learned of his wife's affection for another man—a young Jew, who had wriggled himself into the position of manager of the estate. He had shot and killed the Jew; but his wife had pleaded for forgiveness with so wild remorse and sincere repentance that he had taken her back. But, naturally, he was suspicious and began to watch her, and soon he discovered—no matter how—that she was slowly poisoning him."

Vivi gasped with horror; Stetton muttered an ejaculation.

Aline had looked away, and was tapping the floor gently with her foot.

"Somehow she became aware of his discovery," Naumann finished, "and made her escape. Our friend's journey was a search for vengeance. I shall never be able to forget the expression on his face as he swore to kill the woman who had broken his heart and ruined his life."

Vivi burst out:

"Did he find her?"

"I don't know. I have never heard from him." Naumann turned to Aline: "Is not that enough to cause a man to forswear marriage?"

"Perhaps; it is a matter of opinion, M. Naumann."

She was still tapping the floor with her foot.

"I call it a deuced unpleasant tale," said Stetton. "Come, Vivi; for Heaven's sake, play something lively and get the taste out of our mouths."

He and Vivi moved together to the piano.

Naumann turned round in his chair to make sure they could not hear, then leaned forward and spoke in a low tone to Mlle. Solini:

"I forgot to tell you the name of my friend, did I not, _mademoiselle?_ It was Vasili Petrovich, of Warsaw. Every one in that part of Russia knows him—a huge fellow with a black beard and black eyes."

Aline turned and looked him squarely in the eye.

"Indeed?" she said; and though her face was perhaps a little white, her voice was well under control. "He must be a very interesting man, this friend of yours. It is really too bad you did not get to see his wife; she is, if anything, even more interesting."

"Yes," said Naumann, leaning close to her; "but I know that she is a beautiful woman, for Vasili Petrovich showed me her photograph, and I would recognize her among a million."

Aline started suddenly, then sank back into her chair.

"Ah!" she breathed, looking into Naumann's face with eyes that gleamed ominously. Then, controlling herself with a visibly extreme effort of will, she rose abruptly to her feet and called to Vivi:

"Come, child; it is time for our drive."

—ᴡᴡ—

Three Sides to a Triangle

$\mathcal{I}$T SOON became evident that General Nirzann, in spite of his cox-combry, had given Aline no promises which he was unable to fulfil. Once assured that he was not being played with—which assurance he duly received—he undertook immediately the introduction of Mlle. Solini into the select society of Marisi.

As a beginning, she received a card for a reception at the home of Mme. Chébe.

The affair was anything but exclusive, for everybody in Marisi was there whose name appeared on the biggest list, headed "possible"; still, it served as the point of the wedge.

A week later she and Vivi attended a ball given at the Hotel Walderin by the French minister.

Early in the game Aline began to make her selections of those whom she could most easily use, quite disregarding General Nirzann's advice and substituting her own judgment. This was natural, since the general had no knowledge of her real goal.

"Mme. Nimenyi is perhaps the most important of all," the general would say. "Hers is the richest and oldest family in Marisi. Once she sits at your dinner-table you are made."

"Is she in favor at the palace?" Aline would ask.

"No; a year ago M. Nimenyi refused a loan to the prince, and they are no longer seen at court, as we say. But that is a minor disadvantage. She is almost as important as the prince himself."

"Well, we shall see," said Aline. But she no longer paid any attention to Mme. Nimenyi.

She perceived that her own remarkable beauty was the greatest obstacle she would have to encounter.

Women are always the guardians to the doors of society, and they seem to have found a limit to the physical charms of their own sex beyond which respectability ceases. Whether this is the result of a deep law of nature, or of the instinct of self-preservation, or merely of common envy, no one knows except the women themselves; however, we may be allowed to suspect that they are not disinterested in the matter or they would divulge the secret.

For a week the beauty of the unknown *mademoiselle* who had taken Duroy's house for the season was the chief topic of conversation in Marisi drawing-rooms. Strange things were averred of her; still stranger were hinted. She was a spy in the service of the Sultan; she was a rich American who had killed her husband; she was a courtezan who had fascinated the young King of Spain, and had been paid a million francs by the Spanish government to leave the country.

Then it began to be whispered about that she was a distant relative of General Paul Nirzann, from somewhere in Russia, and that the general intended to introduce her into Marisi society whether they would or no. Society got out its little knives and sharpened them up.

In the meantime Aline appeared daily in her open carriage on the drive with Vivi at her side. Her carriage always appeared early and remained late, for two reasons. One, which she told General Nirzann, was that a face becomes less hateful and less beautiful to people as it becomes more familiar. The other reason she kept to herself.

The young men were eager to meet her, and Aline was willing, but General Nirzann entered a firm negative.

"You must ignore them," he declared, "at least for a time. Everyone is inventing lies about your past. You must make them ridiculous by an irreproachable present. It is a field of battle whose victory will lie with the one who exhibits superior wit and strategy. You have been introduced; it is now a waiting game."

Then came the reception at the house of Mme. Chébe and the ball of the French minister. By that time everyone knew who Mlle. Solini was—a cousin of General Nirzann, Russian by birth, and by inheritance the owner of vast estates in her native land. Vivi, the daughter of a French diplomat, was her ward.

Impecunious young men and their mothers began to look with favorable eyes on Mlle. Solini; not to mention a dozen or so of the old beaus who had stuck to their guns for so many years that they deserved to be called professionals. Such are to be found in every European capital.

The date arrived for Mme. Nimenyi's annual ball. The best of Marisi attended; and one of the minor surprises of the evening was the absence of Mlle. Solini. Questions were asked, and though Mme. Nimenyi did her best to keep the thing secret, it leaked out that the beautiful Russian had indeed received an invitation, but had returned a polite refusal.

It was the sensation of the evening. Knowing Mme. Nimenyi's power, everyone said: "The Russian has killed herself; she is buried. All the same, it is a great joke on Mme. N."

But by this action, seemingly suicidal, Aline had unwittingly made for herself a devoted friend in the person of the Countess Potacci, Mme. Nimenyi's strongest rival for the leadership.

Within three days she was invited to a select musicale at the

home of the countess. This was followed by a party call and an intimate chat. Aline had arrived; discretion only was needed to make her
position secure.

"Let me tell you, Vivi," said Aline, on her return from the
Countess Potacci's, "within a year these people will all be there." She
pointed to the ground at her feet. "But—bah! What does that
amount to? They are merely so many stepping-stones."

"To what?" asked the girl. "Why do you not tell me anything?"

"Have I not?" Aline smiled.

"No; you only tell me what to tell others."

"Is not that sufficient, since it is the truth?"

"Is it the truth?" It was a question.

"Certainly, dear."

Vivi hesitated while a little frown appeared on her clear, white
brow, then she said:

"But if you are so wealthy, why do you take money from M.
Stetton?"

For a moment Aline, with all her cleverness, was taken aback by
this simple, direct question.

"You do not understand," she said finally. "I have my reasons;
you must believe me, Vivi, and trust me."

She smiled with genuine affection; the girl seemed to hesitate a
moment longer, then she sprang forward and threw her arms around
Aline's neck.

"I do believe you," she cried, "and I love you! You are so good
to me!"

And, in fact, she was.

During this month of preliminary maneuvers Stetton was
restraining his impatience with difficulty. He told himself that he
was paying all the bills and getting nothing to show for it. But still
Aline had little difficulty to keep him within bounds; and now
that he saw how highly her charms were regarded by the critical

cosmopolites of Marisi, he felt that his reward was all the more worth waiting for.

He had abandoned his own little scheme with regard to Vivi and his friend Naumann; he had dropped it as one does a match that has burned one's fingers. He could not understand his friend's conduct in the matter; Naumann had seemed to be completely fascinated by Aline, and yet he evinced no desire to pursue the acquaintance, and indeed refused absolutely to discuss Mlle. Solini in any way.

Aline appeared to be equally desirous of forgetting M. Naumann. Stetton felt vaguely that there must be some reason for this apparent antagonism, but he could make only the wildest guesses as to its nature. One morning General Nirzann announced to Aline:

"It is time to begin now; you are safe."

Aline's eyes sparkled. She had been waiting for this word from him, for she knew that in this case the old warhorse could give her instruction to be obtained in no other way. She said:

"Are you sure? Is it not too soon?"

"No, we are timed to the minute," he replied. "The question is, shall it be a reception or a dinner? There is more to be gained by the reception; but the dinner is much safer, for you can make sure of your guests before you send them cards."

"Then it shall be the dinner," said Aline without hesitation, for this question had long before been decided in her own mind. "Come, my dear Paul, you must help me with my list."

The general arranged himself before her in an attitude intended to express mad ecstasy.

"Ah!" he exclaimed, "you call me Paul! Angel!"

"Did I really?" Aline smiled. "But it is not surprising. I call all of my servants by their first names."

General Nirzann stared at her for a moment, then burst into laughter.

"Ha, ha! I see. What a joke! Very good!" Then his face was suddenly filled with portentous gravity and an expression of utter devotion. "All the same, I am your servant in reality. I adore you! I worship you!"

It was quite fifteen minutes before Aline could get him started on the list.

A week later the day of the dinner arrived. It promised to be a complete success; the gathering was small and quite select, and there were no disappointments. Present: the Count and Countess Potacci, M. and Mme. Chébe, Nirzann, Stetton, Naumann, and two or three young fellows whom Aline had added to the list against the advice of the general.

It may seem necessary to account for the presence of Naumann, but only Aline herself could do that. It may have been that she wished to have him under her eye; at any rate, she put the thing so strongly to Stetton that he absolutely insisted on his friend's acceptance. Naumann finally gave in, and he and Stetton went together.

The evening was spoiled for Stetton at the very beginning. He understood, of course, that the Count Potacci would have the honor of taking in Mlle. Solini, but he had counted on the seat at her right. General Nirzann, too, had had his eye on that coveted position; and, behold, it was assigned to one Jules Chavot, a young Frenchman from Munich, who possessed nothing except a fashionable wardrobe, and a somewhat sinister reputation as a duelist.

Stetton sulked and refused to open his mouth, except for the entrance of food; General Nirzann muttered, "What the deuce does she want with that blockhead?" as he glared at M. Chavot with a gaze intended to frighten him off the earth.

The dinner itself was excellent, and Aline performed the duties of a hostess to perfection.

"This is just what Marisi needed," said Mme. Chébe to the general, who had taken her in.

"I beg your pardon?" said the general, removing his ferocious glare from the lucky Chavot.

"Are you getting deaf, little one?" asked Mme. Chébe. Her tongue was the heaviest in Marisi. "I would advise you to be polite to me, or where will you go of an afternoon? I said, this is just what Marisi needed—a woman like Mlle. Solini to give us new life; another dinner-table at which—"

"At which all the homeless puppies can get a square meal," interrupted the general, still thinking of the Frenchmen.

"—one may expect to hear something besides a discussion of Lehar's latest waltz," finished Mme. Chébe serenely, ignoring the interruption.

The voice of the Count Potacci came from across the table.

"How is the prince today, general?"

At these words Aline, who had been chatting with M. Chavot, raised her head quickly, looking at the speaker.

"He is better; much better," replied General Nirzann. "He will probably appear on the drive tomorrow; the doctor has promised it."

Aline turned to Chavot:

"Has the prince been ill?"

"Only indisposed, I believe," replied the young man. "Why—are you concerned, *mademoiselle?*"

"Indifferently so."

"If you would only confess even so slight an interest in myself!"

"M. Chavot, be quiet."

He sighed, and, lifting his eyes, encountered the ferocious glare of General Nirzann, which he immediately proceeded to return in kind.

When the dinner was over, and the gentlemen had smoked their cigars, they rejoined the ladies in the drawing-room. M. and Mme. Chébe left to attend the opera, taking with them two of the young men; the others remained.

The Count and Countess Potacci, with General Nirzann, began

a discussion of Marisi politics in general and the alliance with the Turks in particular; Chavot, Stetton, and a M. Franck gathered round Mlle. Solini; and Naumann and Vivi strolled toward the piano in a corner of the room.

"Do you play?" asked Vivi, looking up at him. Her pretty lips were parted and her eyes glowed with the unwonted excitement of the evening.

"No; I used to, but I am out of practice."

"I am glad; I hate music," Vivi declared.

"You hate music!" he exclaimed in amused surprise.

"Yes. I think it is because at the convent they kept me at dreary, dull compositions until I felt like knocking the piano to pieces."

"Quite naturally," said Naumann. "How long were you at the convent?"

"All my life. Thai is, until Mlle. Solini—" The girl seemed confused.

"You need not guard your tongue with me," said Naumann, looking at her.

"Need not guard my tongue—what do you mean?"

"Nothing," said Naumann hastily, regretting his words. "Except that I am a very discreet person, and am therefore an excellent repository for itching secrets."

"That is really too bad," said Vivi, smiling, "for I haven't any to divulge."

"A pretty girl without secrets! Impossible!" cried the young man.

"That is the second," observed the girl with apparent irrelevance.

"The second—"

"Yes. That makes twice that someone has called me pretty since we came to Marisi. It is delightful to be told so, even when they say it only to be amusing."

"Who was the other man?" Naumann hadn't the slightest idea why he asked.

"The other man?"

"The one who told you you are pretty!"

"Oh! M. Chavot. Aline laughed when I told her of it. She said that M. Chavot was the kind of man who possesses just a certain number of words, and considers it necessary to use all of them every day. I thought it was scarcely nice of her."

They chatted thus for an hour or more without being joined by any of the others, who had formed an animated group round Mlle. Solini. Naumann had no desire to join the circle, and as for Vivi, she found M. Naumann quite the nicest man she had met.

He got her to talking of her life in the convent, then of her future, and she was surprised to find herself revealing thoughts and desires which she had hitherto considered too intimate to discuss even with Aline.

Then Naumann told her a little of life in Paris and Berlin, while she listened with eager ears, declaring when he had finished that her greatest desire was to travel.

"Paris especially," said she. "I was born in Paris, you know. Aline has promised to take me there next winter."

"Have you relatives there?"

"None. None anywhere. I have no one except Aline, but she is so good to me! I want you to know it—you particularly."

"May I ask why?"

"I want you to. Because when I asked her the other day why you did not come to see us"—Vivi seemed unconscious of the fact that she was betraying a special interest in the young man before her—"she said that you had taken a dislike to her. Why should that be, *monsieur?*"

Naumann looked at her: every feature of her face, as well as her words and tone, betokened the most absolute sincerity. He hardly knew what to say, and ended by declaring that he did not dislike Mlle. Solini, but that he had not felt sure of a welcome at her house.

"But she invited you tonight!" cried Vivi. "You are completely in the wrong, M. Naumann. Acknowledge it, and I will forgive you."

At this moment Jules Chavot approached. The group at the other end of the room had broken up; the Count and Countess Potacci were preparing to leave. General Nirzann had taken himself away half an hour before, saying that his presence was required at the palace.

At parting he had pressed Aline's hand affectionately before the assembled company, calling her "dear cousin," and sending a last glance toward Jules Chavot, which was intended to utterly annihilate that young gentleman.

The departure of the count and countess was taken by the others as the signal that the evening was ended. There was an expression of triumph on the face of Mlle. Solini as she bade her guests good night, which carried with it a hint of defiance as she acknowledged the bow of M. Naumann. Stetton and Naumann left together, to walk together down the drive to Walderin Place, where the young diplomat's rooms were situated.

Stetton chatted for an hour in his friend's rooms, then left to return to the hotel. He was in the worst possible humor; he had that evening, for the first time, begun to fear—as he expressed it to himself—that he "was being worked for a sucker." He was filled with anger at Aline, at Nirzann, at Chavot, at himself. He decided at one moment to leave Marisi the following morning; then he laughed aloud in scorn at his own weakness.

He reached the hotel and went to his room. But he did not go to bed; he felt that he could not sleep. All his anger had left—he was now thinking of Aline—the promise of her eyes, the whiteness of her skin, the intoxication of her caress. He allowed his thoughts to dwell on her until his blood was heated and his brain feverish, and he felt that he could no longer contain himself.

He went to the window and opened it, allowing the cool night air to rush across his face. A clock on the church on the side of the square struck twelve.

"I'll do it," Stetton muttered aloud; "by Jove, I'll do it."

He put on his hat and coat, left the hotel, and started afoot at a rapid pace down the drive. It was quiet and deserted, save occasionally when a limousine or closed carriage whizzed rapidly past with those returning from the theater or opera.

Stetton walked with long strides, face set straight ahead, like a man who knows his destination and intends to reach it. As he arrived in front of No. 341 he took out his watch and looked at it by the light of a street lamp. It was twenty-five minutes past midnight.

He ascended the stoop and rang the bell. After a wait of a minute or so he rang again. Almost immediately the door was opened the space of a few inches, and the face of Czean, Aline's butler, appeared.

"It is I—Stetton," said the young man. "Let me in." He was saying to himself, "I'll show them whose house this is."

"But—M. Stetton—" the butler stammered. "Mlle. Solini has retired—"

"What does that matter?" demanded Stetton and, as Czean did not move, he pushed the door open and stepped inside.

He was in the reception hall. The drawing-room, on the right, was dark, but a light appeared through the transom of the door of the library at the further end of the hall. He started toward it.

From behind came the voice of the butler in frightened tones:

"Mademoiselle! Mademoiselle!"

Stetton had nearly reached the door of the library when it opened and Aline appeared on the threshold.

"What is it, Czean?" she asked impatiently; then, catching sight of Stetton, she stepped back with a start of surprise.

Stetton moved inside the room before she had time to speak. The library was flooded with light from a chandelier over the table in the center of the room. At one end two or three logs were blazing merrily in a large open fireplace.

In an easy chair placed before the fire, with his back turned to the door, sat the figure of a man. Stetton crossed to his side with an ejaculation. It was General Paul Nirzann.

The general sprang to his feet.

"Ah! M. Stetton!" said he with a weak attempt at a smile.

Aline had crossed the room.

"I did not expect to see you again so soon," she said to Stetton in an easy tone. "Won't you sit down?"

She was perfectly composed.

The young man remained standing.

"I seem to be intruding," he observed with heavy sarcasm, looking at General Nirzann. "I did not know your house was open to visitors at all hours of the night, *mademoiselle.*"

"Then why did you come?" said Aline, still smiling.

The general broke in with great indignation:

"Do you mean, *monsieur,* to dictate to me the time when I shall be allowed to visit my cousin?"

"Bah!" Stetton exploded in contempt for the little warrior. He turned to Aline: "Listen to me. I am in earnest. Send this man away—at once. I want to talk to you."

"But, M. Stetton—"

"I say send him away! Can't you see I mean it? Otherwise, you leave this house tomorrow."

Aline lowered her lids to cover the glance of hatred she could not keep from her eyes.

"You had better go, general," she said quietly, turning to Nirzann.

"But—" the general began furiously.

"No; you must go."

The general found his hat and coat and crossed to the door, while Stetton followed him with his eyes. There he turned.

"Good night, M. Stetton." This ironically. "Good night, dear cousin."

He was gone.

Aline waited until she had heard the outer door open and close, then she turned to Stetton, who had not moved from where he stood near the fireplace.

"Now, *monsieur,*" she said in a freezing tone. "I shall ask you to explain yourself."

The young man looked at her with eyes as cold as her own.

"Am I the one to explain?" he demanded quietly. "You seem to forget that I pay the rent here, *mademoiselle.* Surely I have the right at least to come and bid you good night, and what do I find?"

"Well, then—yes—what do you find? If I am not angry with you, Stetton, it is only because you are such a fool. You know perfectly well that General Nirzann has been of use to us, and that we are not yet through with him. But because you find him sitting in my library, boring me to death with his silly chatter, you insult me and make me ridiculous! Yes, decidedly, it is you who have to explain."

"It is my house. I pay the rent," said Stetton stubbornly, feeling that he was somehow being placed in the wrong and sticking to his one idea.

"That no longer interests me," said Aline coldly. "I shall leave here tomorrow."

"Leave! But how—you cannot!"

"You are mistaken; what I cannot do is stay here and be insulted by you."

"But hang it all, what could I do? How could I help it when I saw—"

"You saw nothing."

That was all she would say, and Stetton had to make the best of it. Aline stuck to her intention of leaving on the morrow; Stetton, in despair, acknowledged himself in the wrong and begged forgiveness.

In the future he would leave her completely free; he would not presume to dictate to her; he would wait for her own pleasure. Aline appeared to hesitate; he fell on his knees and pleaded with her not to leave him.

"You said you loved me!" he cried. "So I do, Stetton. You know it." She allowed a little tenderness to creep into her tone.

He clasped her in his arms, crying: "You would not be angry with me if you knew how I loved you. These delays are driving me mad—it is more than flesh and blood can stand. Must I wait forever?"

He was completely conquered. She allowed him to embrace her again, then she gently disengaged herself, saying that it was late—she must retire—he must go.

"As for General Nirzann, do not think of him," she said. "He is an old idiot whom I shall discard when he is no longer useful; in the meantime, I shall give you no reason to be jealous of him."

With that promise in his ears, and her kiss on his lips, Stetton walked back to the hotel.

—⁓—

CHAPTER VII

Loyalty For Two

M R. RICHARD Stetton had enough to worry about in Marisi—nobody will deny that; and hence the piece of good fortune that befell him on the morning following the events narrated in the last chapter will not be begrudged to him.

It arrived in the morning mail, and took the form of a draft for five hundred thousand francs from his father in New York. Business was good, it appeared, and Stetton senior wished his son Richard to miss nothing. He wrote: "In another year or so I shall be ready to retire, and then you will be tied down here for the rest of your life. Have a good time; you are old enough to take care of yourself."

"He's a good sort," said Stetton junior, gazing lovingly at the draft.

The unpleasant scene of the night before, while it had not allayed his impatience, had increased his infatuation for Mlle. Solini, and, curiously enough, his trust in her. He was so far from being jealous of General Nirzann that he laughed at him.

"Aline is working him prettily," he said aloud as he made his toilet. "Gad! Won't he be surprised when we go off together?"

After breakfast he wandered into the street, and crossing

Walderin Place, began to stroll idly past the shops on the other side.
It was nearly noon; the sidewalks were crowded with smartly dressed
women and hurrying men.

Stetton paused in front of a jeweler's shop and began to look at
the trinkets displayed in the window. His eye was caught by a necklace of pearls reposing in a box of black velvet.

"Deuced pretty," muttered the young man, assuming the air of a
connoisseur. "Quite elegant."

He thought how well the pearls would look round the white
neck of Aline, and he pictured to himself her delight and gratitude
at being surprised with such a gift; also, he thought of the draft from
New York tucked away in his breast pocket.

He walked inside the shop and asked the price of the necklace.
The clerk told him it was seventy-five thousand francs.

"Ridiculous!" said Stetton—this was premeditated. "At
Lampourde's, in Paris, I got one exactly similar—only I believe the
pearls were a little larger—for forty thousand."

The clerk raised his hands in horror.

"Forty thousand! Impossible" he exclaimed. "This necklace is
worth at least three times that amount. But wait, *monsieur,* I will call
the proprietor."

When the proprietor arrived Stetton again expressed his astonishment and indignation at the absurd price asked for such an inferior trinket.

The proprietor, in his turn, jumped up and down with excitement and declared himself to be perfectly insulted. It was all a part
of the game.

They compromised on sixty thousand francs. Stetton ordered
the necklace delivered at his hotel that afternoon and left the shop,
feeling himself beaten.

"Hang it all, I should have got it for fifty thousand," he said to
himself. "The little man is a sharp one."

That evening after dinner he walked down to No. 341, the Drive. He found Aline and Vivi alone—a fact which added to his good nature and ease of mind. Vivi stayed only long enough to exchange greetings with the visitor, then excused herself and went upstairs.

Stetton, finding himself alone with Mlle. Solini, was a little embarrassed. He wondered if she had entirely forgiven him for his conduct of the night before. They were in the library, before an open fire; Stetton was seated in the very chair which he had found occupied by General Nirzann.

"We did not see you on the Drive this afternoon," said Aline.

"No, I was writing letters at the hotel," Stetton replied. After a short pause he continued: "Also, I had a little business at my banker's. Money must be scarce in Marisi. Really, the fellow nearly fell on my neck when I announced my intention of depositing a draft for half a million francs."

Aline glanced at him. "But that is a great deal of money."

"To some people, perhaps; not to me," said the young man grandly. "I shall probably run through it in a couple of months. By the way, I have spent part of it already on a little surprise for you."

"A surprise for me?"

"Yes." Stetton rose and took from the table a small package which he had laid there when he entered. "A little peace offering," he continued, opening the package. "I don't know if you will like it."

He pressed the spring, displaying the pearl necklace, and handed the box to Aline.

She drew a quick breath with an exclamation of surprised delight, and taking the necklace from its velvet cushion, clasped it about her throat.

"Oh!" she cried ecstatically, unable to say anything. Then she threw her arms round Stetton's neck and pressed her lips to his.

"There!" she whispered in his ear. "I owe you so much now that I must begin to repay you at once."

Never had she been so gracious to him as she was that evening. She allowed him to hold her in his arms as long as he wished, and he got a kiss whenever he asked for it. She expressed a hope that they would be ready to be married and leave Marisi soon—very soon.

In this new tenderness Stetton found her irresistibly intoxicating; he could hardly bring himself to leave, and when he did go he walked on air and sang to the stars.

A few days later Aline informed him that she did not care for any more jewelry. She said that she was afraid to keep it with her in the house, and that otherwise it would be useless.

Nevertheless, she added quickly, she was so in love with the necklace that nothing could make her part with it—it was made doubly dear by the fact that Stetton had given it to her with his own hand. Her reason for bringing up the subject was that, knowing Stetton's princely generosity, she wished to forestall such another gift.

"But hang it all, you do not refuse to accept my presents?" said Stetton, whose ears were ringing with her phrase, "princely generosity."

The controversy ended three days later by her acceptance of a gift of one hundred thousand francs. The poor fellow was actually worked up to the point where he brought it to her in cash and forced it into her hands.

As he walked up the drive after leaving her house he was haunted by a feeling that he had made a fool of himself, but the memory of her caresses and her assurance of love drove it back into the unexplored recesses of his brain—in his case, a not inconsiderable area.

He reached Walderin Place, and turning to the east, entered the door of No. 18. It was one of those old-fashioned residences, abandoned when society moved to the drive, now divided into apartments for bachelors.

Stetton ascended a flight of stairs and knocked on a door at the end of the long, narrow hall. A voice said:

"Come in."

He entered. The room was filled with tobacco smoke and an odor of beer. Frederick Naumann rose from his seat in a large, easy chair by the window and extended his hand to the visitor. Stetton sniffed disagreeably.

"Whew! This smells more like a cheap saloon than the aristocratic apartments of a rising young diplomat. For Heaven's sake open a window."

"Can't help it," said Naumann cheerfully. "This is the proper atmosphere. I am indulging in profound thought. Keep away from that window!"

Stetton pounced on the book his friend had laid on the table at his entrance. It was "Bel Ami."

"Very profound," said he with sarcastic emphasis. "You're nothing but an immoral and morbid devotee of the flesh—that is, your own flesh. Why the deuce don't you show your face once in a while?"

"I've been busy," Naumann declared; "very busy."

"Of course. You forget that I've just caught you in the act. Every one in Marisi thinks you are dead. Come on out and look at the sun."

He ended by dragging Naumann into the street almost by force. They strolled about for an hour or so, then went to Stetton's hotel for dinner.

Naumann was still grumbling that he had been dragged out into a world which no longer interested him, declaring that his entire evening had been wasted, and that he would visit dire vengeance on Stetton's head. He wanted to know why he should not be allowed to sit quietly in his own room when that had come to hold for him the greatest pleasure in life.

"You'll die of dry rot, that's what you'll do," said Stetton in a tone of conviction. "Besides, I have not pulled you out of your hole for nothing. I have a purpose."

"Aha! A plot!" cried Naumann.

"Be quiet and listen. This afternoon I was with Mlle. Solini." A frown appeared on Naumann's face. "Vivi was present, of course— she always is. Well, all she would talk about was M. Naumann. Why didn't he come with me? Where was he? Didn't I think he had pretty eyes? It was pitiful. Why the deuce don't you meander down there once in a while and let the poor girl look at you?"

"I told you the other day I couldn't help you," said Naumann, who appeared to be considerably moved by what the other had said.

"I'm not talking about that. This is a matter of common charity."

"Rot. The girl has forgotten I exist. For the twentieth time I tell you I sha'n't go to Mlle. Solini's."

"And for the twentieth time," Stetton retorted half angrily, "I ask you why?"

"That is my own affair."

"Of course. I suppose it has nothing to do with me. Only, as a friend, it seems to me that you owe me some sort of explanation."

"It would do no good."

"Nevertheless, I want to hear it."

Naumann looked at him and made a sudden decision.

"Very well; you shall. I do not want to go to Mlle. Solini's house, because she is a dangerous and detestable woman; worse, a criminal."

"What the deuce—"

"Wait. Let me finish. You remember the first day you took me there. I told a story concerning a friend of mine, whose wife betrayed him, and after being forgiven for that tried to poison him. Well, Aline Solini is that woman."

Stetton stared at him in amazement. "How do you know this?"

"My friend showed me a photograph of his wife. I cannot possibly be mistaken; the likeness was perfect, in spite of her cleverness. Have you not seen that she hates me? It is because she is aware that I know her secret."

"But why have you not written to your friend—her husband?"

"I did so. I sent a letter to his estate. It was returned by the manager with the information that he had not heard from his employer for nearly a year."

"Then all your proof consists of her similarity to the photograph?"

"Is not that enough? I tell you I cannot be mistaken."

There was a silence, while on Stetton's face appeared a reflection of the struggle between reason and desire. Finally he said, in the tone of a man who has made up his mind:

"I do not believe it."

And nothing that Naumann could say was capable of shaking him. He repeated merely, "I do not believe it," to every argument. When Naumann insisted on knowing how he had met Mlle. Solini, he told of the rescue from the convent at Fasilica, but for some reason or other undefined even to himself he did not mention the episode of the man with the black beard.

"But it is absurd!" cried Naumann exasperated. "She is certainly the same. I would inform the police—I would, positively—but what charge could be preferred against her? There is no evidence. Let me tell you this, Stetton—for I am your friend, though you seem to think otherwise—beware of her!"

"I do not believe it," said Stetton stubbornly. "She loves me."

"She is deceiving you."

"I do not believe it."

In the end, Naumann, perceiving that his friend was immovable, gave it up and departed for his rooms. He had not before admitted to himself the reason for his excessive interest in Mlle. Solini, but now he was forced to self-confession. Only partly was it owing to love for his friend, Vasili Petrovich, and a desire to see him avenged. He was concerned about Vivi.

"Though why, I don't know," he muttered to himself as he paced up and down the length of his room. "It isn't possible that I am really interested in her. Any man would be moved by the thought of a young and innocent girl like her under the influence of that woman. It's an infernal outrage."

He got into bed, but the turmoil of his thoughts kept him awake for several hours.

The following day, early in the afternoon, he called at No. 341, the Drive. He hardly knew what he intended to do or say; he thought that he knew Mlle. Solini too well to expect her to be moved by mere threats, but still he felt himself carried forward by an irresistible impulse to action. At the very door he weakened and turned to beat a retreat; then he turned again and resolutely pressed the bell button.

After all, he was not compelled to face Mlle. Solini, for he found Vivi alone. She said that Aline had gone driving with Jules Chavot.

"And why did you not go along?" asked Naumann, as she led him to a seat in the library. "Have you tired of the promenade so soon?"

"On the contrary. I am more in love with it than ever," said Vivi. "But I do not like M. Chavot."

"That is jealousy," said Naumann, laughing at her frankness. "I have not forgotten that he began by telling you you were pretty, and now he has deserted you."

Vivi began to protest earnestly that she was not the least bit jealous, then, seeing the smile on Naumann's lips, stopped in confusion. "M. Naumann, I really believe you are taking advantage of my inexperience to make fun of me."

It was the young man's turn to protest. He declared that under no circumstances would he make fun of her.

"But yes," Vivi insisted, "it is evident. I need not say that I am offended."

"I assure you, *mademoiselle,* you wrong me," said Naumann earnestly. "I had no such intention. I would not—" He stopped, catching sight of a little provoking smile on Vivi's face. "Now you are making fun of me!" he exclaimed.

Vivi's smile became a rippling laugh. "Well," she cried, "then now we are quits, *monsieur.*"

"What the deuce!" thought Naumann to himself. "She is not so simple as I thought."

He began to speak of Aline. Soon he discovered that Vivi knew absolutely nothing of the woman who was supposed to be her guardian; he knew no more, after half an hour of careful questioning, than he had already learned from Stetton.

But of one thing there could be no doubt: the girl's unbounded affection for Mlle. Solini. She sang her praises in the key of hyperbole; Aline had been both father and mother to her; Aline had opened her heart to her and found a home for her when she was absolutely alone in the world—alone and friendless.

Naumann saw that here again, as with Stetton, his task was next to hopeless, but he decided to venture. He began:

"But what would you say, *mademoiselle,* if you were told that all your confidence and love were misplaced?"

Vivi looked at him. "I don't know what you mean."

"What if you discovered that Mlle. Solini is a bad woman, heartless and criminal—a faithless wife and a murderess?"

Vivi shuddered in horror at the mere force of the words. "I do not know why you say that, unless you wish to frighten me. Of course, it is impossible."

Naumann said impressively, looking into her eyes:

"On the contrary, it is true."

Then, as Vivi sat in silent amazement, he continued: "I repeat, it is true. Mlle. Solini was faithless to her husband, and if she did not murder him it was only because he discovered her villainy barely in time." Then he told her everything that he had told Stetton, arguing with the eloquence of a prosecutor in court, hoping to save the sweet young girl.

When he had finished Vivi said quietly, using the very words that he had heard from Stetton's lips the night before:

"I do not believe it."

He opened his mouth to speak, but she interrupted him:

"M. Naumann, there is some mistake; I am sure of it; I do not know why I am not angry with you; I ought to be. You do not know Aline. She is the best and sweetest woman in the world.

"She has been as kind to me as my own mother could have been. I may not know much of the world, but I am not a silly or thoughtless girl, and I know that what you tell me is impossible."

"But I tell you she betrayed herself to me by her own actions when I told her I had seen the photograph."

Vivi shook her head. "That was your imagination. You wished to convict her." The girl paused for a moment, then she continued in a voice that trembled a little: "You see, *monsieur*, I love her. I cannot listen to you. If you persist I must ask you to—I must say farewell."

"I am sorry—my intentions were good," said Naumann stiffly, rising from his chair.

The girl replied:

"I do not doubt it; but you are unjust to her."

Naumann, standing before her, said in a voice that he tried to keep even:

"Then—since you desire it—farewell, *mademoiselle.*"

He waited for a moment, but she did not speak, and he moved to the door. He was crossing the threshold into the hall when he heard her voice behind him, so low that it barely reached his ears:

"Do not go."

He turned; Vivi had risen from her chair and stood facing him. He crossed to her side.

"Did you speak, *mademoiselle?*"

She spoke quickly, looking into his eyes:

"Yes. Why must you go? Can we not be friends? That is, if you care to."

"But you told me—you said I offended you."

"Well, am I not allowed to forgive?"

Naumann wanted to take her sweet, serious face in his two hands and kiss the pretty, trembling lips. Instead, he lifted her hand and kissed it lightly, saying:

"That is the privilege of every woman."

Vivi smiled—a serious smile. "But you must not say anything more about Aline."

Naumann frowned. "It is hard to promise that."

"But you must. You see, you must be very careful not to make me angry again, since I have just forgiven you."

She stood smiling at him with a new air, half of coquetry, while the young man gazed at her in silence. What was there about the face of this girl, barely pretty, that seemed to interest him in spite of himself? Her freshness and youth? Impossible; he had known a thousand like her. Her naive frankness? But he had always disliked that in a woman. He gave it up, and presently said:

"Then we will talk no more of Mlle. Solini—at least, for the present."

Vivi answered calmly, as though nothing less was to be expected of him:

"That is sweet of you. Now we can amuse each other."

They did so with astonishing success of nearly two hours. It was Naumann who did most of the talking, while Vivi listened to everything from adventures in school to philosophical egotisms with an absorbed interest that was immensely flattering. It appeared that their views on general questions coincided wonderfully, since she agreed to every proposition he honored with his support.

Once, however—probably just to show him that she did have a mind of her own—she undertook to disprove his assertion that Schopenhauer had destroyed Christianity for all thinkers; and (let this be whispered low) he avoided utter annihilation only by demanding, in the middle of the argument, that he be served with tea.

By that time they were as old friends, and the ceremony of tea was exceedingly informal. She remembered, from his previous visit, that he took lemon and two lumps—a circumstance which gave him an unmistakable thrill of pleasure.

The maid announced apologetically that there were no muffins. Vivi looked inquiringly at Naumann.

"Bread and butter?" he suggested.

Vivi nodded.

"And tarts," she added, as the maid disappeared.

The young man declared that the tarts, of apricot, were delicious.

"Of course they are," said Vivi with an air. "I made them myself."

"No! Really? Give me another."

He ate four of them, while Vivi laughed at him.

"You'll be sick—very sick," she declared, shaking a warning finger at him. "Stuffing yourself is no proof of friendship, even if the tarts are my handiwork. It is clumsy flattery."

"You are right," said Naumann. "It is a proof of love—" a pause, then he added, "for the tarts."

He stayed half an hour longer, then rose to go. Evening had

arrived; it was so dark in the little library that they could barely see each other's faces. Vivi rang for lights.

"Good Heavens!" exclaimed Naumann suddenly, "it's after five o'clock, and I had an appointment at the legation at four!" This statement appeared to have no particular meaning for Vivi, but she was plainly puzzled at the lapse in his regard for duty. He prepared to leave hurriedly.

"Then we are friends?" asked Vivi at the door. "You are not going to forget me, as you have done?"

"I am more your friend than you think," he replied. "As for my forgetting you—you will see. *Au revoir.*"

She watched him through the glass of the door as he ran swiftly down the steps and started up the drive.

As she turned slowly to return to the library she heard a carriage stop without, and she hastened back to her chair by the fireplace. Soon the outer door opened and closed, and she heard Aline's voice in the hall.

"No; do not thank me, *monsieur.* I sought merely my own pleasure."

Then the voice of Jules Chavot, more than a murmur:

"Ah, you make me hope for happiness."

Vivi, buried deep in her chair, gazing at the fire, smiled as she murmured to herself:

"Happiness? I really believe that I begin to know what it means."

—m—

M. Stetton Issues an Ultimatum

*T*HAT EVENING at dinner Aline said to Vivi:

"We saw the prince today on the drive."

Mlle. Solini uttered this speech quite in her ordinary tone, and how was Vivi to guess at all that was contained in it?

She knew nothing of Aline's far-reaching and ambitious plans; she did not know that this casual appearance on the drive was the signal for the beginning of the great campaign. And what did she care about this Prince of Marisi, whom she guessed to be gouty and tottering with age? She had her own prince to think about.

In fact, Mlle. Solini had stated only one side of the case of Vivi, and that the least important. She had not only seen the prince, but the prince had also seen her, as she sat beside Jules Chavot in her open carriage, radiant, smiling.

The prince was accompanied by General Nirzann, and as the two carriages came abreast of each other Aline had seen the great man address a sudden question to his companion. She had no doubt that the question had to do with the identity of the golden-haired beauty with M. Chavot; the prince had noticed her. The question in her own mind then was, what answer to the prince had been made by the general?

On that point she received information the following morning when General Nirzann called at No. 341. Almost his first words after greeting her were:

"*Mademoiselle,* you are irresistible. You have caught the eye of the Prince of Marisi."

Aline sent him a quick, searching glance; but her tone was calm to indifference as she said:

"Indeed?"

"Yes, I assure you. He insisted on knowing who you are."

"And you told him——"

The little general raised his penciled eyebrows to show that he considered the question superfluous. "What I have told every one else, of course."

Aline, satisfied for the present, changed the subject abruptly. General Nirzann needed careful handling.

But every day thereafter, for a week, her carriage met that of the prince on the drive, and each day she fancied she noted a growing interest in his gaze. Then came a tea at the Countess Potacci's, which the prince attended. Surrounded as he was by the entire company, he had little opportunity for any speech with Mlle. Solini, but Aline, with her penetrating eye, read the wish on his face. She was satisfied.

The following evening at the opera the prince paid a visit to the box of Mme. Chébe, in which Aline was a guest. Here, again, the conversation was exasperatingly general, but the prince found opportunity to say in an undertone:

"I understand, *mademoiselle,* that you have taken a house in Marisi for the season."

Aline replied:

"Yes; that of Mr. Duroy, at No. 341."

"It certainly must be a very pleasant place if it is as charming as its occupant."

"Your highness is pleased to be kind."

"Not at all; merely sincere."

"If you should find it so in reality, it would make me happy."

At that interesting point they were interrupted by the American Miss Ford, whom Aline thenceforward hated.

But that, as if subsequently appeared, had been enough, for two days later General Nirzann brought to Aline the information that an invitation from Mlle. Solini would be considered acceptable at the palace of the Prince of Marisi. Curiously enough, this commission of the general's appeared to be pleasing to him; Aline could not understand that. She had not yet discovered General Nirzann's one genuine attachment.

"That is my message, *mademoiselle*—a formal one, and so have I delivered it. Now we can talk it over."

"But is this usual?" asked Aline, successfully concealing the drill of triumph that was pounding in her veins.

"You mean this message from the prince?" asked the general. "My dear Aline, it is not only usual, it is necessary. No one would dare send a card to the Prince of Marisi without a previous intimation that it would meet with acceptance."

"Indeed? You know why I ask, Paul. I am ignorant about these things, and a single false step would ruin me."

"Trust to me."

"Do I not?"

"Ah, yes. I am doubly glad now that I have been able to help you. Since the princess died, five years ago, the prince has been interested in only one woman, and that little devil of a De Mide had the blind luck to find her. But she did not last long, while you—ah, we shall show them!"

Aline did not quite like this speech, but she kept her own counsel about it. If General Nirzann were really willing to turn her over to his prince, it meant that she would have so much more freedom in the furtherance of her own plans. At the same time, she hated the little warrior for this hint of his attitude toward her; it was one of the things she laid up against him for the day of reckoning.

Having been informed that a week would be the proper interval before the issuance of the "acceptable" invitations, Aline waited out the prescribed period with ill-concealed impatience. Then she arranged a dinner-party, inviting only those of whose friendliness she was absolutely certain, and who would be pleasing to the guest of honor.

Imagine the surprise of Marisi when it found that Mlle. Solini had already reached that exclusive circle whose houses the prince graciously honored, now and then, with his presence! Why, the woman had not been heard of two months before! When an echo of the tumult reached Aline's ears through her good friend, the Countess Potacci, her only comment was a contemptuous smile.

The evening of the dinner-party arrived. Aline had spent the day with an appearance of outward calm, but with feverish anticipation within her bosom. She had given her personal supervision to every detail of the dinner; she had spent a quarter of Stetton's hundred thousand francs on the decorations and favors.

The gown she wore had been ordered especially from Paris two weeks before, for she had foreseen this occasion and prepared for it. In its selection she had displayed the depth of her shrewdness. She had guessed intuitively that this great man was not to be impressed by the frivolities and impudences of fashion; simplicity, nobility, real elegance were for him. This she achieved.

Jules Chavot, Richard Stetton, and Mrs. and Miss Ford were in the drawing-room when she entered, and she noted with pleasure that her costume failed to impress any but Mr. Chavot, who was in the way of being a man of taste. (As for the Fords, the latest Marisi loan had been negotiated through Papa Ford's New York bank.) A little later the Count and Countess Potacci arrived breathless.

"We were so afraid we should be the last," said the countess, "and that, you know, is frowned upon by *him*. Thank Heaven, he hasn't arrived!"

Ten minutes more and still the guest of honor did not appear. Aline began to be a little uneasy; there was no sign of it, however, as she chatted gaily with Vivi and Mrs. Ford. She heard the countess, some distance away, saying to Stetton and Jules Chavot: "It would not be surprising, you know—he has not been well for several months."

Aline forced a smile to her lips and put down her desire to rush to the window like an impatient schoolgirl. It was twenty minutes past the dinner hour—she was filled with despair.

Then a bell rang, the outer door was opened and closed, and Czean's voice was heard pompously announcing:

"The Prince of Marisi and General Paul Nirzann."

They halted a moment on the threshold—the prince a little in advance.

He was a man in the early fifties, tall and slightly stooped. His brown hair was a little gray round the temples; his keen, commanding eyes, in which the fire subdued all color, looked out from a face habitually pale; added to this, his sharp aquiline nose and firm though sensitive mouth gave him almost the appearance of an ascetic.

Above all, there was something indefinable about both the face and figure that would have seemed more or less to justify, a century or more before, that exploded doctrine of the divine right. (In passing, you are invited to consider what sort of a figure the prince's little general made at his side.)

Mlle. Solini advanced to greet her guest; he met her in the middle of the room. Her conduct, as General Nirzann told her afterward, was perfection.

"I am afraid we have discommoded you," said the prince in his low, agreeable voice. "It was unavoidable—I am sorry."

Then, after a bow to the remainder of the company assembled in his honor, he offered his arm to his hostess, to conduct her to the dining-room.

The prince, of course, had the place of honor; at his right was Aline. On her other side was the Count Potacci, who had taken in Miss Ford; beyond them, M. Chavot with Vivi and Stetton with his fat countrywoman—Mrs. Ford. The table was rounded out by General Nirzann and the Countess Potacci, who sat on the left of the prince. Thus, it will be seen, Aline had given herself as free a field as possible under the circumstances.

She felt that this one evening was more important than all the rest that might follow; here what was needed was not so much fascination—the lure of provoking lips and inviting eyes— as an impression of distinction, of aloofness. The rest could come later.

In this, of course, she was mistaken, and it was just as well for her that she found herself unable to adhere to her prearranged plan of attack. Finding that the Prince of Marisi talked much like ordinary men, she shifted her forces and began to use her ordinary weapons. The result was, that before the roast had been served the prince was saying to her:

"You see, *mademoiselle,* I was right. The house is pleasant—quite the pleasantest in Marisi."

Aline replied merely with a glance, much less incautious, and far more effective, than words.

"You are from Warsaw, I believe," observed the prince, stopping in the act of wielding his knife and fork to look at her. "I have been wondering why you selected Marisi for the winter, instead of going to Paris or Italy, as all Russians do."

"But I am only half Russian," replied Aline. "Perhaps that is why

I go only half as far. I am tired of Paris—and you know Paul is my cousin. It was he who recommended Marisi."

This was safe—she and the general had rehearsed their little story well.

"Then it is to General Nirzann I owe my present happiness?"

"If your highness considers it so, he is the one to receive your thanks."

"I shall give him another decoration tomorrow; he likes nothing better," the prince replied with a smile.

Aline looked across the table at her "cousin," the breast of whose coat was completely covered with ribbons and medals in five mathematical rows. Then, knowing that a thoroughbred must be driven with a tight rein, she turned the conversation to the military exploits of General Paul Nirzann and kept it there.

The natural result was that when, an hour later, the time came for the ladies to withdraw, the prince felt that he had not said the tenth part of what he had wished to say to his charming hostess.

But this slight disappointment of the Prince of Marisi was as nothing compared to the savage-mingled emotions that were tumbling about in the breasts of two of the other gentlemen at the table. M. Jules Chavot and Mr. Richard Stetton were genuinely disturbed by the vulgar sensations of jealousy, anger, and helplessness.

Chavot was thinking: "She is playing for the prince—well! If she succeeds, there is no hope for me."

Stetton was saying to himself: "Here I am in my own house, with my own servants—and what do I get? I'll show her—I pay the rent here—I'll show her!"

This thought was uppermost and came from the depths of the man. "I'll show her!" It appeared even on his face, and caused Vivi to remark to him: "M. Stetton, you are positively gloomy. Indeed, you look at every one as though you hate them."

Stetton merely grumbled in reply; it was all he could do to keep himself from uttering a decidedly unpleasant remark that rose to his lips as he thought that but for this Vivi he would long before have achieved his desire.

He continued morose and sulky over his cigar, and when the men rejoined the ladies in the drawing-room he thought for a moment of going home instead; but he ended by following the others. He got little satisfaction out of that. The Prince of Marisi continued to keep his beautiful hostess to himself, while the others were allowed to amuse themselves as best they could.

Stetton, Mrs. Ford, and the Count Potacci were conversing together in a corner when Vivi approached and said abruptly in an undertone:

"Have you seen anything of M. Naumann lately, M. Stetton?"

"I see him every day," Stetton replied shortly.

"Has he dragged himself into his hole again? He has not been anywhere for a week."

"Not that I know of."

"Is he ill?"

"No."

Stetton turned his back rudely on the girl. He was beginning to hate her, merely because the stock of the emotion that was gathering in his breast had to be bestowed somewhere.

He wandered off by himself and, placing himself where he could not be seen, stood watching Aline and the prince. They were seated side by side on a divan at the further end of the room, engaged in a conversation evidently both animated and amusing. The sight caused Stetton's anger to rise till he could scarcely contain himself.

He made a sudden involuntary gesture of decision, muttering to myself, "I'll show her. I'll not be made a fool of any longer!"

And having thus made up his mind, he walked back to the count and Miss Ford, whom he found discussing the undoubted success of Mlle. Solini's assault on the highest circle of Marisi society.

Stetton smiled grimly to himself, wondering what they would say if they knew the truth about her.

At ten o'clock the prince rose to go, beckoning to General Nirzann, who had been cornered for the past hour by the fat Mrs. Ford, and was therefore hugely relieved at the sign for departure. The prince spoke to the Countess Potacci and Mrs. Ford, bowed to the others, and then said good night to his hostess.

This operation required some five minutes, during which time the room was respectfully quiet, but no one heard any of the prince's words, he spoke in so low a tone. To judge by the smile on Aline's face, they were anything but unpleasant. The general followed, bending over Aline's hand, and a moment later they were gone.

There ensued immediately a scramble; you might have thought it was a race to see who could get away first from their charming hostess, who knew perfectly well that every one had been bored to death.

"My dear," said the Countess Potacci, "was it kind to ignore us so utterly? If it had been for anyone but the prince—"

"If you are walking," Jules Chavot was saying to Stetton, "I'm your man. I go to the Place, you know."

"Thanks," Stetton replied; "I don't think I'll leave just now."

The other looked at him in surprise, but said nothing as he turned to say good night to Mlle. Solini. Czean announced the Potacci car, and that of Mrs. and Miss Ford; in another minute they had departed, and Chavot followed them, with a last curious glance at Stetton, who was standing under the electric light in the hall with a gloomy and determined air.

The door closed. Vivi had gone to the library, and Aline and Stetton were alone. She turned to him, smiling:

"Well, was it not a success?"

Stetton grunted something unintelligible, and stood regarding her for a full minute in silence. Then he turned without a word and began to mount the stairs to the floor above. Aline, still smiling, watched him until he had nearly reached the top, then she called:

"But M. Stetton! Where are you going?"

He stood at the top of the stairs, looking down at her, as he said roughly:

"Come up here. I want to talk to you."

As these words, and the tone in which they were uttered, reached Aline's ears, a sudden and dangerous flash shot from her eyes. She said:

"But why up there? You know very well I will not do that. We can talk in the library."

Stetton replied calmly:

"I would rather not—Vivi is there. I will wait for you in your room."

Before Aline could say anything in reply he turned and disappeared in the hall above, and she heard a door open and close.

Aline stood for a minute without moving, while her eyes narrowed to a thin slit and her face grew pale with anger. She opened her mouth to call to Czean, but checked herself abruptly.

"I am not through with him yet; I must be cautious," she thought, and she smiled.

She walked to the door of the library and told Vivi that she was going to her room and did not wish to be disturbed, and they kissed each other good night. Then she returned and mounted the stairs and entered her room, closing the door softly behind her.

Stetton sat in a chair by the side of a table near the center of the room. He had lighted the reading-lamp and picked up a book from the table, but he was not reading.

As Mlle. Solini entered he raised his head slowly and met her eyes with what was meant to be an expression of grim resolve. But as he saw the anger on her face and met her fiery glance he turned his gaze away.

Aline stood before him saying:

"M. Stetton, you will be good enough to tell me what you mean by this?"

The young man replied doggedly:

"I want to talk to you."

"Well?"

Suddenly, fired into anger by the coolness of her tone and her air of contempt, Stetton sprang to his feet and shook his fist at her, shouting:

"I want you to understand that this is my house! I'm tired of having you treat me like a dog!"

Aline, still perfectly cool, interrupted him:

"M. Stetton!"

Something in her tone quieted him; he sank back into his chair while she continued:

"Do not talk so loud—the servants will hear you! That is better. Let me tell you, you are mistaken. In the first place, you are ridiculous to complain; have you not my promise? And this house—no, this house is not yours, and you know it. You turned everything over to me and put it in my name. That was gracious, I know; but it is not generous for you continually to remind me of what I owe you."

Stetton exclaimed:

"So that's it, is it? You get your hands on what you want and then tell me to go to the devil!"

"*Monsieur,* you are offensive."

"I hope so; I intend to be." The young man rose to his feet, facing her. "You think you can make a fool of me! Don't you think I see what you're after?"

Aline advanced and placed her hand on his shoulder. Then she said:

"Stetton, you do not believe that."

"Believe what? I believe—"

"That I am trying to make a fool of you! Be sensible! Look at me!"

He turned and met her eyes, and as he did so she placed her other arm across his breast and caressed his cheek with her hand. "Now, tell me," she said, "you are jealous of the prince, is that it?"

"Yes," he answered simply; held by her eyes and the touch of her hand.

"Well, that is foolish, because it is impossible. You are impatient, that is all—ah, I do not blame you!" She still clung to him, brushing his cheek with her fingers. "I am not less so myself—you make it hard for me—have you forgotten that I love you? Look at me. There—there!"

Stetton had taken her in his arms and was covering her face with kisses.

A knock sounded on the door of the room and was twice repeated. Aline drew herself away, whispering to Stetton to move to one side, where he could not be seen from the door. Then she walked to the door and opened it the space of a few inches.

It was then that Kemper, Aline's maid, proved to be unfit for her position, lacking the virtue of discretion.

As Mlle. Solini opened the door in a manner surely intended to inspire caution, and showed her face in the opening, Kemper's voice was heard on the outside, in a low but perfectly distinct tone:

"He has come, *mademoiselle!*"

There she stopped abruptly, evidently at some sign from her mistress.

But too late, for Stetton had heard. And, curiously enough—for his brain was not of the quickest—he had also understood. In one bound he was at the door and had thrown it wide open, and started to brush Kemper aside as she stood just without the threshold.

Quick as he was, Aline was quicker still. She sprang past him and ran to the head of the back stairway. There she stopped and called down into the darkness the one word:

"Run!"

Just as Stetton reached her side a door was heard to open and close below. Turning with an oath he ran back to Aline's room and through it to the room behind.

Looking from the window which faced on the rear yard of the house he saw the figure of a man, made plain by the light of the moon, running to the gate which led into the neighboring yard, through which he disappeared. The man was rather less than medium size and appeared to be bareheaded, while flying coattails stretched out behind as he ran.

Stetton threw the window open and, leaning out over the casement, shouted at the top of his voice:

"General Nirzann!"

Suddenly Aline's voice sounded in the room:

"*Monsieur,* close that window, or I shall have Czean throw you out of it."

The figure of the man had disappeared. Stetton turned to face Aline. She was standing in the middle of the room, gazing at him with eyes that blazed with anger.

Outside, in the hall, the moans of Kemper, the maid, could be heard through the door; Stetton, as he thrust her aside in the rush for the stairway, had knocked her head against a corner of the wall.

If Aline was filled with rage, Stetton was no less so. For a moment he stood by the window, then he moved a step toward her, trembling from head to foot. His words, when they came, were so choked with fury as to be barely articulate.

"So," he sneered, "your cousin has taken to using the back stairs, has he? I'll show you, and I'll show him, too! You wouldn't make a fool of me, would you? No, you bet you wouldn't! You bet you won't! What have you got to say?"

Aline's voice was deadly calm as she replied:

"You are mistaken, M. Stetton. That was not General Nirzann."

"Don't lie! Don't try to lie out of it! I saw him!"

"Nevertheless, you are mistaken. It was not General Nirzann."

Stetton glared at her.

"Then who was it?"

"I refuse to tell."

Aline's voice was hard now and her eyes held a dangerous glitter. Stetton, brought up sharply by her words, stood and glared in silence, surprised out of his rage. Finally he said slowly:

"You refuse to tell?"

"I refuse to tell," Aline repeated in the same cold, hard tone.

"But, good Heavens! do you mean to tell me—you admit—"

"I admit nothing. Nor will I explain anything tonight. You are mad—you would not believe me if I told you the truth."

"Tell me who it was?"

"I will not."

"By Heaven, you shall!" cried Stetton violently, advancing with a threatening gesture. Rage again possessed his being. "I say you shall tell me!"

Aline did not move.

"If you lay a hand on me I shall call Czean," she said calmly.

"Tell me who it was?"

"I will not."

For a minute there was silence, while they glared at each other. Then Stetton spoke:

"You know what this means. I will ruin you."

Aline remained silent and he continued:

"I will run you out of Marisi. You know that I have it within my power to do it. And General Nirzann will go, too. At the same time I'll fix both of you."

Aline said:

"You will not do that."

"Won't I? Oh, won't I? I'll show you. I'll give you till tomorrow night—twenty-four hours. You've pulled the wool over my eyes long enough. If you'll leave Marisi with me tomorrow, well and good. I'll keep my mouth shut. You know where to find me. And if you don't leave with me and agree to our immediate departure, I'll fix it so that you'll have to leave without me."

As he spoke Aline's manner had undergone a sudden change. A curious smile appeared on her face; the glitter disappeared from her eyes, and in its place was an expression almost of appeal. She appeared to hesitate a moment before she said:

"Then you would still—marry me?"

"Yes. But there would be no fooling this time," said Stetton grimly.

"And if I do not come?"

"I shall do what I have said," replied Stetton, thinking he had her. "I'll show you you can't make a fool of me! Remember, I'll run you out of Marisi!"

"How much time do you give me?"

"Twenty-four hours."

"Very well," said Aline calmly, and she held out here hand. "Good night."

"But are you coming?"

"I will tell you tomorrow. I must have time to think."

"But I must know—"

"*Monsieur,* you have given me till tomorrow—at midnight."

Stetton looked at her and started to take her hand; then, checking himself abruptly, he merely bowed. Without another word he turned and disappeared into the hall.

Aline stood still in the middle of the room. When she had heard him descend the stairs and leave the house she went into the next room and sat down at her writing-desk.

After a few minutes of thought she took out a piece of note-paper and wrote on it as follows:

Dear M. Chavot:

You told me the other day that if ever I needed you I could make you happy by telling you so. It was a pretty speech; if it was more than that, you may call on me tomorrow morning at eleven. That is all I will say now, except to tell you an old motto of mine: No one should ask for favors who is unwilling to bestow them. Therefore, if I ask one of you—

Aline Solini

Aline read the note over, sealed, addressed, and stamped it. Then she rang for Czean.

CHAPTER IX

━━ ⁓ ━━

M. Chavot Dislikes Americans

M. JULES CHAVOT, some time of Munich, has already been marked as a man of taste. This in what he considered the essentials of life. No. 1 in this list was women.

No one ever knew whether he lived on an income or by his wits, and he generally succeeded in making himself so well liked that no one ever stopped to inquire.

Indeed, nothing whatever was known of him in Marisi, where he had made his home for the past two years, except that he had been forced to leave Munich on account of the death of a young infantry officer who had rashly taken it upon himself to cross rapiers with M. Chavot, merely because he had offered himself as a substitute—and been accepted—in the affections of a certain young lady.

This was all of the reputation of M. Chavot that had preceded him to Marisi, and those who know Marisi will appreciate the fact that it gave him a certain independence of action.

But M. Chavot had really been bored to extinction in Marisi until the afternoon when he first saw Mlle. Solini in her carriage on the Drive. He got an introduction to her and within a week was her devoted slave.

At first he had received no encouragement whatever; then suddenly, as though she had all at once perceived his attractions, Mlle. Solini's attitude toward him had completely changed. Perhaps, in the tangle of intrigue which she was creating in Marisi, she foresaw, even at that distance, her need for M. Chavot; at any rate—to discard speculation—he received her smile.

Her favors so far had been meager, though graciously given, and M. Chavot was preparing himself for a long and delightful siege. Then came the dinner-party for the prince and the sudden shock to the young Frenchman's aspirations.

"The game's up," he said sorrowfully to himself, as, after leaving Mlle. Solini's, he made his way to the establishment of Mosnovin, back of the old Russian House.

There he emptied his pockets completely in two hours at roulette—at the end of the first hour he had been winner by six thousand francs—and returned to his room at two o'clock in the morning in search of sleep.

Seven hours later he awoke, yawned, stretched himself luxuriously, and called for his mail and a glass of vichy. When the mail arrived, a few minutes later, it proved—oh, frailty of woman!—to consist of five delicately tinted, daintily scented notes. There were probably some tradesmen's bills and letters also, but we shall pay as little attention to them as he did.

Four of these notes he glanced at indifferently and threw aside; but when he read the fifth he jumped in one bound from his bed to the middle of the room, calling for his valet.

In forty-five minutes he had shaved, dressed, and breakfasted, and was on his way to No. 341 the Drive.

Czean showed him into the drawing-room, and, after a short wait, during which M. Chavot appeared to restrain his impatience with difficulty, Aline entered. He rose to his feet and bowed, and she crossed to him, holding out her hand. The lucky man was permitted to kiss it.

As he did so the clock in the library struck eleven.

"You are punctual," said Aline, smiling at him.

M. Chavot bowed again. "As a money-lender."

"I did not know that punctuality was a characteristic of money-lenders."

"Ah, *mademoiselle*," said the Frenchman, assuming a sorrowful air, "then it is evident that you have never given one your note. I speak from sad experience."

Aline laughed and, seating herself on a divan, invited him with a gesture to sit beside her. When he had done so she said:

"No; to make a bad pun, I send my notes only to my friends."

"Then I am happy; I received one this morning."

"So I supposed, *monsieur*, and you make me happy by acknowledging it so promptly. I know that what you had said gave me sufficient reason to believe in your friendship, but Frenchmen are great talkers."

"Yet we have been known to act—at times."

"At all times."

"I assure you, you libel us!" cried M. Chavot with a smile. "But we ought not to object to being made a target for wit, since we use it so freely ourselves. In what I said to you, *mademoiselle*, there was neither wit nor dullness—it was simply the truth."

"Then you are my friend?"

"You know it—I am devoted to you."

"It is so easy to say that, M. Chavot."

"And still easier to prove it, when it is true. Try me. You said in your note that you had need of me. Here I am. Try me."

Aline appeared to hesitate, while a little frown gathered on her brow. Finally she said:

"I begin to be sorry that I sent you that note. Do not misunderstand me"—the young man had opened his mouth in protest—"I believe in your sincerity. I would not hesitate to ask a favor of you, but this can scarcely be called that; it requires a greater degree of devotion than I have any right to expect."

"*Mademoiselle,* you wound me and insult yourself."

"No; do not be angry; I mean to be kind, and I am right." Aline paused a moment before she continued: "And now I have made up my mind. We will forget all about that note. It is best."

"But it is impossible!" cried poor Chavot, feeling that he had somehow made a misstep, but unable to imagine how. Then, struck by a sudden thought, he added: "It must be this, that you no longer have need of me."

"No, it is not that," replied Aline. "I will be quite frank, *monsieur.* I need a man who loves me well enough to risk his life for me—a husband, a brother—I could not expect—"

Chavot interrupted her:

"*Mademoiselle,* I beg of you! You say you need a man who loves you well enough to risk his life for you?"

"Yes."

Chavot rose to his feet and stood before her.

"Here I am."

"But, *monsieur*—"

"Here I am," the young man repeated.

"Then—you love me?"

"As well as you could wish."

"Ah!"

Aline's eyes grew suddenly tender and she extended her hand. Chavot took it, dropping to his knees, and covered it with kisses.

"You know it!" he cried passionately. "You know it well!"

"Perhaps," Aline smiled. "At least, I hoped for it."

Her tone and glance caused the young man to tremble with joy. Suddenly he arose, saying:

"But I do not wish to discount my happiness. Tell me how I can serve you."

"Are you so anxious to risk your happiness?"

"No. I am desirous of earning it."

Aline looked at him.

"After all, you may decide that it is not worth it. If you do so you will not offend me."

Chavot repeated impatiently:

"Tell me."

Again Aline hesitated, then she said, without taking her eyes from his face:

"To begin with, a man has insulted me."

The Frenchman shrugged his shoulders. "I will fight him and, if you wish, kill him. What else?"

"That is all."

"That is all?" This incredulously.

"Yes."

Chavot laughed.

"But, *mademoiselle,* I thought you were going to ask me to risk my life. That is absurd; no one in Marisi can stand before me for five minutes."

"So much the better; my revenge is sure."

"This man—do you wish me to kill him?"

Aline allowed the light of hatred to appear in her eyes as she replied: "Yes."

In spite of himself, M. Chavot started in surprise. He had no false notions of women; he knew very well that they usually contain quite as much of the devil as of the angel; but he had not expected this cold and laconic sentence of death. There could be no doubt of Aline's sincerity; she wished the man to die. Chavot looked at her curiously."

"He has insulted you mortally then?"

"Yes. I cannot tell you, *monsieur;* but if I did you would agree with me." But Chavot's start of surprise had not escaped her, and she added: "There is yet time—I have not told you his name—"

"You will tell me now."

"You are sure?"

"Tell me."

"His name is Richard Stetton."

Chavot looked at her quickly.

"Stetton! The American who was here last night?"

"Yes. It was last night—he stayed behind—"

"I remember," Chavot interrupted. "I saw him. I wondered then what the deuce the fellow wanted."

"Some day," said Aline, "I will tell you what he did. He not only insulted me; he threatened me, and—I admit it—I fear him. That is why there must be no delay."

"There shall be none."

"It must be done tonight."

"It shall be."

Aline took the young man's hand and raised it to her lips.

"Ah," she murmured; "if I do not love you. M. Chavot, it is only because I have not dared. What can I say, except to again remind you of my motto?"

"I insist on nothing," the young man exclaimed, his brain fired with rapture. "Only—now, as I look at you—every moment that I wait is a year."

He seized both her hands and gazed into her face with burning eyes.

Aline suddenly drew her hands away and her eyes gleamed coldly.

"Well, your love will receive its reward when it has earned it. Come to me tomorrow and say, 'M. Stetton is dead,' and then—you will see."

In the midst of his passion Chavot felt himself shudder at her

words. For one instant he doubted her and feared her. The indifference of her tone as she spoke of the death of a man, the glitter of
hatred that had twice appeared, unmistakably, in her eyes—these
were not reassuring and almost gave the lie to her tenderness.
Chavot felt a momentary thrill of revulsion in the height of his fascination, curiously intermingled.

Something in her eyes, in her very attitude, appeared tigerish to
him and seemed to warn him to beware. But he laughed at himself
for his weakness, thinking, "I am no baby; I can take care of myself;
I have risked more to gain less," and said aloud:

"*Mademoiselle,* you are right; I shall expect my happiness only
when I have deserved it. There is only one thing to be said. If I kill
this morning—and I shall—it may be necessary for me to leave
Marisi immediately."

"In that case I shall come to you."

"You swear it?"

Aline pressed his hand. "I swear it!"

And five minutes later M. Chavot departed, feeling that for the
first time since he had come to Marisi he really began to live.

In the meantime the intended victim of this pleasant little plot was
going about preparations of his own, wholly unlike a man who has
only a few hours to live. The preparations appeared to be of some
importance and seemed to point to a journey, since luggage was
being packed and several little articles of comfort for travel were
being purchased.

The fact was, Mr. Richard Stetton had fully persuaded himself
that he was at last to have his own way with Mlle. Solini. After leaving her house the night before he had lain awake in bed for two
hours considering his position, which he had found completely

satisfactory. He felt sure that Aline would never allow herself to be exposed to the sneers and insults of Marisi; rather than that, she would meet almost any demand he might make.

The next morning he rose in better spirits than he had known for a month, and after a cold plunge and a hearty breakfast began to make preparations for the journey to Paris. He had decided on Paris for several reasons, of which the chief was that he wished to be seen in the restaurants and on the boulevards with his beautiful wife to be.

Aline would absolutely create a sensation; all Paris would smile at him, whereas previously, on two or three occasions which he would have preferred to forget, Paris had laughed at him. He closed his account at the bank, packed his luggage, and gave notice at the hotel. It is astounding how easily a man can delude himself into regarding a remote possibility as an apodictic certainty.

Toward noon Stetton started out in search of his friend Naumann, and ended by finding him, much to his surprise, at the legation, seated before a desk heaped with paper.

"Not working, I hope?" said Stetton incredulously.

"My dear fellow," said the rising young diplomat, "you insult my profession. I never come in this office but to work."

"Which explains, I suppose, why you come only once a month. I've been looking for you for a solid hour. I came here last."

"That comes of your lack of appreciation of my colossal industry. But what's up?"

"I'm leaving Marisi."

Naumann glanced at his visitor in surprise. "Leaving Marisi. When?"

"Tonight."

"No! But I thought—what of Mlle. Solini?"

"She is going with me."

"Indeed! And the other—Mlle. Janvour—"

Stetton frowned; the thought of Vivi had been the only disturb-ing element in his roseate plans. He replied:

"I don't know. I suppose she will come, too."

It was evident that the young diplomat was considerably affect-ed by this news. He rose to his feet and walked to a window, where he stood for some moments in silence. Then he turned, regarding Stetton with the air of a man who wishes to say something but can-not find the words, and ended by asking:

"Where are you going?"

"To Paris." Stetton glanced at his watch and added, rising to go: "I must get back to the hotel; I'm expecting a message at any moment. What I wanted to say was, will you dine with me tonight?"

"Why—that is—yes."

"All right." Stetton hesitated a moment before he continued: "I don't know—it is just possible that we won't be alone. You won't mind?"

"You mean—"

"Aline and Vivi may be with us."

After a short silence Naumann said with abrupt decision:

"I'll come."

"All right; that's settled, then. At seven sharp."

Stetton returned to his hotel, some dozen blocks away, at a rapid gait, and asked the clerk if any messages had come for him. Being told that there were none, he was plainly disappointed. It was already nearly two o'clock in the afternoon; he had expected to hear from Aline long before this. He went up to his room, not caring to exhib-it his impatience in the lobby and corridors.

There he remained for an hour, having left instructions that any message that came should be delivered immediately. None arrived. He thought of reading, but his books were packed away. For a long time he sat waiting—the most distressful of all occupations.

He took to pacing the floor, and finally, unable to remain inactive longer, he snatched up his coat and hat and sought the street. A minute later he was seated in a cab, on his way to No. 341, the Drive.

Czean opened the door. Stetton pushed his way inside without saying anything, but was halted by the voice of the butler:

"Mlle. Solini is out, *monsieur.*"

Stetton turned abruptly, and after a moments' hesitation asked for Mlle. Janvour. She, too, was out, said Czean.

"Where did they go?"

The butler did not know, and Stetton left, more impatient than ever. He reentered the cab, instructing the driver to join the line of carriages and automobiles farther down the drive. For an hour they followed the stream up and down, but the carriage of Mlle. Solini was not to be seen.

Stetton finally gave it up and returned to the hotel. He rushed to the desk. There were no messages.

Now, for the first time, the young man began to fear that Aline was going to allow him to do his worst, and oppose her word to his. Then he was struck by another thought: what if she had decided to leave Marisi without him?

He would go to No. 341 and force the truth from Czean's burly throat; he would go to the palace and get satisfaction from General Nirzann. A dozen grim resolutions entered his brain, only to disappear as rapidly as they came. All of which had the effect of forcing him to admit to himself that Mlle. Solini had fascinated him beyond all hope of resistance; he was being driven mad by the thought of losing her.

Gradually he compelled himself to become calm. After all, there remained nearly seven hours till midnight, and he had given her until then to come to him. It was inconceivable that she would discard a man who was in the habit of making presents to the amount of one hundred thousand francs in cash.

This reflection restored his ease of mind completely. He sat down at a table in his room and wrote a letter to his father, and one to a friend in Paris, after which he shaved and bathed himself, having nothing better to do, and dressed for dinner. By then it was nearly time to expect Naumann, and he left his room and descended to the lobby to wait for him.

In a quarter of an hour the young diplomat appeared, and they went in to dinner at Stetton's table in the main dining-room, before a window which looked out on the night throng in Walderin Place. The room, a large one, was crowded with stylishly dressed women and men in evening attire, for this was the most fashionable restaurant in Marisi.

As the two young men passed through, Stetton bowed to an acquaintance here and there, and Naumann appeared to know every one; it took them ten minutes to get to their table.

"We eat alone, then?' said Naumann as they took their seats.

"Yes. Aline was too busy to come," Stetton replied, not caring to explain the true state of affairs to his friend. "Why the deuce it should take a woman all day to pack a trunk I don't know."

"My dear fellow, I fail to understand you," said Naumann in a quizzical tone. "If Mlle. Solini was unable to come, why is she here?"

Stetton looked up from the menu.

"What do you mean?"

Naumann replied:

"Turn around and see for yourself. Fourth table to the right, just this side of the fountain. I thought you saw them as we came in."

Stetton turned and looked. What he saw caused him to rise half out of his chair with an exclamation of surprise.

It was Mlle. Solini, with Vivi at her side, sitting at a table with M. and Mme. Chébe and two or three others. At the same moment he saw, at the next table beyond, Jules Chavot with a party of young

men, including M. Framinard, of the French legation, and General
Paul Nirzann.

"Don't stare so," Naumann was saying. "They're looking at you."

"But what—" Stetton began, and then stopped, too astonished
for words.

Immediately his astonishment gave way to anger. So Aline
defied him! She came there to dine, knowing he would see her!
He had not been mistaken; he understood perfectly the contemptuous and hostile glance with which she had returned his gaze.
What the deuce could she mean? How did she possibly hope to
escape exposure?

Why, he could ruin her with two words, and by Heaven, he
would! All these thoughts were pictured on his face as he turned it
toward Naumann, who began to rally him on his deficiencies as a
host.

"It's no joke," said Stetton grimly. "Naumann, you were right
about that woman. And listen here: I'm going to run her out of
Marisi by tomorrow morning."

Naturally, their dinner was spoiled as a dinner. Conversation
lagged; Stetton did not see fit to elaborate on his prophecy of dire
misfortune for Mlle. Solini, and the other evidently had thoughts of
his own, as he sat in full view of Vivi's youthful and animated face.
Once he turned to Stetton to observe that he supposed the contemplated journey to Paris was abandoned, but he received in answer
nothing but an unintelligible grunt.

The room round them became more noisy than ever as the diners grew jolly with food and wine: but no laughter was heard at the
table of Mr. Richard Stetton, of New York.

Suddenly Stetton saw by the expression on the face of
Naumann that someone was approaching from behind. He turned.
Jules Chavot was standing at his elbow.

"You seem to have stuck all the young birds into one cage," Naumann was saying by way of greeting, with a nod toward the table which Chavot had just quitted.

The newcomer bowed.

"Yes. All but yourself and your friend Stetton. Which is as it should be."

Stetton had turned again to his place after a curt nod of greeting, not feeling in the humor for talk with this particular bird.

"And why are we so arbitrarily excluded?" said Naumann with a good-natured smile.

M. Chavot shrugged his shoulders.

"Perhaps I should have differentiated," he admitted. "To yourself there would, of course, be no objection, but there is beginning to be some feeling on the subject of rich young fools with no brains and less breeding."

As he said this the speaker glanced at Stetton with something of a sneer on his lips.

Stetton appeared not to have heard, but Naumann stopped abruptly in the act of raising a glass of wine to his lips and stared at the Frenchman in surprise.

"Chavot! What the deuce—"

Chavot interrupted him:

"Come, Naumann, what's the use pretending? I don't like to see you friendly with the fellow, that's all. You feel the same way about these hanged Americans, you know you do. It's sickening. Cads and cowards, every one of 'em, and it's time we told them so."

During this speech Naumann, guessing instantly at the other's purpose, had tried once or twice to stop him, but without success. Now, feeling that it was too late for his interference, he looked at Stetton and found him gazing at M. Chavot as though he only half understood what was being said.

"You're a fool to do this in here," said Naumann in a rapid

undertone to the Frenchman; and, indeed, the diners at near-by tables were already looking at them. "If there is any difference, you can settle—"

At that moment Stetton found his voice:

"Let him alone, Naumann. It's the same old stuff—dog in the manger. Let him talk."

Chavot turned to him instantly:

"If by that remark, M. Stetton, you mean that I have a desire to possess anything which you possess—"

"That's what I mean," Stetton broke in roughly.

"Then, *monsieur,* you lie."

These words, uttered in a loud voice, were heard over half the dining-room, which had suddenly become still. The smothered cry of a woman came from the next table.

Naumann rose half-way out of his chair to intercept the blow that might be expected, with a face suddenly grown white.

Chavot was looking with a sneer straight into the face of Stetton, who alone appeared to be unmoved by what had been said. He muttered aloud:

"Sit down. Let him talk. Let the fool alone. He's a liar himself."

But though Stetton had graciously given his permission for the Frenchman to talk, it appeared that the Frenchman was not inclined to be so generous.

There was a chorus of cries from all parts of the room, Naumann sprang to his feet and forward, and a dozen waiters came running toward them as Stetton sank back in his chair from a blow delivered on his face with the palm of M. Chavot's hand.

Instantly all was confusion. Half the diners left their tables to crowd toward the scene of excitement. Six or seven waiters grasped the arms of M. Chavot, and as many more were pulling at Stetton, who was choking and sputtering with wrath in his efforts to get loose.

Voices were raised all over the room; the woman who takes advantage of every fairly exciting occasion by going off in a faint was being carried to a parlor. Marisi was enjoying itself.

Naumann, who had grasped Stetton's arm so tightly that he ceased his efforts to get at the Frenchman, was saying in a voice that commanded attention:

"Come, old man, you're making a show of yourself. For Heaven's sake, be quiet. Be quiet."

Then the young diplomat turned to Chavot and said calmly:

"*Monsieur,* what you want is quite evident. I shall call on you in behalf of my friend, M. Stetton, whom you have insulted."

At this the waiters released M. Chavot, who bowed and walked back to his own table without looking at anyone, though the eyes of every one were upon him. The crowd fell back and began to seek their tables. The waiters, grinning delightedly at this pleasing interruption in a monotonous existence, were picking up their scattered napkins and hurrying to their places.

"Come; let's get out of here," said Naumann, starting to thread his way through the maze of tables and chairs to the door.

Stetton, wondering in a dazed sort of manner what had happened, followed him.

~w~

At Marisi Gardens

THIRTY MINUTES later Richard Stetton was sitting on the edge of the bed in his own room, with his brain still whirling in inextricable confusion concerning the cause and meaning of the scene in the dining-room of the Walderin.

His friend Naumann had just left him, after a twenty-minutes' conversation consisting mainly of a most amazing series of instructions and inquiries.

In the first place, what had happened?

Stetton pressed his hand to his brow in bewilderment and tried to bring order to his thoughts. M. Chavot had for no apparent reason called him a liar. He had instantly returned the epithet to the giver, which, according to his way of thinking, made the score a tie. Then Chavot had struck him—Stetton's face grew red at the memory—and then—

Well, then Naumann had led Stetton to his room and begun to ask him the most absurd questions.

First, he had offered to "act" for his friend. To this proposition Stetton had assented vaguely without understanding at all what it meant.

Then the young diplomat had asked if he was a good pistol shot. The answer was, rotten. How about rapiers? Stetton replied that he had fenced some. At that point Stetton lost the sense of things entirely and began to think that his friend Naumann was going crazy.

Finally he managed dimly to grasp the idea that he was expected to fight somebody with swords or something; but, by the time he opened his mouth to disclaim utterly any such intention, Naumann had departed. His last words had been something about returning in the morning as soon as he had completed "negotiations."

The combination of unusual and exciting events left no definite impression on Stetton's mind. There was too much to think about. He said something aloud to himself and realized, in a sort of surprise, that he had pronounced the word "duel." That was a starting-point; his thoughts assumed a degree of clearness.

Then his gaze shifted to his trunks, standing in the middle of the floor, and his mind shifted to the query, "What is that for? Where was I going?"

That in turn brought the thought of Aline, the scenes of the night before at her house, his threat to expose her, and the message that had not come. Then he had seen her in the dining-room, and there was M. Chavot, who had done something or other, and he would avenge himself on Aline tomorrow morning, and he might as well unpack the trunks.

He rose to his feet with a muttered oath, undressed himself mechanically, and went to bed and to sleep.

In the morning everything was different. He awoke early, with a depressing sense of impending misfortune and a feeling that the face of the world had changed entirely in the past twenty-four hours. A cold plunge revivified his body and cleared his mind.

All that had the night before been chaos and confusion now resolved itself into two or three definite facts which suddenly presented themselves with staggering force.

There was the contemplated trip to Paris; that must be abandoned—at least, for the present. He unpacked his trunks and returned the clothing and other articles to their places in the room. By the time he had completed this task, which took a full hour, he felt that he was hungry, and telephoned for breakfast to be sent to his room.

Over his fruit and coffee he reflected on the second problem: the fulfilment of his threat to Mlle. Solini. After all, now that he came to consider the details, it presented some little difficulty. He could not very well make a round of the drawing-rooms of Marisi to carry the information that Mlle. Solini was an impostor and a liar; he still stopped a little short of belief in Naumann's story of her.

He settled it finally with a decision to go to the Prince of Marisi with his wondrous tale, and by one stroke destroy both Aline and General Nirzann.

There remained the matter of the little unpleasantness with M. Chavot. He made short shrift of that. He simply dismissed the whole thing as an outlandish absurdity.

Granting that duels were considered good form in Marisi, they were not so in New York, and he, for one, had the common sense and the courage to stick to the customs of his native land. This phase of the matter he thought important enough to be argued out in detail.

Why, he said to himself, if we believe that when in Rome we should do as the Romans do, it amounts to this, that when we find ourselves among cannibals we should eat each other. Which is manifestly absurd. *Quod erat demonstrandum.*

Nevertheless, he somehow felt himself in this instance to be treading on dangerous and delicate ground, and he vetoed his first impulse, which was to go in search of his friend Naumann and end the thing in two words. Instead, he decided that he had better remain in his room and wait for Naumann to come to him, as he had promised to do.

It was a long wait, for it was then only nine o'clock, and Naumann did not appear until eleven. Exactly at that hour a message came over the telephone to say that M. Frederick Naumann was asking at the hotel desk for Mr. Richard Stetton. Stetton instructed that the visitor be shown up to his room.

The young diplomat entered breezily, yet with a certain air of seriousness which he seemed to consider suitable to the gravity of the occasion. His response to Stetton's slightly embarrassed greeting was a profound bow and a warm shake of the hand.

He wanted to know how Stetton felt, and congratulated him on his appearance of having had a good night's sleep. Then he sat down on a chair with the air of one about to begin an important and lengthy conversation, and said abruptly:

"Well, everything is settled."

Stetton glanced up quickly, with an expression on his face that plainly indicated relief.

"Ah," he exclaimed, "then M. Chavot—"

"M. Chavot had little to do with it," the other interrupted, "though in that little he behaved admirably. M. Framinard, a friend of mine attached to the French legation, acted for him."

Stetton rose from his chair and grasped the hand of his friend Naumann.

"I owe you a world of thanks," he said with some emotion.

"Not at all," declared the young diplomat. "I did my best, of course, and the arrangements are about as advantageous to us as they could possibly be. M. Framinard, who was in a position to make demands, graciously granted all my requests."

This speech appeared a little strange to Stetton; he could not understand why M. Framinard was "in a position to make demands." Had not he himself been the recipient of the blow? A feeling that he must uphold his rights in the matter showed in his voice as he said:

"Of course, M. Chavot will apologize?"

Naumann appeared astonished at this observation.

"Apologize!" he exclaimed.

"Certainly," said Stetton in a firmer tone. "I know you said that everything is settled, but I insist on an apology. Unless," he added, "he sends one through you."

"I don't know what you mean," said Naumann, apparently mystified. "M. Chavot has not apologized, and there is no reason why he should. He is willing to give you satisfaction."

"But you said everything was settled!"

"So it is, and as satisfactorily as possible. You are to fight M. Chavot with infantry swords tomorrow morning at six o'clock behind the old Marisi Gardens on the Tsevor Road."

Stetton dropped back into his chair with a sudden feeling that he needed fresh air.

He was completely taken aback.

So that was what Naumann had meant when he said that everything was settled! Great Heavens! Everything was the exact opposite of settled! He wanted to say something, he wanted to cry, "Impossible!"—he wanted to inform Naumann, who appeared to be as much of a barbarian as Chavot himself, that he (Stetton) possessed the common sense and the courage to stick to the customs of his native land.

He actually opened his mouth to speak, but somehow there seemed to be no words anywhere.

Naumann, in the meanwhile, was talking at some length. He said that M. Framinard had been inclined to choose pistols, but that he had been overborne by his (Naumann's) strategy. He explained that the selection of weapons was in the nature of a triumph, as the heavy infantry sword would be much less dangerous in the hands of the expert, Chavot, than the agile rapier would have been.

It thus became a matter of strength rather than agility, though, of course, they would use only the points. Despite Chavot's marvelous excellence as a swordsman—Stetton shuddered—it really placed the combatants nearly on a par. The young diplomat ended by questioning his principal concerning the nature and extent of his experience in fencing.

Stetton found his tongue.

"Is this thing necessary?" he blurted out.

The other looked at him.

"What do you mean by that?"

"I mean—all this—all this—it's silly. Rank nonsense. I won't do it."

Naumann, beginning to understand, gazed at him oddly.

Then he said slowly: "That's ridiculous, Stetton. You have challenged M. Chavot. You must meet him. It is not only necessary; it is inevitable."

Stetton exclaimed:

"I tell you I won't do it! It's rank nonsense!"

The young diplomat rose sharply to his feet, and when he spoke his voice was clear as the ring of steel.

"M. Stetton, it was with your sanction I carried your challenge to M. Chavot. My own honor is implicated. If you do not fight him as I have arranged, I will be compelled to go to his second and apologize for having acted on behalf of a coward."

There was a silence. Naumann stood motionless, tense, gazing straight at Stetton, who again was beginning to feel bewildered and helpless as he had the night before. The word "coward" was ringing in his ears like the sound of an alarm of fire, and confusing his thoughts.

He managed to stammer something which carried no sense to his own ears, but which seemed to mean something to Naumann, who said, without relaxing his attitude of stern inquiry:

"Then you will fight?"

Somehow feeling that he was speaking against his will, Stetton uttered the word:

"Yes."

Instantly Naumann's manner changed. He resumed his seat, and in a cordial and friendly tone repeated all the details of the arrangements. Stetton understood not a word of it; his brain was engaged in a little civil war of its own.

Then, caught by some phrase, his ear gave attention. Naumann was talking of a man, by name Donici, and by profession master of fencing.

"He has rooms just above mine," the young diplomat was saying. "You'd better spend an hour or two with him this afternoon and freshen up a bit. I'll go over and see him now. Then I must go to the office for an hour or two, after which I'll come after you.

"I shouldn't advise you to go out, unless you want every one to stare at you. Lie around and take it easy—read a book or something. *Au revoir.*"

And on the word he departed.

As the door closed behind him, Stetton rose to his feet. He was glad to be alone—that was his first thought; then, the next instant, he felt that he wanted someone to talk to. He crossed over and sat on the edge of the bed.

Then he jumped to his feet and began to pace rapidly up and down the room. An overwhelming thought, which is only faintly conveyed in the words, "I am going to fight a duel," was hammering at his temples with sickening force and regularity.

He became possessed of a sudden, insane anger—at Chavot, at Aline, at himself, at everybody! "Fool!" he cried aloud, without any idea as to whom he meant to apply the epithet. He crossed to the mirror in the door of the wardrobe and looked at himself, his face, his hands, his clothing, as though the object had never met his gaze before.

He felt himself seized by a sullen lethargy, an irresistible torpor of mind and body; he believed that he was about to faint. He threw himself across the bed and lay there, without moving, for two hours.

He was roused by the ringing of the telephone bell; a few minutes later Naumann entered. He started slightly at sight of Stetton's pale face and rumpled clothing, then announced that he had made arrangements with Signor Donici, who was at that moment waiting for them.

Stetton never forgot that afternoon in the room of the Italian fencing-master, with its two large windows overlooking Walderin Place, and its walls covered with foils, rapiers, masks, and daggers. The bloodthirsty appearance of the room was in direct contrast with that of Signor Donici himself—a little, round man of most astonishing grace and agility, and a face that would have reminded you of the face of a cherub but for the little turned-up mustache.

While the instruction was in progress, Naumann sat on a chair at a side of the room, smoking cigarettes, and now and then offering a suggestion, for he was no mean swordsman himself. He was surprised and considerably encouraged at sight of Stetton's ability with the foils, for, though he was plainly an amateur, he showed that he was acquainted with the principles of the game.

All his tricks, however—those little twists in variation of the four chief movements—were absurdly antiquated, and Signor Donici, noticing this, turned his attention to teaching him new ones.

For two hours, resting at intervals, Stetton lunged and parried, and leaped and slid till he finally threw down his weapon from sheer exhaustion. Sweat was pouring down his face and neck, and he was panting heavily.

"That's enough," he declared. "Gad, I was never so hot in my life!"

Naumann went with him back to the hotel and left him in his room, saying that he would return at dinner time, and Stetton found himself again alone. But the fatigue of his body had communicated itself to the brain; he was too tired even to think. He took a cold plunge, wrapped himself in a dressing-gown, and sat down in an easy chair to rest.

That evening at dinner the table in the main dining-room of the Walderin which was occupied by Mr. Richard Stetton and M. Frederick Naumann was the center of every gaze. Gossip had been busy with the scene of the night before and the one that was expected to follow as its natural sequel, and fancy was flying high.

Many stories were being whispered about; it is unnecessary to pay any attention to them further than to say that the name of Mlle. Solini was mentioned in none of them. Rumor, therefore, was running true to form.

Though the two young men furnished plenty of matter for pleasing conversation at other tables, there was very little of it at their own. To be sure, Naumann talked enough, but his companion found it anything but pleasing.

The young diplomat had somehow got started on a recital of the details of the half dozen or so duels he had witnessed—in one of which he had been a principal—and his descriptions of some of the fancy thrusts and cuts were so just and vivid that Stetton would have sworn he could see the blood flow.

With this difference, that the wounds and gashes appeared to him to be on his own body instead of those of the combatants in Naumann's little tales. By the time they reached the roast he felt like a dead man! He had long before wished to be one.

The dinner ended, and the two young men left the room, followed by a hundred pairs of eyes, and Stetton felt the gaze of every pair. They separated in the lobby; Naumann's last words were, "Don't bother to leave a call—I'll be around in time to get you up." Just as though they were going to spend a pleasant day in the country.

Stetton started for the elevator, realizing that the eyes of everyone in the lobby were turned upon him in open curiosity, perhaps even—he shuddered—in pity. The elevator-boy, too, regarded him as though he were some unusually interesting animal.

Again he found himself alone in his room, this time with a long night before him. He undressed himself and put on a bathrobe and slippers, feeling vaguely that to make his body easy and comfortable might have a similar effect on his mind. In this expectation he was grievously disappointed.

For upward of an hour he alternately lay on the bed and paced the floor; then he walked to the writing-table, took out a sheet of paper and a pen, and began a letter to his father and mother.

The letter was a most curious document, and it is to be regretted that there is not space to give it in full. Never before in all his life had Stetton felt that he had so much to say. He wrote with feverish rapidity, covering page after page, feeling that in the midst of a horrible nightmare he was talking to some one who knew and loved him, and would sympathize with him.

The letter was for the most part tender, reminiscent, and sentimental, though there was in it no touch of philosophy save that of egoism. For three full hours he wrote, and when he finally rose from the table, after placing the letter in an envelope and sealing it, he had worked himself into a frenzy of self-pity that was little short of sublime.

Most of the long night yet remained.

What to do?

He felt that sleep was impossible. Thoughts—plain thoughts, that brought plain pictures—returned in their keenness to torture him. He sat down with a book and gritted his teeth in the effort to bury his mind in it, but the effort was useless.

He got up and walked to the window, which he opened; the cold air rushed across his face. But the sight of the city with its twinkling lights seemed to madden him; he shook his fist furiously at the unoffending night.

Then he closed the window and walked to a chair and sat down, burying his face in his hands.

———

At half past five the following morning Stetton, accompanied by his friend Naumann, entered a big, gray touring-car in front of the Hotel Walderin.

The morning was cold—so cold that the wet snow which had fallen during the night was turned into frosty ice on the pavements and sidewalks.

The two young men were dressed warmly in fur coats and caps, and had just gulped down two hot cups of coffee.

As they seated themselves in the tonneau and the car started forward, Stetton's gaze was riveted on the back of a man, dressed likewise in fur, who was seated beside the chauffeur. He turned to Naumann and inquired with a whisper:

"Who is that?"

"The doctor."

Stetton looked away.

The car sped swiftly down the drive nearly to its end, then turned to the left on the Tsevor Road. The streets were deserted and silent, and there was that odd, splotchy appearance of the atmosphere as though daylight were arriving only in spots. Everything seemed to be covered by a cloak of gray solemnity.

Stetton no longer felt or thought; he sat as one in a dream; but he was being gradually roused by the cold air entering his lungs; he breathed deeply, feeling a pleasure in the sharp twang in his breast and at his nostrils. He knew that the time was not long now; Naumann had told him that the car would carry them to the rendezvous in twenty minutes.

Struck by a sudden thought, he leaned forward to look over the seat in front, then began feeling about on the floor of the tonneau with his feet.

"What is it?" asked Naumann.

Stetton replied:

"I don't see—where are the swords?"

"Framinard is bringing them."

Again silence. They had reached the country now, and the car sped swiftly onward past rows of gaunt, bare trees with layers of icy snow on their black branches, and now and then a farmhouse or a peasant's hut.

The cold seemed to increase; the men buried their chins deeper in the fur collars of their coats. The car crossed a bridge and just beyond turned sharply to the left; ahead was a long, level road, at one side of which, about a mile away, appeared a large, sprawling frame structure that looked like a deserted sheep-barn. As the car neared this building Naumann leaned forward and touched the arm of the chauffeur, who nodded and brought the car to a stop.

The men sprang out and started down a narrow, winding path which led to the rear of the building. Naumann was in front, followed by Stetton; the doctor, who was carrying a black leather satchel, brought up the rear.

They found the others already there in one of the numerous outlying sheds warming their hands over a fire they had made of old boards. As the newcomers entered they straightened up and bowed stiffly.

Stetton noticed a long, black, wooden box lying on the ground at the feet of M. Chavot, and gazed at it in a sort of fascination.

Naumann and M. Framinard moved together to a corner of the shed and began to converse in low tones. The doctor placed his satchel on the ground and sat down on it. M. Chavot remained standing by the fire and assumed an attitude of amazing unconcern.

Presently the two seconds returned from their corner to announce their decision that it was not light enough within the shed; upon which the whole party moved outside. Framinard and Naumann carried the wooden box, which they placed on the ground and opened, displaying to view two swords unsheathed.

"Remove your coats, *messieurs,*" said M. Framinard, who, as the elder of the two seconds, was entitled to the office of spokesman. He added in an undertone to Chavot: "Hurry up, man, we'll freeze to death."

The adversaries removed their coats and hats. Chavot appeared in a tight-fitting woolen jacket, while Stetton wore a heavy-knit jersey.

Stetton, for his part, was acting purely mechanically; a piece of advice from Signer Donici, the finishing touch for one of his tricks, was repeating itself over and over in his head:

"Twist under with the point—twist under with the point."

Stetton closed his lips tight to keep from saying it aloud: "Twist under with the point."

"M. Chavot, you have the choice," M. Framinard was saying. As he spoke he lifted the wooden box and one end.

Chavot approached and put out his hand to take one of the swords. As he did so M. Framinard slipped on the icy snow and fell.

The box overturned and Chavot grabbed at it to keep it from falling.

His hand came in contact with the point of one of the swords, and he drew it back hastily with an oath.

"What is it?" asked Naumann, stepping forward.

"Nothing. A mere prick," said M. Chavot indifferently while picking up his sword.

"But if you are wounded—"

"I tell you it is nothing!"

Framinard had by this time recovered his feet, murmuring

apologies, and handed the other sword to Stetton. He insisted on examining Chavot's hand, but, seeing that it was the merest scratch, motioned the adversaries to their places.

Stetton was biting his lip to keep his teeth from chattering, and found himself, to his own profound surprise, wishing quite naturally that it were not so cold. He was startled by Framinard's voice:

"Messieurs, en garde!"

A quick salute, and there followed the ring of steel. Almost with the first meeting of the weapons Stetton felt his heart sink within him.

The firmness of Chavot's eye was equaled only by that of his wrist, and Stetton felt both of them at once. It was impossible to conquer this man—and yet—and yet—he felt the blood tingle in his veins—perhaps—

They were trying each other out.

Chavot fenced with easy caution, keeping in mind the treacherous ice they had for a footing; Stetton was putting all his brains in his wrist and letting his body take care of itself. Chavot, observing this, pressed closer, advancing the hilt.

There was a sudden flash of steel, a quick turn, and Chavot, bending low, leaped forward like a panther. The point of his sword tore through the jersey of his adversary, who, in leaping aside to avoid the thrust, slipped on the ice and fell to his knees; but he regained his feet as the Frenchman turned to renew the attack.

Naumann had stepped forward with an anxious question, but as Stetton shook his head and remained on guard he stepped back again.

Then, all of a sudden, Stetton felt his adversary's wrist lose half its firmness and cunning, and at the same instant saw an expression of distress and wonder in his face.

"A trick," thought Stetton to himself, and he became more cautious than ever.

But Chavot's sword had inexplicably lost all its fire; once, essaying a mild attack with feint, he quite uncovered himself, and Stetton could have easily run him through but for his own excessive caution.

A look of puzzlement appeared on the Frenchman's face, and an anxiety that amounted to desperation. His arm grew so weak that he was barely able to hold his sword.

Then, so suddenly that no one knew just how it happened, M. Chavot sank helplessly to the ground, while his weapon fell from his hand and slid twenty feet away on the frozen snow.

Stetton, utterly bewildered, stepped back and rested the point of his sword on the toe of his boot. The two seconds and the doctor rushed forward and knelt over the prostrate figure and began feeling all over his body and asking where he was hurt. But Chavot knew no more than they.

He kept turning his eyes from one to the other and saying, in a puzzled tone: "What is it, what is it? He didn't touch me."

Framinard turned to Stetton:

"Did you touch him?"

Stetton shook his head emphatically.

"No."

They were opening Chavot's clothing to see for themselves when suddenly he made a quick movement and uttered an exclamation as though he had discovered something. His body was twisting and quivering now with the little involuntary movements of a man in great pain, and his eyes were rolling from side to side.

He raised his hand—the one that had been accidentally scratched by the point of his sword—and examined it closely, muttering to himself: "Ah—ah—ah!" in the tone of one who understands everything.

With great effort he said calmly:

"*Messieurs,* I am poisoned."

An exclamation of incredulous horror burst from the lips of the onlookers. Chavot silenced them with a terrible glance and continued, speaking with difficulty:

"It was on the point of my sword, with which I scratched myself.

"I am not to blame, but you would not understand. I must speak to M. Stetton. I have only a few minutes." As no one moved, he exclaimed in a tone of furious impatience: "I tell you I must speak to M. Stetton—alone! Leave me!"

The others fell back at the look of command and agonized entreaty in his eyes, and Stetton approached and stood by his late opponent.

"Kneel down," said Chavot, "they must not hear."

As Stetton obeyed the body of the Frenchman writhed and twisted on the ground like one in torture, and a horrible grimace of pain parted his lips. When he spoke again it was in a whisper, and he appeared to force the words from his burning throat with a terrible exertion of the will.

"Listen," he said, and the word sounded like the hissing of a snake. "You heard—my sword was poisoned."

He paused for an instant, trembling violently, and grasped Stetton's arm in a grip of steel in an endeavor to steady himself.

"It was Mlle. Solini—curse her for a demon of hell!—beware—beware—"

Stetton felt the dying man's fingers sink into the flesh of his arm.

"She wanted to kiss my sword—and I—idiot!—I took it to her last night—mine—a string of red silk—I am dying—romance—romance—"

A tremendous shudder ran over the form of the Frenchman,

after which he lay still with closed lips. Stetton glanced round at the others, and they ran forward.

The doctor knelt down and placed his ear against Chavot's breast.

After a long minute he looked up and said in a tone of horror: "He is dead."

They had to pry his fingers loose from Stetton's arm, one by one.

CHAPTER XI

———

A Royal Caller

WHEN RICHARD Stetton found himself again entering his room at the Hotel Walderin, it was with the most curiously mingled emotions his breast had ever entertained.

Relief at his escape from the sword of his adversary and horror at the manner of the Frenchman's death were uppermost, but all was penetrated with the thought of Aline and Chavot's dying words.

He hardly dared to doubt them, for he had a bit of corroborative and convincing evidence of their truth. On picking up Chavot's sword from where it had fallen on the ground, he had seen, just where the blade joined the hilt, a tiny string of red silk thread. He had torn it off and thrust it in his pocket before returning the sword to M. Framinard.

He had said nothing to any of the others concerning the purport of the Frenchman's last words.

In the first place, he himself was not sure of their truth; and even granting that, what good end would it serve to spread the story? If Aline was guilty, nothing could be more certain than that she had so managed that no evidence could possibly be found against her. And Chavot's story was so fantastic, so practically improbable, that it might easily be set down as the delirium of a brain, writhing in agony and burdened with its own crime.

But what of Aline?

He had sworn to be revenged on her—as he phrased it, to "run her out of Marisi." Somehow his desire for revenge was not so keen as it had been two days before. This thought made him uneasy, he did not know why, and he raised his voice aloud in a new vow for vengeance.

First, however, he must see her. Why? Merely to find out if Chavot's story were true. Of course, that would make no difference. In any event, he would ruin her fine plans in Marisi before the sun set.

These reflections occupied his mind as he changed his clothing and ate a hearty breakfast. By then it was ten o'clock, and he got into a cab in front of the hotel and gave the driver the address of Mlle. Solini's house.

Certain of his doubts might have been set at rest if he could have seen the expression on Mlle. Solini's face when she was informed by Czean that Mr. Richard Stetton was in the library. A gleam of surprise and anger leaped into her eyes as she instructed Czean to ask the visitor to wait.

"Chavot has failed me," she murmured to herself; "so much the worse for him."

She hesitated, asking herself whether she should see Stetton. She rose and walked to her writing-desk and unlocked one of the drawers and counted the money it contained—thirty-two thousand francs, all that was left of the American's hundred thousand.

"That is not much," she said aloud, with a smile. Then she closed and locked the drawer and, after a leisurely glance at herself in a mirror, left to meet the visitor.

As she entered the library, where Stetton was waiting, he rose to his feet and bowed stiffly. He had, in truth, a difficult task before him, for never had Aline appeared more beautiful and bewitching. She wore a blue dress that clung to her form as though affectionately caressing her warm body; her golden hair and blue eyes and white skin had the intoxicating effect of white snow and blue sky and the golden radiance of sunshine.

The young man's heart beat faster as he looked at her; he stilled it with an effort as he said coldly:

"You are perhaps surprised to see me, *mademoiselle.*"

Aline crossed to a chair by the fireplace and invited him by a gesture to resume his seat before she replied:

"A little, I confess. After what happened three nights ago, that is natural."

"I do not refer to what happened three nights ago."

"No? To what, then?"

"To my—to what happened this morning."

"Ah! You mean—"

"My affair with M. Chavot."

"But why should I be surprised to see you on that account?"

Stetton looked into her eyes as he replied:

"You know of no reason?"

"None."

"M. Chavot was an excellent swordsman."

Aline gave a start of surprise.

"You say 'was'? But then—what—"

"M. Chavot is dead," said Stetton calmly.

A quick gleam—was it of remorse or hatred?—came and went in Aline's eyes.

"You killed him?" she said, rather a declaration of fact than a question.

"No."

She exclaimed impatiently:

"What then? Why do you not tell me? Is it a riddle?"

Without replying, Stetton rose to his feet and, thrusting his hand in his waistcoat pocket, took forth a little piece of red silk thread.

"Do you recognize that, *mademoiselle?*" he asked, handing it to Aline.

She started the barest trifle, then, after a moment's hesitation, took the piece of thread and looked at it curiously.

"What do you mean?" she said finally. "How could I recognize an ordinary piece of silk thread?"

"I thought you might," said Stetton, looking at her with what he meant to be a searching gaze, "since it is the one you tied on M. Chavot's sword."

Aline returned his gaze with a perfect assumption of astonishment.

"The one I tied on M. Chavot's sword!" she exclaimed. "Are you by any chance gone crazy, Stetton?"

He persisted:

"Do you deny it?"

"It is too silly to deny."

Stetton resumed his seat.

"Perhaps you will change that opinion," he said, "when I have told you what I know. I may as well begin at the beginning."

And he told her the story of the duel, including a detailed description of the death of M. Chavot. At this Aline shuddered; and when he told her of the Frenchman's dying words and his curses for Mlle. Solini, her face blazed with an appearance of honest anger and indignation.

Then Stetton told of finding the corroborative bit of thread on the hilt of the sword, and ended by asking Aline sternly if she still thought his accusation silly. She replied:

"It is not only silly; it is insulting and horrible. I cannot think that you believed it, Stetton. Also, it is impossible; how could M. Chavot have brought his sword to me?"

"Easy enough, in this case. M. Framinard has told me that the swords were left at Chavot's rooms overnight. There was nothing wrong in that."

Aline rose to her feet, saying with an air of dignity:

"Enough, M. Stetton. If you believe that I have done this thing—if you believe that I could do it—"

"I do not say that I believe it," cried Stetton, also rising.

"You have certainly intimated your belief."

"Not at all; I merely asked you to deny it."

"I did so."

"It is not true?"

"No."

"You did not see M. Chavot last night, nor go to his rooms?"

"No. Wait a moment." Aline hesitated an instant, then added: "Yes, I did see him—I had forgotten. He was here only a short time."

"And you did not—not—"

"No." Again Aline hesitated, appearing to reflect, then she said slowly: "M. Stetton, there is something else which I should perhaps tell you. You will understand some things better when you know. You remember three nights ago, when you stayed behind after the dinner party?"

Stetton nodded; as though he could forget!

"Well," Aline continued, "that man whom you thought was General Nirzann was really M. Chavot. No—do not interrupt. He had handed me a note in the dining-room, saying that he wished to see me alone as soon as possible. He did not explain the request, except to say that his reasons were urgent. I told him to come back after the others were gone, and instructed Kemper to show him to my room when he came."

Stetton was silent, drinking in her words. She resumed:

"I had told him to use the rear stairway, because I did not wish any one to see him return. Then, when he came, you were there, and—you know the rest. Since then I have thought that perhaps that was why he sought a quarrel with you, unless—were there any other differences between you?"

"None."

"Then that explains everything."

It would be unfair to Stetton to say that he swallowed this story whole, but there were several points of it that strongly appealed to him.

It disposed of General Nirzann entirely in the matter, it explained Chavot's eagerness for a fight, and it gave a reason why the Frenchman should try to cover Mlle. Solini with obloquy. He wanted to believe it, and he ended by doing so, though not without drawing enormously on his plentiful stock of credulity and vanity.

He looked at Aline. How beautiful she was, and how utterly desirable! After all, if she loved him, even a little—

"But why did you not tell me all this before?" he asked in a tone which suggested that he would withdraw the question if it offended her.

Aline smiled.

"You gave me no chance."

His memory was that he had given her a dozen chances; had, in fact, begged her to tell him who the man was and what he was doing there; but he forbore to press the matter. The real reason, he told himself, was Aline's spirit of independence; he had been too high-handed with her. He said:

"Aline, I am going to tell you this, that I believe you. Perhaps I'm a fool, but it seems to me that the whole trouble has been that you want to have your own way and I want mine. We can't both have it, that's certain. But you ought to do this much for me: marry me and leave Marisi. Come to Paris, Vienna, anywhere. We've made a mess here of everything. Come, will you go?"

Aline cried:

"But what of Vivi?"

"We can take her with us."

There was a silence, then Aline said:

"No, I will not do that. My dear Stetton, you are so impatient!
Give me but a little more time. Two of the wealthiest young men in
town are already nibbling at the bait; another month and we can go.
Really, you must be patient; it would be ridiculous to waste all that
I have done here."

"But, hang it all, I have waited so long already."

"It will be only a little longer. Be patient. You think, perhaps,
that this delay means nothing to me. I do not choose to show it, that
is all. Only, my dear friend, you should know better. A woman such
as I am does not promise herself to a man unless—unless—"

"Well," said Stetton eagerly, "unless—"

"Unless she loves him."

Stetton moved swiftly to her side and enfolded her in his arms.

"Say it," he murmured, kissing her.

"I love you," said Aline in a low and sweet voice.

"Again," commanded Stetton.

"I love you."

"Ah," cried the young man, trembling with joy, "and I love you!
Great Heavens! It drives me mad just to look at you, and to hold you
like this, in my arms—ah!" His voice suddenly became rough: "And
you ask me to wait! How can I?"

"That is easy, if you love me."

"You are wrong; that is what makes it difficult. What is easy is
for you to make me do anything you want me to."

"Well, am I not worth it?" smiled Aline, sure of herself with his
arms round her.

"A thousand times!" cried the infatuated young man in a tone
of ecstasy. In sober truth her caresses maddened him.

When she was in such a mood, or when she chose to make

herself so, there was an irresistible voluptuousness in her every movement, in the mere touch of her finger. And her wonderful blue eyes, when she allowed them to glow with tenderness and the promise of love, set his veins on fire with every glance.

They talked a while longer—talk that consisted mostly of frenzied ejaculations on the part of Stetton, and little tender words from Aline.

Gradually, having thus in a way settled the future, she brought him round to a consideration of the present. And suddenly—he could not for the life of him have told how it came about—he found himself asking her if she were in need of money.

"What a question to ask a woman!" cried Aline, laughing. "Silly! You ought to know"—she tapped him on the cheek—"that every woman—" she tapped him on the other cheek—"always needs money."

They laughed together, and Stetton took her in his arms.

"Extravagant is no name for it," he declared, kissing her. "But there—I shall go to the bank this afternoon, and if there's any left, I'll send it to you."

Soon after that Vivi entered the room and Stetton made ready to depart, after greeting her with a bow. The girl had been out to the hills south of the city with a party of the younger set of Marisi society, skating and tobogganing, and her cheeks and eyes glowed and glistened with youth and health.

Even Stetton was conscious of a feeling of admiration as he looked at her. He lingered a moment in conversation before he went away.

The moment the door closed behind him Aline sprang to her feet with an exclamation of relief.

"Come, Vivi," she cried, "you must help me. It is noon already—I have only an hour—I thought he would never go."

"Still, if you are going to marry him—" said Vivi with a smile.

"Good Heavens! I'll get enough of him then. But come, I must not wait another minute."

She dragged the girl off upstairs.

Judging by the carefulness of her toilet. Aline was preparing for an occasion somewhat out of the ordinary. Vivi and Corri, the new maid, struggled with the great mass of golden hair for thirty minutes before its owner was satisfied.

The gown she was to wear, which had been selected the day before, lay on the bed, a creation of Monsard in black chiffon and velvet, with simple Grecian lines that yet could not hide the air of modishness that clings to some women's clothing as it does to their personality. The hair done, Aline sent Vivi downstairs to ask Czean if her instructions had been carried out to the letter regarding luncheon.

"Tell him if anything is short of perfection he loses his head," said Mlle. Solini.

When Vivi returned fifteen minutes later the toilet had been completed.

"How do I look?" asked Aline, rising from her chair for inspection.

The answer was already in the eyes of the girl, who had halted on the threshold. For a full minute she gazed, quite soberly. Then, "You are the most beautiful woman in the world," she said, with the seriousness of one profoundly and frankly impressed.

Aline laughed, and, crossing the room, passed her arm around Vivi's waist.

"Let us hope others will think so," she said. "It is really important, for both of us."

She began to ask the girl of her morning's sport, and the names of those who had composed the party. Vivi named two or three, and then Aline asked abruptly:

"Was the young Potacci there?"

Vivi glanced at her quickly, and then away, replying simply: "Yes."

Aline smiled. "You do not like him?"

"Not at all."

"He is the best match in Marisi."

"But he would not look at me! Besides, I am afraid of him."

"Well," said Aline, "we shall see."

After a moment's pause she started to speak again, but was interrupted by the ringing of the doorbell downstairs. The next instant they heard Czean open the door, and his respectful tones, and then another voice sounded in the hall, low and pleasant. A minute later steps were heard on the stairway, and Czean appeared at the open door of the boudoir to say:

"The Prince of Marisi is in the drawing-room, *mademoiselle.*"

It will be understood at once that Aline had wasted not a minute of her time at the dinner party three nights before. A *téte-à-téte* lunch with the Prince of Marisi was something that any woman in town would have given her eyes for, though in some cases it would have necessitated a considerable amount of discretion.

Aline herself had felt that she should perhaps have tactfully declined the honor, or postponed it, and she had made no mention of it even to her good friend the Countess Potacci. A long ride and a hard chase make the best game.

As Mlle. Solini entered the drawing-room the prince rose with a profound bow. The greeting smacked of formality, and Aline responded to it in like manner. The prince approached.

"You see I am punctual," said he, taking her hand, with his lips parted in the smile that made women forget he was a prince.

"In my country that is not considered a compliment," said Mlle. Solini. "We Russians have a saying, 'The sooner started the sooner over.'"

"And like most sayings," retorted the prince, "it fails to apply in the present instance. If I wish a thing over I never begin it. Punctuality with me is born of desire."

"Your highness's kindness is ably supported by your wit," said Aline, leading him to a seat. "But I warn you to be careful—the more I get of pretty speeches, the more I want."

The prince had seated himself beside her on a divan, and was regarding her with a gaze that was almost a stare.

"It is impossible to make pretty speeches to you, *mademoiselle*," he declared abruptly. "One doesn't know where to begin."

Aline laughed—a little, musical, rippling laugh.

"Still, if you look long enough—" she said, with an assumption of hopefulness.

"That is hardly possible," said the prince firmly.

"What, to find matter for a pretty speech?"

"No; to look long enough."

Aline, perceiving that the prince was a hard rider, decided to draw away into safety by the old ruse of doubling back.

"But this is absurd!" she cried. "In another minute your highness will be making love to me, and you have not yet had your lunch!"

As though called from some magic domain by the word, Czean at that moment appeared in the doorway.

"Luncheon is served, *mademoiselle*," he announced.

Aline rose.

"Shall we go?" Then, as the prince stood beside her and offered his arm, she added: "We lunch in the dining-room. You know the way, I believe."

As soon as they were seated at the table, Aline took the conversation in hand herself. To tell the truth, this woman who had managed so many men had at last found one who she was afraid was going to manage her.

The tone of the prince's voice and the glance of his eye, the very way in which his head moved on his shoulders, conveyed a sugges-tion of power which, when he cared to use it, would sweep away all obstacles.

"He is dangerous," Aline was thinking; "I must look out for myself."

She began to talk of houses—houses in general, and the house of M. Henri Duroy in particular, which she declared was much too small even for a family of two.

"It is annoying," she said, "to be compelled to lunch in your din-ing-room. It is too—what shall I say?—formal. The library is dingy. And from what I have seen, I would say that all Marisi houses are about the same."

"It is different, I suppose, in Russia," said the prince, without dis-playing any enthusiasm for the subject.

"Yes, but there everything is different. We seem to have more room everywhere, more air, more space. The fact is, Europe is stifling."

"Still, I would hesitate to condemn a continent," said the prince, with a smile.

"That is because it is your own."

"Perhaps. But others seem to find it amusing."

"In which number I beg to be included. It is not that I find it dull. But in Warsaw, for instance, there is a sureness about life that is unknown here. It is as though—but there—I am afraid I am too deep for myself."

Mlle. Solini laughed, but with a sweet seriousness in her eyes.

Changing the subject abruptly, she began to ask the prince of his travels. She said that she had heard that he had visited America, and confessed to a lifelong curiosity concerning that country. The prince sighed, but graciously proceeded to tell her all about the land of freedom.

From that they arrived somehow at a discussion of the alliance with the Turks; the prince professed himself astonished at Mlle. Solini's knowledge of politics. Time flew swiftly; they were both surprised to find themselves sipping coffee, and to hear the clock in the library strike three.

The prince declared it was impossible to believe that two hours had passed so quickly.

"At that rate," he said, "a year with you, *mademoiselle,* would seem but a day. It is not idleness, but pleasure, that is the thief of time."

"An afternoon, then, would be hardly worthwhile," said Aline, looking at him over her cup. "Otherwise I would offer you one—this one."

"Do not!" cried the prince, as though in alarm. "I would not be able to refuse, and I must meet a delegation of petitioners at the palace in an hour. They were to have come at two o'clock; I postponed it—for this."

"You see!" cried Aline, laughing. "I not only understand politics, your highness; I am an influence."

"You are, indeed."

At something in the prince's tone Aline glanced up quickly. He was looking at her in a manner that was not new to her, and yet, in his case, there was a difference.

He spoke again, looking into her eyes:

"You are an influence, *mademoiselle.*"

"In politics?"

"No. I am not talking of politics. That is for old men and fools, certainly not for a beautiful woman like you. I have a habit of frankness. Shall I tell you something?"

He appeared really to mean it as a question, requiring an answer, as he stopped and looked at Aline inquiringly. She replied:

"If you need my permission, you have it."

"It is this," he said quietly: "you interest me more than any other woman I have ever known. With me, that is saying a great deal."

"Your highness is pleased to be kind."

"I have said I am frank."

"Then if it is true, I am gratified and honored."

Aline felt the stiffness of her words, but she also felt herself, for once, genuinely embarrassed. This was not the road she had mapped out for the Prince of Marisi to follow; how could she get him out of it? She said:

"No doubt your highness has been interested in many women."

"A few. It has been my chief amusement in life. You see, *mademoiselle,* I am frank."

Princely this, indeed! Aline had had enough of it. She did not regard herself as an amusement; nor, to do her justice, was she; but the prince did not know that. She pushed back her chair abruptly and rose to her feet. The luncheon was ended.

They returned to the drawing-room. The prince evidently felt that he had received a rebuff; his manner, courteous and amiable to an extreme, nevertheless held a tinge of dissatisfaction.

Aline was smiling and perfectly at ease; she felt that she had begun to take things in her own hand. They had talked but a few minutes when the prince rose to take his departure. His car was waiting in front.

"I need not tell you," said Aline—they were in the reception-room, by the door—"of my gratitude for your highness's kindness."

"It is not gratitude I want," said the prince. "Indeed, there can be no question of gratitude between you and me, *mademoiselle.* I have to thank you for a most pleasant afternoon. *Au revoir.*"

Aline watched him through the glass of the door as he descended the stoop and entered his limousine, the door of which was held open by a footman in green and yellow livery. The car started forward with a jerk and disappeared down the drive.

"If he is piqued," said Aline to herself as she turned away from the door, "so much the better."

Then she murmured aloud, the unconscious voicing of a thought: "The Princess of Marisi."

She moved to the library and, seating herself before the fireplace, was soon buried in thought.

There was a quick patter of steps on the stairs, and Vivi's voice came from the doorway:

"Aline, have you been in my work-basket?"

Mlle. Solini looked round:

"What is it?"

"My red silk thread," said Vivi. "I can't find it anywhere."

Aline hesitated a moment before she replied:

"It is in my room. I was using it last night. You will find it on my dressing-table."

"Thank you," called Vivi, as the quick patter of her feet was again heard on the stairs; and again Mlle. Solini buried herself in thought.

CHAPTER XII

--~~--

A Dangerous Man

$\mathcal{I}$T WOULD seem that the city of Marisi was determined to give Richard Stettin a merry time during every minute that he spent within its limits. It was not even sufficiently hospitable to allow him a good night's rest, no sooner did he dispose of one source of danger and anxiety than another appeared to take its place.

Leaving Mlle. Solini's house shortly after noon, he had walked up the drive toward the offices of the German legation, smiling at the world as he went along.

He did not exactly believe everything that Aline had told him, but neither did he have strong doubt concerning any one point of her story. Nothing that she had said was impossible, and nothing was certain.

He decided that it was the duty of a gentleman to give her the benefit of the doubt, especially when the gentleman had just left her embrace. Besides, had she not declared that he would not have to wait much longer for their marriage.

At the legation, where the clerks eyed him with frank interest, as though he had been a personage, he was told that M. Naumann had not appeared that day and was not expected till the morrow. He continued his walk down the drive and stopped at Naumann's rooms, but found that he had missed him by half an hour. Then he went to his bank for some funds and performed two or three other little errands, arriving at the Hotel Walderin for lunch a little before three o'clock.

As soon as he stepped inside the lobby he was hailed by the desk clerk, who came hurrying to his side with an important and mysterious air.

His message, which he conveyed in a low tone of secrecy, was to the effect that the chief of police had called twice at the hotel to see M. Stetton, and had left word to communicate with him immediately on his return.

"But what did he want?"

"I do not know, *monsieur,* that was all he said."

Stetton took the elevator to his room. He was thinking to himself that somehow Naumann and Framinard had bungled their plans, which had been arranged with the help of the doctor, and that the police were investigating the death of M. Chavot.

This new trouble promised to be considerably more unpleasant, though less dangerous, than the one he had just escaped. Scandal, publicity, perhaps even a scene in court, would be the result.

"Hang it all," he muttered, "what have the idiots done?"

He went to the telephone and called up the office of the chief of police. After fussing and wrangling for ten minutes, and receiving three wrong numbers—without which incidentals no European telephone call is complete—he finally got connected with the office.

"Hello!"

"Hello! This is Richard Stetton. I wish to speak to the chief of police."

"What do you wish to speak about?"

"I don't know. He called to see me while I was out, and left word for me to communicate with him."

"What is your name?"

"Richard Stetton."

"Spell it."

Stetton did so.

"What is your address?"

"Hotel Walderin."

There had been a pause of some length between the questions; the clerk at the other end was evidently carefully writing down the answers. His voice came:

"Wait a minute, please. I will let you know."

Stetton waited not one minute, but twenty. He fumed with impatience; he stood first on one foot, then the other; he swore under his breath; he worked the receiver-hook violently up and down, and he ended by leaning wearily against the wall. As he did so the voice that he had heard before sounded at the other end:

"M. Stetton?"

"Yes."

"Are you the M. Stetton who was present at the death of M. Jules Chavot this morning?"

"Yes."

"Very well. The chief of police instructs me to say that just at present he does not care to talk to you. You will probably hear from him later."

"But what does he—"

There was a sharp click as the man at the other end hung up the receiver. With an exclamation of anger Stetton began to move the receiver-hook up and down; but, as he continued this operation steadily for five minutes without getting any attention from the operator or any one else, he gave it up and placed the receiver on the hook with a vicious bang.

"Idiots!" he muttered to himself, meaning no one in particular.

He snatched up his coat and hat and left the hotel in search of Naumann.

The search lasted three hours, and was unsuccessful. The young diplomat appeared to have suddenly disappeared from the face of the earth. Nor was M. Framinard to be found either at the French legation or at his rooms. At seven o'clock Stetton returned to the hotel, cold, tired, and hungry. He had not eaten anything since breakfast.

After dinner he went out again to continue his search, but with no better success. He finally gave it up as hopeless, and, finding himself not far from No. 341, thought of going to see Aline; but a glance at his watch showed him that it was past ten o'clock, and he returned to the hotel and went to bed and to sleep.

He was awakened in the morning by the telephone. M. Frederick Naumann was asking for him at the desk.

When Naumann entered a minute later he found Stetton sitting on the edge of the bed, dressed in white crepe pajamas and smoking a cigarette. His reception, though not cordial, was warm.

M. Stetton desired to know where in the name of the seven saints the rising young diplomat had been keeping himself for the ten years immediately preceding.

"In two words," said Naumann, when he got a chance to speak, "I have been saving your precious neck from the noose of the hangman. Never in all my life have I worked as I worked yesterday. I am waiting for you to thank me."

"Thanks awfully," said Stetton with irony. "Now, go on. What do the police want with me?"

Naumann smiled broadly.

"Was the old nut here, too?"

"If by the 'old nut' you mean the chief of police, my answer is, twice," said Stetton. "Kindly explain. I thought you and Framinard and the doctor had it all fixed up."

"So we did," replied Naumann, helping himself to a cigarette and taking a seat. "We had our report carefully written out, signed by all three of us as witnesses, and presented it in due order to Duchesne. He's the chief.

"The whole trouble started in the notorious fact that Duchesne hates Germany and all Germans. He tried to make it warm for me, and nearly succeeded, despite the fact that I had the words of Framinard and the doctor to support mine. I spent seven hours yesterday afternoon and night hunting for General Nirzann under guard. When I finally found him and got him to go with me to the prince I received my liberty and Duchesne received a reprimand."

"But what did Duchesne want? What did he say?"

"He accused me of assisting you to poison Chavot."

Stetton shuddered, murmuring: "What an awful mess it might have been!"

Naumann blew a cloud of smoke thoughtfully toward the ceiling, then said:

"It's none too pretty as it is. Listen here, Stetton; you know more about this thing than you've told. Of course, I'm not ass enough to think you had anything to do with it, but why wouldn't you tell us what Chavot said?"

"Because it would have done no good." Stetton paused a moment before he added: "It wouldn't hurt perhaps to tell you. But it doesn't alter anything. Chavot died of his own dirty trick!"

"But what was it he said to you?" Naumann insisted.

The other looked at him with an air of calculation.

"If I tell you," he said finally, "it must go no further. You will understand why."

"I shall not repeat it."

"Swear it."

"On my word."

And once more Stetton repeated the story that had been conveyed to him in the disconnected and painful phrases of the dying Frenchman. He did not, however, for some reason unknown to himself, make any mention of the piece of silk thread.

As the tale was finished Naumann sprang to his feet in excitement.

"But that explains everything!" he cried. "I was sure of it. Chavot may have had his faults, but he was a man of honor. It explains everything!"

"It would," agreed Stetton imperturbably, "if it were true."

Naumann exclaimed:

"True? Why, man, of course it's true! Nothing could be more certain! It all fits in perfectly. Chavot was just the sort of romantic fool to carry his sword round to some woman to let her kiss it, but he was a brave man and no murderer. Of course it's true!"

"I happen to know that it isn't," declared Stetton with the air of a man who knows a great deal more than he has told. "Chavot lied! Mlle. Solini had nothing whatever to do with it."

Naumann looked at him quickly.

"How do you know that?"

"She told me so."

"Told you— How? When?"

"Yesterday. I asked her. She denied absolutely any knowledge whatever of the whole affair."

"You asked her—good Lord!" Naumann sank helplessly into a chair.

Then he again sprang to his feet.

"Stetton," he said slowly, "you positively need some one to look after you. It's amazing! It's incredible! I suppose you went up to Mlle. Solini with a polite bow and said: '*Mademoiselle,* kindly tell me if you are a murderess.' And when she answered no, you believed her. Stetton, you're worse than a baby. You're an imbecile! If any—"

"Hold on!" the other interrupted. "Perhaps I'm not such a fool as you think. I did not, as you amusingly suppose, bow to the lady and ask if she were a murderess. I questioned her for a quarter of an hour before she even knew what I was driving at."

"Well, there's no use arguing about it," said Naumann in a sudden tone of determination. "This is a matter for the police."

"It is nothing of the sort," said Stetton firmly, "and you know it."

Naumann looked at him incredulously.

"Do you mean to tell me you are going to say nothing whatever about it?"

"I am not."

"Then I shall."

"No, you won't. You gave me your word you'd mention it to no one."

"But, hang it all, it's infamous! Why, if we—"

Stetton interrupted him:

"Wait a minute. Even granting that Aline is guilty, how would it do any good to inform the police? Where's your evidence? Chavot is dead. You couldn't possibly connect her with it in any way."

"But he told you—"

"The ravings of delirium. No one would believe it against her word, with no evidence to support it."

The truth of this was so apparent that Naumann was forced to admit it. Still he argued, saying that they owed it to Chavot to clear his name of the odious blot that had been placed upon it; but he could do nothing with Stetton, who continued to affirm his belief in Mlle. Solini's innocence.

As Naumann's impatience increased, the American became more obstinate; at one point of the controversy it began to appear as though Stetton would soon have another duel on his hands. But they gradually calmed down, and when the young diplomat rose to go an hour later the two young men shook hands warmly and parted in friendship.

Naumann left the hotel to go directly to the legation, where he expected, and received, a severe reprimand for having become involved in so unsavory an episode as that of M. Chavot's death.

"It is unfortunate for me," said Baron von Krantz, with a look of disapproval from under his heavy eyebrows, "that you possess so small a share of discretion. You are very well aware that we are already regarded with disfavor in Marisi, and you should take every precaution to avoid giving it anything to feed upon. I have not yet decided whether I shall make a report to Berlin."

Naumann sought his desk and began an assault on the pile of papers that had accumulated during his absence of two days. It was not a very successful assault, for his mind was elsewhere, as indeed it had been now for something over a month.

He was thinking of a sweet, girlish face with laughing black eyes and a crown of lustrous black hair; and by the side of this picture there came, unbidden, another—that of a wondrously beautiful woman whose eyes, to Naumann's fancy, had no laughter in them, but the cunning of a devil and the infamy of one.

His interest in Vivi, he had often told himself, was purely romantic; he had merely felt pity for her at her helplessness in the clutches of Mlle. Solini. But of late he had not been quite able to persuade himself that his interest was limited to this.

He was conscious of an increasing desire to see her, to touch her; more than once he had found himself wondering what it would be like to hold her in his arms, to kiss her—

At such times he would shake himself impatiently and ask himself, with furious indignation, why he should take the trouble to theorize concerning a sensation which he had so often experienced. As though he had never held a woman in his arms!

"But not Vivi," something would whisper within him; "not Vivi, with the laughing eyes and lustrous hair— "Then he would swear at himself aloud and go out for a walk.

Today he was frankly and increasingly worried for Vivi's welfare—even, he told himself, for her life. He was firmly convinced, in his own mind, that Mlle. Solini, as she called herself, was responsible for the death of M. Chavot, with the poison intended by herself for Stetton.

As he thought over that dreadful scene he was amazed at the woman's fiendish cleverness. For if her scheme had been successful; if Chavot had wounded Stetton instead of himself with the poisoned sword, the result would have been that the Frenchman would probably have been condemned and executed as a murderer, and she would have been rid of both of them.

Whatever accusations Chavot might have made, she would have so arranged it that no slightest proof could be found against her, and the Frenchman would simply have earned the additional odium of having attempted to place the blame for his own crime on the shoulders of a woman.

And Vivi was in the power of this creature—more, she even loved her! And who knows where Aline would strike next?

Naumann shuddered.

Suddenly the face of Vivi, trusting, innocent, with smiling lips, appeared before his eyes as plainly as though she herself were standing there in front of him. Beside it, as always, there was slowly outlined that other face, fair indeed and beautiful, but which appeared to him to lose all its beauty in its wickedness.

A sudden, swift resolve entered his brain. He set to work feverishly, and in less than an hour had cleared away the mass of papers on his desk, dictated a score of letters, and filled a pad with memoranda and recommendations for Baron von Krantz.

Then he snatched up his coat and hat, and, finding a cab outside the legation, got in and gave the driver the address: "No. 341 the Drive."

As the cab rolled smoothly along Naumann tried to formulate some plan of action. A dozen ideas offered themselves, only to be rejected all.

"There is one thing that would frighten her," he said to himself, "and that is an encounter with Vasili Petrovich. She is afraid of him, and well she might be. If I could only find him! I know of nothing else."

He was undecided what to do when the cab stopped in front of No. 341.

He wondered curiously how he would be received by Mlle. Solini, or if he would be received at all.

When she came to him in the drawing-room with outstretched hand and a smile on her lips he took the hand and bowed over it without returning the smile. If Aline was surprised to see him, she betrayed no sign of it, as she motioned him to a chair and took one for herself.

"We have not seen you for a long time," she began in a tone of friendliness. "Though, to tell the truth, we have hardly had reason to expect you."

But Naumann was in no humor for preliminary courtesies. He said abruptly, looking straight into Mine's eyes:

"I do not come as a friend, *madame,* and you know it."

"Ah!" said Aline quietly, with a flash of her eyes. "I admire you for that, M. Naumann—it is frankness, and that is what I like. For what have you come?"

"I don't know."

A smile of real amusement appeared on Mlle. Solini's face.

"You don't know?"

"No. That is, I do know, and yet I wonder why. I come to warn you."

"To warn me?" Aline's eyebrows were lifted.

"Yes."

"Are you so interested in my welfare?"

The young diplomat made a gesture of impatience.

"At least, I did not come to play with words," he said. "Let us not pretend, *madame*. You know very well what I know and why I came. Let us both be frank."

"Well, then, frankly, I do not understand you. You say that I know what you know. What is that?"

Naumann looked straight at her as he replied:

"I know, for instance, that you are responsible for the death of M. Chavot. No—do not start with indignation and surprise—you do it very well, but it is quite useless. I am not telling you what I guess at, but what I know. I repeat, it was you who poisoned the sword of Jules Chavot."

Suddenly, as he spoke, a change appeared on the face of Mlle. Solini. It was as though she had lowered a curtain from before her eyes, as she returned the gaze of M. Naumann with a frank expression and mocking. She said, in the tone of one uttering a challenge for amusement:

"If it is as you say, *monsieur*—and I will not presume to contradict you—what then?"

For an instant Naumann was taken aback, then he recovered himself and said quietly:

"I expected that. I knew you were capable of it. Perhaps you are right in your insolent security; perhaps it is impossible to fasten this particular crime on your shoulders, where it belongs. But that is not all I know. I know also that you are the wife of Vasili Petrovich, and that you betrayed him and tried to kill him."

"Well—for the sake of argument, I will grant that also—and what then?" Aline smiled sweetly.

"Merely this, that you are in danger of overreaching yourself. And now I will tell you why I came. I came for Mlle. Janvour. Depraved and wicked as you are—you asked me to be frank, *madame*—you know that as long as she remains with you she is approaching her ruin.

"I want to take her away from you. I will have a guardian appointed for her; I will see that her welfare and happiness are assured. I have no ulterior motive, *madame;* you who read men so easily can see that for yourself. I do not—" He hesitated for an instant, then continued: "I do not pretend to love her, but I am sorry for her. That is all."

There was a long silence, while Aline sat looking into the young man's eyes, without a trace of emotion in her own. Then suddenly she rose and walked to the door and pressed a button on the wall. In a moment a servant appeared, and she said:

"Tell Mlle. Janvour to come to the drawing-room."

Then she returned to her chair to wait. They heard the heavy footsteps of the servant on the stairs, and shortly the quick patter of Vivi's little feet.

As the girl entered the room, Naumann rose and bowed. Vivi's rather effusive greeting came to a halt when she observed the profound seriousness on both their faces.

Aline said abruptly:

"Vivi, I sent for you to ask you a question. M. Naumann and I have been talking of you. There is no need to repeat what he says about me, since you have heard it before from his lips—and in my absence.

"He now says that I am unfit to take care of you—that I am depraved and wicked—that he wishes to find a home for you among his people—that he wishes you to leave me. I will add that he does not pretend to love you, but declares that he is sorry for you. I called you to let you decide for yourself."

Vivi was looking first at Naumann, then at Aline, with a face suddenly grown pale. Her lips quivered as though she wanted to speak, but could not find the words, and the expression in her eyes told of the struggle that was going on within her breast.

As for Naumann, he, too, found himself without words when he felt that he most needed them. "He does not pretend to love you—" It sounded harsh and somehow false.

Did he love her, then? But before he could crystallize his tumbling thoughts he heard Vivi's voice:

"*Monsieur*, you have no reason to be sorry for me." The voice trembled and was very low. "You know that I love Mlle. Solini; you are wrong to say such things of her. But I—I assure you—I appreciate your kindness—your interest—"

Suddenly her voice broke and stopped, and, covering her face with her hands, she turned and ran from the room.

There was a silence. Then Naumann turned to Aline, and his voice also was trembling as he said:

"*Madame*, you have taken advantage of me. You will regret it. You did not wait for me to tell you all that I know; I will now tell you the rest. This morning I received a letter from Vasili Petrovich. I shall answer it tomorrow. I shall expect to hear from you before then."

And then, while Mlle. Solini remained standing motionless and silent in the middle of the room, for once in her life startled out of speech, the young diplomat walked to the hall, took up his coat and hat, and left the house without another word.

For a long minute Aline stood still where he had left her. Then she moved slowly to the door and down the hall to the library, where she seated herself in her favorite chair in front of the fire.

She remained thus a long time, buried in thought; then, glancing at the clock, she rose and started for her room to dress for dinner.

"Decidedly," she murmured aloud, as she began to ascend the stairs, "this M. Naumann is a dangerous man."

~~~

CHAPTER XIII

The General Runs on an Errand

IF ANYONE in Marisi had been asked what was the most interesting room in the palace of their prince, the answer would have been: "The one at the rear of the main corridor on the left, on the second floor." And if they had been further questioned why, they would have replied, "Because no one is ever allowed to enter it."

In this room, which the prince permitted no one to enter, he was seated alone on the morning of the day of the events narrated in the preceding chapter. There appeared to be nothing in the room or about it that would justify the mysterious exclusion of the curious; nor, in fact, was there.

On three of its sides were shelves of books, above which hung paintings and etchings, distributed in a somewhat haphazard fashion. On the fourth side, which faced the drive, were three double windows and a wide-open fireplace. A large table was in the center, heaped with books and papers.

The fact was that the prince, who found himself in a position considerably more public than he would naturally have wished, had simply chosen this den as a retreat from the importunities of subjects and sycophants.

The prince was half sitting, half reclining, in a big easy chair placed between the table and the fireplace. His eyes were closed and his chest moved regularly up and down with his breathing; it might have been thought that he was in reality asleep.

But young De Mide, his secretary, would at once have noticed the two little lines of wrinkles extending across the high white forehead, and would have known from that sign that his master was engaged in deep and profound consideration of some weighty and important subject.

Suddenly the prince opened his eyes, sat up, and rose to his feet with a short laugh greatly resembling a grunt—certain indications, De Mide would have said, that he had reached a decision. He left the room, walked down the corridor to its farther end, and mounted a flight of stairs on the left. In the corridor above he halted before a door at about its middle, and knocked on it sharply. A voice sounded:

"Come in."

The prince entered.

As he did so General Paul Nirzann jumped up from a chair he had been occupying near the window and bowed half-way to the ground.

"Ah! Your highness, I am honored."

"You usually are," said the prince dryly. "As, for instance, last evening."

The general looked at him with a deprecatory air, saying:

"The decision was left with your highness."

"I know, but you had already decided for me."

"Is that possible? I beg your highness's pardon; I simply made a request."

"Yes, and it led to another offense for poor old Duchesne, whom you hate, but who nevertheless loves me as well as you do."

The face of the little general grew red with indignation.

"You will pardon me, your highness," he cried, "but that pig of a Duchesne has never—"

The prince interrupted him:

"That will do, Nirzann. You are hardly to blame, after all, for I really believe that young Naumann was in the right. But that is not what I came to discuss; let us forget it."

General Nirzann remained standing while the prince walked to a chair and seated himself. Then the general resumed his own chair and sat in respectful silence, waiting. Presently the prince spoke abruptly:

"Some time ago, Nirzann, you introduced me to a Mlle. Solini, who you said was your cousin."

The general looked at him quickly.

"Yes, your highness."

"She came, you said, from Russia. She herself has since informed me that she selected Marisi for this season on your recommendation. One or two things have led me to believe that this recommendation was owing to—well, let us say, for my benefit."

"But that—your highness knows—" The general halted in confusion.

"You need not deny it," said the prince with a smile. "I shall not make it a matter for reproach; indeed, I owe you a debt of gratitude. Mlle. Solini interests me."

"I am not surprised at it," said General Nirzann, who had recovered himself instantly at hearing the word "gratitude."

Disregarding this slightly impertinent observation, the prince continued:

"Yes, I admit it, I am interested in her." He paused for a moment, then asked abruptly:

"Is she really your cousin?"

But the general, who had been expecting just this question, had an answer ready:

"Certainly, your highness. Why do you ask that? If you doubt me—"

"No, I do not doubt you; I am merely seeking information. She is your cousin, then?"

"Yes."

"From—"

"Warsaw."

"She is Russian?"

"Yes. That is, on her father's side. Her mother was German—it is through her that we are connected."

"I see. Her estates, then, are near Warsaw?"

Again confusion appeared on the face of the general. He started twice to speak, without saying anything, and ended by declaring abruptly, in the tone of a man who has determined to speak the truth:

"They would be, your highness, if she had any."

"Ah!" The prince lifted his eyebrows. "But I expected that. This little tale of her fabulous wealth is a child of your brain, Nirzann?"

The prince's tone was friendly, and the general grinned as he replied:

"Yes, your highness. For the—let us say—amusement of Marisi. Otherwise she would have been ignored."

"Quite right. I applaud your acumen. She is not of noble birth?"

"No."

The prince frowned slightly at this answer, and walked to a window, where he remained for some minutes looking down into the street. The general sat silent, knowing perfectly well what was going on within the other's mind, and well satisfied with his knowledge. Suddenly the prince turned:

"I repeat, Nirzann, I am interested in her."

The general said:

"And I repeat, your highness, that it is not at all surprising."

"But she is your cousin?"

"A distant one."

"Then you think——"

"I think exactly as your highness does on all subjects."

"And Mlle. Solini?"

"I cannot answer for her. You have, no doubt, already discovered that she has a mind of her own. Most of her life she spent in a convent, but in the past two or three years she has been from one end of Europe to the other."

"When do you expect to see her?" the prince asked abruptly.

"I don't know. Perhaps this evening."

"Could you see her this evening?"

"Yes, your highness."

"Alone?"

"Certainly."

"And ask her——"

"Whatever your highness wishes."

"Then do so. I need not tell you what to say. I would advise you to use as much strategy and delicacy as possible. And if you are successful, in the end, there is a vacant Cross of Buta that I should know how to make use of."

The general fell on one knee, his face pale with joy.

"Your highness—I am overwhelmed—it has always been my desire——"

"I know," the prince smiled. "That will do, Nirzann. Earn it, and it is yours."

And, adding that he would expect the general to ride beside him at three o'clock as usual, the prince departed.

All of which goes to explain the expression of mingled hesitation and resolve on the face of General Paul Nirzann as, a little after eight o'clock that same evening, he rang the bell at the door of 341 the Drive.

All afternoon he had been impatiently awaiting this hour; now that it had arrived, he found that he had not yet decided what to do with it. At one instant his thought was that everything would be plain sailing; the next, remembering Aline's ambitious schemes both for herself and Vivi, the chance of success appeared slim.

He had indeed chosen an unfortunate time for his strategic assault on the fortress of the fair. Only two hours before his arrival Aline had heard from Naumann's lips the words, "I will write to Vasili Petrovich tomorrow," which had caused her to pay M. Naumann the compliment of declaring that he was a dangerous man. A doubtful one, indeed, not without its conjectural effect on his future—which he should have foreseen.

But General Nirzann, who was not skilled in the detection of subtle shades of expression on faces, saw nothing out of the common on that of Mlle. Solini as she welcomed him in the library.

There was restlessness and impatience in her manner, but he had been noticing that for some time now. For the rest, he was too absorbed in the difficulties of his own mission to give much study to its object.

They talked for an hour on various subjects. A dozen times the general began cautiously feeling the ground to lead up to the purpose of his visit, but invariably was taken away from it by Aline, until he began to think she had guessed it and was consciously avoiding it—in which supposition, of course, he flattered himself.

At length, having discussed the details of Aline's successful campaign in Marisi and offered one or two tentative suggestions for the future, he approached the subject of money.

"There is no want of that," said Aline, replying to his question. "I have over a hundred and twenty thousand francs in cash."

The general whistled in surprise.

"What the deuce!" he exclaimed. "Is this American made of gold?"

"So it would seem. But have you nothing to say of my dexterity at getting it from him?"

The general looked at her quizzically.

"That depends. You know what I have said before. It seems to me impossible that the man is fool enough to give up so much for nothing."

Aline laughed. "He has expectations—of marrying me."

Nirzann snorted.

"To be frank," he said, "I wish to know whether he is going to be in a position to interfere."

"Interfere? In what way?"

"With—certain plans."

Aline looked at him with quick suspicion. "But we have discussed all this before."

"I know. But if it becomes necessary to get rid of him, what then?"

"I have told you I will do so whenever you are ready."

"Whenever I am ready to leave Marisi with you, yes. But what if we abandon that intention?"

Aline regarded the general for a moment with a quizzical air, then said dryly:

"My dear Paul, you are trying to find out something. Have I not told you twenty times that your attempts at subtlety are ridiculous? Come—what is it you want? Out with it."

"Shall I be frank, then?" asked the general in the tone of one who is willing to come out in the open rather than take any unfair advantage.

"Yes," Aline smiled. "I beg of you, general, do not deceive me."

He was saying to himself, "I must use strategy; I must be tactful."

After a moment of thought he said aloud, impressively:

"Aline, this morning the prince came to see me in my room at the palace." General Nirzann never pronounced the words "my room" without adding "at the palace."

"Indeed!" said Aline, glancing at him.

"Yes; and he came to talk of you. Actually. He pretended that the object of his visit was to discuss that unfortunate affair of M. Chavot's death, but I saw through him. He came to talk of you."

"Indeed!" Aline repeated. "His highness is very kind."

"But it was not kindness. I assure you, he was thinking only of himself. *Mademoiselle,* you have said that you love me. I have been compelled to believe myself secure in your heart. But what if I have the Prince of Marisi for a rival?"

Aline looked at the general, and so faint and subtle was the mockery in her eyes and on her lips that she safely dared his blunt observation.

"My dear Paul," she said, "the only reason I repeat that I love you is that it gives me pleasure to say it. You know it well. Not even the prince himself can displace you—in my heart."

For the first time in two months the general neglected to fall on his knees before her in rapture at words of love from her lips. The fact was that he was being torn cruelly by conflicting emotions.

In so far as he could love a woman, he loved Aline, but his capacity in that direction was limited. The true passion raged not within his valorous breast. Stronger than his love for any woman, for all women, was his attachment to his prince and the desire to stand first in his graces—and, besides, there was that little matter (not little, however, in its importance to the general) of the Cross of Buta.

These thoughts being uppermost in his mind, Aline's protestations of love merely brought a smile to his lips—a smile that, on the face of a common man instead of a general, might have been called a simper. He said, attempting a sigh:

"Nevertheless, dearest, I begin to fear. The prince is irresistible."

"Not against you, Paul."

"Alas! I fear so—even against me."

"Do you not hear what I say? I love you."

"But if the prince should attempt—"

"He would be unsuccessful."

"I cannot believe it."

"I swear it."

"I do not believe it." The general was getting desperate.

Aline laughed outright.

"My dear Paul, you say that very much as though you do not want to believe it."

But against this insinuation the general protested warmly.

"How can you say that? Good Heavens! Have I not risked my reputation—my very existence—for your sake?"

"Still, it is plain that you are willing to give me up."

General Nirzann was getting a little bewildered, seeing that he was going round in a vicious circle and getting nowhere. Decidedly, he must admit something or give it up. Between the two alternatives there was but one choice. He cleared his throat. How to say it? He opened his mouth and closed it again. Then he plunged forth recklessly:

"No, I am not willing to give you up. But, *mademoiselle,* I am the servant of my prince. Everything that I have—my purse, my honor, my life—belongs to him. And even what is dearer than all else—"

Aline interrupted him sharply:

"Stop, general!"

He continued with increasing firmness:

"You must understand me, dearest Aline. You know that I love you; but where my prince would enter I must step aside. That is what I came to tell you. Not as an emissary, I assure you—not that—but his wishes are plain. What can I do? Unhappily I have nothing but a choice of two evils."

"And to lose me is the lesser one?" She was enjoying herself immensely.

"No—that is—you must understand—" The general wondered why the deuce she should think it necessary to put things in so unpleasant a manner.

"I do understand," said Aline dryly. "And this is my answer: I love you!"

"Of course, of course; and I love you," replied the general, beginning to show signs of impatience. "But do you not see? It is impossible to refuse the prince."

Aline said calmly:

"Then I shall accomplish the impossible."

At this plain statement of intention the general rose to his feet in excitement.

"I know what it is!" he exclaimed. "It's that American! I have suspected this all along. You won't give him up—that's what it amounts to."

"Do you mean M. Stetton?"

"Yes, I do; and it's true!" cried the general, getting more excited every minute.

Aline said sharply:

"It is absurd, and you know it."

"It is true! You love him!"

"Ridiculous."

"You love him! You have been deceiving me!"

Aline shrugged her shoulders contemptuously; then, after a moment's reflection, looked at General Nirzann with a sudden air of decision.

"Listen to me, Paul. The American is a fool. I care not that for him," snapping her fingers. "No—let me finish! Or, rather, answer a question. You came here today as an emissary from the prince. Am I not right?"

The general began to protest; but, seeing the uselessness of it, ended by admitting that it was as she said.

"And what does the prince want?"

The general, seeing that she knew everything, anyway, replied simply:

"He wants to displace me in a position which he does not know I possess."

"You are sure of that?"

"Of what?"

"That he does not know."

"How is that possible, *mademoiselle?*"

Aline sighed with something like relief.

"Very well. I am glad to know that if you have ceased to love me, you at least have not betrayed me. As for the prince's desire, this is my answer: a fortress worthy the name neither invites a siege nor surrenders without one. You are a man of war, general; you will understand me."

"But—"

"No; do not say anything more; I will not listen to you."

Aline inserted a tremor into her voice.

"As for you, Paul, I will not say that you have broken my heart; but you have made me unhappy. Ah—Paul—no—do not speak—"

Aline sank back into her chair and covered her face with her hands.

General Nirzann, delighted and confused and dissatisfied all at once, after endeavoring vainly for ten minutes to get her to listen to him, turned reluctantly and left to go with his somewhat cryptic message to the Prince of Marisi.

———

CHAPTER XIV

A Peace Offering

AT THE hour that General Nirzann left No. 341 to return to the palace, which was a little after ten o'clock in the evening, M. Frederick Naumann was seated in his furnished rooms on Walderin Place, gazing moodily at the wallpaper and confessing to himself that he was in the very deuce of a quandary. He had been seated thus for two hours, and he remained two hours more. Then he rose wearily and undressed himself and got into bed.

It was another hour before sleep reached him, and when it came it was accompanied by unpleasant dreams and frequent awakenings. All night he tossed about like one in a fever, and when the first ray of the light of morning entered at the window he rose, feeling that to lie still another instant would drive him mad.

Dressing hurriedly, he went for a walk in the cold morning air in search—Heaven help him!—of peace of mind.

He had ceased asking himself if he loved Vivi Janvour. He had no sooner left Mlle. Solini's house the night before than that question had met with a decided and desperate affirmative. But that only made matters worse.

In the first place, he had no reason to believe that his love was returned. Secondly, he was a man of considerable wealth and social position, of whom much was expected, both matrimonially and otherwise—and who was she?

He groaned. She was Vivi, and that was enough for him, he told himself furiously. But there was Mlle. Solini. He groaned again.

He had turned east, toward the poorer residential portion of the city, and was walking rapidly along the silent streets, neither knowing nor caring where he went. After an hour of this he felt that he was hungry, for he had eaten no dinner the evening before, and he entered a cheap lunch-room for some eggs and coffee, not noticing the chipped, stained dishes and soiled oilcloth.

Then he resumed his walk, still with his back turned to the heart of Marisi. In another half-hour he found himself approaching the country. Still he kept on; the turmoil and restlessness of his brain had communicated itself to the body.

Vivi, offered her choice between him and Mlle. Solini, had turned her back on him. That was his thought; it was followed immediately by this, that he was not being fair to himself. Considering the way in which Mlle. Solini had presented the alternative, what else could Vivi have done?

The words, "He does not pretend to love you," were ringing in his ears, in the voice of Mlle. Solini. He exclaimed aloud in a sort of puzzled fury: "How the devil did I happen to be idiot enough to say that?"

Then, carried away by a sudden bewildering burst of anger, he had threatened Aline, saying that he would communicate with Vasili Petrovich.

Would to Heaven he could! Of course, he thought, Mlle. Solini was too clever not to have seen that his threat was a mere empty bluff. He would not have been surprised to know that she knew much more of where Vasili Petrovich might be found than he did.

It was next to certain that Vasili, with his energy and furious desire for revenge, had found her long before this, and a meeting between them could have resulted only in her death or his. And she was very much alive.

Naumann was brought suddenly to a halt at finding that he had reached the end of the narrow, winding lane he had been following. Thus reminded of his surroundings, he looked about him in some surprise. He seemed to have got far out into the country.

On all sides nothing was to be seen but barren fields and gaunt, skeleton-like trees. He looked at his watch; it was nine o'clock. With an exclamation of wonder at the distance he had walked, and feeling himself a little tired, he turned about and began to retrace his steps toward the city.

Three hours later he arrived at his rooms all but exhausted in body and with his mind more unsettled and restless even than before. He had decided on nothing; indeed, he asked himself, what was there to decide?

He loved Vivi; well, what of that, since she did not love him? Even if Mlle. Solini, moved by his threat, should renounce her claims on the girl, what good would that do if Vivi was unwilling to leave her?

He sat down in a chair by the window of his reading-room, looking out across the place at the buildings on the opposite side without seeing them.

Clearly, the only sensible thing to do was to forget all about it. Surely that was simple enough. As though he had never been in love before! Dozens of times! Something whispered within him: "But Vivi is different." Bah! How different?

Was a man of the world like Frederick Naumann to succumb to the old trick of an innocent face and baby eyes? What a fool he had been! That was the thing to do, of course—forget all about it. He would begin at once—let us see, exactly how does one begin to forget?

There was a knock on the door. Naumann, startled, jumped in his chair, then called out an invitation to enter.

The door opened, disclosing the form of old Schantin, the *concierge*. He entered, closing the door behind him, and bowed awkwardly. In his hands he held a parcel wrapped in brown paper, about the size of a cigar-box.

Naumann's impatience at the interruption showed in his tone as he said: "What is it?"

"A package, *monsieur*. Left by a messenger. You were out. He said it was to be delivered to you personally, and you know, *monsieur*, I am always—"

Naumann interrupted him.

"All right. Lay it on the table and get out. I'm busy."

When the *concierge* had left, with an expression of utter amazement on his stupid old face—for never before had he left the room of M. Naumann without having received a kind word and a substantial tip—Naumann sat back in his chair to begin again to forget. He flattered himself that the matter promised to be quite simple.

"Bah!" he thought. "Why the deuce did I work myself into such a stew? In a week I won't even remember her name."

Then, realizing suddenly that it was well past noon and that a considerable amount of work was awaiting him at the legation, he rose to change his clothing, which had become soiled during his tramp in the country. He had tied his scarf and was crossing to the wardrobe to take out a coat and waistcoat when his eye happened to fall on the parcel left on the table by the concierge.

"What can it be, anyway?" he muttered, lifting it curiously and taking out his knife to cut the string.

Inside the paper was a gray pasteboard box. Removing the lid, his astonished eyes beheld a tiny, pink-tinted envelope resting on what appeared to be the product of some Marisi bakery shop.

The envelope was inscribed in a small round hand: "M. Frederick Naumann."

He tore it open and took out a small sheet of note-paper, on which was written the following:

Dear M. Naumann:

If I offended you last night I am sorry, but what could I do? You will say, perhaps, that I acted with foolish pride, and you will be telling the truth.

Do not think that I undervalue your friendship, or that it is not dear to me. Of course, I cannot ask you to come again to the house of Mlle. Solini—you must not come here, I beg of you—it makes me unhappy.

But here is a peace offering, monsieur—you see I have not forgotten a happy hour you gave me once. I shall always be your friend.

Vivi Janvour.

Naumann read the note three times and pressed it passionately to his lips as many dozen. How like Vivi it was! His Vivi! For she should be his—he swore it. He forgot all about his vows to forget.

And evidently, though it was too much to say that she loved him, she did actually think of him and care for his friendship. To be sure, she told him plainly not to come to see her; but that was only natural, considering the hostile relations existing between himself and Mlle. Solini.

He turned his attention to her peace offering. It consisted of half a dozen apricot tarts, exactly like the ones they had eaten together the day he had taken tea with her, which she declared she had made herself.

This, he said to himself with a smile, was even more like Vivi than the note. He could see her little white hands dabbling daintily in the flour—her brow, he decided, would be puckered up in a little serious frown.

The tarts, with their delicate brown crust and reddish amber fruit, lay side by side in two neat rows. Naumann had not eaten anything since his hasty breakfast in the cheap lunch-room early in the morning. He took up one of the tarts in his fingers, feeling as he did so that he was performing a rite of love.

The tart was half-way to his mouth when a loud knock sounded on the door. The rite of love was interrupted in mid air. Naumann turned, calling out "Come in," and hastily returned the tart to the box.

It was Richard Stetton, who was dropping in, as he said with his first words, in the expectation of being amused. At sight of Naumann in his shirt-sleeves he demanded to know if it was fitting for a hard-working young diplomat to stay in bed till the middle of the afternoon.

"My dear fellow," said Naumann, motioning the visitor to a chair, "it gives me pleasure to inform you that I rose this morning exactly at six o'clock. Kindly apologize."

Stetton helped himself to a cigarette from a box on the table and settled himself comfortably in the easiest chair in the room.

"Apologize?" he asked scornfully. "Never. In the first place, I don't believe you. Secondly, if you really did get up at six o'clock in the morning, it merely proves that you are insane. What the deuce did you mean by it?"

"Oh, nothing. I went for a walk."

"For a walk?" This incredulously.

"Of course. My dear fellow, it is the most pleasant hour of the day."

"Yes—for sleeping. However, I find the subject tiresome. How about our friend Duchesne? Is he still trying to make trouble?"

"Not since his little interview with the prince," replied

Naumann over his shoulder. He was standing in front of a mirror, buttoning his waistcoat. "Don't worry about that any more; it's all settled."

"Chavot's funeral is tomorrow morning."

"Yes? Are you going?"

"I haven't decided. Hardly know whether I ought to go or not."

Stetton rose from his chair and walked to the table, depositing the stub of his cigarette in a tray and taking a fresh one from the box.

"Hello!" he exclaimed suddenly. "What's this? Fixing up for a bachelor tea?"

Naumann turned to find his friend gazing curiously at the box of apricot tarts.

"Oh—that," he said with a touch of confusion; "why—it's just a sort of present."

"Made especially for your consumption by the fair hands of some fair lady, I presume," observed Stetton. "Who is she?"

Naumann replied:

"Mlle. Janvour. Not that it's any of your business, you know."

"The deuce you say!" Stetton looked at him in some surprise. "Vivi, eh? Guess I'll take one."

"I guess you won't," the other retorted, springing across the room and snatching the box away.

Stetton shrugged his shoulders and walked back to his easy chair. "All right, keep your old tarts—I've eaten 'em by the hundred, anyway." After a second's pause he continued with a grin: "By Jove, I know what it is. I know why you're so careful of 'em. Naumann, you're an ass."

"What are you talking about?"

"You. You and your fertile imagination. Don't blame you a bit. Can't be too cautious. You're perfectly right. Since the tarts come from No. 341 they're probably poisoned."

The tone was that of heavy sarcasm. He exclaimed in mock terror, as Naumann took one of the tarts from the box and started it for his mouth: "Look out there, man—don't eat that! It'll kill you!"

"Don't be so funny," replied Naumann dryly; but, nevertheless, his hand stopped half-way to his mouth, as it had before at the sound of Stetton's knock.

For a moment he gazed at Stetton in silence, then he slowly returned the tart to the box, which he placed on a shelf in the wardrobe.

Stetton was laughing in high glee.

"By Jove, he believes it!" he exclaimed. "I'll be hanged if the man doesn't actually believe it!"

There was no answer from Naumann, who remained standing by the door of the wardrobe, gazing at his visitor with the expression of one who has just discovered something to think about. For a full minute he stood thus while Stetton continued his ejaculations of gleeful amusement, and ended by demanding:

"You don't mean to say you seriously believe it possible? Come; don't be an ass. I was joking, of course."

"Maybe it isn't a joke," replied Naumann slowly. "I don't know whether I believe it or not. You don't understand; you don't know all the circumstances."

He stood again considering for a time, then suddenly took forth a pink envelope and, drawing forth the note, handed it to Stetton, asking:

"Do you happen to know Mlle. Janvour's handwriting?"

Stetton took the note and read it through, still with a grin on his face. Then he returned it, saying:

"It looks like it, but I can't tell for sure. Haven't seen anything but her signature. But say—better be careful—the note may be poisoned, too, you know."

Naumann paid no attention to this observation.

"It isn't possible," he muttered to himself, frowning. "It isn't possible."

For a minute he stood looking at the note, while the frown deepened. Then, with a quick gesture of decision, he walked to the table, took up the telephone, and asked the operator to give him the number of Mlle. Solini's house.

Stetton, who began to see that his friend, for some reason or other, was really treating the matter seriously, sat in his chair and listened in silence. Naumann quarreled with three or four operators, trying to get the number he wanted. At length he was successful; he heard a voice on the wire which he thought he recognized, saying:

"Yes, this is Mlle. Solini's residence. What is it, please?"

Naumann replied:

"Please let me speak to Mlle. Janvour."

"This is Mlle. Janvour."

"Oh!" For a moment Naumann was confused. Then:

"This is Frederick Naumann."

"M. Naumann?" There was a flutter in the voice at the other end. "I did not recognize your voice."

"No? I recognized yours. I called you up, *mademoiselle,* to thank you."

"To thank me?" The voice held a puzzled tone.

"Yes; to thank you for the note you sent me this morning."

"The note I sent you?" This in a tone of amazement.

"Yes. I received it an hour ago, when I returned to my rooms."

There was a slight pause before the response came:

"But, M. Naumann, there must be some mistake. I have not sent you any note. What did it say?"

"Pardon me—then you didn't send it?"

"No."

"Nor a box—a sort of—er—parcel, containing a peace-offering?"

"No. Really, I don't know what you are talking about. What was in the box? What did the note say? Where did they come from? Are you making fun of me, *monsieur?*"

Naumann replied soberly:

"No, *mademoiselle*—please do not think that I would ever try to make fun of you. But this—I am afraid this is serious. I can't explain now. Perhaps later. I'll call you up again."

Vivi's voice sounded vaguely and inaudibly at the other end; she was evidently talking to someone standing near her. This for perhaps a minute; then suddenly her voice sounded clearly over the wire: "*Au revoir,* M. Naumann."

Instantly there was a click in his ear; she had hung up the receiver.

Naumann turned about, facing Stetton.

There was a short pause, then he said abruptly: "Your joke isn't a joke, after all. She didn't send it."

Stetton exclaimed: "Rot! That doesn't prove anything."

"No, but something else will," said Naumann grimly. He took his overcoat from the back of a chair and put it on, then took up his hat. "Come on."

"Where are you going?"

"You'll see. Come on."

Stetton began to protest: "Not if you're going out on a wild-goose chase with your imagination for a guide. I'm no detective."

"This is no wild-goose chase. I've got an idea, and I want to use it. Come on. I need you."

Stetton rose, still grumbling, and took up his coat and hat. A minute later the two men were in the street together; Naumann, who appeared to know exactly where he was going, halted a cab and, getting in after Stetton, gave the driver an address in the eastern part of the city.

"The reason I want you," the young diplomat explained as they were carried rapidly along, "is that our errand has to do with the police, and since my quarrel with Duchesne over the Chavot affair I prefer not to ask them for anything."

Stetton looked at him in amazement.

"You don't mean to say you're going to the police with this! Are you crazy?"

"Not exactly. I'm not going to the police—at least, not in the way you mean. Our errand is at the city pound. The police are in charge of it."

"The city pound!" Stetton's amazement increased. "My dear fellow, I really believe we'd better go to the insane asylum instead."

Naumann vouchsafed no reply to this, but sat gazing steadily ahead as the cab jolted steadily over the rough paving stones. The ride lasted for something like half an hour, and was ended when the driver stopped in front of a low, red-brick building with barred windows and an iron padlocked gate for a door.

Naumann glanced up in surprise to find that they had reached their destination, and began to tell Stetton in as few words as possible what he wanted him to do. Stetton appeared to be both amused and astonished at what he heard, but, seeing his friend's seriousness, promised to obey orders.

Stetton jumped from the cab, advanced to the iron gate, and rang for admittance. After a wait of a minute or so the gate was opened the space of a few inches and someone from the inside questioned him. His answers appeared to be satisfactory—the gate was opened further and he passed within.

There followed an interval of ten minutes or more, while Naumann, seated in the cab, eyed the gate with increasing impatience. At length it again swung open and Stetton reappeared, carrying in his arms a small black and tan dog, evidently of the breed commonly known as "cur."

"Good!" cried Naumann as Stetton walked to the cab and handed in the dog. "Did you have much trouble?"

"None whatever," Stetton replied, entering the cab and brushing off his hands. "They have fifty or more in there. You ought to see 'em. They gave me my pick for five francs."

"He'll do. Go ahead, driver. Back where we came from—No. 5 Walderin Place."

During the return journey Stetton, having performed his mission, gave his opinion of it in no uncertain terms. It was absurd—a huge joke—a ripping, roaring farce—blessed if he wouldn't tell everybody in Marisi he knew. The town would be too hot to hold M. Frederick Naumann, who was making a profound ass of himself. The whole thing was ridiculous.

To all this Naumann made no reply whatever. He sat sunk in meditation, so far as circumstances would permit—for the black and tan dog, which he was holding on his lap, appeared strongly to disapprove of riding in a cab, judging by his struggles to get free. Naumann clutched him tightly in his arms, nor paid any attention to Stetton's unfeeling observations concerning the absurdity of the performance.

Arrived at No. 5 Walderin Place, they dismissed the cab and mounted the stairs together to Naumann's rooms, carrying the dog with them. As soon as he was put down on the floor of the reading-room the animal began to scamper about, barking furiously.

Stetton threw himself into a chair, still calling Heaven to witness that his friend Naumann had gone completely crazy, and ironically commiserating the dog on the dire misfortune about to befall him.

Naumann opened the wardrobe, took forth the pasteboard box and took out one of the tarts.

"Here, doggie!" he called, and began to chase the animal round the room. "Here, doggie! Nice doggie! Here, doggie!"

Stetton was exploding with laughter.

The dog stopped, approached cautiously and sniffed at the tart. Then he backed off, shaking his head as though in grave doubt.

"Wise pup!" yelled Stetton in glee. "He's as crazy as you are, Naumann—those tarts are the best stuff in Marisi. I know—I've eaten hundreds of 'em."

The dog approached again, sniffed more eagerly than before, snatched the tart suddenly and gulped it down. Then he stood looking up at Naumann, wagging his tail, which in dog language is usually taken to mean, "I want more."

Naumann stood regarding him with intense gravity, quite as though he expected him suddenly to blow up.

"Ladies and gentlemen," called Stetton in stentorian tones, "we will now present the last act of the soul-stirring drama, 'The Modern Borgia.' Look at him, ladies and gentlemen! Observe him well!

"He is perhaps the crudest man now living. He eats 'em alive. At his present rate of activity it is estimated that he will destroy the entire population of Marisi within the space of one year and two months. Note the viciousness of his eye! See the blood-lust in his—"

"For Heaven's sake, stop it!" cried Naumann. "Perhaps you won't feel quite so funny in a few minutes. I have a reason for all this, Stetton, and a good one. Watch the dog."

"He seems to be all right, so far," replied Stetton, grinning. "In fact, he's a good, sensible pup. Why don't you give him another one—don't you see he's asking for it?"

"That might be a good idea," said Naumann, taking the suggestion seriously.

He went to the wardrobe and came back with another of the tarts, which the dog gobbled with apparent relish. Immediately Stetton started off again on his oration:

"Ladies and gentlemen, we will now present the last act of the soul-stirring drama, 'The Modern Borgia.' Look at him—"

He kept this up for five minutes, warming up to his topic as he went along. Then suddenly his tones lost their vehemence, he lost the thread of his discourse, and his voice stopped.

Indubitably something was happening to the dog.

The animal had ceased wagging its tail for more. Instead, it was looking up at Naumann with a pitiful expression in its eyes and a hanging lip.

Suddenly it turned and walked toward the door, whining dismally, then changed its course and went through an open arch into the bedroom. The two men following it heard a low whine coming from under the bed.

"What the deuce does it mean?" asked Stetton, suddenly become serious. Naumann did not answer.

For several minutes they stood silent, while the whine became continuous and louder. Suddenly Naumann bent down and, reaching under the bed, seized the dog by the hind leg and pulled him forth.

Involuntarily he started back at sight of the misery and agony in the beast's eyes.

It was frothing at the mouth, and its head was rolling from side to side; the whine had become a low, heartrending moan. The little body was quivering and trembling all over.

"This is horrible," said Naumann with a white face. "I was a brute to do this. It's horrible!"

It was soon over.

The moan became more and more feeble, and the head scarcely moved. The expression in the dog's eyes as he turned them up to the two men standing over him was horrible, indeed, and seemed to Naumann to hold an accusation; he turned his own eyes away.

Suddenly there was a violent twitching of the animal's legs; the moan ceased, and the body became still. Naumann looked round again when he heard Stetton say in a low tone:

"He's dead!"

"Poor devil!" said Naumann with deep feeling. He added: "But the Lord knows I'm glad it wasn't me!"

"And the question now is," said Stetton with an attempt at facetiousness that did not hide the tremor in his voice, "Who made the tarts?"

—〰—

CHAPTER XV

Love and Stubbornness

PERHAPS THE most difficult thing you can ask of a man is that he either forgive or forget a deliberate and premeditated attempt on the part of another to take his life.

Life gives value to everything and holds all values in itself; it is, of course, trite to say that a lover loves it better than his mistress and a miser more than his gold. Otherwise they would both starve to death.

Frederick Naumann liked life as well as the next man; you can imagine his feelings when he discovered that the woman he already hated had tried to take it away from him. His hate increased tenfold and was seasoned with fear.

He swore revenge on Mlle. Solini; and when Stetton took occasion to observe that there was no proof that Mlle. Solini was the author of the attempt on his life, Naumann gave his friend the lie direct, but apologized immediately after.

He set out at once, however, to find the proof, and went about it in a manner which indicated that he meant business. He took the paper in which the box had been wrapped and the box itself, containing the four remaining tarts, and locked them in his wardrobe.

This done, he went below in search of the concierge to obtain information concerning the messenger who had delivered the parcel.

But old Schantin, whose eyesight and hearing were none too good anyway, remembered very little.

Was the messenger a man or a woman? A man.

Was he in uniform? Schantin didn't know.

A man or a boy? He wasn't sure.

What did he look like? The concierge was completely at sea on that point; he only knew that it was some sort of a man.

Which way did he go after delivering the parcel? Out of the door. At this answer, the only definite one he received, Naumann lost patience entirely and left Schantin blinking helplessly on his chair near the door of the outer hall.

It was then three o'clock in the afternoon, and Naumann hastened to his desk at the legation for the first time that day. His duties were performed in a perfunctory and hasty manner, but still there was enough to keep him busy till after six o'clock. Then he went to the Hotel Walderin to dine with Stetton.

That night in his room he considered the question that confronted him from every possible angle. One thing he had decided at once—he would not report the affair to the police.

For one thing, they probably could not help him; for another, they certainly would not, so long as Duchesne was in command; and for still another, if he became thus associated with another unsavory episode it would in all likelihood result in his being recalled to Berlin. If he succeeded in finding proof of Mlle. Solini's guilt, that would be a different matter; he would see that she was punished for it, if he had to move heaven and earth.

But how to obtain the proof? As for tracing the messenger, that appeared to be utterly hopeless, since Schantin had no recollection of him whatever. The tarts could be chemically analyzed and the sale of the poison traced; but that was a long chance, and besides, only the police could make such an investigation with any promise of success.

There remained the parcel and the box itself and the note. If only he dared to ask the assistance of the police! Surely Mlle. Solini, clever as she was, had not succeeded in covering every track.

In his own mind Naumann was as thoroughly convinced of her guilt as though he had seen the act with his own eyes. Also, he was just as certain that Mlle. Janvour had had nothing whatever to do with it, and he was more than ever resolved to get the girl away. How, was another matter.

Evidently Mlle. Solini had not thought so lightly of his threat after all, since it had led her to the daring and all but successful attempt on his life. But the bluff would no longer serve; she had declared war, and his only chance was to fight back.

In his bed that night a thousand schemes and surmises raced back and forth through his brain until he finally fell asleep through sheer weariness.

The one clear thought that he possessed when he awoke the following morning was that he must save Vivi. He felt that if he could only see her and talk to her she must perforce listen and believe.

He started to the telephone, to ask her to meet him at a restaurant for lunch; then, on second thought, decided to take a more open course. He waited till eleven o'clock; then, unable to restrain his impatience longer, took a cab for 341 the Drive.

He half expected that Mlle. Solini would refuse to allow him to see the girl; perhaps would see him herself, feeling her position impregnable, to ask him with her mocking smile if he had written to Vasili Petrovich. In that case he could do nothing but swallow her defiance, and then—well, and then he would see.

No doubt in this expectation he was correct; but luckily Mlle. Solini was out. So said Czean, at the door.

"And Mlle. Janvour?"

"I will see, *monsieur*. Step into the drawing-room, please."

In a few minutes Czean returned to say that Mlle. Janvour was in her room and would be down shortly. Naumann sighed with relief. He had no sooner composed himself to wait than the door opened and Vivi appeared on the threshold.

She was dressed in a loose house gown of gray, caught together at the waist with a rope girdle; Naumann thought he had never seen her look so charming.

"I am glad to see you, *monsieur*," said Vivi, approaching with outstretched hand. In her manner was ill-concealed curiosity, mingled with an air of reserve.

"And surprised, of course," said Naumann, bowing over her hand.

"Perhaps—a little," the girl confessed, smiling at him. "I see you so seldom that it is something of an event. Won't you be seated?"

"And usually an unpleasant one," said Naumann, finding a chair for her and taking one himself. "As the day before yesterday, for instance. I know it was unpardonable of me, *mademoiselle*—I should have come to you first—"

"Not at all," Vivi protested, recovering in a degree her natural ease of manner. "You were most kind and thoughtful, M. Naumann; if I did not thank you I do so now. Only, it was impossible."

"Impossible for you to accept my offer, you mean?"

"Yes."

"And why?"

"Is it necessary for me to repeat my reasons?"

"No. I do not know why I asked. I know I have no right to annoy you as I do."

"You do not annoy me, *monsieur*."

"It is evident that I do."

"Pardon me—it is not so—you must not say that." Vivi's eyes were looking earnestly into his. After a short pause she added, as though involuntarily: "You know very well you are the only friend I have in Marisi."

Naumann smiled:

"It is hard to believe that."

"Nevertheless, it is true."

"You do not treat me as though I were."

"Do I not?" cried Vivi warmly. "You are wrong, *monsieur;* it is you who treat me badly. You never come to see me, and what can I do? One day—do you remember it?—I thought we were really going to be friends. The day you promised not to say anything more of Aline. It is true you kept your promise, but by saying nothing."

"Am I not here now?"

"Yes, but with some terribly serious purpose; I can see it in your eyes. You come to tell me something; I would much rather you came to tell me nothing. Is it about that mysterious note you received the other day?"

"Yes. Yesterday."

"Well, I admit I am curious about that. I've been waiting for the explanation you promised me. You have discovered, of course, that it was written by someone else. What was in it? How was it signed?"

For reply Naumann reached in the breast-pocket of his coat and took out a pink-tinted envelope, from which he extracted a sheet of paper. Then he said:

"I received this day before yesterday morning, *mademoiselle,* in a box of apricot tarts. It is signed with your name." He handed the note to the girl.

At the first glance Vivi exclaimed in wonder: "Why, this is my handwriting!" Then, examining the note closely, she continued: "No, I believe not, but it looks like it. Exactly. All except the T's; I make very funny T's."

She read the note over twice; then, looking up at Naumann,

added: "It is precisely my signature. And it is on my note-paper.
Where did it come from?"

"I have told you; it came in a box of apricot tarts—the peace
offering."

"Apricot tarts!"

"Yes. Exactly like the ones you gave me once at tea. Do you
remember? You said you made them yourself."

"Yes—so I did."

Vivi stared at him a moment in silence, then continued:

"But where could they come from? Who could have sent them?
And why?"

"I can answer the last question. There is one thing I haven't told
you. The tarts were poisoned."

A look of horror came into Vivi's eyes. She cried:

"Poisoned!"

"Yes, *mademoiselle.* When I telephoned you and discovered the
note was a forgery, I grew suspicious. I fed one of the tarts to a dog.
He was dead in ten minutes."

"But that is horrible!" said Vivi in a low tone, gazing at him as
though half in doubt of what she had heard. "It is impossible. Who
could have done anything so dreadful as that? And who could know
my handwriting, and get my note-paper, and know about the
tarts—"

The girl paused abruptly, while her eyes began to fill with a new
expression of dread and fear.

"*Monsieur,* what is this you are telling me?" she cried half
angrily.

"The truth, *mademoiselle,*" replied Naumann earnestly. "It is
unnecessary for me to say more; you are beginning to draw your
own conclusions, and you are right."

"You mean—it was someone in this house?"

"Yes, and someone who hates me."

There was a long silence. On the face of the girl appeared an expression of understanding and doubt and fear. Naumann sat silent, waiting for her to speak. Finally she said:

"I know. I know what you are thinking, M. Naumann. You think it was Aline who—who did this. You have come here to tell me so. I can't believe it—I can't—I can't!"

"But it is true. Think, *mademoiselle,* how is it possible that it could have been any one else?"

"I do not believe it!" cried the girl.

And to that assertion she held steadfast, despite everything Naumann could say. A dozen times he recapitulated the proof, which was overwhelming, but Vivi remained loyal.

He ended by becoming impatient and declaring that no one in their senses could doubt such a chain of evidence. Vivi, up in arms instantly, retorted that he had better go to the police if he felt so sure of his knowledge, and accused him of bias and malice.

"But I don't understand!" cried Naumann in despair. "I don't see how you can possibly doubt! And I am not prompted by malice— you wrong me when you say that."

"I know; forgive me," said the girl, softening instantly. After a short pause she added: "M. Naumann, I want to ask you a question; then perhaps you will understand. Would you believe this thing of your mother on this evidence? Would you believe her a murderess?"

"Great Heavens," cried Naumann, "of course not! You do not know my mother."

Vivi replied earnestly:

"But Aline has been a mother to me, and more. Do you not see? I love her. *Monsieur,* you are mistaken—I feel it—I am sure of it!"

Naumann perceived at length that his case was hopeless. To argue with a woman against a genuine and deep affection is the business of a fool.

Still he did not despair. Vivi had not been angry with him; that was surely a sign of something. She had said that he was her only friend in Marisi. He looked at her, and began where he should have begun in the first place. He said:

"Then, *mademoiselle,* if you look upon Mlle. Solini as a mother, I will talk no more of her."

"That is what I asked of you two months ago," said Vivi with a sudden smile.

"I know; I should have obeyed you. You think, perhaps, that I can talk of nothing else."

The girl protested that that was exactly what she did not think.

"Do you not remember that day in the library? You were charming. There! Is not that a confession for me to make when I ought to be angry with you?"

"I like you to be angry," declared Naumann irrelevantly. "It makes your eyes flash. If the truth were known, it might be that that is why I say things you do not like."

"I hope not," said Vivi, suddenly serious, "for it hurts me. To have to be angry with you, I mean. And the worst of it is, you can be so pleasant. Quite the pleasantest man I know."

Naumann laughed at her tone of a critical woman of the world, and at the little serious twist of her lips.

"It is not much to be champion of Marisi," he declared. "Wait till you get to Paris. I should be doing well if allowed to call your carriage at the Sigognac."

"Paris!" cried Vivi, forgetting everything else at sound of this, to her, magic name. "Oh, I can hardly wait! We are going in the spring."

"With—"

"With Aline."

Naumann frowned, and there followed an awkward silence. He knew very well what he wanted to say, and was only trying to decide how to say it. He ended by observing lamely:

"I should like to show you Paris myself. And Berlin, and London—don't you think we could have a good time together?"

"Hardly," laughed Vivi mischievously. "I wouldn't go without Aline, and fear you wouldn't be very gay."

"But I don't mean with Aline. I mean alone—just you and me."

"Oh! That would be very pleasant if it were possible."

"But why is it not possible?"

Vivi looked at him quickly. Yes, his face was like his tone—quite serious. She felt somehow that she had given herself away, or was going to, and she said with a touch of dignity:

"Do not let me think you are in earnest, M. Naumann."

"But I am in earnest!"

"Then, do you mean to insult me?"

"Insult you!" Naumann stared at her in amazement. Then, slowly, his face filled with the light of understanding, and at the same time grew eloquent with denial and protest.

"*Mademoiselle!* Surely you could not think that I meant— You could not! How could I insult you when I love you?"

"*Monsieur!*" cried Vivi, her face blazing.

But Naumann, having pronounced the word, felt himself well started and plunged recklessly on.

"I love you!" he repeated. "You know it. I have loved you ever since the first time I saw you. Great Heavens! Insult you? I worship you, Vivi! Let me call you that! Vivi, don't turn away from me—let me look at you! Dearest!"

Then, struck suddenly with the thought that what he was saying was of some importance and deserved a measure of dignity, he rose to his feet and said distinctly:

"Mlle. Janvour, will you marry me?"

Vivi's face had gone from white to pink, and from pink back to white. Her eyes refused to meet his, and when she finally spoke her voice trembled and was so low he could scarcely hear the words.

"But M. Naumann—you know me so little—it is impossible—that you—you—"

"Vivi, look at me! I love you!" His voice, too, was trembling.

"*Monsieur*—I do not know—"

"Do you love me?"

"*Monsieur*—"

"Do you love me?"

There was a sudden tense silence. And then, before either of them quite knew what was happening, his arms were round her, holding her close, while he knelt beside her chair. She struggled—a little; their lips met; her arms were round his neck.

"Ah—ah—ah—" she breathed, sighing like a breeze of spring.

"Vivi, darling—you do love me—look at me—"

Again their lips met.

"Do you love me, Vivi?"

He repeated the question over and over, and finally there came from somewhere near his shoulder, in a voice muffled and scarcely audible with emotion, the word:

"Yes."

He held her tighter. Presently he spoke again:

"Will you marry me, Vivi?"

At this question, uttered in a tone which, though tender, was not without insistence, Vivi drew away as though in sudden fright.

"I don't know—I must think—" she stammered.

Naumann cried, as though astonished:

"But you love me!"

"Yes," said Vivi simply, recovering herself. "Yes, *monsieur*, I love you. I think I have always loved you. But when you ask me to marry you, that means a great deal, doesn't it? Perhaps you don't realize—are you sure you want me?"

"Want you!" Naumann encircled her again with his arms. But she held him off.

"You know, *monsieur,* there are many things to consider—your family—your position—"

"I know," replied Naumann, a little sobered by her tone. "I have thought of everything, Vivi. But nothing else matters. Will you marry me?"

"Then—yes."

Again she submitted to his embrace, but with a curious hesitancy. It was not that she was cold; her eyes, eloquent with love, spoke of the sweetness of her surrender; but still she was troubled with some secret thought. After they had remained silent for a long time she gave it voice.

"Of course," she said abruptly, "you will ask Mlle. Solini."

It was like a bombshell thrown into the midst of a peaceful camp, though it lay smoldering for some time before it burst.

Naumann, to begin with, allowed himself an expression of surprise, saying that he did not think it at all necessary to ask Mlle. Solini for the hand of Mlle. Janvour. Vivi protested that she could not marry without Aline's consent, and added:

"I told you she has been a mother to me."

"But surely you see that it is impossible for me to ask anything of Mlle. Solini!" cried Naumann.

Thus the argument began. Vivi, warm with loyalty, declared that she owed everything to Aline, and that to disregard her in this most important question of her life was unthinkable. Naumann retorted that he could not see how Mlle. Solini was in any way concerned in the matter.

Vivi replied that Aline was concerned in anything that concerned her, and wanted to know if Naumann would prefer the girl he would marry to be entirely without protection or connection— a thoroughly indiscreet question, since it led the young man to

declare that he would certainly wish his intended wife to be anything rather than the protégée of a murderess.

The bomb exploded at this point with a deafening roar. Vivi said
coldly:

"I have told you that you wrong Aline. You must not insult her,
monsieur, if you wish me to think well of you."

"But what has she to do with us?" cried Naumann. "You ask me
an impossibility. I would not speak to Mlle. Solini; I would not ask a
favor of her if it were to gain the world."

"Then, I am sorry."

The girl's face was white.

"Do you admit that you are unreasonable?" Naumann
demanded.

"How can I? There is no use in discussing it, M. Naumann. It is
you who are unreasonable."

"Child!" cried the young man angrily. "You are stubborn, that is
what it is, and you know it."

Vivi said, trying to smile:

"I would not make a very good wife, if I am stubborn and
unreasonable. That is enough, *monsieur.*"

"You mean—"

"We need not quarrel longer."

"Then you send me away?"

"Yes," she replied bravely.

"You want me to leave you?"

Incredulity, astonishment, despair—all were in his voice and eyes.

"Yes," Vivi repeated.

There was a silence, while they stood gazing at each other.
Naumann's face went red and white by turns; he was trembling with
emotion; once or twice he essayed to speak, while a look of entreaty
and appeal appeared to fight with the anger in his eyes, but found
not their way to his tongue.

Suddenly a voice sounded from the doorway:

"Vivi! Ah, M. Naumann!"

They turned. It was Mlle. Solini, wearing a toque and furs; evidently she had just entered by the street-door. For a moment there was silence, while she stood looking keenly from the girl to the young man and back again; then Naumann, bowing deeply to Vivi, proceeded to the hall without uttering a word, took up his hat and coat and left the house.

Mlle. Solini watched the door close behind him, then turned to Vivi, who had sunk back in her chair and covered her face with her hands. In the woman's eyes was an expression of compassion and genuine affection; an expression that no one else had ever seen there or ever would. She crossed to the girl's side and, bending over her chair, took her in her arms and laid her cold cheek against the girl's warm one, wet with tears.

"Vivi, what is it?" asked Mlle. Solini tenderly. "Tell me, dear, what is it?"

"Nothing," replied Vivi, raising her head and trying to smile through her tears. "Nothing is the matter—nothing whatever. Only—oh, Aline, my heart is broken!"

—w—

The Prince Makes Love

O N LEAVING the house of Mlle. Solini, Naumann returned directly to his rooms at No. 5 Walderin Place, in a state of mind not easily to be described.

There could be no more nonsense about forgetting Vivi Janvour—that he knew. He loved her, and he would always love her. He wanted her as he wanted nothing else in the world.

He called himself a fool, an idiot, a thundering imbecile. After all, had she asked him anything unreasonable? Was not her attitude toward Mlle. Solini perfectly understandable—more, was it not commendable? Should she be condemned for her loyalty?

Still, if she loved him, could she not make concessions to his prejudices and beliefs—beliefs well founded on knowledge?

One thing was certain—he could do nothing about the poisoned tarts. The note might possibly be proved a forgery, but Vivi herself had been nearly deceived by it. It was written on her own paper.

Any activity of his in the matter would probably result in more trouble for her than for the one he knew to be guilty. Aline Solini possessed the cleverness of the devil himself. So thought Naumann as he took the box containing the four remaining tarts and threw it on the fire.

Then he sat down to watch it burn, railing at Fate, as many another man has done with less reason before and since.

There we will leave him, to return to No. 341 the Drive, after passing over an afternoon and a night. You may be sure Mlle. Solini was wasting no time in railing at Fate; she was not in the habit of leaving her affairs to the management of that dame's capricious hands.

Nevertheless, her great campaign was not prospering. Her ship of intrigue was caught in a dead calm. Her subtle and powerful attack appeared to have been repulsed not only with ease, but also with contempt.

In plain English, she had received no message nor hint of one from the Prince of Marisi since General Nirzann's diplomatic mission of two days before. True, she had seen the general several times, but all he would say of the prince was that Aline's message had been delivered, and that there was no reply.

So much being explained, you will understand the light that flashed in the eyes of Mlle. Solini when, on the day following that on which Naumann had won and lost his love, she was informed by Czean, as she sat at her writing-desk in her boudoir, that the Prince of Marisi was awaiting her in the drawing-room.

"Tell him I will be down shortly," said Aline, while her eyes flashed with joy. Fifteen minutes later she descended, having made a hasty but by no means ineffective toilet.

In the first minute, after greeting the royal visitor, she saw that the message carried by General Nirzann had had its effect. The prince had descended from the attitude of a man who takes what he wants to that of one who takes what he can get.

It was not exactly that he treated her with increased respect, for he had never been lacking in that; it was something subtle and indefinable in his manner of looking at her and speaking to her that seemed to say, "You make the rules; I will follow them."

They conversed for an hour, amiably but quite impersonally, on every conceivable topic. The prince made no mention whatever of the message he had sent by General Nirzann, or the one that had been returned to him.

He appeared to think it quite natural to drop in for a little chat with Mlle. Solini, though Aline knew that no one else in Marisi had ever been similarly honored. As he rose to go the prince said:

"No doubt you received a card from De Mide?"

Aline answered in the negative. The prince continued:

"Perhaps he hasn't sent them out yet. I am giving a dinner at the palace tomorrow evening, and I have placed your name on the list. I shall see you there?"

"Is it not a command?" smiled Aline carelessly, concealing the elation that rose within her. Had not the Countess Potacci tried to console her the day before because she had not been invited to this dinner?

"I would not have you consider it so," the prince was saying in answer to her question. "When we are willing to ask a favor of anyone we do not presume to command them."

"If it is a command, I obey."

"And if it is a favor?"

"I grant it."

A minute later the prince departed. The door had no sooner closed behind him than Aline rushed to her room to send a note to the dear countess.

When the card of invitation arrived that evening it was found to contain the name of Mlle. Janvour as well as that of Mlle. Solini. This struck Aline as a little curious; nevertheless, she went with it at once to Vivi's room to acquaint her with the news and consider what dress she should wear.

But Vivi declined flatly to go at all. She was lying on the bed with a damp cloth tied round her head; her eyes were red and swollen and her face white.

"Come," said Aline, "this is absurd! And all for that little fool of a Naumann! Dear child, he isn't worth a single tear. You must go; an invitation from the prince is a command."

Vivi said stubbornly:

"I can't help it. I won't go! Say I'm sick; say anything you want. I won't go!"

Aline was forced to give it up.

Accordingly, the following evening, at a little before seven o'clock, Mlle. Solini departed for the palace alone in her limousine. Strictly speaking, of course, it was Stetton's limousine; but no one knew that.

It was her first glimpse within the palace, and the truth was that she was more than a little uneasy at her lack of knowledge of the proprieties and ceremonies to be observed. Once inside the great bronze gates at the entrance, she was conducted by a servant down the shining marble corridor to an apartment at its farther end. She had no sooner stepped on the threshold than she heard the voice of General Paul Nirzann:

"Ah! We have been expecting you, cousin."

In another instant he was at her side, and they crossed the room together, surrounded by a low murmur of admiration from the assembled company at the appearance of Mlle. Solini. Aline was at home.

Three hours later she returned to No. 341 flushed with triumph. She had outshone every other woman in the room—that much she could see with her own eyes, even if she had not seen it in the eyes of the men.

At dinner she had sat at the right hand of the prince, and throughout the evening he had paid her marked attention, to the exclusion of everyone else. This, of course, had not pleased the ladies present; the old Countess Larchini had been moved to the point where she administered a direct snub to Aline loud enough for all to hear. Shortly afterward Aline had heard Mme. Chébe ask the countess the cause of her quarrel with "the beautiful Russian."

"I have no quarrel with her," Larchini had replied. "She is an upstart, and must be shown her place."

To which Mme. Chébe had retorted:

"Take care, countess; you are indiscreet; what if her place turns out to be the palace?"

At the recollection of which Aline was still smiling as she mounted the stairs to her room after returning home; the smile was a scornful one.

"Bah! They are of no importance one way or the other," she said to herself as she rang the bell for her maid. "Well, we will see."

Whatever were the prince's thoughts, it soon became evident to all of Marisi that they were concerned with the beautiful Russian. On the afternoon of the day following the dinner-party his limousine was seen standing for two hours in front of No. 341. The next day it was the same, and the next, and many days thereafter.

Marisi began to talk. What was worse, Marisi began to whisper; and some slight echoes reached the ears of Mlle. Solini. At each succeeding report, carried to her by her faithful friend, the Countess Potacci, she frowned and said nothing.

Receptions and entertainments were now being given at the palace almost daily, and the beautiful Russian was always present, and the place of honor was always hers. She no longer accepted any invitations save those of the Countess Potacci and Mme. Chébe, who—as she was perfectly well aware—were engaged with the others in tearing her to pieces behind her back. Aline smiled at them, biding her time in patience.

It soon began to appear that she would need all the patience she possessed, and more: She had given up her afternoon drives, for the prince called every day. But when that is said, everything is said.

He did not speak the words that Mlle. Solini wanted to hear; he did not assume the attitude she expected and desired. He had attempted once or twice in his masterful way to make love to her; but Mlle. Solini, whose quick ear had detected at once the fact that he was pitched in the wrong key, had repulsed without offending him.

Each time he had responded to her desire with the most perfect good nature.

At length Mlle. Solini grew impatient. One evening after the prince had gone she sat for two hours alone in the library, meditating on her tactics and trying to discover the error in her strategy. There could be no doubt, she told herself, that the prince was fascinated by her.

He spent several hours of every day with her; he humored her slightest whim, when she thought it advisable to have any; twice, to try her power, she had actually dictated his policy on affairs of state, one of which had been of some importance.

What was it, then, that held him back? The mere fact that she was not of royal birth? She turned that suggestion aside with scorn; she knew the prince; he was not a man to be hindered in his desires by ordinary or conventional obstacles.

It must be—and this thought had occurred to Mlle. Solini many times within the month—it must be that General Nirzann had betrayed her by revealing to the prince the truth of his own connection with her. Ah, if he had! Aline's eyes blazed dangerously.

"At any rate," she said to herself as she arose to dress for dinner, "I shall know tomorrow. I shall risk all, and I shall either win or lose. We shall see."

The following afternoon the prince called at a little after two o'clock, as usual. Aline received him in the library quite informally,

for they had come to know each other very well indeed, and had
long since dispensed with all ceremony. On this occasion, however,
there was a certain constraint, an air of aloofness, in her manner, and
the prince observed it at once, glancing at her curiously. The glance
did not escape Mlle. Solini; she had resolved that on that afternoon
nothing should escape her.

"I am moved once more to observe," said the prince, drawing
up an easy chair before the fire, "that this is easily the pleasantest spot
in all Marisi. And if you knew how I love my study, *mademoiselle,* you
would appreciate the compliment."

Aline, who was seated in a chair by the table, merely smiled
for reply.

"And all it needs for perfection," continued the prince, "is for
you to be reading aloud. Poor De Mide! I have grown to detest the
very sound of the man's voice. Yesterday morning, if you will believe
me, I came nearly throwing a book at him. What shall it be today?
Turgenef?"

Aline replied:

"I don't believe I shall read today, your highness. I don't feel
inclined that way."

"No?" The prince turned around in his chair to look at her.
"Not the headache, I hope?"

"No, I have not a headache today." (The reader will understand
that Mlle. Solini's headaches had occurred on those rare occasions
when she had been unable to refuse an afternoon to Mr. Richard
Stetton, of New York.) "I don't feel like reading; that is all."

"I am sorry; I had really counted on something of Turgenef
today," said the prince in the tone of a man who has been unjustly
deprived of a privilege. "Well, then we shall talk. You will be glad to
hear that young Aschovin has been pardoned."

"Your highness is most kind."

"Come, now!" Again the prince turned around in his chair. "That is not a tone for you to use to me, *mademoiselle*. You know it."

"Nevertheless, I use it, your highness."

The prince rose to his feet, facing her, and said abruptly:

"Something is wrong. What is it?"

"Nothing, your highness."

"Have I offended you?"

Aline did not reply. She sat for a moment, returning his gaze in silence; then she also rose to her feet and stood facing him, with eyes that were clear with the light of a sudden resolve. Finally she spoke:

"Your highness is right; there is something wrong. I have something to say—something unpleasant—unpleasant, that is, for me."

The prince frowned; when there was anything unpleasant to be said he much preferred to say it himself. As he did not speak, Aline continued:

"It is possible that your highness will be offended, and that is why it is unpleasant. Still, you ought not to be; you have told me often to be frank with you. It is this, that your highness must not come to see me anymore."

The prince gazed at her as though he had not understood.

"Not come to see you anymore?" he repeated blankly.

"No. You will understand. Do you not know that all Marisi is talking about me? Perhaps your highness does not hear these things; then I will tell you that every one is saying that I am your mistress. There, you see I am quite frank. It is absurd, of course; but I must preserve the shred of reputation that is left to me."

Certainly the prince could understand that. He did so, and was instantly on his guard, though he could not quite conceal his astonishment as he looked at the beautiful Russian with a gaze that tried to force its way into her heart. There was a long silence.

Aline resumed her chair; the racing of her pulse was not

betrayed by any expression of her face. The prince walked to the fireplace and stood for a long time looking down on the red coals. When he turned it was with a gesture of determination. He spoke abruptly:

"You say it is absurd for Marisi to suppose that you are my mistress. Why? You are playing with me, *mademoiselle,* and that is a dangerous game."

Aline interrupted him with a voice quite as firm as his own:

"Pardon me; your highness is mistaken."

"*Mademoiselle,* it is hard to believe you."

"Believe it or not, your highness, it is the truth."

"Then, if that is so," demanded the prince, taking a step toward her, "tell me why you have given your time to me. You have made me love you—you have made yourself necessary for my happiness— and now you send me away! *Mademoiselle,* there is something behind all this!"

"Nothing more, your highness, than a desire to preserve my honor."

The prince glanced at her with quick suspicion. "And what do you mean by that?"

"I mean that whatever my own happiness might require, I would not take it with a burden of shame."

"Ah," said the prince slowly, while the light of understanding appeared on his face, "I see!"

"I expected nothing," Aline interrupted. "Or if I did, I do so no longer."

Her voice was tremulous with emotion.

"Do you not see that you are being cruel to me? That what you say is more painful to me than death? It seems I expected the impossible. I am paying for it now."

Her voice trembled so that she seemed scarcely able to go on.

"Yes, I admit it. I expected—everything. Now leave me—go—go!"

She leaned forward in her chair and buried her face in her arms on the table.

For a moment the prince stood looking down at her uncertainly; then suddenly he bent over and placed his arm across her shoulder. Her sleeve, flowing open, exposed her arm; his hand rested on her delicious white skin; his head was so close to hers that her hair was against his cheek and about his eyes. He said in an uneven voice:

"Aline—I did not think—it is impossible—come—you must love me—look at me—you must—"

Aline's shoulders were shaking under his touch, and when her voice came it was mingled with sobs.

"Go!" she cried. "Leave me—please—you are brutal—go—go—"

He pulled at her; she would not move, but kept begging him to go. Then, feeling perhaps that a prince cannot afford to make himself ridiculous, he straightened up abruptly and turned away.

With a last, lingering glance at Aline's shaking figure from the door of the library, he left the house without another word.

Aline waited till she had heard the outer door close behind him.

Then she jumped up from her chair and ran to the window in front in time to see him enter his limousine and drive away. When she turned there was a smile on her face—a smile of joy and triumph.

She said to herself aloud:

"He is mine!"

—⁓—

CHAPTER XVII

Stetton Makes a Proposal

WHEN THE Prince of Marisi returned to the palace he went at once to his study, as he called it—that room at the end of the corridor on the second floor about which all Marisi was curious, because no one was ever allowed to enter it. Arrived there, he threw himself into a chair and buried himself in meditation.

In that, however, he could find no relief. He rose to his feet and began to pace up and down the room, with his forehead wrinkled in a deep frown. It had been many years since the prince had been moved so profoundly as he was at that moment.

He stopped before the fireplace and stood looking up at a portrait that hung over it—the portrait of a woman about thirty years of age, with dark hair and large, serious eyes.

"Sasoné," the prince murmured aloud, "Sasoné, it is not you who can help me, but you can forgive."

For a long time he stood looking at the portrait in silence; then, with a sudden gesture of decision, he turned and rang a bell on the table. When a servant appeared an instant later, the prince asked if General Nirzann was in the palace.

"Yes, your highness; the general is in his room."

"And De Mide?"

"He went out, your highness, saying that he would be here before your highness returned. He did not expect you—"

"Very well; that is all."

As soon as the servant had disappeared the prince also left, to make his way to the room of General Nirzann on the floor above.

It was evident that General Nirzann, like De Mide, had not expected his prince to return at so early an hour. He was seated in an armchair, dressed in a pink dressing-gown, reading a book. As the prince entered he jumped up with an exclamation of surprise, threw down his book, and bowed half-way to the floor.

"Remain seated," said the prince with a wave of his hand, crossing to a chair.

The general, with a merry twinkle in his eye, wanted to know if his cousin Aline had lost her charm or was merely indisposed.

"It is of her I came to speak," said the prince, with so serious an expression on his face that the general instantly altered his own to agree with it.

"What the deuce has she done now?" thought he with an inward frown.

As usual, the prince plunged immediately into the heart of the matter. He began abruptly:

"General, there are some things about Mlle. Solini that I wish to know, and to know positively. If you can tell me, so much the better. If not, I shall send De Mide to Warsaw to find out."

The effect of these words on General Nirzann may be easily understood. Send De Mide to Warsaw! That would mean the discovery of the general's deception: it would mean his ruin, his banishment from Marisi; the end of everything. The general, trembling inwardly, took a firm grip on himself. He said, in as calm a tone as possible:

"I cannot understand why you say that, your highness. If you doubt me—"

The prince interrupted:

"No, Nirzann, I do not. I have never entertained a very glowing opinion of your abilities, but your fidelity is beyond question. That is why I come to you. I do not need to explain why, but this has become a serious matter. In the first place, Mlle. Aline Solini is your cousin?"

"She is, your highness."

The general's tone was calm and firm; it would appear that he was capable of both courage and resolution in a crisis.

"She has estates near Warsaw?"

"She has had, your highness. They are no longer even in her name."

"Has she an equity in them?"

"No. She has nothing."

The prince looked at him sharply:

"She is spending a great deal of money in Marisi. Where does she get it?"

The general was prepared for this question; he and Aline had long before decided what answer should be given to it. He replied:

"She has told me, your highness, that she has a balance of cash left from the disposal of her estates."

"I see." There was a short pause, then the prince continued: "Now be frank with me, Nirzann. What do you know of your cousin?"

"Very little, your highness. I have often told you so. Most of her life was spent in a convent. At one time she even considered taking the veil, and I believe she has not yet entirely abandoned the idea."

"Has she any relatives besides yourself?"

"None."

"Absolutely none?"

"Absolutely. I have often told your highness that my family has its last male representative in me. We are doomed, it seems, to extinction."

The general actually achieved a tone of mournfulness.

"That is right; you have often told me that." The prince paused; he appeared to be thinking. Then he said abruptly: "I have sometimes wondered, general, why you do not marry your cousin."

General Nirzann smiled.

"Surely that is not a matter of wonder, your highness. In the first place, she has but little money, and I have none. Secondly, she won't have me."

"Ah!" The prince's eyebrows were lifted. "You have asked her, then?"

"Many times, your highness. Would it be possible to see such a prize without making an effort to possess it?"

The prince smiled; he was pleased to hear this sentiment, which had been his own echoed by other lips, even those of General Nirzann.

"You are right," he declared; "you are positively right, Nirzann. She is indeed a prize."

"A prize for princes," said the general, beginning to feel more sure of himself.

"Yes, a prize for princes." The ruler of Marisi frowned. "But one for which even a prince must pay the full price. That is why I came to talk with you, Nirzann. I know I can depend on what you tell me.

"I shall not send De Mide to Warsaw—it would be useless; I know everything that can be known. I shall see you tonight at dinner. *Au revoir!*"

And he departed as abruptly and unceremoniously as he had entered.

As soon as he had left, General Nirzann sprang to his feet in swift and uncontrollable agitation. At that last speech of the prince's he had had all he could do to contain himself. Great Heavens! What had he done?

"One for which even a prince must pay the full price." That could mean but one thing. But it was unthinkable! A prince of Marisi to marry an adventuress, a peasant courtezan? General Nirzann sank back in his chair, groaning in dismay and despair.

To this had he been brought by that demon in the form of a woman! He felt bewildered and crushed by the sudden rush of misfortune. What could he do?

To allow the prince to accomplish his design was impossible. Rather anything than that; for the prince had judged correctly of General Nirzann; if he was nothing else, he was loyal. He had meant to toss Mlle. Solini to him as a plaything—and now this!

The little general swore that he would cut her throat and his own into the bargain before he would allow her to become Princess of Marisi; and he meant it.

Something had to be done, and at once. His first thought, of course, was to go to Mlle. Solini; but a moment's reflection showed him the uselessness of it. He knew very well what would happen.

He would threaten her with exposure; she, knowing that in betraying her he would also betray himself, would defy him to do his worst. Next he thought of going to the prince and telling him the truth. But that held the extreme of danger.

If the prince really contemplated marrying Mlle. Solini in spite of her comparatively humble birth, he must indeed be infatuated with her, and he would not deal lightly with the man who, by his own confession, had so deceived him.

For an hour the general remained irresolute, while a thousand schemes raced in and out of his brain. Now he would throw himself into a chair in despair; again he would spring to his feet and pace rapidly up and down the room.

Was there no way out of it? That devil of a woman! He would

like to wring her neck! What was to be done? The general tore his hair and called to the heavens.

Suddenly, struck with an idea, he stopped short. Ah, Perhaps— perhaps— He considered for a moment; then, suddenly making up his mind, snatched up his coat and hat and ran through the hall and down the stairs to the *porte-cochère* of the palace.

A limousine was standing at the foot of the steps. The general sprang in, calling to the driver:

"The Hotel Walderin—and hurry."

Ten minutes later he was asking at the desk of the Walderin for Richard Stetton.

"M. Stetton?" said the polite clerk. "I will see if he is in, general."

A wait of five minutes, which to the general seemed an hour, and a message came from M. Stetton to show the visitor up immediately.

To say that Stetton was surprised to receive a call from General Nirzann would be to put it mildly. But he was usually content to take things as they came, and he merely allowed himself to wonder, "What can that fellow want with me?" However, his surprise showed on his face as the general entered the room.

The two men bowed politely and looked at each other with an expression which, though not exactly hostile, was certainly not over-cordial. As for the general, he was in no mood to humor petty antagonisms. This was a matter of life and death to him, and he came straight to the point.

"M. Stetton," he began abruptly, "no doubt you are surprised to see me."

The young man admitted that the call was somewhat unexpected in its nature.

"I have come to you," continued the general, "concerning a matter which is equally important to both of us, and—"

Stetton interrupted him to ask him to be seated. The general, moving in quick little jerks, placed his hat on one chair and himself on another and resumed:

"My errand has to do with Mlle. Solini. I believe that you are interested in her."

Stetton, wondering what on earth would come next, admitted that this surmise was not incorrect.

"What I have to say will surprise you," continued the general, "perhaps as much as it surprised me. As you know, I have been— er—more or less intimate with Mlle. Solini, and I am perfectly aware of the relations that exist between you and her.

"Well, she is playing you double. She is betraying you. *Monsieur*—" The general halted for a moment; then continued impressively: "Unless you or I do something to interfere, Mlle. Solini will marry the Prince of Marisi within a month."

Stetton did not appear so surprised, after all. Instead, he smiled as one who possesses superior knowledge and said:

"You are mistaken, general."

Then, when the general began to insist that he knew only too well what he was talking about, Stetton continued, interrupting him:

"Pardon me—just a moment. It is no wonder that you have been deceived, with all the rest of Marisi. Indeed, for a time I was deceived myself, when I saw that the prince was spending every afternoon at Aline's house. I demanded an explanation, as my right, and she explained everything in two words. It is Mlle. Janvour the prince goes to see—if he marries anyone, it will be she."

"Rot!" cried the general. "I tell you it is Mlle. Solini herself!"

"Mlle. Solini says otherwise," smiled Stetton, unmoved.

"Then she is deceiving you."

"It is hardly likely. She would not dare."

"But it is! *Monsieur,* I see I shall be forced to tell you the source of my information." The general paused a moment, then continued: "It is the Prince of Marisi himself."

This made its impression. A look of doubt and astonishment appeared on Stetton's face.

"The prince!" he exclaimed.

"Yes. Perhaps now you will believe. Mlle. Solini has been lying to you, which is not surprising. She intends to marry the prince; it has been her game all along. What is worse, the prince intends to marry her."

Stetton leaped to his feet with an oath, advancing toward the general.

"This is the truth?" he demanded.

"It is the truth, *monsieur.*" The idea of resenting the implication did not enter the general's head.

"The Prince of Marisi told you that he is going to marry Mlle. Solini?"

"Not in so many words. No. But his meaning was unmistakable."

There was a silence. Stetton resumed his chair. The general regarded him anxiously. What was he going to do? The question was soon answered, when the American again rose to his feet, walked rapidly to the wardrobe, and took down his coat and hat. Then he turned:

"General, I thank you. It is true we are not friends, but you were perfectly right to come to me, and I thank you. We stand together in this matter. There is no time to be lost."

The general also rose. "Where are you going?"

"To see Aline. Will you come with me?"

But the general had already decided that he would allow Stetton to fight the battle alone. He had a dozen excuses ready, and he recited them glibly as the two men left the room together and descended in the elevator.

Stetton did not insist; he was glad, indeed, of the other's refusal. They parted in front of the Walderin; General Nirzann to return to the palace in the limousine, and Stetton to take a cab to 341 the Drive.

The truth was that Stetton by no means held implicit belief in the general's story. With him Aline had done her work well, playing on his vanity with the expertness of a master musician fingering the keys of a piano-forte.

She had allowed him just enough encouragement to lead him to believe that she longed for their wedding as much as he. She had explained all her activities with perfect logic. Still, the tale of the general was enough to cause even him to doubt, and he was consumed with impatience as he sat waiting for Mlle. Solini in her—or his—library.

Entering, she crossed to his side and offered him her lips to kiss. Stetton accepted the offer with alacrity, but with a lack of warmth that did not escape her attention. Her thought was: "A few days more, M. Stetton, and I shall say good-by to you forever." She said aloud:

"My dear boy, you have something on your mind. See how easily I can read you! That is a proof of love. But come, out with it."

Stetton had long before given up all attempts at finesse with Mlle. Solini. He replied simply:

"It is not pleasant."

"Good Heavens! It never is."

"It will require a great deal of explanation."

"It always does."

"It amounts to this, Aline, that you have been lying to me."

"Monsieur!"

"Now, don't fly into a rage. You have found out by this time that I am plain-spoken. I say what I believe. I repeat, you have been lying to me."

"What do you mean?"

Stetton eyed her for a moment in silence, with a look that was meant to be searching and disconcerting.

"I'll tell you what I mean," he said finally. "Sit down!"

When Aline had obeyed this command he told her word for word what he had just heard from the lips of General Nirzann.

Aline heard him through in silence. When he had finished she observed calmly:

"Well, what of it?"

"It is true, then!" cried Stetton, suddenly enraged, for he had expected an immediate and vociferous denial. "You admit it!"

"I admit nothing. I simply say, if it is true, what then?"

"Answer me! Is it true?"

There was a silence, while he stood looking down at her with blazing eyes. He repeated his question a dozen times, in varying tones of insistence and anger; she sat motionless and silent, with lowered eyes. Suddenly she spoke, and there was something in her tone that compelled attention:

"M. Stetton, I will answer your question, but in my own way. Will you listen to me?"

"You can answer yes or no," he insisted, "and talk afterward. Is it true?"

But she persisted, and he was forced to give way. He took a chair across the table, saying with a frown:

"Go on. But to begin with, you know what I know, and what I will do."

"I know," said Aline. "I know only too well. That is why I want to talk to you. I am going to appeal to your generosity, and that is something I have never done before with any man."

"I have not too great a stock of it left," said Stetton dryly.

Aline replied:

"No, and that is why I do not count on success. But I feel that I owe myself the chance, if there is one. *Monsieur,* it amounts to this, that it rests with you to save me."

"That is exactly what I am trying to do."

"I do not mean that. I mean to save me from yourself. I am at your mercy; I admit it. I am asking you to be generous."

Stetton grew impatient.

"But what do you mean? What do you want? What are you talking about? It occurs to me that I have been fairly generous already."

And indeed, so he had; was there not at that moment over two hundred thousand francs in cash locked away in Mlle. Solini's desk upstairs?

"You have been generous," agreed Aline, "more so than I had any right to expect. But that is not what I mean. I do not want money, *monsieur;* I want my freedom."

"Your freedom?" This suspiciously.

"Yes. Do you not see? *Monsieur,* three months ago—it seems as many years—I promised to marry you. I understood at the time very well what I was doing. I made that bargain willingly; indeed, what else was there to do? I was in great danger—I was alone—I had to think of Vivi as well as myself. But since then I have grown to detest and hate myself for it. You are a gentleman, *monsieur.* I ask you to release me."

"What! What! You—"

"Wait—let me finish. Despising myself as I did, I yet had every intention of living up to my word, desiring only first to dispose Vivi safely in marriage. I had that intention till yesterday. But yesterday"— here Mlle. Solini's voice faltered—she appeared to be overcome with emotion—"yesterday, *monsieur,* an honorable man—a gentleman— asked for my hand in marriage."

"The prince!" cried Stetton furiously.

"I do not say who it was, *monsieur.* It would not be fair to him. But now you know what I want. His offer is honorable. I ask you to permit me to accept it."

She stopped, looking at Stetton through lowered lids. He appeared to be really touched, as he gazed at her in silence. He said finally:

"But it is impossible! I love you!"

"*Monsieur,* you cannot refuse me. I beg of you—I plead for your mercy—"

He replied more firmly, in a tone of finality:

"It is impossible. I cannot give you up."

Aline's manner suddenly changed. She raised her head with an air of defiance and looked straight into his eyes as she said:

"You will not give me my freedom—you will not release me from my bargain?"

"I will not."

"What if I do as I please?"

"You dare not."

"You would betray me?"

"If you force me, yes."

There was a silence. Again Aline's eyes were lowered. Then she looked up again and said in a tone of hopelessness:

"Very well, *monsieur.* But of one thing rest assured—I will not allow you to cover me with shame. My bargain with you is ended."

Stetton gazed at her in astonishment. "But what are you going to do?"

Aline replied in the same tone of hopelessness and despair:

"What can I do? There is but one thing left to me—a life of resignation and piety. You found me in a convent, *monsieur.* I shall leave you to go to one."

Instantly Stetton was jumping up and down in frantic protest. She should not go! He would not permit it! He loved her—he could not give her up! He would follow her to the door of the convent—he would prohibit her entrance!

Stetton stormed, threatened, and pleaded by turns. She had made the bargain—she should live up to it! Did she not love him? He would not give her up—he could not! He would do anything— he would go anywhere—he would give her anything in the world she wanted.

But she would not move from her decision.

Her eyes were wet with tears, and, seeing them so for the first time, he thought them ravishingly beautiful. He felt an irresistible desire to kiss the tears away. But she would not let him touch her.

"Never," she cried, "never, never."

He exclaimed in despair:

"But you must—you must! I can't live without you! To lose you now? It would drive me mad! Aline—my darling—listen, Aline— you must marry me!"

"Ah, *monsieur,* it is too late! No—no—do not tempt me—I have decided—"

Instantly he was on his knees, begging and pleading with her to marry him. Suddenly she murmured something—he protested violently—it appeared that she doubted his sincerity. He swore by everything sacred that he had never been more in earnest in his life.

She looked up and asked abruptly:

"Would you marry me now—tonight?"

"Why—that—I don't see—" he stammered, completely taken aback.

"But I do see, *monsieur.* Forgive me, but I have reason to doubt you."

"What can I do?" cried Stetton. "To marry you tonight is impossible. There are arrangements to make—it would appear strange— Anything I can do I will do."

"You are willing, then, to bind yourself?"

"Utterly! You mean a contract? Gladly!"

"No, I do not mean that. I would not ask that. But why—I wish to feel assured—will you write to me tonight?"

"Write to you?" He appeared not to understand.

"Yes," she answered. "Write what you have said."

This was a close game she was playing now. She risked a smile— a little tantalizing smile that softened her words.

It was unnecessary. Stetton could see no reason why he should not write a proposal of marriage to the woman he seriously intended to marry. He said as much, and expressed a willingness to execute the document at once on the table in the library.

Aline thought quickly. There was no paper in the house except her own and Vivi's, tinted and scented, and that, she decided, would be dangerous for her purpose. She replied that it was unnecessary to do as he suggested; it would be sufficient for him to send his formal proposal from the hotel.

Stetton replied in the tone of one who intends to make good his words, "You will receive it tomorrow morning," and went his way.

CHAPTER XVIII

—◆—

Proposal Number Two

*C*ZEAN!"

"Yes, *mademoiselle*."

"Has the mail arrived?"

"Yes, *mademoiselle;* I am bringing it."

It was ten o'clock in the morning.

Mlle. Solini was in the library, reading aloud to Vivi, who sat by the window with some embroidery. In the earlier mail Mlle. Solini had been disappointed; there had been many letters, but not the one she was looking for.

As she took this which had just arrived from the tray, which Czean held out before her, there was an expression of expectation that approached anxiety on her face. She ran through the little bundle eagerly—ah! There it was—"Hotel Walderin."

She opened the envelope and quickly glanced over the letter. Then, laying her book on the table and telling Vivi she would return in a moment, she went upstairs, opened a drawer of her writing-desk, placed the letter inside, closed the drawer, and locked it.

"There!" she breathed with a sigh of satisfaction. "So much for him!"

Then she returned to the library and resumed her reading—a play of Molière's—for Vivi's instruction and her own amusement.

The morning passed. Noon arrived. Then one o'clock, and luncheon. By the time that was over it was nearly two, and Mlle. Solini began to exhibit signs of restlessness.

She told herself that she had no reason to be uneasy—had not General Nirzann told Stetton that the prince had signified his intention of marrying her? Nevertheless, her restlessness increased.

She walked to a window of the drawing-room and stood there, looking out on the street, for half an hour. She went to her room and quarreled with her maid about nothing at all. The afternoon wore away.

Four o'clock found Mlle. Solini again in the library, reading; only by a conscious effort of the will could she force her mind to follow the words in their sequence. Dinnertime came, and with it the end of hope. The Prince of Marisi had not appeared.

In the evening Stetton called, and Mlle. Solini was compelled to humor him for three weary hours, in order not to rouse his suspicion. As an alternative, he must be preserved.

This was difficult; the young man was burning with love, and appeared to expect his affianced to be similarly afire. She managed somehow to satisfy him, and when he left quite late she threw herself on her bed, thoroughly exhausted in mind and body. Waiting was a dreary performance for Mlle. Solini; she preferred to act.

The following day she waited till half past three o'clock; then, as the sky was sunny and the air warm and pleasant, she ordered the open carriage and went with Vivi for a ride.

It was her first appearance on the drive in nearly a month, and it created a small sensation. Wherever she passed people could be observed whispering to one another, but none failed to greet her with the utmost politeness. All that they said of Mlle. Solini might be true; in the meantime they preferred to practice caution.

They had just made the last turn at Savaron Square, and Aline had ordered the coachman to drive home, when, on swinging again into the drive, she found herself looking directly into the eyes of the Prince of Marisi, seated by the side of General Nirzann in the royal carriage.

He was looking straight at Aline. In spite of herself, the color mounted to her face; she inclined her head in a dignified bow, and the prince returned it, she thought, somewhat coldly.

That was all. The two carriages rolled on in opposite directions. Aline bit her lip in vexation, and failed to recognize Stetton, who passed them soon afterward in a touring-car.

On the following day Mlle. Solini did not leave the house. Through a window of the drawing-room she watched the afternoon promenade for an hour; several times she saw the royal carriage containing the prince and General Nirzann. Again the thought occurred that the general had betrayed her.

"But," she argued to herself, "the prince would never forgive him. No; he is mine; I must be patient."

Despite this, she was uneasy; and when Stetton called in the evening she was as gracious and kind to him as she had ever been. He would talk of nothing but the happiness that was soon to be his, and was so insistent in his demand for a definite date for its consummation that Aline finally named a day early in June.

M. Stetton also had a little project on foot for her amusement. He had happened to hear that morning at the hotel of an old French château some miles out of Marisi on the Tsevor Road, which had been turned into an inn. He wanted to know if Mlle. Solini would drive out there with him the following day in his motor-car. He hastened to add that he would, of course, expect Vivi to accompany them; upon which, after a moment's reflection, Aline accepted his invitation and said they would be ready to start at ten o'clock.

The day proved to be a happy one for Vivi and Stetton, and, to all appearances, for Aline also, save for one little incident that occurred as the car sped swiftly through the pleasant hilly country to the west of the city.

They had just passed a little wooden bridge and turned to the left down a long stretch of straight, level road, at the right of which, some distance ahead, appeared a cluster of low, rambling sheds.

Stetton glanced at the spot with a start of recognition, and then, he scarcely knew why, turned to Aline and observed:

"That is where I fought Chavot."

She glanced up quickly, and he fancied that she shuddered, but she said nothing.

The château was about fifty miles from Marisi, and they reached it a little after noon. Everything was delightful. They had luncheon on an enclosed terrace, into which the sun shone brightly; off to the right the mountains rose, a majestic line of purple.

For an hour or more they lingered over their coffee, served in little earthen cups, while Stetton and Vivi chatted pleasantly about nothing at all, and Aline gazed toward Marisi, thinking of a great deal. Then they made ready to return.

It was nearly five o'clock when Aline and Vivi were set down by Stetton at the door of No. 341. Vivi ran upstairs to her room; Aline went to the library and rang for Czean.

"Has any one called?" she asked when he appeared.

"Yes, *mademoiselle.* The prince was here at two o'clock, and again at four."

"Did he leave a note, a message?"

"Nothing, *mademoiselle.*"

Aline's eyes sparkled. At last! She did not regret her absence; on the contrary, she considered it a lucky stroke. Still, she must contrive that the prince should see her, and as soon as possible; she knew where her strength lay.

After a few minutes' thought she went to the telephone and

called up the Countess Potacci. The countess was delighted to hear from her dear Aline; she complained of having been neglected.

What was that? Mlle. Solini wished to invite herself to occupy a seat in the countess's box at the opera that evening? Certainly! The countess would be glad to have her.

They would stop at 341 for her on their way. Aline said that was unnecessary, as she could go in her own car; but the countess insisted. They would call for her at eight o'clock.

Aline hung up the receiver, calling for Czean to serve dinner half an hour earlier than usual. Then she ran lightly up the stairs to her room. All her fatigue from the day's long ride was forgotten; she was in the best of humor and spirits, and spoke so kindly to her maid that she lost a considerable portion of the reputation she had acquired in that quarter.

When she went down to dinner two hours later Vivi ran up and threw her arms round her, exclaiming impulsively:

"I can't help it! You are so beautiful!"

Aline laughed and kissed her. The truth was that she enjoyed no one else's praise so much as Vivi's.

She received enough that night, though most of it was not for her own ears.

No sooner had she entered the Potacci box at the opera on the arm of the count than every glass in the house was leveled in their direction. But it was not for this that Aline had come, and a hasty glance at the royal box across the auditorium showed her that it was empty. It was yet early, however, and the prince was always late.

The lights grew dim and a hush fell over the house, while the orchestra commenced the overture. Then—the opera was "Rigoletto"—the curtain arose on the scene of much color and little music in the palace of the Duke of Mantua, and the hunchbacked jester began the antics that were to lead him into the path of grief and death.

But Aline had not taken her eyes from the royal box; and soon she was rewarded by seeing the curtains slowly open and the prince appear, followed by General Nirzann and one or two other members of the household. Aline turned her eyes to the stage.

The curtain fell; the auditorium was again lighted; the hum of conversation was heard on every side. Half a dozen of the young sparks of Marisi appeared in the box of the Count Potacci, attracted thither by the presence of the beautiful Russian.

Aline received them graciously and chatted pleasantly; all the time, however, she was watching the royal box out of the corner of her eye.

The visitors disappeared; the curtain again rose; all was again darkness and silence, save on the stage, where the *Duke* and *Gilda* soon began their amazingly amiable duet.

At the end of the second act the Potacci box became crowded; it would seem that Marisi fancied it could read the thoughts of the beautiful Russian by looking into her eyes, and no one is so interested to discover the truth or falsity of a piece of gossip as those who have started it.

General Nirzann appeared to pay his respects to the countess and Mlle. Solini; evidently he had been apprised by Stetton of the success of his mission three days before, for he greeted his cousin Aline with warmth and effusion.

Aline was listening to him and a dozen others who were trying to talk all at once, when suddenly she heard a new voice behind her greeting the Countess Potacci. It was that of the prince.

As he came toward the front of the box the others fell back before his imperious glance, looking at each other significantly. Aline kept her gaze steadfastly ahead. Suddenly she heard his voice quite close to her, low and musical:

"Good evening, *mademoiselle.*"

She replied calmly, without turning round:

"Good evening, your highness."

Again his voice sounded, this time lower still and full of significance. He uttered the one word:

"Tomorrow."

Then he fell back to the side of the Countess Potacci, who
would have given her eyes to know what that whispered word had
been, and the others again crowded round the beautiful Russian.

The face of one, however, was filled with something besides
admiration; General Nirzann was trying to guess at what the prince
had said. To be sure, Stetton had told him that he himself had Mlle.
Solini's promise of her hand, but the general was beginning to appreciate Aline's capacity for intrigue, and he feared her.

During the last act Aline watched the stage without seeing it;
what did she care for murdered maids or betrayed jesters? She
allowed herself, however, a feeling of contempt for poor *Rigoletto*—
the weak fool, to entrust his vengeance to the hands of another.
Assuredly that would not have been the way of Mlle. Solini.

On the way home in the Potacci carriage she paid no heed to
the comments of the count and countess; she kept repeating to herself the word: "Tomorrow."

An hour later, alone in her own room, she surveyed herself in
the mirror with satisfaction and approval.

"Tomorrow," was her thought, "tomorrow."

The following morning she awoke late. Stretching herself luxuriously, she rang for her maid; then followed her chocolate and mail,
after which Vivi came in to say good morning. She was sitting on
the edge of the bed, playing with Aline's golden tresses, when there
came a sudden knock on the door. In response to Aline's invitation
to enter, Czean appeared.

"M. Stetton is in the library, *mademoiselle*."

Aline appeared to reflect for a moment. Then she said in the
tone of one who has made sudden decision:

"I am not at home."

Czean stammered:

"But, *mademoiselle*—he already knows—I have told him—"

"I am not at home," Aline repeated sharply. "Tell him so."

Czean disappeared to give the lie to Stetton. As for Vivi, although she was greatly surprised at this sudden change in the fortunes of M. Stetton, she made no observation on the matter. She had long before learned that the more inexplicable a thing appeared to be the less likely was Mlle. Solini to explain it.

The burning of bridges is a pastime that only the sure-footed should allow themselves; this Mlle. Solini knew, and yet she had applied the match. The prince's "tomorrow" had arrived.

This should be her day of triumph; everything was well in hand. She had the confidence of her genius; and when, at a little after two o'clock in the afternoon, she heard the outer door open and the voice of the Prince of Marisi in the hall, her pulse remained as steady and composed as her face. Czean, who had received his orders, escorted the royal visitor at once to the library, where Aline was sitting alone.

As soon as Aline looked into the prince's eyes as he crossed the room to take her hand, she saw that the battle was over and the victory won. He had come to claim his prize, and to pay the price that was demanded for it.

Aline resolved that it should not be too easy for him; she remembered that scene in the same room three days before, when he had left her in the midst of her humiliation. True, it had been assumed, but he did not know that. Today he should answer to her pride.

The prince appeared, in fact, to be a little ill at ease. He began with some conventional remark concerning his disappointment of the day before. Aline, delighted to have the cue, replied with a long and circumstantial account of their trip into the country, and ended

by observing that she and Vivi had about decided to go by automobile to Paris, for which place they intended to depart in the course
of a week or so.

"You are going to Paris?" asked the prince in a tone which
implied that no one ever went there.

"Yes. Does that surprise your highness?"

"I thought you intended to stay in Marisi."

"So we did, for a while. We have changed our plans."

Aline said this, not as one who expresses an intention for the
sake of evoking a protest, but quite naturally as a matter of fact. It
had its effect on the prince. He regarded her for a moment in
silence, then said abruptly:

"You are less acute than I thought, *mademoiselle*. Did you not
understand what I said last night?"

Aline smiled.

"Was it so cryptic, your highness? I took it to mean that you
would honor me with a visit today." She glanced at him, as much as
to say, "And here you are."

"A quite natural deduction," said the prince dryly. "But had you
no idea of the nature of my visit?"

"I am not good at guessing riddles, your highness."

"But you are an adept—do not deny it—at reading the hearts
of men."

"Perhaps—of men. But not of a prince."

"It is all the same."

"Your highness will forgive me; experience has taught me the
difference."

The prince's face suddenly became quite grave. He gazed
toward Mlle. Solini as though he were looking not at her, but
through her; his thoughts, serious ones, appeared to be elsewhere.
Suddenly he said:

"If there is a difference, you must admit that it is not a fictitious one. Let us be frank, *mademoiselle*. I did not come here today to play with words, though you do it so delightfully." He paused; as Mlle. Solini did not speak, he continued:

"The other day I said something that angered and offended you. I am not going to apologize, though I hope for your forgiveness—and more. You know, *mademoiselle,* that my life does not belong to myself; and perhaps you are right, for therein lies the difference between a prince and a man.

"My family has ruled in Marisi for two hundred years. We have not the ostentation of the larger thrones, but our pride is equal to theirs. Behind the familiarity and democracy of our relations with our people there exists a tradition stronger even than that of the family of your own Czar."

The prince paused, regarding Mlle. Solini expectantly, but she said nothing. He resumed:

"I do not need to explain why I am saying all this to you, *mademoiselle*. You know very well. You know that I love you, for you are able to read the hearts of men, and to play with them. I speak calmly and gravely, because it affects others than myself when I ask you to become my wife and share with me the throne of Marisi."

Aline drew a sharp breath. She felt the eyes of the prince upon her, with their sternness and gravity. To tell the truth, she was not a little embarrassed. Quick, hot, passionate words—these she could command at will; but to dissemble in the face of this deep and calm sincerity was not easy. She finally murmured:

"I do not know—I have not sought this honor, your highness—if it is a sacrifice, I will not accept it."

"It is a willing sacrifice, *mademoiselle*. Do not misunderstand me. For myself"—and here, for the first time, the prince's voice held a note of passion—"for myself, I would hesitate at nothing. I love you;

that is enough. It is of others I am thinking when I speak of sacrifice. But they will make it willingly for me. Do you accept, *mademoiselle?*"

"I—I—" Aline faltered and stopped.

A note of eagerness crept into the prince's voice.

"Tell me. Do you accept?"

Aline extended her hand. The prince took it in his own and pressed the fingers to his lips quite gravely.

"I accept, your highness," said Mlle. Solini in a low voice, moved, in spite of herself, by his manner.

The prince straightened up, drawing a long breath.

"Ah!" he said in a new tone.

It was more than an exclamation; it was a prayer. Then, in a sudden burst of passion, long restrained, he made a quick step forward and took her roughly in his arms. He held her close, and sought her lips with his own.

"This—this is what I wanted!" He was breathing heavily. "I love you—you witch—you witch—I love you!"

"No—no—" Aline pushed him away. "Your highness must not—your highness—"

The prince half released her, still keeping an arm around her shoulders.

"Not that any more," he said, in the voice of love. "My name is Michael. Say it."

"But—your highness—"

"No! Say it!"

Again he drew her to him, this time with firm tenderness; still he was trembling from head to foot.

"Say it," he repeated.

She whispered in his ear: "Michael."

"You love me?"

"Yes."

"Say it."

"Michael, I love you."

After that, silence. A long silence, broken here and there by soft murmurings and little electric words. At length the prince released her from his embrace and began to talk to arrangements—it appeared that a great deal of ceremony was connected with the betrothal of a prince.

When he announced that he would send General Nirzann with a formal proposal, in writing, on the following morning, Aline turned her head quickly to hide the smile that appeared on her lips. She could guess how General Nirzann would relish that mission.

The prince went on to say that he had selected the general for that office as being peculiarly fitted for it on account of his relationship with Mlle. Solini. He added that everything must be kept strictly secret until the time came for a formal announcement from the palace.

To all his suggestions Aline listened respectfully and assented as a matter of course. The prince made ready to leave. They had been together over three hours; night was beginning to fall, and the library was dim with the ghostly and melancholy light of dusk.

"I shall see you tomorrow," said the prince, holding her in his arms and kissing her. "Tell me again that you love me."

"Michael, I love you."

A moment later he was gone.

Aline rang for lights.

But not the brilliance of all the lamps in the world, nor of the sun itself, could have equaled that in her own eyes.

—∿—

CHAPTER XIX

The General on Guard

*I*MAGINE A man—for we are nothing if not modern—imagine a man in a thoroughly tested and guaranteed aeroplane, with a warranted stabilizer, sailing along peacefully—and not too swiftly—through the warm and pleasing air of a spring in Arcadia.

Below, not at too great a distance, appear smiling green valleys and silvery winding streams; from a grove of trees, a little to the right, arises the song of thrushes and nightingales. Above, the blue sky, with the glare of the sun softened deliciously by a few light, fleecy clouds.

Imagine all this; and then think that suddenly, almost without warning, the sky is overcast, great clouds of rain begin to fall, the wind howls and sweeps in a whirlwind of fury, all grows dark, and the aeroplane, trembling violently, breaks squarely in two and goes crashing toward the earth.

Picture to yourself that man's emotions and sensations, and you will have an approximate idea of how General Paul Nirzann felt when, on meeting the prince after his return to the palace, he was greeted with the words:

"General, I am going to marry your cousin."

True, at first he was conscious of no sensation whatever. He was completely stunned. He gazed at the prince with the look of a man who has been unexpectedly knocked on the back of the head, and stammered:

"Your highness—I—what—your highness says—"

"Are you so amazed?" asked the prince, laughing. "You should not be. I surely made myself clear enough the other day."

"But it is impossible!" cried the general, beginning to find his tongue.

"Ho!" exclaimed the prince in great good humor, with a twinkle in his eye, "I see what it is! You are jealous—you admitted you wanted her for yourself. You are too late, Nirzann; besides, you yourself called her a prize for princes."

Then, more seriously: "Of course, you must not breathe a word of this—not a word to any one. Come to me tomorrow morning at ten o'clock; I have an errand for you. If you—Well, De Mide, what is it? Oh, yes, I had forgotten. Remember, general, not a word."

The prince walked off on the arm of his secretary.

The general stood like one paralyzed, feeling the world tumbling about his ears. He was unable to think. By some queer trick of the brain a phrase he himself had used and the prince had just repeated was running over and over in his head: "A prize for princes—a prize for princes."

He was not sure but what he was saying it aloud, and, observing a footman regarding him with a stare of curiosity, he somehow made his way down the great hall and up the stairs to his own room.

There he remained for two hours, pacing up and down in feverish agitation. There was a knock on the door; a servant appeared. The prince desired to know if they were not to have General Nirzann's company at dinner.

The general replied in the negative, saying that he would dine out. Again he took to pacing the floor, but he could find no loophole of escape. He sighed, and came to a sudden determination; then he stood still in the middle of the room, surveying the familiar objects about him with the air of one who says farewell; tears were in his eyes.

To do him justice, the general's decision was in the way of being heroic; let him have his due. Again sighing, he left the room and sought the street. Fifteen minutes' walk brought him to the door of 341 the Drive.

Mlle. Aline Solini fancied that she knew very well what was in store for her when Czean appeared at her door to announce that General Nirzann wished to see her. An unpleasant scene, that was all. Her first impulse was to refuse to see him.

"After all," she thought, "it must be done sometime, and as well get it over with." Then, aloud: "Tell him I will be down in a few minutes, Czean."

As the prince had said, Aline knew well how to read men's hearts, and, he might have added, their minds. With her first quick glance at the face of General Nirzann, torn with regret and despair, and at the same time firm with the strength of an unalterable resolution, she saw that her task was not to be so easy as she had expected. Nevertheless, she had no doubt of the outcome.

The general rose to his feet and approached her with a majestic strut. He wasted no time in preliminaries; he said abruptly and almost fiercely: "We are alone?"

"Yes, we are alone." Aline smiled, saying to herself with a touch of amusement: "The little general is going to be theatrical."

The general was speaking: "*Mademoiselle,* three hours ago the Prince of Marisi told me that he is going to marry you."

She replied calmly: "That is true."

"Pardon me, *mademoiselle,* it is not true; it is impossible."

"How impossible?"

"I will not allow it."

"You cannot help yourself."

"I can, and I will."

These sentences were shot forth with the rapidity and incisiveness of the reports of a Gatling gun. At this last declaration of the general's, uttered in a tone of the utmost determination, Aline made a gesture of incredulity.

For a moment she stood still, returning the general's gaze with one quite as firm as his own; then she said, as one who is forced to argue a matter which has already been decided:

"General, listen to me. I understand your position perfectly—both its strength and its weakness. I do not deny that you have certain claims on me, and let me tell you this—that you will always possess my gratitude. I am going to marry the Prince of Marisi. I warn you not to attempt to hinder me."

"You are not going to marry the prince."

"I am."

"I will prevent it."

"How?"

"By telling him the truth about you."

"Bah! You dare not, my dear general; it would be to ruin yourself."

"I know that very well; I have resigned myself to it."

Aline looked at him quickly; the fellow had actually said that as though he meant it! Which, of course, was absurd. She said dryly:

"That is quite useless, general. You are trying to frighten me. I know you too well to believe you. You are too old and too wise a man to cut your own throat. I am willing to talk with you sensibly, but I will not listen to your foolish threats."

She stopped, expecting the general to break out into loud protestations of his sincerity and earnestness; but he did not speak. Instead, he stood regarding her in silence, with a little, forlorn smile on his lips, but with clear, determined eyes.

For the first time a tinge of foreboding crept into Aline's thoughts. Was it possible that this little man was going seriously to oppose her—that he was willing to drag her down with him to double ruin?

But why?

Did the fool really love her?

But, no—she would manage him. Bah! To carry the thing thus far and be foiled at last by the little general? Impossible!

"If you think my threats are foolish, you are mistaken, *mademoiselle.*"

The general was speaking quite slowly and distinctly, as if he wished to make himself very plain. "I mean every word I say. You see, I owe everything I have in the world to the Prince of Marisi." The general's voice became plaintive in its earnestness. "Everything.

"I love him; I would die for him, as I have served him. Do you know what he said to me the other day? And we were talking about you, too. He said: 'General, your fidelity is beyond question.' That is great praise from his lips, *mademoiselle!* I can honestly say I deserved it. You tell me I am too old and too wise a man to cut my own throat. I would cut my own throat—literally—rather than betray my prince."

"Betray him!" cried Aline. "My dear general, who is asking you to betray him? Is it betraying him to permit him to marry the woman he loves?"

Mlle. Solini realized with a feeling of anger that she was descending to argument.

The general replied calmly:

"Pardon me, *mademoiselle;* when that woman is you—yes."

"Ah!" cried Aline, while a glance, furious and keen as the flash of steel, darted from her eyes. Unmoved the general continued:

"I may seem brutal; I cannot help it; I shall speak plainly. You have deceived me and tried to outwit me. You are betraying and deceiving M. Stetton, and accepting money from him. These things alone would make you unfit to become Princess of Marisi. But in addition to that, there are so many ambiguous things about you— indiscretions—shall we say—more than enough; I am determined."

"Ah, what a gentleman you are!" Aline spat out these words in one furious breath.

"I am no longer a gentleman, *mademoiselle;* I am merely the servant of my prince."

Aline was compelled to believe. Every tone of the general's voice, every glance of his eye spoke of the deepest earnestness. There was no doubt of it; these were not mere empty threats; the man would actually do as he said.

Aline looked at him, and if looks could kill the general would assuredly have dropped dead in his tracks. Her brain was working with the rapidity of lightning. There had been a time, she thought, when the general could not have spoken to her as he just had done. What a fool she had been to loosen her hold on him! If only she had not neglected him when she began to feel that he was no longer useful to her! She glanced at him swiftly, speculatively. Perhaps—

She crossed to the general's side and placed her hand on his shoulder. He appeared to take no notice of the movement, but stood in silence, as though awaiting her decision.

"Paul," she said—he had always been childishly pleased when she called him that—"Paul, I cannot believe that you will do what you say."

"Do not doubt it," replied the general grimly. She fancied that his shoulder moved slightly under her touch—a good sign, she thought. She said, allowing a note of tenderness to creep into her voice:

"But I do doubt it. You cannot be so cruel to me. Have you forgotten everything? Do you no longer love me?"

Her arm crept round his neck; she moved a little closer to him.

"Can you blame me, Paul, for wanting a home, a position, a

name? You know the one I would take if I could; I do not need to tell you where my heart is. If you will not marry me yourself, Paul, why do you refuse to allow me to find happiness where it is waiting for me?"

There was a pause, while the general regarded her with an air of sadness and commiseration. But when he spoke his voice was quite firm; more, final.

"Aline, I am sorry—believe me—I am sorry, but it is impossible. I am determined." And he repeated, as though to strengthen his resolution, which, indeed, was quite strong enough already: "I am determined."

Aline thought: "He is weakening." Her other arm crept around his neck; her hands met on his shoulder.

"Paul," she murmured, looking into his eyes—"Paul, listen to me. Do you think I have ceased to love you? I could not, dear. Because I marry the prince I do not need to give him my heart. It is yours; it will always be yours. And—"

She got no further in her mistake. The general, suddenly understanding her, tore her arms from his neck and pushed her away with such violence that she would have fallen but that her outstretched hand fell on the back of a chair. Nirzann stood breathing heavily, regarding her with eyes of horror and disgust.

"My God!" he cried, choking with wrath and contempt.

Aline sank back in a chair, turning her face away. She was no longer angry; on the contrary, she was composed and deadly calm. She perceived at last that the case was desperate; that only a miracle or a stroke of genius could save her. She must think—she must have time to think! She turned to the general:

"You have made up your mind to betray me?" She asked it as one asks an ordinary question for the sake of information. For reply, the general merely nodded. "And what you demand is that I voluntarily cancel my engagement with the prince?"

"I demand nothing. I offer you an alternative."

There was a short silence; then Aline said:

"I don't know—my brain is confused—I don't know what to say. Give me time to think—leave me and come back in an hour."

He replied roughly:

"There is no need to think; it is a simple choice—yes or no."

"But I must think—my brain is whirling—what harm can that do? You would be wise to humor me, if you expect me to consider your desires in my answer."

"I do not expect you to consider my desires, *mademoiselle;* I do not wish that you should." He paused, but she did not speak, and he continued: "I am not thinking of myself, but of the prince. And let me tell you this, I will not wait an hour, nor ten minutes. Nor will I trust your word—I will not even allow you to remain in Marisi. When I go the limit I do not stop on the way, and I fear you."

"Really, general, you flatter me." Aline, playing for time, spoke sarcastically. "You will not trust my word? What else can I give you?"

"I don't know—something—a letter—an agreement—I must have something in writing. If I do not have it when I leave this house I shall go straight to the prince and tell him all."

A letter! Aline turned her eyes away quickly, lest she betray her thought. A letter! Wait—how could it be done—oh, for a minute to think! Ah! She nearly breathed it aloud. An idea! Wait—wait—yes— Her brain was working like lightning, in swift, brilliant flashes of inspiration. She turned to the general:

"You insist on my answer now?"

"Now."

"And you say—a letter—"

"Yes. A letter to the prince. That would be best."

"And I must leave Marisi?"

"At once."

There was a silence, while Aline sat apparently reflecting. The

general stood regarding her with the calmness of a man who is prepared to die, and who therefore can be moved by nothing. Suddenly
Aline spoke:

"I will go."

"You will go?" the general cried, startled. He had not expected
this.

"Yes. I will go. At once. Tonight—or tomorrow morning. And I
will give you your letter. Some day, general, you shall pay for this. I
do not know how nor when, but you shall pay for it." She arose.

"I expect to, *mademoiselle*." The general was unmoved by her
threat; he had expected that. "But let me warn you, don't try any
tricks with me. I must have the letter now, and you must be out of
Marisi for good by this time tomorrow." Then, as Aline was moving
toward the door leading to the hall, he called out sharply, "Where are
you going?"

"To my room, to write the letter," was her answer.

He made no reply, and she disappeared.

The general sat down to wait. After all, it appeared that he was
really going to escape with a whole skin. He was conscious of a certain feeling of gratitude toward Mlle. Solini, not very strong, perhaps,
but still it was there; and when, after an interval of fifteen minutes,
she returned, holding in her hand a pink envelope, he regarded her
with somewhat less contempt than he had half an hour before. Now
that it was all over, he felt, indeed, rather kindly disposed toward her.

Aline, approaching him, held the envelope out in her hand. It
was unsealed. On its face was a postage-stamp: below it was
addressed: "Michael, Prince of Marisi. Marisi Palace, Marisi."

The general took it and, after glancing at the address, put it in
his pocket.

"That is the end of everything," Aline was saying, "of everything." Her tone was one of sorrow and resignation, not unmixed

with anger. "Now, general. I am going to make some demands of you—I deserve something from you—you cannot deny it."

The general bowed and started to speak, but she interrupted him:

"I shall leave Marisi tomorrow morning. I would not stay anyway, after this. I do not want the prince to get that letter till after I have left. I do not want you yourself to read it till tomorrow morning; I need not explain why now; you will understand when you read it. You must promise me, general; you must swear to it."

"I promise, on my word," said the general, moved in spite of himself at this calmness in the face of disaster. "I promise gladly, *mademoiselle*. And if there is anything else—"

Aline appeared to think for a moment.

"Only this," she said finally, "that if M. Stetton asks you about me, tell him you know nothing. Nothing. Promise me."

"I promise, on my word," repeated the general, thinking that he was getting out of it rather cheaply.

"Remember, you are not to read the letter till tomorrow. And of course it must go through the mail—that is why I stamped it— the prince must not know you have seen it."

"Indeed not!" thought the general, and he said:

"You have my word, *mademoiselle*. I shall do exactly as you say."

There was an awkward pause. Aline drew back, as though to signify that there was nothing more to say. The general began uncertainly:

"*Mademoiselle*—Aline—I am sorry—"

She looked straight at him:

"That will do. I do not want your sympathy. Leave me—it is over. Leave me."

For a moment the general returned her gaze in silence; then, without a word, he turned and left the house.

—⁓—

CHAPTER XX

The General Keeps His Word

GENERAL PAUL Nirzann slept well that night. His aeroplane—to return to our dashing metaphor of the previous chapter—had righted itself and was again sailing peacefully along. The only cloud on the horizon was the loss of his Cross of Buta; the general really regretted that. But he had to acknowledge, though not without a sigh, that it was cheap at the price.

He was thoroughly glad that he was at length finished with Mlle. Solini. Of course, he had never really loved her, and for some time past he had feared her. In all conscience, he and Marisi were well rid of such a woman.

He did not doubt but that she would leave in the morning, as she had promised; indeed, Marisi would be the last place where she would want to remain, after the destruction of all her plans.

For his own part, he kept his word with her. He deposited her letter in a drawer of his desk without looking at it, wondering at the same time why she had placed this curious restriction upon him. For some time he lay awake; his dominant thoughts were of security and thankfulness. He slept soundly.

In the morning he rose rather late. He sang—or, to be strictly accurate, uttered noises—while he dressed, and ate a hearty breakfast in his room. He was lingering over the coffee when a glance at his watch showed him that it was twenty-five minutes past nine.

He remembered that the prince had commanded his presence at ten o'clock—for what purpose the general easily guessed—and, thinking that the matter of the letter must be attended to before then, he went to his desk and took it from the drawer.

The envelope itself held memories for him; he had himself received several exactly similar. He could see now, in his mind's eyes, that little corner of Aline's dainty writing-desk where they lay scattered about in an ebony box—two colors, pink and blue. This one was pink. The general sighed, took out the letter, and read:

To His Highness the Prince of Marisi:

What I am going to say will no doubt astonish your highness. As for me, it breaks my heart.

I shall be brief; I must either say too much or too little, and I prefer the latter.

In four words—I cannot marry you.

Your highness knows that I would not write this without a reason, and a powerful one. Forgive me if I do not tell you what it is.

By the time you read this I shall have left Marisi; I shall never see you again. Ah, Michael—I may call you that once more, may I not?—I had thought that the first letter I should write to you would be very different from this.

I can say no more—*adieu*.

Aline Solini.

The general read this letter over three times, and each time the frown on his brow deepened. Not that he had any fault to find with it, considering its purpose; indeed, he thought it perfect. It had an air of finality.

But why had Aline insisted so strongly that he should not read it till this morning? He could not understand that. He read it over again. Decidedly, there was nothing in it to explain that curious request.

But—he shrugged his shoulders—what of that? There was the letter; it was sufficient; quite sufficient. He returned the letter to the envelope, moistened the mucilage on the flap with his tongue, and sealed it.

Then he pressed a button on the wall beside his desk.

"But that would not do," he thought. "I must mail it myself."

When a servant appeared a moment later he dismissed him, saying that he would perform his errand himself. He rose, put on his coat and hat, and sought the street, and, walking some distance down the drive, deposited the letter in a mailbox.

As he heard it fall to the bottom of the box he breathed a sigh of satisfaction, and turned to retrace his steps.

By the time he reached his room it lacked but a minute till ten o'clock, and; stopping only to deposit his hat and coat on the back of a chair, he left it again to hasten to his appointment with the prince, in that room on the floor below, at the end of the corridor, which we have seen twice before. The general, being of the household, had the privilege of entering its sacred precincts; and he never did so without a little straightening of the shoulders at the thought of that privilege.

The prince, as it appeared, was in great good humor. When the general entered he was engaged with De Mide, his secretary, but their business was soon ended, and De Mide prepared to leave.

General Nirzann moved ostentatiously out of his path to the door. He did not like De Mide, and took advantage of every occasion to show it.

"You are punctual, I see, Nirzann," said the prince, as the door closed behind the departing secretary.

"Am I not always so, your highness?"

"I suppose so. The fact is, my dear general, you have so many virtues it is difficult to remember all of them."

The general smiled politely at his prince's little joke. "Your highness is kind to remember even one of them," he declared, quite as though he meant it.

"That will do, Nirzann; you will never be a courtier; you are too clumsy," laughed the prince, seating himself in a chair and motioning the general to one on the other side of the table. "But come; we must get down to business. Of course you know what I want you for?"

"I can guess."

"To be sure. You are to carry my formal proposal to your cousin." The prince arranged some papers on the desk before him. "I have been working at it with De Mide. I think we have it in proper form, but there are some gaps to be filled in. To begin with, what was her father's name?"

The general called on his wits, realizing that the farce must be played through. After a moment's hesitation he replied:

"Nicholas—Nicholas Solini."

The prince wrote something on the paper. "And her mother?"

"I—really, I do not know," stammered the general. "That is, I forget the name of her family. Her given name was the same as that of my cousin—Aline."

Again the prince wrote on the paper. Then he looked up with a frown:

"Now, about those estates in Warsaw. You say they are no longer in her name?"

"No, your highness."

"Then I suppose her residence could hardly be said to be there," observed the prince. "Let us see; I think this will do." He looked at the paper for a minute in silence, then began to read aloud from it:

To Mlle. Aline Solini, of Marisi, daughter of Nicholas Solini, of Warsaw, and his wife, Aline, greeting from Michael William Feodor Albert Keff, Prince of Marisi, Duke of Gernannt, Chevalier of the Order of Mestaniz. His highness, by these presents—"

The general sat listening respectfully while the prince read the somewhat lengthy document from beginning to end.

Once before the general had heard such a paper read in this same room—many years before.

As this thought crossed his mind he glanced up involuntarily at the portrait over the fireplace—the portrait of a woman of about thirty years, with dark hair and serious eyes.

She would have thanked him, the general thought, if she could; it was well that Mlle. Solini was not to take her place.

"You will take this to Mlle. Solini at once," the prince was saying. "I want all preliminaries arranged without delay so that we can make the public announcement as soon as possible. You will conduct the affair, of course, with due formality. You will understand, Nirzann, that I am eager for haste in this matter."

The general managed a smile.

"I can well understand that, your highness."

"Yes. Since you are Mlle. Solini's only living relative, you will be expected to officiate in that capacity at the wedding. And before I forget it, I have a little present for you."

The prince opened a drawer of the table and took out a little ivory box, which he opened, displaying to view a cross of gold, with yellow and green ribbons.

"Your Cross of Buta, general. Here, let me— What is it? What's the matter?"

"I—I—nothing, your highness." A swift spasm as of pain had

distorted the general's face. "That is—I felt something—it has passed now."

"That is what comes of dining out," said the prince with a smile. "You know your weakness, general."

"It has passed," said the general, who was looking relieved. "Your highness will forgive me—I should not—in your presence—"

"Good Heavens, man," the prince interrupted, laughing, "don't apologize! Indigestion has no respect for princes."

"Your highness is always kind." The general rose. "I am ready to go with your—er—proposal whenever your highness pleases. If there are any—"

The general's voice stopped suddenly, while his features were again distorted with a spasm of pain. This time it continued twice as long as before.

"What is it?" again cried the prince, looking at him in quick sympathy.

The general sank back weakly in his chair, while his eyes grew wide and staring and his lips twitched convulsively.

The prince crossed hastily to his side with an exclamation of alarm.

"What is it, Nirzann? Are you ill? What is the matter?"

"I don't know, your highness." The general appeared to be speaking with difficulty. He tried to struggle to his feet, but fell back again into the chair. "Perhaps—if I—if I—"

Then, quite suddenly, there came from his lips a great cry of pain—the cry of one who is being tortured with insupportable agony.

"Help!" he cried, again trying to rise. "For God's sake, help me!"

The thing had come so suddenly that for an instant the prince stood as one paralyzed. The next he was ringing the bell on the table and calling to the footman without. Then he sprang back to the general, who was slowly slipping from the chair onto the floor, and supported him in his arms.

In another moment two or three servants rushed into the room, attracted by the prince's cries. One he sent for water; another for the doctor, who was in the palace; and still another helped him support the general.

They had all they could do to hold him; he was struggling in their grasp like a crazy man, uttering screams of agony that sounded throughout the palace and reached even into the street. Other servants and members of the household rushed in, crying out in startled tones; all was confusion and uproar; they had thought the prince was being murdered.

De Mide, arriving breathless, offered to take the place of the prince beside Nirzann; but the prince shook his head, crying:

"The doctor—get the doctor!"

At that moment the doctor arrived—a man of sixty or more, wise and competent, who had served the prince's father before him. He pushed his way through the throng to the side of General Nirzann, who was a terrible sight to behold as he struggled in the arms of the prince and the footman.

His eyes were rolling wildly about, his face was red and distorted, and froth was coming from his mouth. The old doctor gave him but one glance before he turned to the De Mide and said sharply:

"Clear the room!"

Then the doctor turned and gave some swift instructions to a servant who had entered with him and who now disappeared at a run. De Mide ordered every one from the room; it was cleared in three seconds. No one remained but the prince, the doctor, and De Mide.

General Nirzann had slipped to the floor. The doctor knelt beside him, holding him down with both arms. The general's movements were more feeble now; his body was moving from side to side with little convulsive twitches. A low, continuous moan came from his lips.

The servant who had taken the doctor's instructions entered, carrying a case of instruments and bottles. De Mide hurried him forward, crying:

"Here, doctor—here you are!"

There was a silence, broken only by the moans of the general, now so feeble they were scarcely heard. The doctor raised his head and said gravely:

"Send him away. It is too late. Send him from the room."

"But what is it?" cried the prince. "This is horrible! In Heaven's name, what is it?"

The doctor did not reply. He was gazing at General Nirzann, whose body was trembling with spasmodic shudders that ran from his head to his feet. But his eyes were steady and seemed once more to hold the light of reason. The doctor leaned forward and spoke distinctly:

"Look at me, general. Do you know me?"

The eyes shifted, and the general's voice came, painful and gasping, as though every word were torn from his throat by force:

"Yes—Anchevin—yes." Again the eyes shifted toward the prince. "Your highness—listen—before—I am dying—Aline—Aline—"

He stopped; more would not come. The doctor took a pitcher of water and poured some over his mouth; then he leaned forward and spoke:

"Answer me if you can, general. Use all your strength. You have been poisoned. Do you know who did it?"

A sudden light flashed into the general's eyes—the light of comprehension. Then their expression changed as quickly to one of the most intense fury and hatred—so plain, so fiercely malignant, that De Mide and the prince recoiled involuntarily.

And again words came from the general's lips, but this time in a whisper, barely audible, though he was plainly making a terrible effort to speak intelligibly.

"Poison!" he gasped. "Yes—I know—yes—mucilage—mucilage—"

That was all. Several times more he opened his lips; it could be seen that he was exerting himself tremendously to speak; but no words came. His fingers were plucking convulsively at the edge of his coat; his eyes closed, then opened again; a tremor passed all over his body, and he lay quite still.

The doctor rose to his feet, turning to the others; they saw by the expression on his face that all was over. Their own faces were filled with a question—a question of horror; the doctor answered it without waiting for them to speak. His voice was very grave.

"Your highness, the general was poisoned. And with some quick poison—something that he has taken within the hour. Do you know—"

The prince interrupted him in a voice of agitation:

"I know nothing, Anchevin. He was sitting there, talking to me; the attack came suddenly and without warning. Why—I can't believe—it was only ten minutes ago—"

He stopped abruptly and stood looking down at the body of the general as though he were just beginning to understand what had happened. This for a long time; then he murmured gently: "Poor old Nirzann—a faithful servant and a true friend."

No one will deny that the little general deserved the epitaph.

Then the prince, suddenly rousing himself, turned to the others:

"Anchevin, you must repeat to no one what you have just said. Call it anything you like; there must be no mention of poison. De Mide, you will do what is necessary. Get Duchesne on the telephone and let him confer with Anchevin, but let him understand that whatever investigations he makes must be kept strictly secret. We owe it—to him."

The doctor began:

"Your highness, there must be an autopsy—"

"Good Heavens!" cried the prince. "Anchevin, you are ghoulish. Do what is necessary, but don't talk about it. De Mide, the general must be removed to his own room."

"Yes, your highness."

"And don't forget to impress Duchesne with the necessity for secrecy. If there is any—"

He was interrupted by the ringing of a bell. It was the telephone on the prince's desk. De Mide crossed to it and took up the receiver. The others heard him speak, and, after a short pause, say:

"Yes, the prince is here."

Another pause, then De Mide asked:

"Who is it?"

Then:

"One moment, please." De Mide placed his hand over the mouth of the transmitter and then turned to the prince.

"Mlle. Solini wishes to speak to you."

With an exclamation of surprise the prince hastened to take the receiver from his secretary, at the same time saying:

"You may go—both of you. Return in five minutes."

Then, when the doctor and De Mide had disappeared, he spoke into the telephone:

"Aline! Is this you, Aline?"

"Yes, your highness."

"Ah! I recognize your voice."

"And I recognize yours." A short pause. "I wanted to ask your highness—I wanted to know if you have received a letter from me this morning?"

"A letter? No."

"Oh! Then it hasn't been delivered. I am glad of that. I mailed it this morning, and then, half an hour afterward, found it on my desk."

"You found it on your desk?" repeated the prince, puzzled.

"Yes. I had placed a letter to someone else in the envelope addressed to you." There was a little silvery laugh in her voice. "And it is a letter which I would much rather you didn't read. That is why I telephoned you—I don't want you even to open it." Again the laugh. "Your highness knows that all women have their strictly private secrets."

"I know," said the prince, and began to return her laugh; but his eye rested on the body of General Nirzann, lying on the floor almost at his feet, and the laugh stuck in his throat.

"I will return your letter unopened, Aline. I shall speak to De Mide about it at once."

"That is what I was afraid of—that someone else might read it."

"I'll see that they don't. I'll guard your secret for you; I have the right, haven't I?"

"Yes, your highness."

"Not that!"

"Then—yes, Michael."

The prince was wondering if he ought to tell her of the death of her cousin, and how, but decided that it would be too rude a shock, coming thus suddenly over the telephone. But neither should she learn it through the cries of newsboys or the headlines of a newspaper.

He asked if he might call on her at her home in half an hour, saying that he had something of importance to tell her that could not be entrusted to the telephone. That arranged, he hung up the receiver and turned just as a knock sounded on the door.

It was De Mide, come to say that servants were preparing the general's room and would soon arrive to carry him there. The prince nodded gravely, without speaking.

Then, when the secretary had gone, he walked over to the body of the little general and stood looking down at him in silence.

His thoughts reverted to the general's dying words. They had been of Aline and of the prince himself, perhaps—so thought the prince—the only persons he had ever loved. But then—at the very end—

The prince's brow was wrinkled in a puzzled frown. He muttered aloud:

" 'Mucilage!' Now what the devil could he have meant by that word 'mucilage?' "

Which was one of those questions that never find an answer.

——

CHAPTER XXI

Stetton Goes Hunting

THE YOUNG are always with us."

The man who wrote that called himself a philosopher; but he would have shown clearer claim to the title if he had written instead: "The young are always with themselves."

Youth is the age of conceit, arrogance, vanity and egoism. It was the age of Richard Stetton. Thus much given, you can guess at the young man's feelings when, upon calling four different times at the house of Mlle. Solini—twice a day—he was told each time that she was not at home.

At the first call he believed it. The next he wondered. The third he doubted. The fourth he pushed his way past Czean at the door and went stalking through the drawing-room, library, dining-room and kitchen. The place was empty, except for the servants, who tittered behind his back.

What to do? He had not quite worked himself up to the point of daring to mount the stairs to her room and force an entrance. Besides, he felt that he was making himself ridiculous. He left the house with a threatening glance at Czean, who had followed at his heels throughout the search.

On his way back to the hotel he bought a newspaper. The first thing in it that met his eye was an account of the death of General Paul Nirzann.

The following morning, feeling that the situation was getting a little beyond him, Stetton went to his friend Frederick Naumann for advice; and then, for the first time, he told the whole story of his relations with Mlle. Solini, even to that burning proposal of marriage on which he had exercised all his epistolary genius a few nights previous. When he had finished Naumann was staring at him in incredulous amazement.

"You don't mean to say you were ass enough to propose to her in a letter!" cried the young diplomat.

Stetton saw no reason why he should be considered an ass.

Naumann groaned.

"My dear fellow, it was bad enough to propose to her at all! And to put it in writing! Of course, the worst trick she could play you would be to marry you, but the Lord knows what she'll do.

"Don't ask me for advice. The only thing I can say is, get that letter, burn it, take the ashes to San Francisco and drop them in the Pacific Ocean. She's too much for me; I've washed my hands of her."

With which Stetton was perforce contented.

After that he stayed away from No. 341 for two whole days. On the morning of the third day he attended the funeral of General Nirzann at the Church of Montrosine, in the company of Naumann. The service was public, and the church was crowded; but in all the throng Stetton had eyes for only one figure—that of a slender woman, dressed in black and heavily veiled, who sat far to the front on the right, by the side of the Prince of Marisi.

It was Aline, who, as cousin of the general, was of course the chief mourner.

As he sat listening to the chant of the priest, Stetton conceived an idea. Perhaps, after all, he thought—for seeing Aline dressed in the garb of grief, hypocritical though he knew it to be, disposed him to generous thoughts—perhaps, after all, she had really not been at home when he had called.

He had been too impatient. He should have done—well, he should have done what he was going to do now, that very day.

At the conclusion of the ceremony at church Stetton accompanied his friend Naumann back to his rooms. There they chatted till noon. Stetton calculated that it would take two hours for the funeral procession to go to the cemetery and return; at one o'clock, therefore, he left Naumann and went afoot down the Drive to a point nearly opposite No. 341.

After a wait of fifteen minutes he saw the royal carriage drive up and halt in front of that number. Aline and Vivi got out, assisted by the prince, who took them to the door, and then returned and reentered the carriage, which resumed its way to the palace.

Stetton waited five minutes by his watch, then crossed the street, ascended the stoop and rang the bell.

"I'll know this time," he muttered grimly to himself. "I'll show this smart *mademoiselle* a thing or two."

He stood close to the door in order to be in a position to push his way in as soon as it was opened.

But the door did not open. After a minute's wait he again rang the bell. Another minute, and still there was no sign from within.

He pressed his finger against the bell-button and kept it there; then he began punching it with little vicious stabs. Still there was no sign.

He put his face against the glass of the door and tried to look within; he could see nothing, but he knew that anyone standing at the farther end of the hall could see him plainly. For five minutes he stood alternately ringing the bell and pounding on the door, which was locked; then, muttering a string of oaths, he gave it up and returned to the street.

It was now quite evident, even to him, that Mlle. Solini neither desired nor intended to see him. He perceived the fact, but he could not understand it. Why, he was going to marry her—he, Richard Stetton, of New York, rated—or soon to be rated—at ten million dollars!

Was the woman crazy? Aline Solini, a nobody, penniless, an outcast—it was absurd! In all America there were not ten girls who would not have jumped at the chance! Positively, she was out of her senses!

But out of her senses or not, it was perfectly plain that she would not see him. That, in short, he had been cut dead. Refused the house! The house for which he himself had paid the rent! By the time Stetton reached his room at the hotel he had worked himself into a raging fury.

He forced himself to calmness and began to consider possibilities. He could not very well break in the door. He thought of waylaying her on the street, but decided that it was beneath his dignity. As for an appeal to the agent of M. Duroy, owner of the house, that was impossible, for the simple reason that it had been taken in Aline's name.

He ended by deciding to leave Marisi for good, charge his expenditures, of something like half a million francs, to the account of experience, and forget Mlle. Solini finally and forever. He even leaped to his feet with an oath and began to pack his trunks. He stopped almost before he had started. The face of Aline was before him.

The lips, with their inviting curve, the white, soft skin, the glorious eyes, filled with promise—and with this, the memory of her arms about his neck, her delicious breath against his cheek, her soft words of love whispered in his ear. No—another oath—he could not give her up—he would not! He sat down at his desk and wrote her a letter of nine pages.

After that he waited for three days. No answer came to his letter. He sent another, longer than before—one that was surely calculated to move a heart of stone.

To this he confidently expected an answer, and it was with a feeling of despair that he found none on the following morning. He wandered dejectedly into the reading-room of the hotel and picked up a newspaper. The first thing that met his eyes was the following, in bold headlines:

THE PRINCE TO WED

Announcement Made of His Engagement
to Mlle. Aline Solini of Marisi

No Surprise to Society, Which Has Admired
and Courted the Beautiful Russian
Since Her Arrival

Betrothal Approved by Council—
Wedding to Take Place Late in July

Stetton stared at these headlines for five minutes without moving, while his face slowly assumed the expression of a man who is reading his death sentence. Then, mechanically, as one in a dream, he read the article from beginning to end.

Many details were given of Mlle. Solini—her parentage, the date of her birth, *et cetera*. It was called a genuine love-match. The wedding would have been set for an earlier day but for the fact that Mlle. Solini was in mourning for the recent death of her cousin, General Paul Nirzann.

Messages of congratulation had been received from all over the world. *Et cetera, et cetera.*

Stetton rose and walked out into the street. He was dazed; he knew not whither to go or what to do. He started rapidly down the Drive, then halted, cursing aloud.

What was the use? He would not be admitted.

Another thought came—he would go to the Prince of Marisi and tell him the truth about Mlle. Solini. He was filled with savage fury; he wanted to strike her, to crush her. He started off down the Drive toward the palace, in long, rapid strides; he could not get there soon enough.

Suddenly a hand fell on his arm and a voice sounded in his ear:

"Hello! What's up? You look as though you were marching in the face of a thousand cannon!"

It was Naumann. Stetton halted.

"Aline is going to marry the prince," he said, as though he were announcing the end of the world.

"I know it," said Naumann dryly. "It's the talk of the town. You're well rid of her, old chap. But won't the prince have a merry time of it!"

"He will, indeed," Stetton replied grimly. "And he won't have to wait long, either. I'm on my way to the palace now."

The other looked at him sharply.

"What's that? What are you going to do?"

"I'm going to cook Aline's goose for her. I'm going to tell the prince all about her."

The face of the young diplomat suddenly became serious—very serious. He said emphatically, grasping Stetton by the arm:

"My dear fellow, you are going to do nothing of the sort."

"No? Watch me!"

"But it's folly—madness—suicide!"

"I don't see why. Anyway, I'm going to do it."

There was a pause, during which the two young men glared at each other. Finally Naumann spoke:

"Stetton, you can be more different kinds of an ass than any ten men I've ever seen. Listen to me a minute! Do you realize how serious this is? Have you any idea what it means to go to the Prince of Marisi and tell tales of the woman he has publicly announced he is going to marry? Unless you have proof—double riveted, apodictic, instantaneous proof—of every word you utter, you'll find yourself in jail in two minutes."

Hesitation and doubt replaced the determination in Stetton's eye; the strength of these words was impressive. He said:

"But what can I do? Hang it all, don't you see I've got to do something?"

"Come over to my rooms," said Naumann, placing his arm through that of Stetton. "We'll talk this thing over."

Half reluctantly Stetton allowed himself to be led back along the Drive. Here and there they met boys with papers, shouting the news of the prince's engagement to Mlle. Solini, the beautiful Russian. On the street corners groups of people were gathered, talking; it was easy to guess of what. Everywhere they saw smiles and beaming faces.

"Why the deuce are they all so happy about it?" demanded Stetton.

Naumann replied:

"On account of the future heir."

At which the American grunted as though such a sentiment were beyond his comprehension.

Arrived in Naumann's rooms they began, as the young diplomat had said, to "talk it over." At first Stetton refused to be impressed. He declared with an air of bravado that the Prince of Marisi was the same to him as any other man, and that nothing and no one in the world should balk him of vengeance on Mlle. Solini, the perfidious, the treacherous, the odious.

"I agree with you," retorted Naumann, "that she is all that and more. But what can you do about it? Come; get down to cases; what specific charge can you make against her?

"When you get your audience with the prince, what are you going to say?"

"I—I—why, a dozen things."

"What, for instance?"

"In the first place, I'll tell him that she is not General Nirzann's cousin. It was that lie that got her in."

"How are you going to prove it?"

By the look on Stetton's face when he heard this question, you might have thought he had been asked how he was going to prove that the world was round. He repeated:

"How am I going to prove it? Why, you know it yourself! She's no more General Nirzann's cousin than I am!"

"Quite true," said Naumann patiently; "but you must remember that the general is dead. You must have proof."

Stetton ended by admitting that he had none.

"But," he cried impatiently, "what does that amount to? That is the least of what I have to tell. How I found her in the convent in Fasilica, how she bargained to marry me, how she shot the man that saved us—the one you think was her husband—how she poisoned Chavot—"

Naumann interrupted wearily.

"But, I repeat, of all these things you have no proof—absolutely none. You yourself don't believe she poisoned Chavot."

"Yes, I do now. And also, how I've given her four hundred thousand francs since she came to Marisi."

"Good Lord!" Naumann looked at him in amazement. "You don't mean to say you've given her that amount of money! How? In checks? An account?"

"No. Mostly in cash and jewels. There were no checks."

Naumann shrugged his shoulders and spread out his hands.

"There you are again. Where's your proof?"

"But I paid the rent for the house personally; gave it to Duroy himself. That's something."

"Not much. Couldn't she say you were acting as her agent? Stetton, you haven't a leg to stand on. The worst of it is that only a week ago you sent her a written proposal of marriage; it is the most powerful weapon she could have against anything you might say. You can't go to the prince with more accusations; believe me, if you do you'll regret it."

In the end Stetton was forced to admit that his friend was right. If General Nirzann were alive it would have been a different matter—so said Stetton grimly, and Naumann agreed with him. As it was, nothing could be done. Nothing.

But still Stetton could not smother his desire for revenge. He brought his hand down on the table with a bang, crying with an oath:

"I'll tell you what, Naumann, I'd give one million dollars in cash to get even with her! I mean it!"

Naumann was standing in front of a window with his hands in his pockets, looking out with a frown across Walderin Place.

As Stetton spoke he turned and said abruptly:

"Well, there's a chance."

"A chance? What do you mean?"

"A chance to get even with her, as you say."

"In Heaven's name, how?"

"Find Vasili Petrovich."

Then, as the other stood gazing at him in slow comprehension, the young diplomat continued:

"You have told me that he was only wounded that day in Fasilica—that you saved his life. Then depend on it, he is still very much alive and searching for the woman who injured him. If you can find him he will soon see to it that she doesn't marry the Prince of Marisi or anyone else. You'll have all the revenge you want."

"But where is he?"

"That's the question. He isn't at Warsaw; that much I know, for I've written there several times. But he's somewhere. Find him. Advertise all over Europe; go yourself if you find a clue anywhere. It's just possible he's still in Fasilica. Find Vasili Petrovich, and he'll do the rest."

"By Heaven," cried Stetton, "I will!"

In another minute they were discussing details and plans for the search. There was plenty of time; according to the announcement, the wedding was to occur late in July, and this was early in April.

Now that something had been decided upon—something that bade fair to be productive of results—Naumann laid bare a corner of his heart to admit his own vital interest in the proceedings, on account of his love for Mlle. Janvour. Stetton had no time to waste on thoughts of Vivi or Naumann; his head was filled with one exclusive, overmastering idea.

In the first place, they prepared an advertisement which Naumann was to insert in every newspaper of any importance in Europe and Russia. It read as follows:

> Vasili Petrovich, of Warsaw, will please communicate at once with Frederick Naumann either at Berlin or Marisi.

Secondly, Naumann gave Stetton all the assistance and information possible for his search, regretting that he could not assist personally.

He gave him letters to his father in Berlin, acquaintances in Warsaw, St. Petersburg, and Paris, and a dozen men in the diplomatic service stationed in different cities. Stetton had suggested asking the aid of the police, but Naumann had vetoed the idea, explaining:

"It would be dangerous on account of what will follow if we find him. We may use them as a last resort."

Finally, after a discussion lasting four hours, everything was arranged, and it was decided that Stetton should leave Marisi without delay.

On the following morning the Tsevor Express had for one of its passengers Mr. Richard Stetton, of New York. His destination was Fasilica.

It was three months before Stetton saw Marisi again, and in that time he traversed all of Europe and most of Russia.

He began, as they had decided, with Fasilica. There he found nothing.

He went on to Warsaw, where the manager of Vasili Petrovich's estates, upon reading the letter of Frederick Naumann, received him with open arms. But of his master he could tell him nothing—absolutely nothing—he had not heard from him for a year. Still, he did have a clue, a very slight one.

On the strength of that clue Stetton proceeded to St. Petersburg. Still no trace.

Next he journeyed to Berlin and sought out Naumann's father, who gave him suggestions, but nothing more, and they led nowhere. Thenceforth it became a mere wild-goose chase, and nearly attained to the dignity of a mania.

He visited Paris, Rome, Budapest, Vienna, Moscow, Marseilles, Athens; and the first of July found him back at Warsaw. Time then was short; and Stetton, worn out in body and mind, headed himself for Marisi and the advice of his friend Naumann, from whom he had heard but once or twice in the entire three months.

He arrived at Marisi at eight o'clock in the evening and went

directly to the Hotel Walderin for a bath, a change of linen, and dinner. That done, he went to Naumann's rooms at 5 Walderin Place.

Naumann was delighted to see him, but in despair at his lack of
success. Stetton, however, refused to lose heart, saying that they still
had nearly a month before the date of the wedding, and that by
procuring the aid of the police they might yet be successful. He was
stopped in the middle of this speech by the look of surprise that
appeared on Naumann's face.

"Haven't you heard?" cried the young diplomat. "Have you
been out of the world altogether? Haven't you got any of the dozen
or so letters I've written you in the past few weeks? Don't you ever
look at a newspaper?

"My dear fellow, the Prince of Marisi and Mlle. Solini were
married two weeks ago!"

—m—

Back Again

$\mathcal{T}$HAT NIGHT Stetton and Naumann sat together in the latter's room until well past twelve o'clock. Many things were said.

Naumann told of his repeated efforts to see Vivi and his final success, only to be interrupted by Mlle. Solini and ordered from the house. Also, that since the prince's marriage it had been delicately hinted to the German minister that his secretary, Herr Frederick Naumann, was *persona non grata* in Marisi, as a result of which hint Naumann was to be transferred to Vienna within the month. He had even been denied entrance to the palace when he had called there in a final desperate attempt to see Vivi.

These, and many other occurrences, were related by Naumann; but when Stetton finally left to return to his hotel he remembered none of them. His mind was occupied with the attempt to realize that Aline was lost to him irrevocably; that Aline, the woman who had promised to marry him, who had given him her kisses and embraces and words of love, was now Princess of Marisi.

It was only now, for the first time, that he fully realized the extent of his infatuation for her. When he reached the room and once more found himself alone, he gave himself up to a very delirium of despair. He did not sleep that night.

The morning brought no relief. A thousand times during the night he had tried to tell himself that all was over; that he might as well say farewell to Marisi forever, and the sooner the better. But he could not bring himself to the point of a decision to go.

He was constantly haunted by the face of Aline; it was ever before his eyes. He did not know whether he loved or hated her; he only felt he could never forget her.

Then suddenly his humor would change, and he would curse her with every oath in his vocabulary. He would drive her to ruin, to death itself; above all, he would have his revenge.

As for Vasili Petrovich, he had given up all hope of finding him. He was certain in his own mind that Aline's bullet, on that never-to-be-forgotten morning in Fasilica, had, after all, been fatal. Vasili Petrovich was dead—so he told himself—revenge would come from his own hand or not at all. He swore that it should come.

It was in this mood that he sought the street, after a late and unsatisfactory breakfast. Having no place to go in particular, he proceeded in desultory fashion to 5 Walderin Place and ascended the stairs to Naumann's rooms.

The young diplomat was not in. He returned to the street and wandered down the Drive to the German legation. There he remained for an hour, chatting with Naumann, whom he found in almost as low spirits as his own.

At eleven o'clock he was again on the Drive, strolling along at random, wondering where to go and what to do. Suddenly he halted, turned, and found himself directly in front of the white marble palace of the Prince of Marisi. He had, in fact, been carried there by his own mind and will, though quite subconsciously.

As he stood there, gazing at the great bronze portals not a dozen paces away, he was possessed of a sudden, overwhelming desire, which was, in fact, nothing but the crystallization of a thought that had entered his mind many times during the night and morning. Now it grasped him fiercely, so that he did not hesitate even to argue the matter with himself.

He walked down the marble flagging, entered the bronze gates, and handed his card to the servant at the door, saying that he desired an immediate audience with the prince.

He was led down the broad corridor to a reception-room and left there to wait. There were four or five other people in the room, evidently likewise waiting for an audience with the prince. In a few minutes a servant appeared and beckoned one of them to follow him. Another ten minutes and Stetton heard his own name from the door:

"M. Stetton, the prince will see you now."

Stetton followed the servant for some distance down the corridor, up a flight of stairs, and into a large room of state, hung with rick tapestries and old savars, with an air of formality and ceremony even in the rugs that covered the polished floor.

Before a table, in a great armchair of ebony, was the Prince of Marisi; at a smaller table nearby a young man sat, writing. As Stetton entered, the servant at the door called out his name in a loud voice. He crossed the room, stopping a few paces in front of the prince.

The prince extended no greeting to him, though they had dined at the same table three or four times not long before. Instead, he looked up and said abruptly:

"You wished to see me?"

"Yes, your highness."

"What is it?"

Stetton hesitated, then said in a low voice:

"Your highness would prefer—that is, what I have to say is for your highness's ears alone."

"You are sure of that *monsieur?*"

"I am sure of it."

The prince turned to the young man writing at the table.

"De Mide, leave us. Return when M. Stetton is gone."

De Mide rose without a word and departed.

"And now," said the prince, "be brief, M. Stetton. There are others waiting."

"I will try to, your highness." Stetton was calling on his courage. "What I have to say will both surprise and displease your highness, but you must believe that my only motive is to serve you. It is of Mlle.—the princess that I want to speak."

"The princess?" The prince frowned and looked at him sharply.

"Yes, your highness. There are certain things about her which you ought to know, and which I am sure you do not know. Things that are unpleasant, but are unhappily true. Your highness will be offended to hear them, but in the end you will thank me."

The prince's frown was deepened.

"Do you mean to say that you have accusations to make against the princess?"

Again Stetton gathered his courage together. He replied in a firm tone:

"Yes, your highness."

"Of what nature?"

"I can only answer that by relating them in detail."

"They are grave?"

"Yes."

The prince rang a bell on the table. When a servant appeared he said:

"Tell the princess that we request her presence."

The servant disappeared.

"But, your highness—" began Stetton in a voice of protest.

The prince interrupted him:

"That will do. I manage things my own way, *monsieur.*"

There was a wait of five minutes. Stetton consumed it in speculation, as to what was going to happen; the prince looked through some papers on the table.

Then the door opened softly, and Aline entered. Evidently she had questioned the servant who had summoned her, since she gave no sign of surprise or any other emotion on beholding Stetton. She crossed the room and stood beside the prince, who was the first to speak.

"*Madame,*" he said, "I have sent for you to hear what M. Stetton has to say. He wishes to speak of you. Now, *monsieur,* you may proceed. Be brief."

M. Stetton suddenly became conscious of a great desire to sink through the floor. He realized that Naumann had been right—eminently right. There was nothing he could say; nothing he dared to say.

He saw very plainly in the prince's eye what would happen to the man who tried to bring odium on the woman who bore his illustrious name without—as Naumann had said—indubitable and instantaneous proof. Several times he opened his mouth to speak, but could find no words. He was seized by an ignominious but overwhelming desire to cut and run.

The prince spoke with brusk impatience:

"Well, *monsieur?*"

Then, as Stetton remained silent, the princess's voice suddenly sounded:

"Your highness, I can understand M. Stetton's embarrassment and reluctance. I know very well what he wishes to say, and it is quite natural that he should hesitate to speak before me. I am sorry that he finds it necessary to speak at all, but your highness is already aware that I am not perfect."

Judging by the little smile that appeared on the prince's face at this observation, his highness was aware of nothing of the sort. The princess turned to Stetton:

"*Monsieur,* if you wish me to explain for you, I shall be glad to do so."

Stetton nodded, and the expression on his face was one of gratitude.

"Your highness will be surprised and displeased at what I have to say," began the princess, unconsciously repeating almost the very words that Stetton had used a few minutes before; "but I hope for your forgiveness, though I have been unable to forgive myself. I shall be brief.

"Your highness will remember a day when you left me—I thought forever—unhappy, miserable, in tears. On the very next day M. Stetton asked me to be his wife, and I accepted. Indeed"—the princess glanced at Stetton, then continued, without noticing the prince's start of surprise—"I still have the letter he sent me, which I assure him I shall always treasure.

"Three days later your highness came to me at the opera and gave me reason to believe—that is, told me you would call on me the following day. That same night I canceled my engagement with M. Stetton. I am to blame; I do not deny it; it was a perfidious action, and M. Stetton is perfectly right to feel that he has a grievance against me."

The princess paused, looking first at the prince, then at Stetton, her lovely face filled with humble and touching appeal. The prince appeared to be somewhat astonished. He looked at the young man, saying sternly:

"What is this, M. Stetton? Do you consider it a grave accusation against a woman to say that she has changed her mind?"

As for M. Stetton, he stood speechless. Rage at his helplessness,

wonder at Aline's devilish cunning and ready wit, and withal a certain gratitude at being lifted out of his dilemma—all these mingled
emotions left him confused and silent.

In the meantime the prince was eyeing him steadily, waiting for
him to speak. He wanted to break out in bitter denunciation of this
woman who was Princess of Marisi, but he dared not and could not.
He ended by not speaking at all.

He made a deep bow to the prince and princess, turned without a word and made for the door.

As he reached it he heard Aline's voice behind him, saying: "Let
him go, Michael."

Another minute and he was on the street.

Well, this was the end of everything. So ran his thoughts. Not
only was Aline lost to him forever, but all hope of vengeance was also
gone. The adventure, which at one time had appeared certain to lead
him to the altar of happiness, had landed him nowhere, empty-handed.
The chapter was closed. For his part, he would waste no time crying over spilled milk; he reached this philosophical conclusion as he
entered the door of his room at the Walderin.

He ate lunch without any appetite for it, wandered about the
streets for an hour, and chatted another hour with an acquaintance
he met in Walderin Place.

Three o'clock in the afternoon found him seated in the reading-
room of the hotel with a book in his hand, though his crowded
thoughts would not permit him to read.

Suddenly feeling a hand on his shoulder, he looked around to
find Frederick Naumann standing at his elbow. Naumann was saying:

"I've been looking for you for two hours. What the deuce have
you been doing with yourself?"

Stetton, seeing no reason for taking his friend into his confidence concerning his brilliant performance at the palace, replied that
he had been nowhere in particular.

Said Naumann:

"I want to talk with you. Come up to the room."

Stetton, who didn't want to talk with Naumann or any one else, reluctantly led the way to the elevator and to his room. It was true that the young diplomat had the air of a man who brings news; but what news could interest him now?

When they had lit cigarettes and found seats, Naumann began abruptly:

"I got a letter this morning."

This did not appear to Stetton to be exactly catastrophic, and he said nothing.

"A letter from Mlle. Janvour," continued the young diplomat in a tone of elation. "What do you think of that?"

"I can't say that I think much of anything."

Naumann snorted:

"No? Well, I do. In the last two months I've written her a dozen times and spent a small fortune in bribes, and this is the first word I've had from her."

"What does she have to say?" This in complete indifference.

"Not much. But it's something. Stetton, I'm going to marry her. I can't live without her. But the princess has forbidden her to have anything to do with me—and she won't. She says so in this letter."

"Then how the deuce do you expect to marry her?"

"But that isn't all she says," continued Naumann, disregarding the other's question. "She says she still loves me; that she can never love anyone else, in the same sentence that she tells me not to send her any more letters. This decides me. I'm going to write to Berlin tonight. Within two days the police of all the world will be looking for Vasili Petrovich."

"They won't find him."

"And why?"

"Because he's dead."

Naumann glanced at him sharply:

"What do you mean by that? How do you know—"

"I don't know it. At least, I have no knowledge of it. But I am perfectly certain that he is dead. Good Lord! Haven't I myself looked into every corner of Europe big enough to hold a microbe? It's useless."

"You talk as though you didn't care whether we find him or not," said Naumann with some heat. "What has happened?"

"Nothing. I'm through, that's all. Through with the whole business. I'm sick of it. Let me tell you something, Naumann—the man never lived that could hand Aline Solini anything she didn't want to take. She's too much for me, and she's too much for you. I've given it up. I leave for New York tomorrow morning."

"Ho!" cried Naumann. He insisted: "Something has happened. You weren't talking this way last night. What is it?"

In the end Stetton gave a detailed account of his visit to the palace.

When he had finished Naumann protested that he could not see why the occurrence, humiliating as it was, should decide Stetton suddenly to renounce all his plans; indeed, it should naturally have increased his eagerness and energy in their performance.

But Stetton, not to be moved, persisted in his determination to leave Marisi the following morning. When Naumann rose to go, three hours later, they shook hands and told each other good-by. Naumann was dining out that evening, and Stetton expected to leave the following morning too early to see him.

After all, he did not go. He had made all preparations; there was nothing to detain him; he simply didn't go. He seemed to the unable to bring himself to the point of departure.

Naumann hinted, not without a touch of malice, that he was probably waiting for the Carnival of Perli, which was to begin in a week or two. The Carnival of Perli, he explained, was an annual midsummer event in Marisi, and the street pageant of the opening day would be led by the prince and princess in a golden chariot. No doubt, said Naumann, Stetton would want to see that.

"I would," Stetton answered, "if I could have Vasili Petrovich at my side. I think the prince would return to the palace in his golden chariot alone."

Three days passed, and the morning of the fourth found Stetton still in Marisi. A dozen times he had decided to leave on the next train for the west; each time he had failed to do so, for no apparent reason whatever. He had met Aline once with Vivi on the Drive; she had bowed to him politely and amiably, and he had felt a savage satisfaction in pointedly turning his back.

But on the fourth day he finally made the jump. At one o'clock in the afternoon he called on Naumann at the legation to say farewell. Naumann shook hands with a laugh.

"If I thought you were really going," he declared, "I'd remonstrate. The carnival is on next week, and, really, you shouldn't miss it. It's no end of fun. But you'll be here, all right."

"You'll see," was Stetton's retort. "This is final. Good-by, old chap. I'll see you some day somewhere, perhaps."

And three hours later found him actually seated in a compartment on the Berlin express as it roared through the valleys at the rate of sixty miles an hour.

He told himself that he had seen the last not only of Marisi, but of Europe. The place sickened him. He wanted to get back to America. New York! Everything would be different. He would forget all about Aline Solini in a week. And he would get to work. The Lord knew it was time, anyway. Marisi! He hated the very name.

He stopped for a day in Berlin to pay farewell calls to friends and acquaintances, and two days in Paris, for the same purpose. Then he went on to London, where he transacted some business with the branch office of his father's manufacturing company, and lingered three days more, in the meanwhile having secured passage on the Lavonia, which was to sail from Liverpool in a few days.

That night he attended the theater and had supper at the Savoy with an old acquaintance—a Harvard classmate who had come to England as agent for an American automobile.

What with his manner of talk and string of reminiscences, it seemed to Stetton that he was already breathing the air of the States. How good it sounded! How good it would be to set foot once more on Manhattan pavements!

But the following morning, though this feeling had not departed, it was accompanied by one of sadness and regret. There was nothing definite about it, and by the time he boarded the train for Liverpool it had left him free to enjoy happier thoughts.

He told himself that he had not realized, until he was actually ready to begin the last lap of his journey home, how much he had wanted to be there. The faces of his father and mother were before him; he was surprised to find himself actually longing to see them. He could hardly wait for the train to reach Liverpool.

He was the first to descend at the station, which was crowded.

It was three o'clock in the afternoon. Cabbies were shouting themselves hoarse, men and women were running hither and thither in every direction, the station announcers and agents of the steamship companies were bumping into each other with true British clumsiness, and newsboys were completing the din by crying out an extra edition of an afternoon paper.

Stetton beckoned for a cab and gave directions to take him to the pier, and at the same time tossed a boy a penny for a paper.

He handed his bag to the cabbie, told him where to go, and entered the cab. Once inside, he opened his newspaper.

In the upper left-hand corner, in big black letters, was the word "Extra"; and just below, in letters quite as black but not so big, was something that made Stetton's face turn suddenly white.

For a long while, as the cab rattled over the rough cobblestones of Liverpool toward the steamship pier, he sat gazing at the headlines like one paralyzed; then he read the short article printed below:

Marisi, July 19.—The Prince of Marisi was shot and killed by an anarchist today while leading the pageant of the Carnival of Perli with the princess.

The princess narrowly escaped, and is prostrated by the shock. The assassin was captured.

Below this meager account were the words:

More will follow in a later edition.

The cab stopped; the door flew open; they had arrived at the pier, Stetton was startled by the voice of the cabby:

"We're here, sir!"

Stetton looked up with a face as pale as though he had just seen a ghost, and said:

"I've decided not to go. Drive back to the railroad station, and drive like the devil."

In another thirty minutes he was again on a train, headed for Marisi.

―᙮᙮―

CHAPTER XXIII

Price—Two Million Dollars

THERE ARE many kinds of power in the world, and though some of them are able to stand alone, most are rendered useless without money to develop or uphold them. Political power certainly belongs to this latter and larger class, though in some instances it manages to live by what it feeds on. When this fails, destruction follows.

Thus, roughly, might be summarized the thoughts of Aline, Princess of Marisi, as she sat alone one afternoon in her boudoir in Marisi palace.

It was three days after the final obsequies had been performed over the body of the prince; a week had passed since his assassination. The princess had secluded herself in the palace and refused to see any but one or two of her most intimate friends.

She had, indeed, plenty to think about. During the life of Prince Michael she had known little or nothing either of state affairs or his personal ones; she had just begun to make her influence felt in little matters of detail, and that was all. But with his death she had become in fact the ruler of Marisi; on the very day following she had sat on the throne at a meeting of council.

Since then she had learned many things; among them being this from the lips of De Mide, that the state coffers were sadly depleted and those of the dead prince empty; worse, somewhat in debt.

For the coffers of the state the princess felt little concern; they could be made to attend to themselves. But those of the prince—that is to say, her own—were a different matter. According to De Mide, it was difficult to procure cash even for the household expenses.

There was six hundred thousand francs due Latorne, of Paris, for the magnificent diamond cross which the prince had given Aline for a wedding present. As much more was owed in Marisi.

Since the death of Prince Michael the creditors were clamoring for their money; what was worse, they refused to advance more. The princess was already in debt to the state treasury, and, besides, it also was practically empty. It was impossible, De Mide had said, to get cash even to pay the servants of the palace.

Not a very pleasant situation, surely, for a newly bereaved princess. So thought Aline; but, true to her character, instead of wasting time in bewailing the difficulties of her situation, she set about finding a way to remove them.

Her first thought was increased taxes. When she pronounced that word De Mide smiled.

"Very little of the revenue is derived from taxes," he asserted, "and that little goes to the state. The funds of the ruler of Marisi come from Paris and St. Petersburg, in recognition of certain services rendered those governments in connection with the Balkan States and the Turks. France pays two hundred thousand francs a year, Russia two hundred and fifty thousand. Prince Michael collected these sums three years in advance; nothing can be expected there."

Thus Aline found herself confronting a real problem. And by dint of thinking a great deal of money she came, by a natural chain of association, to Richard Stetton, of New York. With her to think was to act; she went to the telephone and called up the Hotel Walderin.

At the first sound of Stetton's voice, eager and joyful when he discovered to whom he was talking, the princess knew that he was still hers. That was all she wanted to know. She asked him to come to see her at the palace the following morning at eleven o'clock.

When Stetton arrived, twenty minutes ahead of time, he was shown at once to the apartments of the princess on the second floor, and into a little reception-room, daintily and tastefully furnished. He had waited but a moment when he heard the rustle of a curtain behind him.

He turned and saw the princess.

Aline expected little difficulty in this interview; nevertheless she came prepared for the battle. Never, thought Stetton, had she been so beautiful, so desirable.

Dressed in mourning purple from head to foot, her white skin and golden hair possessed almost a supernatural loveliness, while her gray-blue eyes glowed—with what, Stetton wondered—with welcome?

For his part, he was plainly embarrassed and ill at ease. He bent over her hand as of old, but dared not kiss it. Truth was, he was more than a little afraid of her. In addition to everything else, was she not a princess?

"I cannot say how glad I was to find you were still in Marisi," Aline was saying. "I had feared you would have returned to America."

"I did," said Stetton, looking at her as though he were trying to fill his eyes. "That is, I started. At Liverpool I read of the prince's death and returned."

"Ah!" Aline smiled. "Then you knew, after all."

Stetton looked at her, puzzled.

"I mean, you knew I would expect you," Aline explained.

"I do not understand that."

"But, *monsieur*—then why did you return?"

"I don't know. Yes, I do know. To see you."

"There!" said Aline, as though he had admitted something. "You see, I am right."

"Perhaps," Stetton agreed, "but I don't know what you are talking about."

Aline laughed.

"You knew I would send for you."

"How could I know that? I hoped, perhaps."

"And why, *monsieur?* I thought you hated me."

"And so I do."

"Then why did you hope I would send for you?"

"Because when I do not hate you I love you."

Aline glanced at him approvingly.

"My dear Stetton, you are developing a tongue. That is well. You are going to need all the accomplishments you can muster."

"For what purpose?"

"That is the secret, to be divulged later. Now, let us be frank— the preliminary skirmish is over. Tell me exactly what you think of me, and tell me the truth."

"You know very well what I think of you."

"Nevertheless, tell me."

"I cannot tell you."

It was easy enough to tell what the young man meant by the expression of his eyes.

Aline smiled as she said boldly:

"Then show me."

The next instant Stetton had her in his arms, pulling her against him roughly, passionately, and raining kisses on her cheeks and eyes and lips.

"That is what I think," he cried in a voice hoarse with feeling.

What he was doing then he had been dreaming of for months. Her breath against his face maddened him; her lips, though they did not respond to his pressure, were soft and yielding.

"This is what I think," he cried again, intoxicated.

"But, Stetton, you must remember," Aline began, trying to free herself.

"I remember nothing—nothing but this, that I love you! You would tell me that you are a princess, that I must respect the memory of the prince. I respect nothing. I love you!"

"But you should not tell me—now," Aline protested in a voice that was an invitation to tell her again.

"I should not tell you at all," said Stetton grimly. "I know it very well. I am a fool to love you, and a still bigger fool to tell you so. You see, Aline, I am beginning to know you. You have never loved anyone, and never will. You never loved me; you merely played with me, got what you wanted, and then threw me over. And still I love you, in spite of your—"

The princess interrupted him.

"You are wrong."

"Wrong to love you?"

"No."

The princess paused for a moment, then with a sudden air of decision continued:

"Stetton, you are wrong; I repeat it." She looked at the young man with tender eyes. "Why should you say I do not love you? Because I married the prince? Surely you do not think I loved him? Can you not understand that a woman's ambition may be stronger than her love? Well, my ambition is satisfied"—she looked at him meaningly—"my love is not."

"You mean—" cried the young man, trembling with joy, not so much at her words as at the expression of her face.

"I mean, Stetton, that I still have your proposal, and that I am willing to accept it."

This was a little sobering. A sudden frown appeared on Stetton's brow.

"Ah, that——" he began, and stopped.

"Do you hesitate?" asked Aline, fixing him with her eyes.

The truth was, he did. He could not understand it. A month ago—nay, a day—two hours ago—he would have asked nothing better for happiness than this which was now offered to him.

In all conscience, had he not had enough of this woman and her wiles? Did he not know her to be treacherous, perfidious, dangerous? Still, to have her for his own—to realize in actuality the desires that had possessed him for so many months—was it not worth any price?

And was she not a princess? Another thought, fed by his vanity, and therefore growing rapidly, entered his mind. Aline had everything she wanted—position, wealth, everything. If she still desired him, it must mean that she really loved him. Besides, for what had he returned to Marisi, if not for this?

"Do you hesitate?" Aline repeated.

For all reply he took her again in his arms. Again his lips sought hers, and this time met with a response as ardent as his own. For a long time they stood, holding each other close; then Aline gently disengaged herself and held him off with her two hands on his shoulders.

"You see, Stetton," she said, looking into his eyes, "we are going to be happy after all. We will forget everything, will we not? Except each other. Now, do you not see that I love you—that I have always loved you?"

The only reply came from his burning eyes. He was too filled with the rapture of her presence to speak.

Soon after she told him he must leave. For the present, she said, they must practice extreme caution; they must give no basis for rumors so soon after the death of Prince Michael. The event that had opened the way for their happiness would at the same time defer its consummation.

But if Stetton was impatient, she declared that he was no more so than she. He need fear nothing more than the temporary delay; she was his—his forever.

Stetton departed with a lighter heart than he had known for many months.

When he had gone Aline stood looking at the door which had just closed behind him for a full minute.

"For the purpose," she said finally to herself, "I could not do better in all the world. Easily managed, vain, passionate, ignorant—in short, a perfect fool. And with his fifty millions, which, by the way, must be investigated—"

She turned and rang a bell, to send for De Mide.

A week passed. Stetton called at the palace daily and had long conferences with Aline; it began to appear that it was not so easy a matter to become the consort of a princess.

Aline had not yet broached the subject in council, but she had sounded two or three of its members privately, and she reported that their final approval was almost certain. The difficulties of the matter were presented to Stetton in so strong a light that he declared his inability to comprehend how they had any chance whatever of success.

"We would not have," said Aline, "but for one thing."

"And that is?"

"An heir to the throne is expected in six months."

Stetton's face reddened, and he abruptly changed the subject.

A week later Aline informed him that two of the council members who remained obstinate could be won by bribes.

Old Duplann, she felt sure, could be had for fifty thousand francs. As for Cinni, a shrewd young Italian who had conducted the late prince's negotiations with the French and Russian governments, that was a different matter. It would require twice that amount with him. A mere hundred and fifty thousand francs in cash—which she did not happen to possess—would turn the scale in their favor.

Stetton provided it, without a murmur. Indeed, he had not expected to get off so cheaply.

The day of the council meeting arrived. Stetton remained in his room at the Walderin, awaiting a message from the palace. The meeting was scheduled for twelve o'clock; an hour before that time he was fuming with impatience. He thought the time would never pass. Noon came; he could scarcely contain himself.

Then one o'clock; and exactly on the hour the telephone-bell rang, and he received word that the princess desired to see him at once. He rushed from the room and to the street, where he had kept an automobile waiting all day. In five minutes he was at the palace.

His first glance at Aline's face, as she met him in her reception-room, told him that all was over. It was eloquent with disappointment, rage, and despair. He cried out without waiting for her to speak:

"What is it? What have they done?"

"Ah, Stetton!" sighed the princess, taking his hand and looking sorrowfully into his eyes.

"They have refused!" cried the young man, feeling his heart sink to his boots.

"No." Aline shook her head.

"They have not refused? What then?"

Aline did not reply at once. Still holding Stetton's hand, she drew him down beside her on a divan. Then she said, seeming to have difficulty to find the words:

"No, they have not refused. But they might as well have done so, for they have imposed conditions that are utterly impossible. They are stubborn, impudent, detestable—I hate them!"

"But the conditions! What are they?"

"It would do no good to tell you." Aline was holding his hand in both her own.

"Tell me!" he insisted frantically. "What are they?"

"No; indeed, I cannot."

But he insisted so earnestly that she was finally forced to yield. She began:

"In the first place, they demand that you be given no power whatever in Marisi politics, either domestic or foreign."

"Bah! What do I care for their politics? What else?"

"They ask that you sign away all claims of whatsoever kind on the State of Marisi for your—our children, if we have any. Under certain conditions this clause may be abrogated later, but only by their will."

"Well, that is not impossible. Is that all?"

"No. The last is the worst. They demand that you furnish ten million francs to the state, to be used in the treasury of the throne."

Stetton jumped to his feet in amazement.

"Ten million francs! Two million dollars!"

"Yes. Of course, it is merely another way of refusing. They knew very well that you would be unable to furnish that amount. It was Cinni who did it—and he took our money! The greasy wretch!"

Stetton kept repeating: "Two million dollars!"

"They would listen to nothing," Aline went on. "I pleaded with them, threatened, stormed; you may be sure I did not let them off easily. But they were immovable. They would not reduce the amount by a single sou."

"Two million dollars!" said Stetton.

Aline pressed his hand. The expression in her eyes was one of sadness and despair.

"Ah, Stetton!" she sighed. "This, then, is the end. You must know this, my disappointment is as bitter as your own. To have so nearly approached happiness, and then to lose it!"

Stetton sighed. "Two million dollars!"

"Yes. It is monstrous. 'Twas Cinni who did it—the oily, wily Italian. I hate him! Some day, Stetton, you may be sure we shall be revenged. They pretend—well, it makes no difference what they pretend. We shall be revenged; I shall make it the task of my life.

"If only I dared defy them! But no—the people are with them—I would lose everything. I thought that today we would be betrothed; instead, we must say farewell!" Her voice trembled. "You will not forget me, Stetton? You will think of me, as I shall think of you? And to know—"

She was interrupted by a quick movement from the young man. He had risen to his feet and stood facing her, his face lit up by a sudden resolve. He said abruptly, in the tone of one who has made a momentous decision:

"Aline, I will get that ten million francs."

She also rose to her feet, with an appearance of astonishment. "Stetton," she cried, "you cannot! It is impossible!"

"I will," he replied firmly.

She doubted it, and said so. He stuck to his assertion, and finally persuaded her. She applauded his sublime resolution and threw herself into his arms, crying that after all they would be happy, their love would receive its reward.

She declared that she hated to give in to Cinni and the others, but if Stetton thought her worth it she would see that he did not regret his bargain. Besides, she added somewhat ingenuously, would he not have a ruling princess for a wife?

So much decided, they entered into a discussion of details. It would be necessary, of course, for Stetton to go to America to see his father.

As a matter of fact, he did not expect much opposition in that quarter. His father certainly would not be overjoyed at the prospect of handing over two million dollars, but how his mother would jump at the chance of having the Princess of Marisi for a daughter-in-law! She would consider such an acquisition cheap at double the price. No, there would be no opposition there.

He did not explain all this to Aline; he merely told her that he would have no difficulty to procure the necessary amount, but that he would have to go to New York to get it.

"I did not imagine," said Aline playfully, running her fingers through his hair—they were again seated on the divan—"that you carried that much money around in your pocket."

It was decided that Stetton should leave for New York the very next day; they were both anxious, though for very different reasons, to have the matter settled as speedily as possible. It was thought that he would be able to return to Marisi within a month.

"And then," said Aline, "we shall not have long to wait. The wedding must not take place until a year after Prince Michael's death, but we shall be assured of our happiness, we shall be together, and the time will fly swiftly. We shall be a happy family, Stetton—you, Vivi, and I."

"That reminds me. I had almost forgotten. I saw Naumann last night—Frederick Naumann. He wants to marry Vivi."

Aline frowned. "I know it."

"Well, why not?"

She replied dryly:

"For a dozen reasons. I think you are acquainted with most of them."

"But all the same, Naumann is a good fellow, and he is a good friend of mine. Can't you forgive him for my sake? If we are going to be happy we ought to be willing to extend our happiness to others. You see what your love does for me; I am beginning to be unselfish. Indulge me in this, won't you?"

Aline laughed.

"So you are beginning to be unselfish? Well, it would be a pity to hinder you. We shall see about it when you return; if you are successful no doubt I shall be ready to forgive anybody anything.

"And now"—she glanced at her watch—"you must leave me. I must have a talk with De Mide before dinner, when I shall see Cinni and one or two others. If you see your friend Naumann tonight, tell him not to despair."

Stetton rose to go.

"There is no question about my seeing him. He is probably waiting at the hotel now."

"All right. Tell him. And, of course, come in the morning before you go, and say good-by."

Stetton kissed her hand and left.

~m~

At the Gare du Nord

*A*FTER ALL, Stetton did not get away from Marisi on the following morning. When he called on Aline at the palace, quite early, to say good-by, he found her engaged with De Mide and Cinni, and was forced to cool his heels in an antechamber for three hours. By the time he finally obtained an audience it was long past his train-time, and he postponed his departure till the afternoon.

He had intended to go straight to Hamburg and sail from there, but altered his route at the request of the princess, who had errands for him to perform in Paris. She had discharged Cinni from her service that morning, though not without a struggle; and at De Mide's suggestion had decided to entrust Stetton with a message to the French government.

He canceled his booking from Hamburg, and procured a passage on a steamer sailing from Cherbourg four days later.

With the feel of Aline's parting kisses still on his lips, and after a hearty hand-shake with Naumann, who went to see him off, he boarded a west-bound train at Marisi station at five o'clock in the afternoon.

His thoughts during the two days' journey were somewhat

confused and not entirely pleasant. True, he was at last sure of having Aline for his own; on the other hand, he did not relish the task of confronting his father with a request for two million dollars in cash. Indeed, long before he reached the French border he had decided to leave that part to his mother.

Arriving in Paris late at night, he went to the Continental Hotel. By noon the following day he had delivered the princess's message to the French premier and, since his sailing time was still thirty-six hours away, decided to remain in the city on the Seine another night.

He passed it somewhat hilariously with Mountain-Richards, of the American embassy. They traveled the usual route, from the Café de Paris to Montmartre; Stetton returned to his hotel and bed at seven o'clock in the morning.

At four o'clock he rose, broke his fast, and ordered a cab to take him to the Gare du Nord, having arranged the matter of luggage on the day previous.

At the railway station he bought a book or two and some magazines, which he stuffed in the traveling bag he was carrying. As he straightened up and started toward the doors leading to the trackway, he felt a heavy hand on his arm and a gruff voice sounded in his ear in French:

"Young man, I want to talk with you."

Stetton turned, startled, and found himself looking into a pair of piercing black eyes.

Their owner, a giant of a man with a black beard that covered all the lower part of his face, was holding Stetton's arm in a grip of steel.

Recognition flashed into the young man's brain with that first glance, and left him speechless.

It was the man of Fasilica, whom he had last seen, many months before, lying prostrate with Aline's bullet in his body!

"I want to talk with you," the man repeated, in a tone that meant much more than the words. He added, gazing into Stetton's eyes:

"I see you recognize me."

Stetton tried to free himself from the other's grasp.

"Really, *monsieur*," he stammered in a voice that he tried to keep calm, while his face turned suddenly pale, "you have the advantage of me. Take your hand from my arm."

The other did not move as he said in a hard voice:

"Don't try to lie to me. You recognized me at once. Come. It is useless to try to escape me. I want to talk with you."

Stetton's brain was whirling in confusion. He glanced round. The room was crowded. People were rushing about in all directions. Not ten feet away a *sergent de ville* stood against a pillar, his eye roving idly over the throng.

People who passed were beginning to glance curiously at the two men, one holding the arm of the other, who was struggling feebly to release himself. Stetton opened his mouth to call to the *sergent de ville*. He was stopped by the voice of the man with the beard:

"Don't do that."

His tone, and the look of his eye, showed Stetton the futility of his intention. This man could not be shaken off in that way. He would follow him to America, around the world, anywhere above or below the earth, before he would forego his purpose.

He must do something—say something—what? He looked at the man whose fingers were still around his arm, and said with an effort at impatience:

"Well, what is it you want?"

"Come with me. We can't talk here; people are beginning to notice. I have some questions to ask you."

Stetton protested:

"But my train leaves in three minutes. If you have a question to ask, ask it. I am listening."

A sudden gleam appeared in the eyes of the man with the beard—a cold gleam and menacing.

"Monsieur," he said, and it was evident that he was forcing himself to speak calmly, "if you knew me better you would not argue with me. When I become angry I neither know nor care what I do. I would advise you to do as I request."

Stetton did not risk another protest. He was struck with a sudden thought—that is, sudden for him—to the effect that his wisest course was to make friends with this man; to deceive him, since he was unable to combat him. He said in a tone of conciliation:

"I do not wish to argue with you, *monsieur,* I am merely anxious to make my train. But there is one two hours later; I suppose I can take that. What is it you want?"

For reply the man with the beard uttered the one word "Come."

Then, with his hand still on Stetton's arm, he guided him to the door of the railway station and across the street to a cheap café on the corner. They entered and seated themselves at a table on one side of the room, which was half filled with cab-drivers, clerks, and railway employees.

A waiter approached. The man with the beard ordered a bottle of wine and laid a five-franc piece on the table to pay for it. He remained silent until the waiter had brought the wine and filled the glasses, then he looked at Stetton and began abruptly:

"In the first place, *monsieur,* I wish to know if you have recognized me?"

Stetton, who had made up his mind what to do, replied promptly in the affirmative, and added:

"You are the man who saved us that night in Fasilica. The night of the siege."

The man with the beard nodded.

"I am. And in addition to that, I am the man whom you left to die."

Stetton tried to smile.

"You seem to be very much alive, *monsieur*." Then, at the light that leaped into the other's eyes, he added hastily: "But what else could I do, under the circumstances? My first duty was elsewhere."

"That is not my opinion," said the man with the beard dryly. "It was a base action, and you know it. But let it pass. It is unimportant; as you say, I am alive. The truth is, I do not know whether I owe you anything or not. That is what I want to find out. You entered my house that night with a woman."

"With two women," put in Stetton.

"You know the one I mean. The other—the girl—I do not know her. I mean Marie Nikolaevna. How came you to know her? What was she to you?"

Stetton frowned.

"By what right do you ask me that?" Then, as the other leaned forward in his chair, he added quickly, "But there is no reason why I should not tell you. She was nothing to me, *monsieur*. I did not know her. I met her quite by accident."

Stetton went on to explain how he had found the two women in the convent and helped them to escape, up to the point where they had entered the house of the man with the beard.

"That is all," he finished. "You know the rest, *monsieur*."

The Russian was eying him steadily.

"You had never seen her before?"

"Never."

"Then why did you leave me to die? You did not know how badly I was wounded. I had saved your life. Why did you attempt to take mine?"

"But I did not!" cried Stetton hotly. "In fact, I saved it. When you moved on the floor she pressed the revolver to your head and would have pulled the trigger if I had not snatched it from her hand."

His sincerity was so apparent that there was no room for doubt. Still the man with the beard insisted:

"But why did you leave me helpless, and, for all you knew, fatally wounded?"

Stetton replied: "That would be a long story. She told me—but does it matter what she told me? I was made to believe that you were a monster, a rogue, unfit to live."

The man with the beard nodded.

"That was like her. That is what she would do. I see, *monsieur,* that you were not to blame. It is not strange that Marie Nikolaevna was able to fool you—she who fooled me so easily. It is not easy to fool Vasili Petrovich. We are quits when you tell me one thing. Where is she?"

As he asked this question the Russian's voice trembled with expectation and his hand grasped the edge of the table.

Stetton tried to meet the piercing black eyes, but could not, as he replied promptly and in a tone of firmness:

"I do not know."

There was a silence. Stetton forced himself to meet the other's eyes, but quickly turned away, unable to withstand that searching gaze.

The man with the beard spoke in a grim voice: "*Monsieur,* I want the truth. Where is Marie Nikolaevna?"

Stetton merely repeated: "I do not know."

Then, suddenly furious with himself for allowing this man to address him thus, he exclaimed angrily:

"Are you trying to quarrel with me, *monsieur?* Why should I tell you anything but the truth? Of what interest is this woman to me? I have not seen her since that morning in Fasilica."

The Russian laid a hand on his arm and said:

"I do not say I do not believe you. I want to know. You say you have not seen Marie Nikolaevna since that morning?"

"No."

"Where did you leave her?"

"In Fasilica."

"Where in Fasilica?"

"In—" Stetton hesitated; he had no time to think—"in the convent, where I found her."

The Russian's glance was like a flash of lightning.

"The convent was destroyed."

"I know—" Stetton stammered—"I know—that is, part of it. There was a room—some rooms—she said friends would take care of her—"

There was a pause. Stetton was cursing himself for a fool, and trying to think of a way to repair his blunder when suddenly and inexplicably the Russian's manner changed. He lowered his eyes, then raised them again to look at the young man with an expression of confidence and friendliness. He said:

"*Monsieur*—pardon me, but this is a vital matter to me—you are telling me the truth?"

Stetton replied with all the firmness he could muster:

"I am. Why should I tell you other than the truth?"

Another silence. Stetton glanced nervously at his watch. The waiter approached to see if the gentlemen required another bottle of wine, but found that they had not touched the first one. Then suddenly the man with the beard rose to his feet and said:

"I thank you, *monsieur,* and beg your pardon for having detained you. *Adieu.*"

And with the word he departed, so rapidly that by the time Stetton turned round in his chair he had already disappeared into the street.

Stetton sank back in his chair.

His first thought was: "So Aline's name is Marie Nikolaevna!"

A hundred others followed, of more importance and infinitely more disturbing. This was Vasili Petrovich, Aline's husband, for whom he had searched all over Europe; and now that he no longer wished to find him—

Aline, then, could not marry him. That, in a way, brought its consolation; there would be no need for that two million dollars. But to lose her! After all his struggles, all his attempts, all his disappointments—to lose her!

Then came a most vivid picture of the man who had just left—his piercing, stern eyes, his grim, significant tone, his grip of steel, his massive, muscular frame. No, it would not do to risk crossing the path of Vasili Petrovich.

As for Aline, she was doomed; it was certain that he would find her sooner or later. And as for Richard Stetton, the best thing he could do was to go on to America as he had intended, and stay there.

But to lose her! It was impossible. Her face appeared before his eyes, as he had seen it three days before. To lose her! It was more than he could ask of himself, now that success was in his grasp, to relinquish it.

Did she not love him? Possessed of everything that her heart could possibly desire, had she still not desired him? And for the man who warned her that Vasili Petrovich was alive and searching for her, there would be in addition unbounded gratitude.

Stetton sat in his chair in the café for two hours, while these thoughts surged back and forth in his brain. The thought of giving up all hope of possessing Aline was unbearable; the thought of the certain revenge of Vasili Petrovich was terrifying.

But it was not for nothing that he had come and gone at the snap of Aline's fingers for many months. At the end of the two hours he rose, left the café, hurried across the street to the Gare du Nord and found a train for the east then on the track. When it pulled out, ten minutes later, he was on it.

Having once decided, and finding himself actually headed for Marisi, he was filled with burning impatience to reach his destination.

The train, rushing across the Continent at the rate of fifty miles an hour, appeared to him barely to move. He could not sit still for five minutes at a time; he kept walking up and down the aisle between the compartments with his watch in his hand; each village that they passed brought its measure of relief—he was that much nearer. When the train stopped at a station he would leave the car and stand on the platform, fuming with impatience till they were again under way.

What would Aline do? Would she yield to him? Would she start a search for Vasili Petrovich? He knew she was capable of it, and of a great deal more if she found him. Clearly, it would be an ugly business, but he could not help that.

He must have her at any cost; it was impossible to give her up. Good Heavens! How the train crawled along like a decrepit old man with a cane! Would he never get there?

They had reached Berlin; the train was slowing down as it entered the outskirts of the city. There would be a wait of forty minutes there; Stetton wondered how he could make it bearable. He wandered into the next car to the rear, and, as he entered from the platform, found himself looking directly into the face of Vasili Petrovich!

Stetton stood for one moment as one struck dumb; Vasili Petrovich did not move.

Then the young man turned and bolted precipitately into his own car and compartment, closing the door after him, and sank back on the seat. His face was pale, and he was trembling from head to foot.

His first thought, when he had recovered sufficiently to have any, was to leave the train at Berlin and return to Paris—in short, to give it up. This, he told himself, could be no coincidence; Vasili Petrovich was following him—a black nemesis.

He shuddered as he reached for his bag on the rack above. Why should this giant Russian suspect him? But it was enough that he did.

Then, suddenly, he was seized with blind rage at the fate which was tearing the prize from his grasp just as he had his fingers on it. It should not be!

He burst out into a string of oaths. He would show this Vasili Petrovich! He would outwit him—this burly giant with the piercing black eyes and the brain of a child. He forced himself into calmness in order to be able to think.

By the time the train halted at the station in Berlin, a few minutes later, he had conceived a plan and prepared to act on it. He knew Berlin well, and with that knowledge had perfected his plan.

The train had barely stopped when he dashed from the steps and into the station. A quick glance over his shoulder showed him the man with the beard leaping from the car behind; he bounded forward. He rushed through the gates, waving his certificate of passage in the face of the official who stood there, out into the street, and to the right.

A short block down, a turn to the left, and there, as he had expected, was a group of motor-cars, standing for rental. He rushed up to the man in charge:

"Which is the fastest car here? Quick!"

The man gave him a glance which indicated that he strongly disapproved of such indecent haste, and slowly pointed to a big, gray touring-car on the other side. Stetton leaped in; the chauffeur was on his seat.

"To Augburg!" he called; and he added, as the car started smoothly forward, "a thousand francs if you make it in two hours."

The car leaped ahead; in ten seconds it had disappeared down

the street. The man whom Stetton had first accosted turned to make
an observation on mad foreigners to another of the chauffeurs, and
was surprised to find himself confronted by a man about twice his
own size, with glowing black eyes and a black beard.

The man with the beard was speaking:

"That man who just rented a car—where is he going? What
directions did he give?"

The car-starter looked at him superciliously and informed the
questioner politely that it was none of his business.

The man with the beard thrust his hand in his pocket; when he
brought it forth there was a flash of gold. He drew the car-starter
aside; their hands touched; there was a single whispered word:

"Augburg."

The man with the beard turned and ran back to the railroad station. Entering, he approached the clerk at the information desk.

"Does this train for Marisi stop at Augburg?"

"Yes."

"At what time?"

"Two thirty-nine."

A gleam of satisfaction appeared in the Russian's eyes as he
turned, walked back to the trackway and boarded the train he had
left less than five minutes before.

In the meantime, Stetton, in the gray touring-car, was threading
the streets of Berlin. Slow work, that; but after thirty minutes of it
they reached the city limits and the car leaped forward. During that
wild ride Stetton had no time to think; he was too busy holding
himself in his seat.

As they reached the railway station at Augburg, eighty-five miles
from Berlin, he glanced at his watch; it was twenty-five minutes to
three. He shoved ten one-hundred-franc notes into the grinning
chauffeur's hands and leaped from the tonneau into the station.

"Has the Marisi express passed?"

"No; due in three minutes."

"It stops here?"

"Yes."

And five minutes later found Stetton back in the same compartment he had left in Berlin.

He was certain that Vasili Petrovich had been left behind. He had seen him rush after him into the station at Berlin; no doubt he was at that moment searching that city high and low. No, he need no longer fear Vasili Petrovich. The wily Russian had found his match.

Stetton thought of searching the train for him, to make assurance doubly sure, and did in fact start to explore the car to the rear. But the doors to most of the compartments were closed; the attempt was fruitless. He returned to his own compartment and sat down, as easy in mind as possible under the circumstances.

It would be hard to say which was the clearer picture in the eye of his mind: that of Aline or the man with the beard.

The nearer he approached his destination the more nervous he became, the greater his impatience and anxiety.

What would Aline say? What would she do?

He worked himself up to a point where each second made the next more intolerable. The meeting with Vasili Petrovich had thrown him completely off his balance; he was little better than a man guided solely by the impulse of a mania.

When the train finally reached Marisi, at eight o'clock in the evening of the following day, he rushed through the station like one possessed, leaped into a cab, and shouted to the driver:

"To the palace!"

CHAPTER XXV

On The Balcony

On that side of Marisi palace which faces the east, shut off from view of the drive by the trees and shrubbery of the grounds and garden, there is a broad marble balcony running from one end of the wing to the other.

This balcony, which is some twenty feet above the ground, is reached from the palace through a series of French windows, those in the front leading to the apartments of the prince and those in the rear to the rooms of the princess.

Over its marble balustrade the branches of century-old trees wave majestically, and, in the summer, stir softly about the thousand scents rising from the garden below. On a hot summer night it is the most comfortable spot in the city, as well as the most pleasant.

On this balcony sat the Princess Aline and Mlle. Janvour, at a little after eight in the evening. They had left the dinner-table only a few minutes before, and Aline had brought Vivi with her partly to escape the intrusion of other members of the household, and partly because she wished to inform her of a certain decision which she had that day resolved upon, to the effect that if she still wished to marry Heir Frederick Naumann the princess would give her consent and blessing.

The woman and the girl sat for a long time without speaking.

The evening was soft and mild, and sweet with the fragrance of the garden. The noises of the city sounded at a distance; its clamor was reduced to a soothing and pleasing hum.

All was quiet and peaceful, even in the breast of the princess; for not only were her plans in a fair way of completion according to her desires, but she was about to confer happiness on her Vivi, the only creature in the world for whom she had ever felt any genuine affection.

She pressed Vivi's hand and opened her mouth to speak, but was interrupted by the entrance of a servant through one of the windows leading onto the balcony.

The princess turned impatiently:

"What is it? I was not to be disturbed."

The servant approached apologetically:

"I know, your highness, but M. Stetton insisted. He is—"

"M. Stetton!" cried the princess.

"Yes, your highness. He is below. He would not be refused. He says it is of the utmost importance that he see you at once."

The princess had recovered herself. She said calmly:

"Show him up. I will see him here."

Then, when the servant had disappeared, she turned to Vivi:

"You had better go, dear. I had something to tell you—it must wait. Kiss me."

Vivi kissed her, not once, but many times, then turned to go. As she passed through the window to the hall within she met Stetton. He was making for the balcony almost at a run and gave her the merest nod in passing.

His pale face and excited manner roused the girl's curiosity, but she said nothing as she continued on her way down the hall to her own rooms.

Stetton stepped through the window. The balcony was comparatively dark, and coming as he did from the brilliantly lighted palace, he could see nothing.

He heard Aline's voice:

"Here, Stetton, I am here. What is it? Why have you returned?"

He made his way to her side, where she stood against the marble balustrade, and took her in his arms and kissed her. She endured his embrace with ill-concealed impatience, repeating:

"Why have you returned?"

Stetton began:

"I got as far as Paris—"

"Did you see M. Candalet?"

"Yes."

"His answer?"

"Was favorable. But—" Stetton hesitated, then said abruptly:

"Aline, Vasili Petrovich is alive. I have seen him."

The face of the princess turned suddenly pale; so pale that Stetton observed it in the dim light from the windows. She put out a hand and grasped his arm.

"Vasili! You have seen Vasili Petrovich? Where? When?"

"In Paris. At the Gare du Nord."

"But he did not see you?"

"Yes, and followed me to Berlin. I shook him off there."

Then, while the princess stood looking at him in amazement, he related his experiences of the past two days, from the interview with Vasili Petrovich in the Paris café to his arrival at the palace a few minutes before. Never had he seen Aline so moved; her eyes flashed fire; her whole body was tense.

"Fool!" she cried, when he had finished. "You should not have returned to Marisi at all! Why did you not remain in Paris and write to me? Why did you not—but there!" Her tone was one of furious scorn. "An eagle does not catch flies; nor should we expect a fly to catch an eagle."

Stetton did not exactly understand this observation, but the tone was enough. He protested hotly that he had done the best thing possible; at least, he had not gone on to America and left her in ignorance of her danger.

"*Mon Dieu!* What a man!" said Aline with increasing scorn. "But that would have been much better than to lead him straight to me!"

"I tell you I ditched him in Berlin!" cried poor Stetton, who had expected the most profound gratitude for his heroism.

"Perhaps," said the princess, forcing herself to be calm. "But you are no match for Vasili Petrovich, my dear Stetton. I have no doubt that he is in Marisi—perhaps in the street, in the garden there, now."

The princess glanced about uneasily, then suddenly crossed to the windows through which the light shone from the hall, and drew the curtains across the glass, leaving the balcony in darkness. Then she made her way back to Stetton's side and continued:

"You do not know this Vasili Petrovich. He is capable of anything. He is the one person in the world that I fear. You acted for the best—I know that—but you have plunged us in danger. I shall send for Duchesne in the morning, and have the entire city watched for him. Ah, if I once get him in my hands—"

Aline's eyes glittered so brightly that Stetton saw them in the darkness. After a pause she began again abruptly:

"But, after all, why did you return? Why did you not go on to America, and write me of this meeting?"

Stetton stammered something about coming back to find out what to do.

"Do?" cried the princess. "We shall do as we intended, of

course!" Then, at a movement from the young man, she moved close to him and put an arm around his shoulders. "Do you think, Stetton, that I will let this Vasili cheat me of you?"

"But he is your husband!"

"Bah!" Aline snapped her fingers. "That only makes it the more imperative to get rid of him."

She moved closer to the young man and put her other hand on his shoulder.

"It will not be necessary to make any change in our plans. Go to America—start tomorrow—and by the time you return there will be no Vasili Petrovich."

Stetton shuddered at the calmness of her tone. For the thousandth time he tried to tell himself of the danger he was putting his head into, and for the thousandth time he forgot everything else in the promise of her eyes and the sweetness of her kisses.

Her arms were round his neck; she was breathing words of love in his ear; he held her against him roughly, feeling the beating of her heart on his breast, filled with a mad fire.

"Aline," he whispered, "Aline! You know I love you—I love you—I love you—"

Suddenly the princess started and turned about quickly.

"What was that?" she whispered in a tone of alarm, but without removing her arms from the young man's neck.

"What? I heard nothing."

"That tree—that branch there—it moved—see, that one over the balustrade—"

"It was the wind."

"But there is no wind. Stetton, let us go in. I confess it, I am alarmed."

"Bah! You are fanciful. It was nothing." He held her again in his arms and pressed his lips to hers. "Come, Aline—I shall leave tomorrow, then—be kind to me tonight! I love you so! As for Vasili Petrovich, you are right; we will not let him rob us—"

The sentence was never finished.

Stetton suddenly felt his throat gripped in fingers of steel, and at the same moment saw an arm stretched round him toward Aline.

She started back with a cry of terror as she saw herself confronted by a man with a black beard and piercing black eyes, that were brilliant even in the darkness of the balcony.

But she was not quick enough; the fingers of the man's free hand closed about her own throat, slender and white, and sank into the flesh.

After that there was not a sound. The man with the beard stood towering above them, holding them at arm's length; against his great strength they were as babes.

They grasped the sleeves of his coat and tried to pull themselves free; they tore frantically at his fingers, which closed ever tighter about their throats; all was futile.

"Marie"—the voice of Vasili Petrovich came, merciless and terrible—"Marie, demon of hell! Look at me—ah—look in my eyes—what do you see there, Marie Nikolaevna? It is the wrath of God!"

They struggled more feebly. The man with the beard laughed aloud.

"No, no—it is useless—it is the hand of fate around your throat—and yours, you lying dog. I have waited—I have waited—"

Slowly, inexorably, they were pressed to the floor by his overpowering weight and strength—to their knees—down—down—they lay on their backs on the marble pavement; the fingers of steel sank ever deeper in their throats.

Vasili Petrovich was on his knees between them; his arms moved up and down; there was a dull, sickening thud.

A second time, a third, a fourth; then, without releasing his hold, he bent over closely and examined first the face of Stetton, then that of the princess. This for a long time; but what he saw was death.

Vasili Petrovich rose to his feet and stood looking down at the body of the woman.

"Marie," he muttered, and repeated it several times. "Marie—Marie."

He turned abruptly, walked to the balustrade and swung himself onto the branch of a tree that hung over the balcony, and disappeared in its dense foliage.

There was the sound of bending limbs, and, a moment later, the muffled noise of his feet landing on the grass of the garden below.

The branch swayed gently back and forth over the marble balustrade.

Its movements became slower and slower, until the trembling of the leaves finally ceased entirely and became still.

All was night and silence on the balcony.

Somewhere in southern France—exactly where does not matter—perhaps at Nice—on the white sand of the beach, under a large multicolored parasol, sat a young man and a girl.

They were dressed for bathing, but their costumes were dry; it was perhaps not the first time that they had found something on the beach more interesting than the waters of the Mediterranean. They had been silent for a long time, gazing steadfastly into each other's eyes; between them, on the sand, their hands were clasped tightly together.

Suddenly the girl spoke:

"And yet—I believe—my sadness makes me happier." She smiled soberly. "So you should not be jealous of it."

The man looked at her. That is, he would have looked at her if he had not been doing so already.

"I am jealous of anything and anyone that gets the smallest fraction of your smallest thought," he declared emphatically.

"No; I am serious," replied the girl. "You must not expect me ever to forget Aline, and if I want to talk of her it must be with you, for there is no one else. How could I forget? How horrible it was!"

The girl covered her face with her hands.

"Vivi! Vivi dearest!" The man tried to pull her hands away. "You must not think of that—you positively must not. To please me, dear. As for Aline, I shall not ask you to forget her, and I shall talk of her with you whenever you want me to. Dear, you must not—the doctor has forbidden it and you must take heed. Come, talk of me a while—you know what I want you to say."

Evidently the young man knew what he was about, for at this request the girl suddenly uncovered her face and looked at him.

"M. Naumann," she said emphatically, "if you begin that again you will regret it."

"But Vivi! To wait a year is impossible! Six months at most—make it six months. You know very well what mother thinks—"

Vivi interrupted him:

"Your mother agrees with me, young man, and you know it."

"But, hang it all, I tell you I can't wait a year! I won't! In the autumn I go to Rome and you will stay at Berlin—what the deuce do you expect me to do?"

The girl sprang to her feet.

"As you please, *monsieur*," she cried gaily. "Always do as you please; that is my motto, as it was that of the Abbey of Saint Thélème. And now farewell, *monsieur*."

Waving her hand at him mockingly, she raced down the beach toward the surf. In an instant he was on his feet and after her, and they entered the water together with a tremendous splash.

And thus, finally, it happened that Vivi Janvour, who was distinctly French from the tip of her toes to the top of her head, changed her nationality as well as her name and became a German *frau*.

No one will say that she didn't deserve her happiness or reproach her for remaining loyal to the only friend her early years had known. Content in a convent and modest in a palace, she made the best and most obedient of wives; and yet—this should be whispered—if you wish to procure a favor from Herr Frederick Naumann, who has become somewhat of a power in politics and diplomacy, it would not be a bad idea first to gain the approval of the mistress of the house.

Still, Naumann had his way in the matter of a certain date.

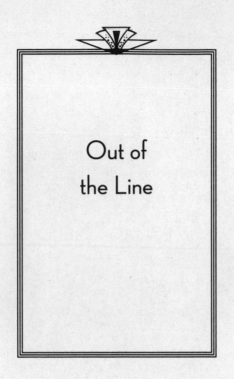

Out of
the Line

*M*RS. SAM Rossington pulled aside the curtain of her bed and gazed out upon the world beneath the window-shade which her maid had drawn only a minute before.

Then, as she stretched out her hand toward the chocolate tray on the table at her elbow, her mouth opened with the deep, frank yawn of solitude, and she propped herself comfortably against her pillow to sip and to ruminate.

Today was Mrs. Sam's— or Agatha's—birthday, and she was paying the white-bearded Father his inevitable tribute of regret and consideration. Old Time is never discreet or tactful.

At this moment he was reminding Agatha with brutal frankness that she had passed her thirty-first summer, and that henceforth his sickle would descend with increasing rapidity and more disastrous stroke. For Agatha, comparatively young as she was, had already reached that melancholy point in life where one's thoughts lean rather to the past than to the future.

Though, to be sure, Agatha's fluttering brain was seldom long disturbed by anything so uncomfortable as thought. Like one who "wandered in a forest aimlessly," she had taken life as it came—and taken all she could get—with hardly a thought for yesterday, and with none at all for tomorrow.

Like most human lives, which are in their development of soul and sensation curiously similar, however they may differ in incidents and experience, Agatha's existence had been distinctly divided into periods.

The first, which might be called the Romantico-Innocent, she had almost completely forgotten, save where here and there the fragrance of some sweet remembrance had refused to succumb to malodorous disillusionment.

The second, or Domestic-Hypocritical, she remembered, but with a shudder. Willing as she had been to be amused, Sam Rossington had come near being too much for her. Agatha had been for him neither a wife nor a friend, but merely a sensation; and, since she had originally been planned by the Creator for something a little better than an ornament or a plaything, she had more than once repented of her blindness and folly.

Having married Sam Rossington for the sake of his wealth and the worldly comfort and security it represented, she had stuck to her bargain with commendable constancy, and it must be admitted that he got his money's worth; on the other hand, it is true that Agatha had not been wholly free from regret.

It had taken various forms, having at times ascended even into the region of pious aspiration, but being more often distinctly of the flesh. In short, Agatha was one of those unfortunate beings who are endowed with a soul, and then left without a will to support it. Nothing is quite so uncomfortable as a loose conscience.

The passing years had blurred, but not effaced, the past. Disturbing glimpses of it now and then visited her dreams, though they no longer caused any deeper emotion than a mild wonder as to whether her life could, after all, have been made to contain any more happiness than she had known.

One face, which always appeared to her white and drawn with suffering, was of most frequent recurrence in her visions. Even yet she wondered that she had been able to dismiss such a man as John Carter; and even yet she admired his manly ways of accepting defeat.

To be sure, he had signified his intention of going straight to the devil as rapidly and thoroughly as possible, after the immemorial custom of disappointed youth; but he had really been very decent about it.

Ah well! Agatha sighed as she rang for her maid—what had she, a sophisticated widow, to do with youthful fancies? That had been ten years ago. For seven of them she had lived with her husband, when he had suddenly shown an unwonted consideration for her by contracting a fever during the festival at Havana, and dying in less than a week—an act which Agatha felt had almost justified her choice of him.

"And the funny part of it is," said she aloud, as the door opened to admit her maid, "that I have really missed the poor devil!"

"I beg your pardon?" said Jeanne.

"Nothing," said Agatha. "Take away the tray. Was there no mail?"

"No. Mrs. Cranshaw and Miss Carson telephoned, and there are some roses and a basket of orchids—shall I bring them up?"

"Lord, no!" said Agatha. "The room already smells like the Temple of Allah." She lay back on her pillow and watched the girl silently. "Jeanne," she said suddenly, "do you know that today is my birthday?"

"Certainly, *madame*," came the answer from the depths of a closet.

"Well, aren't you going to congratulate me?"

Jeanne emerged from the closet carrying a gown, which she placed on the arm of a chair.

"Why—" she began uncertainly, embarrassed by this unwonted display of friendliness on the part of her mistress, "I—I wish you many happy returns of the day, *madame*."

"Thanks," said Agatha dryly. "I suppose I could hardly expect you to be enthusiastic about it." She regarded Jeanne curiously, as though seeing her for the first time. "I have never given you much encouragement, have I?" she said.

"You have been very good to me, *madame*."

"Perhaps—in a way," said Agatha, pondering. "It is curious," she continued impersonally, "that I have never taken the trouble to know you. Sam used to say I was unsympathetic. Perhaps that is why I have no friends. I tell you, Jeanne, I am growing old; for I am beginning to be lonesome—this morning I am positively unhappy. What was Mrs. Cranshaw's message?"

Jeanne looked up from the dressing-table, where she was arranging the articles for a somewhat complicated toilet.

"To ask if she could expect you this evening. The bath is ready, *madame*."

Agatha did not find her usual delight in the cold, bracing water, nor in the mysterious and fragrant ceremonies which followed her emergence; and by the time Jeanne began to dress her hair she was almost irritable.

This was alarming; Agatha was anything but a creature of moods; and Jeanne, who possessed a sensitive soul, found herself speculating on the possible reasons for this unexpected development of nerves.

Meanwhile her deft fingers moved rapidly, arranging the golden brown coil of which Agatha was justly proud, while Agatha gazed absently at the array of bottles and jars on the table before her.

"Jeanne," she said suddenly, "I shall not go to Mrs. Cranshaw's tonight."

The maid was silent.

"I am sick of it all," Agatha continued presently, half to herself. "It is so utterly idiotic—though, thank the Lord, it's not respectable.

This is a fit, Jeanne—and the first I've ever had. I'm just beginning to realize that I've wasted ten years and I suppose I'll waste the rest. It's a habit. And yet—today—"

She interrupted herself suddenly—"Jeanne, if you were me, what would you do with a birthday?"

"I don't know, *madame*," the maid stammered, hesitating.

"No, you must answer," Agatha persisted, "I'll leave it to you. I am *Haroun Al Raschid,* and you're my grand vizier. But I warn you I'm devilish melancholy, and you'll need no little imagination. I want a positive adventure. Come! What shall it be?"

The maid laughed uncertainly.

"*Madame* might give a party," she suggested.

Then, at Agatha's impatient gesture of derision, she walked round and in front of her chair stood looking down at her.

"If *madame* is serious—" she began.

"I am," Agatha declared.

Whereupon Jeanne, in her capacity of grand vizier, and with a preamble which, though interesting enough, has nothing to do with this story, made a most unique suggestion. As she concluded, Agatha rose and clapped her hands gleefully.

"Jeanne," she cried, "you are positively a jewel! Better than that, you are right! For the first time in my life, I shall try to make some-one else happy!"

In more ways than one, New York is a city of distances. At midnight in winter it is, for instance, a million miles from Tenth Street and Broadway to West End Avenue, where Agatha's cozy apartment was situated.

At exactly half past eleven in the evening of her birthday Agatha, closely wrapped in furs and attended by Jeanne, entered a limousine

at her own door and startled the chauffeur by directing him to drive
to Tenth Street and Broadway. A minute later they had turned south
from Ninety-Sixth Street and begun their journey.

This Broadway is easily the most interesting street in the world.
It contains the world—in miniature and caricature. The Lucia of
Naples, the Champs Elysées of Paris, the Muski of Cairo, the Grove
of Damascus—all are to be found here, if you only know where to
look for them. With an open eye and a ready soul you can circum-
navigate the globe in one night between the Battery and Washington
Heights.

Even Agatha, who had been partially awakened by Jeanne's
unexpected eloquence of the morning and the excitement of her
own unusual errand, felt a new sense of interest and life as the limousine sped southward past endless rows of apartment houses, darkened shops, shabby moving picture theaters and glittering cafés.

On through the Circle, dominated by a screaming advertisement
of a Sunday newspaper and a general appearance of loud vulgarity;
past Fifty-Third Street, darkened by the L tracks overhead and the
dusky skin of its inhabitants underneath; into the realm of fur-lined
overcoats, painted faces, dazzling lights, and popping corks.

Then through a quiet length of a mile or so, bursting suddenly
into the cheaper and noisier gaiety of Fourteenth Street, the car carried them, now rapidly, now more slowly, until at last they passed
into that strip of comparative darkness which is left by right to the
tender mercies of the watchman and policeman.

Agatha, buried deep in her furs and lost in thought, was roused
by a touch on her arm.

"Look!" said Jeanne, pointing to the right. "There they are,
madame!"

There they were, indeed; a line of silent men, in single file,
beginning at the corner of Tenth Street and reaching up Broadway

almost a full block. There could not have been less than eighty or ninety of them. In the semi-darkness—the street is dimly lighted here—it was barely possible to perceive that they were poorly and scantily clothed, and shivering from the cold, and that their faces presented a haggard, almost a sinister, appearance.

They had been waiting here in the bitter cold, some of them, for over an hour; it is easy to believe that they were really in need of that for which they waited; miserable in themselves, and companions of misery. One would hardly go through such an experience for the sake of a fortune; they were waiting for a chunk of bread and a cup of coffee.

By now they shuffled and stamped with impatience; for the hands of a clock in a nearby window pointed at five minutes to twelve, and midnight was the hour for which they waited.

"Poor devils!" Agatha shuddered.

Then she leaned forward and spoke to the chauffeur, and the car came to a stop close by the curb at the head of the dark line.

As the door of the limousine opened and Agatha stepped to the sidewalk, a policeman who had been pacing up and down beside the line approached her and touched his cap respectfully.

Agatha accosted him; he nodded; and as she continued somewhat hurriedly, explaining the nature of her errand, his face broadened with an expansive grin and he wagged his head appreciatively.

"Lord, ma'am!" said he. "There's no objection in the world. Sure, and I'm glad to see you make the poor devils happy. I'll keep watch down the line so as to make sure they don't repeat on you. They're sly ones."

"Thank you," said Agatha. "And now if you'll tell them—"

"Sure," said the policeman. He turned to the line and raised his voice. "Men," he said, "here's a lady givin' a birthday party, and she wants to play a little game of 'Hold fast to all I give you.' The rules are to stay in line till it's over. You won't have to go around the corner tonight."

As Agatha stripped a crisp new bill from the package she held under her cloak and handed it to the man at the head of the line she felt a curious fluttering of her heart, unlike anything she had ever before experienced. And as she saw the man's eyes fill with tears and heard his fervent "God bless you," her hand trembled with so unusual and divine an emotion that it could scarcely find the pocket inside her cloak.

And so with the second and the third and the fourth—on down the line she went, while she gradually controlled her fast-beating heart and began to give words of cheer and good wishes along with her bounty.

Half the men in the line—those white, drawn, haggard faces—were in tears; she felt half smothered by the shower of blessings and gratitude. Never before had she been so utterly happy.

She was about three-quarters of the distance down the line when one poor fellow, on catching sight of the figure on the bill she gave him, fell on his knees at her feet and began mumbling incoherently his thanks and blessings. Agatha patted his shoulder and added her tears to his own. And then, as she turned to the next man in the line and looked up into his face, she uttered a cry, tottered backward, and probably would have fallen but for his prompt spring forward to her support.

"John!" she breathed. "God in heaven! John!"

The man shook her rudely.

"Fool!" he whispered. "Don't recognize me!"

Then, as the policeman came running up, "She stumbled," he said sullenly.

The policeman returned to his position. Agatha, by a supreme and violent effort of the will, controlled herself and, taking a bill from the package, held it out to the man.

"Take it," she said as calmly as possible. Then, pressing closer to him, "Listen," she whispered rapidly. "Come to me—tonight—at once—" and then, at the look of refusal in his eyes, "you must. I shall not leave till you promise." The man next him in line leaned forward curiously. "For God's sake, John!"

He shook his head and opened his mouth to speak, then, hesitating, glanced around at the white, strained faces peering intently at them through the dim light. When he turned to Agatha his face wore a grim smile, and when he spoke his voice, low and grave and strained, was tinged with a bitter humor.

"I will come," he said. "The address?"

Agatha whispered it in his ear; he nodded his comprehension and turned an impassive face to the policeman, who approached to inquire the cause of the delay. Agatha passed him, unheeding, to continue on down the silent line, and five minutes later she reentered the limousine.

"Jeanne," she said calmly, "I want to cry. Let us get home!"

"But, *madame*," said Jeanne as the car turned about and started up, "you are so pale—surely—what has happened?"

"Nothing," said Agatha shortly. "Only—I have seen a ghost. Please Heaven—" she broke off and laughed bitterly.

"Well, at least I shall see him. After all, what does it matter?"

She sank back into her corner, motionless and silent, while the car sped on swifter than before. Once more they passed through the glare of Fourteenth Street, the glitter of Times Square, and the monotonous irregularity of upper Broadway.

Arrived in her rooms, Agatha threw off her furs and turned to her maid. There was a feverish restlessness in both her manner and tone; her eyes glowed with excitement; from head to foot she quivered with repressed emotion.

"Jeanne," she said, "I expect a caller—Mr. Carter. He will probably be here at any moment. When he comes, show him in."

Then she went into her own room and sat down to wait.

Five, ten, fifteen, thirty minutes passed—tense, strained with suspense and expectation; minutes during which thought and feeling were so closely packed and of so intense a nature that they resulted in a sort of numbness or nothingness, and left both brain and body wearied to exhaustion.

Then came the reaction; for Agatha was quite old enough to be cynical. She walked over to a mirror and surveyed herself critically, a cold, sarcastic expression in her eyes.

"Lord, what a fool!" she said aloud. "Sam was right, after all. If he could only see me now, how amused he would be! And he wouldn't care a hang!"

Then the door opened and closed; and she raised her eyes to meet those of John Carter.

The man before her was well worth a study. Here, in the glaring, penetrating light, many things were revealed that had been mercifully hidden in the dimness of the street. His suit was shabby and ill-fitting, but clean; his shoes, that had at one time been tan, were spotted and cracked; his linen though white, considerably the worse for wear; and the hat under his arm was a shapeless mass of dirty felt.

But at the sight of his face these items were forgotten. The square jaw, the hollow cheeks, the white, sloping forehead, the severely straight nose, all were dominated by the fantastic, bitter humor and grim inscrutability that looked out at you from the steady steel-gray eyes.

Knowing, cynical, and yet somehow expressionless, they gazed steadily at Agatha until she was forced to turn aside nervously and motion him to a chair.

Carter remained standing.

"Here I am," he said quietly. "What do you want?"

Agatha, hearing his voice and looking into his eyes, began to understand why she had been unable to forget John Carter. And she began to be afraid—of what, she could not have told.

"Won't you sit down?" she said, advancing toward him with outstretched hand. "You haven't even said 'Good evening,'" she laughed nervously.

Carter regarded the hand for a moment quizzically, then, taking it in his own, led her to a chair and seated himself beside her.

"Perhaps you are right," he said, after a pause. "It may be better for both of us to have it out. But what is there to say? As for you, I know all about you; and as for me, you know all about me, too—after tonight. I had forgiven you, and you had forgotten me. What else is there to say?"

"Perhaps," said Agatha, looking directly at him—"perhaps I had not forgotten."

Carter laughed mirthlessly.

"My dear Atha," he said, "it is useless for us to pretend. Especially for you. I am no longer twenty-five. In some ways, I am no longer a man. If I am bitter, you will please remember who sowed the seed for me. Against my will I promised to come here tonight to save you from your own folly—you were completely unnerved, and you were capable of anything. Why did you ask me? Was it merely curiosity? Or pity?"

"I don't know," said Agatha. "I think—I wanted to help you."

For some minutes there was silence. Carter sat motionless, his face turned away from Agatha, expressionless and grave. Then, suddenly, he felt the touch of a hand against his cheek, and the sound of a voice—the merest trembling whisper—sounded in his ear.

"Jack! I don't want to help you! I want you—to help me! I have not forgotten you Jack—I have never forgotten you, Jack—I have never forgotten you! Oh, I am silly and helpless, and I love you; I have always loved you—"

Agatha was crying silently on her knees by the side of Carter's chair, her head resting against his shoulder. Her arm crept around his neck, and she clung to him, quivering.

With an effort Carter controlled his voice. "Atha."

There was no answer. For a moment the man sat silently staring straight ahead, the merest quiver of an eyelid betraying the battle that was raging within; then, placing his hands on Agatha's cheeks, he lifted her head from his shoulder and arose, trembling, to his feet.

"By God," he said quietly, "you almost got me. Listen, Atha. There was a time when I wanted just what you want. But now—you're too late."

To Agatha, still kneeling by the chair he had left, the words came as in a dream. The strain under which she had labored for two hours; the reaction from ten years of repression and restraint, left her numb almost to the point of unconsciousness.

She heard, but she was incapable of movement. And Carter's voice, grave and measured, came to her as from a distance, and as though it were the voice of fate itself.

"You think you want me, Atha, but you are mistaken. The man you're looking for died ten years ago—you know best who killed him. You and I are as far apart as the poles—we'd hate each other in a week.

"You want to bring back the past—well, give it up. It's the most hopeless and utterly impossible task in the world. We had our chance; we'll never have another. We're through, you and I.

"I don't love you; I don't even pity you; for you are not the Atha I loved—you are not Atha at all. My life is not the only one you've ruined. Don't think I am deceived by your display of emotion and feeling, and don't deceive yourself. It's all a lie.

"It's merely a yearning for the past; a desperate and hopeless effort to make your dreams come true; a memory; an echo of what once was, and can never be again. There's nothing left to either of us but bitter experience and perhaps a passion or two; and we were not made to satisfy each other's passions."

The voice ceased suddenly, with a little throb, a catch of pain. Agatha heard his steps approaching, and was aware that he stooped above her, though she felt nothing; then she heard his steps again receding, and the door open and close.

He was gone.

She struggled to her feet with an effort; then stooped and picked up something which her movement had shaken from the chair by which she had knelt.

It was the bill she had given to Carter in the line. Summoning her strength she called Jeanne, then sank back into the chair, while the bill fluttered from her hand to the floor.

Agatha gazed at it stupidly as it lay crumpled at her feet.

"He might have taken it," she said plaintively, wearily. "He might have taken that."